The Kindling

of

GreenFyr

Book One of the Reunification Conspiracy

By
Mark Freeman

PublishAmerica
Baltimore

PublishAmerica has allowed this work to remain exactly as the author intended, verbatim, without editorial input.

Cover art by R.J. Freeman.

ISBN: 1-60563-161-2
PUBLISHED BY PUBLISHAMERICA, LLLP
www.publishamerica.com
Baltimore

Printed in the United States of America

For...

Heather, my love, partner in life, and best friend.
You're my muse; you inspire me to be more than I ever could have
dreamed to be. I could fill volumes and still never find the words to
express my thanks and love.
AML

And for Barrett and Logan, my Happiness and Joy; every day you
prove to me magic does truly exist in this world.

Thanks…

and love to my parents for their unending support. Without your love, caring, and generosity, none of this would have been possible.

And with much thanks to my brothers for being heroes to their little brother in a world desperately lacking in them; you taught me the true value of my imagination. This book is as much yours as mine.

Special thanks to R.J. for the cover art, you breathed life into my words.

The Kindling

of

GreenFyr

Book One of the
Reunification Conspiracy

1

As the snow lightly touched his face, Owen smiled and breathed in the crisp morning air. It was the first snowfall of the dwindling autumn and he hoped it meant no school for the day. The snow was coming down heavily and had been for the last hour. It was just now starting to actually accumulate on the fir branches overhead. The morning had yet to dawn; even through the heavy gray snow clouds he could tell that the sun had yet to break from behind the Green Mountains to his east. Everything lay in silence and monotone shades of gray.

He stepped hesitantly through the trees further away from his yard and the protective yellow lights of the kitchen window. His father was long gone on his way to work while his mother was just starting to pack his lunch for school, thinking him still in bed. This, however, was his time, before the world was awake and moving, when only he and the snow were alive in the forest, when no one knew where he was or what he was doing.

That was when he noticed the track in the snow.

It was certainly a cat track, but the biggest he had ever seen. He knew it was a cat track for two reasons. First, because he had a cat named Piper—who was his best friend, possibly his only friend—and she would often lie next to him in bed and gently touch his face with her paw. And second, because his father worked for the state as a biologist and had shown Owen bobcat tracks before, but this track was bigger than any bobcat track he had ever seen. His first thought was that this must be a catamount. Something that folks in his part of the country seemed to wish was still in the woods, but that his dad told him were long gone from the Green Mountains. Occasionally, his father said, some kook might let a captive animal go in the forest, but other than that, catamounts didn't roam these hills anymore.

But that didn't change the fact that there was now a very large cat track at his feet in the snow. He bent down to look at it more closely, holding his hand, fingers splayed, just over it to compare the size of it. The track was easily the size of Owen's hand. Owen was suddenly very nervous about being alone this far in the forest. He slowly stood up and started to turn away when he saw the gray and tawny flash streak across the trail in front of him. At first he thought it was a mountain lion, but then he saw the large rosette pattern spots along its flank.

Snow leopard! Owen thought. He'd known immediately.

Owen had a book in his room, *Encyclopedia of Cats of the World*; he'd even seen television shows on them, so he had known at once what the animal was running through his back woods. Owen had even seen leopards in person once, when his parents had taken him to the Bronx Zoo in New York. And he knew very well that they didn't live here in his woods. They lived in the Himalayas. *What was it doing here in Vermont?*

Just as he was wondering why a Himalayan leopard was here, in his back woods, three very large, dark hounds burst from the forest after the cat. The hounds had sickly, charcoal gray coats and large paws tipped with long nails that tore into the duff and newly fallen snow. They had enormous heads with large floppy ears and glowing green eyes.

Glowing green eyes? Owen thought as they sped after the leopard. But before he gave it another thought he had taken off after the four animals. He cut through the forest on an intercept course, guessing they would follow the old rail bed path through to the creek. It was not the most direct way of going, but the easiest in the direction they were heading. He wasn't as fast as the animals, but he knew this land better than they did, and he could make up the time by steering straight down the bank and up the frozen creek bed. He sped through the woods down the short incline towards the creek, over the now snow covered angel hair ferns and horsetails and into the small grove of willows that flanked the creek.

As he reached the frozen brook, he grabbed two baseball size rocks without even thinking or stopping, and raced up the basin to where the animals would cut across the streambed if he'd guessed right. Just as he turned the bend in the creek, the snow leopard leapt from the bank, practically over his head. Owen ducked, and just as he was beginning to stand back up the dogs exploded from the top of the hill and scampered down the bank after the cat.

Owen shouted and threw the rock in his right hand at the lead hound hitting it just off its shoulder. It yelped and slipped on the icy stream crashing into the bank on the far side. Quickly he switched the second rock into his right hand and fired at the next hound, now turning towards him, and hit it square between the eyes. It too yelped in pain. The third dog, however, had already changed course and was bearing down on Owen. It charged Owen with its sickly green eyes and thick strands of spit and saliva spilling from its jowls. The beast growled, deep and guttural, making the hairs on Owen's arms and the back of his neck stand on end. As it opened its ghastly maw, Owen could see large, dark teeth, and a faint green flickering light coming from deep within the beast.

Owen turned and ran, but slipped on the frozen creek. As his ankle twisted he spun to see the hound leap at him, and just as it left the ground, its back raised above the bank of the creek bed, a single ray of sun broke through the thick, gray cloud cover and touched the dog's back. In that blink of an instant, as the light of the sun gleamed off the unhealthy dark coat of the dog, the beast vanished with a whine. In the ray of sun there floated a cloud of dust that in the minutes following the dog's disappearance soon dissipated into the air.

Owen turned his attention to the other two dogs, but they too were gone in the coming of the morning.

2

Owen stood up and brushed the snow from his pants. He looked around for the three dogs and leopard that had been there only minutes before but were now gone. *It had been real, hadn't it?* he thought as he climbed up the bank. *The tracks!* he remembered, looking at the ground where the animals had burst through the forest. The hounds had done a good job of tearing up the snow where they had followed the leopard through the forest.

Owen followed the tracks back to where they ran into the old rail bed and further on until he found a snow leopard track again. He smiled with pride as he thought of how he had backtracked just as his father had taught him.

"When in doubt, follow it out," his dad always said when they found tracks in the woods. They were usually deer or coyote, once, they had found the tracks of a mother black bear and cubs.

He knelt in the snow and the excitement grew, he really wished that school would be cancelled for the day. His dad had shown him how to make a cast of a print using something like plaster called *Permastone*. If school was cancelled he'd come back out and cast the track to show his father. Owen stood back up and rushed back down to his house. He snuck back in through the basement slider beneath the deck, so his mom wouldn't hear or see him. He kicked off his boots, and hung his parka on the pegs by the stairs. Tiptoeing up them, careful to step over the fifth stair from the top because it always squeaked, he listened for his mother.

As he reached the top of the basement stairs, he poked his head from the door to make sure the coast was clear. He then slipped out and gently closed the door behind him. He now needed to make his way down the hall past the kitchen on the right, which was where his mom was, and up the stairs. Once at the stairs he was home free. As he stepped down the hall, and just before he reached the doorway to the kitchen, he heard his mom call, "Owen, time to get up. School's on today, Hon."

"OWEN?" she called again, more loudly this time. He then heard her start walking towards the doorway, *Oh no; she's coming to wake me up,* he thought. Which really wasn't the end of the world, but a lecture from mom was not the best way to start the day. He'd been read the riot act before for sneaking outside on his own without telling anyone. Once, he had snuck out at three in the morning to watch a meteor shower, but had fallen asleep on the deck only to awaken to his mom standing over him. Another time before that, when he was younger, he had snuck out on Easter Morning to try and find rabbit tracks in the back yard. He had instead found a skunk. His parents had bathed him in tomato juice that morning, and even though it had turned his skin orange, he still smelled like a skunky tomato for their dinner at his grandmother's. Both events had happened years before, but he'd still never lived them down. Luckily, he was the only grandson of an only child, so there hadn't been any aunts, uncles or cousins who had to smell him that Easter Sunday.

"Owen? You would sleep through a train wreck, wouldn't you?" she said, as she was just about to step into the hall. Owen had plastered himself up against the wall and was willing himself invisible, a trick that had never worked before, but it didn't keep him from trying again. He was beginning to think his theory of mind over matter just had too many holes in it when the phone rang.

"Hello?" his mother said answering it. Owen chanced a quick peak into the room, she had her back to the door, and so he bolted across the open doorway and hit the stairs at a full run. He didn't hear who had been on the other end of the phone conversation because he had taken the opportunity to dash to safety. Once in his room, Owen began pulling off the clothes he'd been wearing and began pulling on his clothes for school. Piper sat in the middle of his bed with the bed sheets clumped around her and watched him change. Owen stopped in mid-changing and looked to the top shelf of his bookcase, his favorite books bookshelf: McInish, Tolkien, Rowling, Lewis, Jaques, Funke, and Colfer. *Glowing green eyes,* he thought, *it's something out of one of my books. Must have been the light, but the leopard? At least that's explainable, almost.*

He was almost dressed when his mother knocked at his door.

"Owen?" she said as she stepped into his bedroom. "Oh, you're awake."

"Yeah, I think the phone woke me, did someone call?" he said, feigning a yawn.

"Yes, it was David." David was his mom's agent. "He wanted to see how the book was coming." His mom's latest book was coming along slowly as Owen knew. She had dashed upon the scene as a writer of young adult, fantasy books, but after her first two, she had to go on book tours for almost a year straight. A weekend in New York, a week in San Francisco, two weeks in Europe, the whole experience had drained her, and when it came time to write the third book in the series, she had just been too exhausted to be inspired to write anything at all.

"What ya tell him?"

"That it's coming along quite well, thank you," she said with a smile.

"You know, when I lie, I get in trouble," Owen said smiling back.

"It's not lying, exactly…."

"MmmHmmm," Owen hummed, smirking.

"I've made some progress in the last few days, and you're too smart for your own good, Owen McInish. Now finish getting dressed for school." Owen's mom turned and left the room.

Owen looked over at Piper snuggling into the covers on the bed and said, "You'll never guess what happened."

3

Owen turned and waved to his mom peaking out the front window at him; once she'd turned away he pulled his fleece hat off and tucked it into his pocket. This way his head might be cold, but at least the kids on the bus wouldn't get the satisfaction of taking it away from him. He ran his hand through his dark hair and tried to neaten and flatten it from the static electricity that was making it stand on end. Owen stamped his feet in the snow and took some pleasure in turning the powder to packed slush.

He stopped stamping his feet when he heard the bus begin to climb his hill, shifting to its lowest gear to make the climb. Owen tried to think of the snow leopard to distract himself from the growing knot in his stomach. After he'd thrown the rocks at the hounds he'd lost track of the leopard and assumed she'd kept running into the woods. *Why hadn't she just climbed a tree?* he thought as the bus came into view around the corner of his road. The large yellow vehicle, even coated in sand and salt from the plowed and sanded roads, was in bright contrast to the snow covered balsams of his driveway.

Invisible, be invisible, he thought as the bus approached. *Be invisible and it will drive right by.* The bus slid to a stop in front of him while the doors popped open with a hiss of warm air in his face. *I'm really going to have to start reworking that theory,* he thought as he climbed onto the bus. The bus was already mostly full everyday when it got to his house, and so Owen looked for the few open seats available to him. He started working his way down the aisle when Zack Harris called his name.

"Owen, I gotta seat open right here, next t'me."

"No Owen, sit here," Brian Wigby said with a smile that could make a timber rattler look innocent.

Maybe I can make THEM disappear if I try, he thought as he sat next to Harris, the lesser of two evils in Owen's opinion.

"What, no hat today? It's pretty cold to be with outta hat," Zack said as he further messed up Owen's hair.

"What's the matter, Owen? Don't like me as much as Zack?" Wigby asked as he slid down his seat to the aisle so Owen was within arm's reach. "Maybe you gotta crush on him or somethin'."

"Gross! You girl," Zack said, punching Owen in the arm.

Harris and Wigby were a grade ahead of Owen in school and had been riding him from the first day Owen stepped onto the school bus in kindergarten. He had no idea why, just like the two bullies he thought, they probably had no idea why either. Because of it, Owen had a lot of trouble making friends. Most kids were scared to even talk to him for fear of becoming targets of Zack and Brian. At first it had been really hard going to school everyday, knowing they would be waiting for him. It hadn't gotten any easier, but he had grown used to it. He had even found some ways of avoiding them while at school, some places he could be by himself during his free periods where they hadn't found him yet.

"Hey everybody, Owen likes Zack!" Wigby yelled above the roar of the bus. The rest of the bus laughed out of fear of retribution more than from the humor of it; Owen looked straight ahead as his cheeks turned crimson, and he wished he could teleport himself back home to his bed and Piper.

When the bus stopped at school Owen stood and exited quickly, vanishing into the crowd of students. He worked his way to his home room and distracted himself by thinking of the leopard running through the woods and chasing rabbits and deer. The snow had already begun to melt so he knew that there would be no tracks to cast when he got home, but he hoped he'd find one in the mud that was beginning to form. *If it gets cold again tonight maybe it will freeze and I can caste it in the morning.* He was lost in his thoughts as the bell rang.

As he stepped onto the bus at the end of the day he was thankful to see that neither Zack nor Brian was on board. It wasn't unusual for them to be serving detentions at the end of the school day. Owen worked his way to the back of the bus and squeezed in next to the window. He wiped the fog and condensation away with his sleeve and daydreamed about the morning's events. He'd spent the whole day in a fog and his first period teacher twice had asked if he was okay. He assured her he was, and after the second time he tried to pay more attention to his classes. He knew if he didn't, he'd be risking a phone call home to his mom, and he didn't want to mention the leopard to his parents until he had proof. Owen was still having trouble believing what he'd seen that morning, how could anyone else believe him without some sort of evidence. He was lost in thought, when the bus pulled up at the bottom of his driveway.

As it came to a jarring stop and the doors popped open, he suddenly realized where they were and quickly scrambled off the bus to the giggles of the other passengers.

4

Owen was sitting at his desk in his room looking through his cat books and trying not to think about his disappointing afternoon. When he had gotten home from school, his mother had met him at the driveway like most days while she was getting the mail, and they walked back up to the house together. He'd dropped off his backpack with his schoolbooks and raced out to the woods behind the house. He looked all afternoon until his mother had called him for dinner, but he hadn't found a single track.

At dinner, he talked to his father about his day at work and his father asked about Owen's day at school. In the beginning of Harris and Wigby's harassing, Owen had told his parents, but there was very little for them to do about it. They had spoken to Owen's teachers and Owen's father had even called Mr. Wigby once, but it had only made things worse for Owen with the two boys in the end, so Owen had begun to keep most of the bullying to himself. He knew his father and mother would try to help, but he also knew that the two boys wouldn't stop and would probably only be meaner if his parent's got involved again. Mr. McInish suspected as much and often offered hypothetical advice to his son about dealing with bullies and sticking up for himself, but he also knew that his involvement hadn't helped the matter much in the past. Sadly, when he had been Owen's age, he faced the same treatment in school and knew how his son felt.

Owen turned from his desk and found Piper sitting on his pillow watching him. She squinted at him from across the room, and Owen squinted back at her. She yawned and stretched on his pillow before padding over to the edge of the bed, to lean as far as she could towards him without falling off. Owen leaned back in his chair and scratched the top of her head, just behind her ears, which induced instantaneous purring.

Piper arched back and tipped her head, leaning closer into Owen's hand as he scratched her. She opened her eyes, and tilted her head, tipping her ears from side to side towards the open window. Owen had opened the window wide to allow the night air to cool his room; for some reason his room was always the hottest in the house, and he usually tried to cool it off every night before going to bed. As Piper looked towards the window, Owen glanced towards the opening just as the snow leopard leapt into view.

The large cat landed on the windowsill and perched itself in the opening, long tail balancing, watching Owen. It too tilted its head from side to side as if listening to Owen's thoughts. The snow leopard made no further movements to enter the small bedroom. Owen chanced a glance back at Piper and to his surprise the smaller cat was very calm. She sat still on the corner of the bed, squinting her eyes at the larger cat in the window.

Owen looked back to the window and was unnerved to see the snow leopard staring at him.

"Knock, knock, Owen. May I come in?" Owen's dad asked from just outside his door. The knock on the door pulled Owen away from the window for only a split second, but when he looked back the leopard was gone.

"Sure, c'mon in," Owen said as he leapt from his chair and ran to his window. The leopard was nowhere to be seen as Owen leaned out of his window for a better view.

"Geezum crow it's cold in here!" Owen's dad said, walking into the room.

"Sorry, was kinda hot."

"Well, you should probably be closing that window, I'll turn the heat down. We aren't quite Rockefellers just yet. I can't be throwing heat out the window!"

"Yeah, okay," Owen said as he closed the window, knowing he'd open it again once his father left the room.

"And don't think I don't know you'll open it again as soon as I leave," Owen's dad said with a smile. "So, seriously, how was school today? You seemed pretty distant at dinner tonight. I figured I had a little over a year left before you got your license, became an even moodier teenager, and stopped talking to me all together." His dad sat on the edge of Owen's bed and began scratching Piper behind her ears. Owen could hear her purring all the way over by the window. He walked over and sat back at his desk.

"Things are fine at the school. The same, you know."

"Yeah, I know," his dad said, knowing exactly how things were.

"Well, I know the last time that I tried to help with things, I just made them worse, so I won't butt in this time, but I can offer advice or just be a sounding board if you want."

"Okay," Owen said, turning his attention back to the window.

"I know I've said this before, but there will always be people out there who will feel the need to try and make other people feel small, Owen. And sometimes, there's an amount of their garbage that someone has to take, but other times, people need to make a stand. Personally, I always found it easier to stand up for someone else getting picked on than when I was the target."

"Yeah, I know dad, thanks," Owen said smiling weakly at his father.

"No, I don't think you're really getting what I'm saying, Owen. I don't want you to think I approve of you fighting or to think that I believe violence solves anything, but sometimes bullies need to be knocked down too." He stood up and walked over to Owen and put his hand on his son's shoulder. "It's your battle, Owen, you'll have to decide how best to fight it. Just know that I'll support you however you choose to handle it. I'm always around if you ever need, or want, to talk about it." He rubbed his son's hair and left the room.

Owen looked after his dad as he walked out the door and closed it behind him. "Oh, and lights out in a few more minutes, it's getting late, okay?"

"Alright," Owen said, turning his attention back to the closed window.

Owen walked over to his bed and pulled his bed sheets back, walked over to the window, opened it wide again, climbed into bed, and turned the light off.

"G'night Pipe, let me know if we have any visitors in the middle of the night, okay?"

5

When Owen woke up in the morning, dawn hadn't quite broken. His room was cast in shades of gray in the very cool morning air. He blinked twice while trying to get his eyes to focus before he saw the snow leopard sitting in the cushy chair in the corner of his room. Piper was curled up lying with the larger cat, while the leopard watched Owen with its head resting on its front paws.

Owen immediately froze and stopped breathing. Of all the scenarios he had played out in his head before falling asleep, this had not been one of them. The cat didn't seem to be aggressive or even remotely dangerous at this point, but Owen's dad had always told him that wild animals are unpredictable and that's what makes them dangerous. *This was unpredicted*, Owen thought as he sat still in his bed watching the snow leopard watching him not even three meters away.

"Well, good morning, I guess," Owen said while he slowly sat up a bit in bed, but even with that slight motion the leopard leapt from the chair and in one jump landed in the windowsill, disappearing out into the gray morning.

Owen leapt from his bed and went to the window. Looking out the opening the crisp morning air stung his face, but the cat was already gone from sight.

"Owen, time to get up!"

"I'm up, mom." He walked over to his dresser and pulled some clothes out without bothering to see if they were what he wanted to wear or not and got dressed. He grabbed his backpack and headed down stairs. Breakfast was on the table. He ate the cereal not knowing what kind it was. His mom watched him while he ate and finally sat down next to him.

"Owen, what's on your mind?"

"Hmmm? Oh, nothing, mom, just thinking about school," he said filling his mouth with another mouthful of cereal.

"I know your father spoke to you last night, but if you want to talk to me about…"

"I'm alright, ma." Owen usually didn't brush his mom off, but how could he tell her a snow leopard had spent the night in his room. It was bad enough they were always trying to *talk* about the kids at school, but he would be on the first bus to a shrink if he mentioned the leopard.

"Well, you better get going then, the bus will be here any minute," she said with a sad sigh as she stood from the table and walked back towards the sink with Owen's breakfast dishes. Owen watched her go, feeling badly for snapping, but then again, what was he going to do now?

Standing from the table he grabbed his bag, "I'll see ya later, ma."

"I really hope you have a good day, sweetheart."

6

As Owen reached the bottom of his driveway, he noticed the leopard sitting across the road from him. She sat next to a large sugar maple that grew on the edge of the road, her light coat in stark contrast to the brown bowl of the tree and the yellow, red, and brown leaves on the ground beneath her. Owen was struck with a thought just then. *Certainly someone else must have spotted her by now?* And as if she was reading his mind, she stood, turned, and slowly started to walk up the bank behind her. Just as she began to walk away Owen heard the grind of the bus shifting gears, beginning its climb up his hill.

And without a second thought, Owen bolted across the road. He made tree cover just as the bus cleared the top of the hill. Stepping behind the trunk of a large yellow birch, he caught his breath and waited, listening to the bus driving by him. Owen heard it slow, but not stop. He knew if he wasn't there it would crawl by his house, but keep going. The driver didn't like having to stop on his hill if he didn't have to, so he would just creep by the driveway at a snail's pace. Owen had to be driven to school several times for not being there when the bus drove past.

He knew the problem would be later when the school called because he didn't show and they had not received a phone call from his mother saying he wouldn't be in today.

Once the bus was clear of his house, he started up the hill after the cat. She hadn't moved very far from the road, which surprised Owen.

He thought for sure she would have taken off as soon as he ran across the street, but she had simply sat down when he stopped to wait for the bus, and now that the coast was clear she stood and started walking up the hill again. Her pale coat on the dark forest floor was easy for Owen to follow as he trudged up the hill behind her.

As he walked he silently hoped he'd find some evidence of the leopard to show his parents and try and ease their disappointment from his skipping school. He'd never done anything like this before and could only imagine how disappointed they'd be with him. He looked back up towards the leopard, just to reassure himself that he wasn't crazy, and that he really was following the cat as she stopped, turned, and looked back at him.

Am I crazy or does she want me to follow her, he thought as he kept climbing. The leopard stopped in a small depression in the ground surrounded by hemlocks. As Owen got closer, she moved deeper into the grove where Owen was just beginning to have trouble following her. His father had called this type of area a deeryard because of the thick hemlock cover that actually reduced the accumulation of snow on the ground during winter while the thick bows helped keep in the warmth. The shallower snow was easier on the deer and the thick foliage made for better cover.

Is she trying to lose me? Why doesn't she just bolt instead of walking then?

As he walked deeper into the grove he noticed her sitting as if waiting for him again. She was perched on a downed red oak tree and yawned wide as he came into the small clearing. The yawn gave him pause, even in the shadows of the forest, her teeth gleamed in the little light. Owen stepped closer while the cat watched him until he came to a large stone that was across from the leopard. He stood for a moment and the cat didn't move, so he sat.

"You could have eaten me last night and didn't, so I'm thinking you won't eat me now," the boy said, trying to assure himself.

The rock was cold and he squirmed on it until his behind finally became numb, while the leopard just stared at him, occasionally tipping her head from one side to the other.

"So, why are you here then?" Owen asked. The leopard tipped her head towards him. "Well, you're certainly not from around here. Did someone turn you lose; my dad says people do that sometimes." She tipped her head and Owen thought he saw a glint of something metal around her neck. "You were just dropped off, weren't you? That's a collar around your neck, isn't it?" he asked slowly standing from the rock. The leopard stood with him and took a step backwards off her log. He sat back down. "Okay, I'll stay here; just don't go anywhere, okay?"

The leopard stepped back onto the log and then stepped off it in Owen's direction. His heart began to race as she slowly walked towards him. He held his breath when she was only a foot from him, and when she rubbed her chin along his knee he let out a long, trembling sigh. It was oddly reminiscent of Piper and how she would rub her chin along him. She stopped and looked up into his face. She didn't squint the way Piper would, she held his attention and looked deeply into his eyes as if trying to tell him a story. She looked at his hand, and he slowly lifted it to her face, she sniffed it and then looked back into his eyes. Owen slowly brought the hand up to her face and gently brushed the fur along the side of her cheek. A loud purr emitted from somewhere deep in the leopard's throat, the sound of a revving motorbike, which startled him for a second before he recognized the sound. He ran his hand down a little farther along the leopard's neck, thankful that he hadn't worn gloves today, when he touched what he had seen glinting in the light. The metal was cold in his hand, but before he could take a look at it, the leopard was startled and leapt clear over his head.

She was three meters behind him before he realized he was holding the collar in his hand.

7

Owen stood and quickly turned to see if the cat was gone already from behind him, but as he turned the leopard stopped in her tracks and was slowly turning around to face him. If a cat can have one, then the leopard had a surprised look on her face.

"Please don't go, I didn't mean to take it, it just came off in my hand!" Owen pleaded as he laid the collar on the rock in front of him and took a step back. He noticed it for the first time really. It looked as if it was made of a deep, rich, silver metal; it gleamed in the faint forest light. Owen could see, but not make out very well, writing all along the outside of the collar. As he looked back up at the leopard, he realized he hadn't seen a clasp on it at all. He would have looked back down at the collar to double check, if the leopard hadn't started walking back towards him.

She stopped at the rock and looked down at the collar laying on it. Owen heard, or more accurately felt, a deep rumble in his stomach. Realizing it was a growl coming from the leopard he took two quick steps backward. The leopard looked up at him immediately and silenced her growling. Her eyes locked on Owen's again and he imagined they looked less like an animal's this time. He instinctively took another step back.

The large cat stepped up onto the rock, careful not to touch the collar lying on it. She stepped off and approached Owen, stopping only two feet in front of him. She could sense his heart racing, and a part of her enjoyed his anxiety. She could almost taste his fear as she made eye contact again and changed shape into her true form.

8

Where the snow leopard once stood, now stood what Owen could only have described as an elf girl. She stood only four and a half feet tall, with long tawny and white hair and bright green, one might say, cat-like eyes. Her features were sharp, yet delicate, with an under current of power and fierceness. Her skin was a light, acorn brown with a healthy ruddiness to her cheeks. Her ears poked out from under her hair, which flowed freely down her shoulders and back. She wore only an off white, light cotton tunic and soft, light brown, leather breeches. She wore a small bracelet on her left wrist, and three silver rings, one on her right thumb, one on her right middle finger, and the last on her left index finger.

Owen fell down. He just dropped down onto his rump before he could even try to stop himself. He couldn't believe it. *The snow leopard just...and then a girl...with pointed ears...* His mind stumbled over what he had just seen and just couldn't make sense if it. Owen looked up and met the girl's green eyes, and in that moment he realized that she and the snow leopard were one. They were the same person, animal, being, he couldn't explain how, but after meeting her eyes, he just knew.

She stepped forward and offered him her hand. Owen stared at the fine, long, bird-like fingers offered him and just couldn't help staring. He tentatively held his hand up to hers, and with strength that surprised

Owen, she helped him to his feet. He held her hand and just couldn't take his eyes off her; he made a conscious effort and closed his mouth before she looked down at their hands still clasped. He let go, and she smiled at him, and it filled him the way hot-chocolate warms you on the coldest winter days.

"My name is Orla, and you Owen McInish have set me free," she said with a voice that reminded Owen of forest warblers in spring.

Owen walked over to the stone and sat down. He rubbed his eyes with the balls of his hands and looked back at Orla who had hopped up onto the log again. Owen noticed that she wasn't wearing any shoes, and that on her left foot she wore a small silver toe ring on the toe next to her big toe. He also just realized that when she walked soft bells in her hair danced, sounding like rain drops on dry leaves in autumn.

Great, now what? I've gone insane, he thought as the girl turned and looked at him.

"You seem to be able to accept me as a leopard much more easily than in my true form," she said, smiling at him.

"Yeah, well, at least snow leopards exist. What are you? What next? An old Wizard in a floppy hat, or better yet, are you going to whisk me off to some school for wizards and witches?"

"I'm not sure that I exactly follow you, Owen. To be honest, I'm not sure exactly how I got here. As for what I am, I realize that a human hasn't seen one of my kind in a very long while, so a bit of explaining on my part would seem polite. I am *Fey*, or elf, one of the faerie folk. To be exact, I am Sylvan, or a forest elf. And I meant what I said: you set me free. That collar on the rock, that you were able to unlock, was preventing me from changing back to my Sylvan shape. But even before that, you saved me yesterday from those three hounds."

"Yeah, I've been trying to forget about them. I figured I'd work on proving you existed first, and then I would worry about them. What were they anyway?"

"Death Dogs. Sent after me by someone, but I don't know who would send them for me. To be honest, I don't really remember much before yesterday. I remember that I had left Quailan to visit with my father while he was at Council, but then I can't remember the rest until yesterday and running from the hounds."

"Why didn't you just climb a tree to get away from them?"

"Once the hounds tree their quarry, they bay for the Houndsmen to come, and then it would have been too late. I could feel dawn coming, and was hoping I could out run them until the sun broke the clouds. The hounds cannot exist under the light of day."

"Where's Kway-lan?"

Orla smiled, but didn't answer; she went back to pretending to focus on balancing on the log, which is something she didn't have to do. She placed one foot in front of the other, carefully, as if the log was a high wire, and then without any hesitation, did a back flip back to where she had started. She looked at Owen and smiled.

"Impressive, but you didn't answer my question. Is that in the faerie handbook: "If you should come upon an unsuspecting human, do NOT divulge the location of our secret hideout?"

"No, we don't have a "handbook" as far as I know, but we haven't revealed ourselves to humans in a very long time—even by our standards—and that's for a reason. It's bad enough that I've shown myself to you, but to reveal all our secrets is asking a bit much, don't you think? I've shared more with you than anyone else has in over several thousand years, or more, because you have proven yourself a friend. But some things I cannot share, sorry." She watched Owen now. She was solemn in her sincerity. She was thankful, but she really didn't know Owen, and there was a reason the *Fey* had stopped associating with humans. She hoped she hadn't already shared too much with him, but there was something about him that made her feel she could trust him.

"So what are you going to do now? Don't you have to go back?" Owen was starting to realize that he wasn't going to have any proof of the snow leopard to show his parents and that he was going to be in an awful lot of trouble when he got home. He'd never done anything of this magnitude before, and he was thinking they were going to be pretty upset with him.

Orla, sensing the change in his mood, misinterpreted it, thinking it was related to lack of trust in him. "Owen McInish, there is something more I can show you, without betraying the privacy of my people anymore than I have already." She stepped off the log and began heading farther up the hill, slowly, hoping Owen would join her. In the short time she'd been watching him since her arrival, she had become very found of the young human.

Owen began to walk along beside her through the trees. He stopped, turned, and went back to the stone. Grabbing the collar, he turned and sped after Orla, placing the collar in his coat pocket. He noticed that the only sound she made walking through the dry leaves was the soft raining sound from the bells in her hair.

9

When they finally reached the destination Orla had in mind, Owen was so warm from walking he wished he'd worn a lighter jacket. He was sweating under the one he had on. Orla, however, looked perfectly comfortable in her tunic, breeches, and bare feet.

"Don't you get cold?"

"Of course I get cold. Why do you ask?" Orla asked. She enjoyed having someone whom didn't know all about the *Fey* to talk with. Back home, no one would ever even question her about being cold, or warm, or affected by the climate.

"Well for starters it's like 40 out right now, and you're walking around in a shirt and no shoes." Owen sensed that the elven girl was playing with him, but he really wasn't in the mood. He thought this whole thing was pretty neat, but right now he was distracted about the punishment waiting for him at home and he was rather short on patience. His parent's disappointment was going to feel a lot worse than any punishment they dished out.

"Well, because this isn't really that cold. *Fey* are much more *resistant* to changes in the climate and environment than humans. It's quite like when some humans are more comfortable in warmer climes and some in cold."

"Like flatlanders trying to live in Vermont," Owen said under his breath.

"I'm not sure I understand your analogy."

"Nothing, not important. So, what are we looking at exactly, or are you just taking a break?"

"No, we are looking at something, or at least I am. Tell me what you see," Orla said as she held out her hands to the landscape in front of her.

What Owen saw was some large boulders dropped willy-nilly along the top of a small summit in the hills around his house. Dispersed amongst the boulders was a good cross section of species and ages of different trees, nothing out of the ordinary.

"Some rocks and trees."

"Well, honestly, that is what you're supposed to see, but now watch," as she spoke she took his hand in hers, which was quite warm to touch.

Owen looked back to the spot which Orla indicated and saw something completely different. Instead of random boulders emerging from the surrounding forest floor, he saw large stones hewn into blocks carefully placed in a circle around a small depression in the top of the summit. Surrounding the stones were large, ancient Yellow Birch trees whose bark shown a brilliant gold in the morning light.

"But how?"

"You are seeing the forest, and this place in particular, through my eyes. When we left your world we left markers and places behind that were still ours and placed incantations on them to keep humans from venturing into them, or more importantly, investigating them. When someone comes upon this place they see just the top of a hillside. When this land was pasture more than a century ago, this place looked just like a pasture to anyone who looked."

"But when someone walks through it, they must?"

"No, the spell keeps anyone from walking through the circle. If you were to attempt to do so after I let go of your hand, you would just walk astray of the mark, or if you had never seen the true place, you would not have the desire to even walk that way."

"What is it?"

"A door. It's called an enchanted hollow by some and a sacred circle by others," she said taking a step closer and bringing Owen with her.

"So is this how you got here?" Owen asked feeling a bit overwhelmed at this whole experience.

"I believe so, but I'm not sure. I can't remember anything of how I came here or how the collar was placed upon me. I should be able to use it to travel back home tonight though, and hopefully find out what happened to me. It's disturbing having a whole piece of my memory missing like this."

"Why not now?" Owen asked leading Orla deeper into the depression that the stones surrounded. He was surprised now how unremarkable the site was. In some ways, it reminded him of the place in England, Stonehenge.

"Well, for one, you're here, and when I leave your world, I shouldn't have any observers," Orla was beginning to like this young human. He was nothing that she had envisioned of humans from the stories she had heard from the elders. *He's innocent, kind, and brave.* She wasn't sure if many others from her world would have come to her aid against foes that much stronger than they. *If dawn hadn't been breaking when Owen had engaged the hounds he wouldn't have lasted long against them,* she thought as she let him lead her through the hollow.

"Well, if you're not holding my hand, what difference does it make if I'm here or not?" Owen asked, stopping in the middle of the hollow and turning to Orla. "Would I still be able to see you, or would the spell hide you from me as well?"

"I would hide me, from you, to begin with, but if I didn't do that, no, the circle only disrupts the appearance of itself. You would see me as well as you see a deer walking through. However, you cannot witness the ceremony, and I have never done it before. If you were here, I would be nervous, and worried about doing this ceremony for the first time."

"Ah, okay, makes sense."

"Owen, please do not come back this evening looking for me. I showed you this site in confidence and hope you will respect my wishes. After tonight you may come back as often as you like, actually I hope you do."

"Believe me; I won't be coming back tonight. After my parents get through with me, I wouldn't be able to make the walk up here. So, if you don't remember coming here, how did you know about this place? Or do you know where all of these places are?" Owen was beginning to feel cold again. To him it seemed as if it was actually getting colder. He didn't remember anything remarkable about the weather report last night, but as he looked at the sky, it seemed as if a snowstorm was moving in quickly.

"I sensed it in leopard form. These places emit power that a *Fey* can feel. I came here after you chased off the Hounds, but in leopard form I couldn't complete the ceremony, so I came back to your house for the evening. Thank you, by the way, for your hospitality last night.

"I do apologize for any trouble you might be in with your parents. There was something I was drawn to; possibly something about you that indicated you might be able to help me further, which you did. If not for you, I would still be trapped as a leopard."

"Glad I could help. Listen, I don't mean to be a jerk, but I should be getting home. I'll kick myself later for not spending more time here, or asking you more questions—that I'm sure you wouldn't answer anyway—but I'm sure the school has called by now and my mom is probably freaking out as we speak."

"I understand. Do you mind if I walk back with you? I truly have enjoyed meeting you." *More than you realize, Owen,* she thought.

As they exited the hollow, Orla let go of Owen's hand and it never fazed him that the circle returned to its more natural, yet false, facade. Orla was relieved that the spell still worked. As Orla let go of his hand Owen immediately thought there was something he should be remembering. It was there in the back of his mind, but the more he reached for it, the less he held onto it, so he let it go and concentrated on his walk home.

The two companions walked slowly through the forest, enjoying the quiet of the day, and the light snow that began to fall on their way back to Owen's home. By the time they reached the road and driveway, the snow was coming down much heavier and had already begun to accumulate on the ground

Figures, Owen thought, *I skip school on a day they would have sent us home anyway.*

They stopped on the edge of the road, but neither boy nor elf knew what to say at their parting. Owen noticed his father's truck in the driveway and realized his mom must have called his dad when she had gotten the call from the school.

Orla was also amazed at how different this human was compared to what she had feared she would meet when first realizing she was in this realm.

"So, any chance you could shift back to your snow leopard form and leave a few tracks in the snow for me to find tomorrow? It may help get me off the hook with my parents," Owen said smiling, even though he didn't feel much like smiling. He wondered if this was what it felt like to have a friend to adventure and joke with.

"I'm not sure that would be the best," Orla said smiling despite herself. "Besides, do you really think your parents will be allowing you to wander the woods tomorrow after not going to school today?"

"Yeah, you're probably right. Well, maybe I'll get my dad to take a look anyway."

"Then maybe I can leave some sign, but I'm wary of leaving any indication I was actually in your world, Owen. It truly was a pleasure meeting you, though, Owen McInish, I owe you my life, and I pledge you my friendship." Orla extended her hand.

Owen took her hand in his, and held it for a moment. He willed himself to remember every feeling and thought at that moment. He slowly let go and began to cross the street to his house.

Orla watched him cross the street and begin to head up his driveway; she began to turn back towards the forest when a strange sensation struck. She looked back to Owen and the house when she realized what that sense meant.

10

By the time Orla was able to reach Owen, he had already taken a step up onto his front porch.

"Owen, don't go in there!" Orla said from right beside him.

"What, how?" Owen began and then realized the questions were pointless. "Why?"

"I sense something very wrong from inside your home. I feel presences from my world inside, and they're not friendly," Orla said, reaching out for Owen's hand to lead him back to the woods.

"My parents!" Owen said while bolting for the door. Bursting through, he almost ran straight into a statue standing in the front hallway. *What the? This doesn't belong here,* Owen thought until he recognized the statue. It was his father.

His dad was holding a baseball bat pulled back over his shoulder as if getting ready to swing. The bat, Owen knew, was always kept in the front closet. His father's expression was a mix of fear and anger, frozen in stone.

Owen couldn't believe it. "Oh no, mom," he said almost to himself and then louder, "MOM!" Orla stepped in behind him; "Gaia no, preserve us, Owen BE QUIET!" she hissed through clenched teeth chasing after him.

Owen ran through the downstairs, and when he didn't find his mom, he ran upstairs. He found her just before his parent's bedroom, holding his father's hunting rifle. *He must have sent her upstairs for it while he was going to try and hold them off downstairs. But who, what?* He thought as he felt the first tear begin to slide down his cheek, his eyes welling up. He slouched down onto the floor at his mother's feet. The expression on her face was one of fear and disbelief.

Orla stepped along side him. "Owen, we must leave this place at once. It is not safe here." She put her hand under his arm and began to lift him to his feet.

"But my parents, can you?" he started and then stopped, choking on the words.

"I can not change them back, but I can place a spell on them to keep their minds safe while in this state, until we can bring them back. We must move quickly, however."

She let go of Owen's arm, hoping he wouldn't sit back down. Orla closed her eyes and began mouthing words Owen couldn't understand or follow. She raised her right hand to her forehead and her left hand to Owen's mother's and with her two first fingers touched her own and the other's head. A soft blue glow appeared on his mother's forehead as Orla let go and repeated the motion, only this time touching hers and his mother's lips. The same glow appeared as she let go. Orla opened her eyes and in a slightly distant voice said, "Let's go."

She grabbed him by his arm again and ran down the stairs. Owen really had to run to keep up even though it only appeared that she walked quickly. They approached his father and she repeated the ceremony to the same affect.

With her voice even softer Orla said, "Now, we really need to get out of here." The smashing of the front and back doors drowned out the end of her sentence. Orla pushed Owen out of the way from the door's debris as a huge creature walked in. It stood taller than Owen's father by more than a meter, hunching to squeeze through the broken doorway. The creature had huge bore like tusks growing out of its mouth. It wore thick pieces of hide armor and from under the iron cap on its steeply sloping head, long black, braided hair strewn. In its clawed hand it held a very large hammer. The creature's eyes glowed a pale red and it roared as it charged Owen and Orla.

"What?" Owen started.

"Trolls! Run!" Orla said as she leapt at the troll. Owen noticed that as she jumped her arms from her elbows down changed. They grew whitish fur and her fingertips unsheathed small leopard claws. Owen stood, but before he turned from the room he watched as Orla dragged those claws across the face of the troll, turned in mid-air, pushed of its face with her feet, and landed running beside Owen before he knew it.

"Out the back," she said as they ran into the kitchen.

"*Not so fast faerie,*" a harsh voice said from behind them. Owen turned and saw another troll grab Orla by the back of her shirt and lift her clear off the floor. He was dressed similarly to the first but held a large scimitar instead. As he spoke yellow spittle sprayed from his mouth and he gnashed his tusks together. Owen turned and saw a third troll entering from the hole that had been his backdoor. Without thinking, he reached under the island-counter in the middle of the room, and pulled out the fire extinguisher. Pulling the pin he fired it in the face of the troll holding Orla. It growled and threw her across the kitchen and out the bay window over the sink. As the window crashed, Owen threw the can at the troll coming in through the backdoor. The troll swung its huge battle-axe and cut the can neatly in two resulting in a loud explosion and blast of white, powdery fire retardant. Owen barely ducked in time behind the counter before the explosion sent shrapnel spraying through the room.

He raced for the door, over the now fallen troll with the axe, and out the back. Owen heard the troll he sprayed close behind him. He was hoping that if he had gotten it in the troll's eyes that it might take him a while to recover, but it didn't appear that way. As he ran down the steps of his deck, the troll lumbered out the back door.

"Remember me?" Orla said from the roof above the kitchen door, and as the troll looked up, she dropped a stone gnome from Mrs. McInish's garden. The stone statue broke across the forehead of the troll, temporarily dropping him.

"Go!" Orla shouted as she leapt off the roof, landing next to Owen in the yard. The two companions raced into the forest behind Owen's home and along the railroad bed where they had first seen each other.

11

The snow had really picked up since they had gone inside the house, and there was already a dusting covering the ground. Within the hour there would be several inches of snow on the forest floor. As Owen ran through the woods beside Orla, he knew there was already enough snow for their pursuers to track them.

Orla stopped at the crest of a small hill and looked back towards Owen's house. She held her hand over her eyes to block the snow that was now falling in big wide flakes.

"This snow isn't natural," she said quietly to Owen.

"No, it doesn't seem it, does it?" Owen said feeling hollow and vacant.

"It's not, but I've never met a rock troll that had elemental abilities."

"Have you ever met one that could turn people to stone?" Owen asked.

"No. No, I haven't. There is someone else involved here, someone the trolls answer to," she whispered as she dropped to her knees trying to get a better view beneath the tree limbs. "It looks like there are only two following us. I think the one you felled with the explosion isn't with us anymore."

Owen thought hearing that should bring some satisfaction, some evenness for what had happened to his parents, but it seemed that void in his chest only grew deeper.

"How did you do that, Owen?" she asked genuinely. She had heard many stories regarding humans, but none of them ever spoke of powers like that. She knew that humans were resourceful and had a hunger and adeptness for technology, but she hadn't seen Owen wield anything with power enough to subdue a rock troll.

"He did it himself. I was just trying to hit him with it. He cut it, and the extinguisher blew up. If I hadn't fallen when I threw it, and ended up behind the island when it blew, I'd probably be back there too."

"Thanks to Gaia, you are not," Orla said touching her hand from her forehead, to her heart, and to the ground. "We must keep moving, trolls are not the brightest lot, but rock trolls are the more advanced of the different species. They won't have any problem tracking us in this snow and we still don't know who else is with them." She let the last word trail off as if lost in thoughts of her own.

"Where are we heading? We, I, can't, run all night," Owen said, almost embarrassed to admit he wouldn't be able to keep up with the elf.

"Neither can I, I was hoping to work our way back to the enchanted hollow."

"So you're just going to bail on me, leaving me here with these things?" Owen said more angered than afraid at the possibility.

"No, I have a feeling they are here for me, but they won't leave you as a witness now either. Things have changed, I am afraid you will have to come," she said as she turned and began moving through the forest again.

12

Owen, stunned only for a moment, quickly took off after Orla into the worsening storm. *Take me with her?* He couldn't believe his ears. *First off, why is she in charge? What if I don't want to go? Okay, of course I want to go, but I'm getting tired of her calling all the shots. Although, she did kick some major troll butt back there. But I've saved her life twice now! I should have some input.* He stopped just before walking into Orla.

"If you were thinking any harder I might hear you," she said smiling for the first time since sensing the trolls in the house.

"Yeah, well, what if I don't want to go?" Owen asked, sounding angrier about going than he actually was. He was still pretty upset about his parents and it was finding other ways of coming out. Owen could feel that void in his chest filling in with a deep ache and longing. He decided it was better to become angry. Being angry was easier.

"You don't have to," Orla said staying annoyingly calm. "Most likely, the two remaining trolls will follow me, and send a squad back to deal with you later. I didn't mean to make any decisions for you, I just figured that you would be coming along now because there is no way here, in your world, you can help your parents, but back in my world, we might find a way. I figured you would be very obstinate in that choice and found no point in arguing it with you, seeing how I would want to do the same myself. Was I wrong?" she asked, softening her voice and stepping closer to him to use his body to hide from the wind.

"No. You weren't wrong, but I want to be part of all decision making from now on. No more secrets from you, either."

"Done. As long as you don't ask about anything that might compromise me with my people," she added quickly.

"Okay, so you said "we". Does that mean you'll help me find a way to turn my parents back?"

"Of course. I pledged my friendship didn't I? That's not something a Sylvan does lightly." She blew into her hands to help warm them.

"I thought you didn't get cold?" Owen asked realizing for the first time that her lips were looking a bit blue.

"That's not what I said. You don't listen very well, do you? We're more resistant than humans, but we still get cold. This storm has lowered the temperature quite a bit, but it's also not natural. I'm more susceptible to super-natural elementals than to normal climate changes. I've also used up a bit of my strength and don't know how much more we'll need to get back home, so I don't want to waste it keeping myself warm."

"Well, you can have my coat then," Owen said starting to slide out of his parka.

"No, you'll need that. There is one thing I can do, but I wasn't sure how you'd react."

"What? After everything I've seen, just do what you've got to do to keep yourself warm."

"I could turn into my leopard form again, but then I wouldn't be able to talk with you. I have an in-between shape that combines characteristics of both forms. I just didn't want to upset you by doing it."

"Oh, just do it and get it over with. I think I can handle it," Owen said a bit more sarcastically than he meant.

Without another word Orla shifted shapes right in front of him. There was a dim blue light that flowed over her entire body, and in the soft rustle of leaves there stood her new shape. She was a little shorter, covered in thick snow leopard fur, and her hands were the ones Owen had seen before when she attacked the troll. Her feet were now big snow leopard paws, but her legs were the same shape as her elven form. Her eyes were still the same brilliant green, but her face was more cat-like. Her nose had flattened some, but not entirely like a cat's, and when she smiled at Owen, he could see she had the dentition of a large cat. The one thing that Owen did notice, that embarrassed him a little, was that her clothes had disappeared as quickly as they had appeared the first time. Were it not for her dense fur, she would be naked in front of him.

"Well, what do you think?" Orla asked in a voice resembling a purring cat.

"Wicked. But, I, uh, I thought, you'd still, you know, have clothes," Owen stammered.

"No, they're too cumbersome when we change, so mine are magically stored for me in the ring I wear on my thumb." She held up her hand and showed Owen that her ring was indeed the only piece of clothing or jewelry that she still wore in this form. "Besides, I'm the one without any clothes on; I should be the one embarrassed, not you. All Sylvans change forms. We are so accustomed to changing that we are no longer modest in our animal forms. Besides, my fur covers me more than any piece of clothing I could wear. You humans are an uptight bunch, that one bit of folklore about you is correct," Orla said as she turned and began trotting through the snow. Owen, shaking his head, followed closely behind her.

13

When the two companions reached the hillside at the base of the enchanted hollow, Orla stopped them from moving any further. She sniffed the air, but the wind from the storm was swirling in so many directions she couldn't tell where any of the scents were coming from. Owen searched the snow around where they had first ascended the hill and found several sets of foot prints, certainly large enough to be troll prints.

"Trolls are close, but I can't tell where exactly." She was looking to where Owen was studying some tracks.

"Can they feel the circle like you? Isn't that how they would have come here?" he asked standing up and walking back to Orla.

"Yes, they should have, and yes, they should be able to feel its pull, but I'm more concerned about who's directing them."

"Well, they're probably waiting for us up at the circle, expecting you to make a run for it, right?" Owen asked.

"Maybe."

"How long does the ceremony take?"

"Not too long, but I'll need to concentrate, and if they're up there, I doubt they'll let me," she said as she started heading back up the hill.

"Well, only one way to find out I guess."

As they reached the outer ring of the circle they couldn't see any of the trolls around, but Orla picked up a stronger scent amongst the trees.

"They're here, I just can't tell where." The wind and snow was making visibility very poor.

"So what do we do, we know they're here, and we know they're just waiting for us to show ourselves in the open. Can we wait them out?" Owen asked, already knowing the answer as he began to shiver.

"Well, we've managed this far. We'll make a break for the hollow, once in the center I'll start the ceremony to open the portal, and you do your best to buy me some time."

"Um, sure. You know back at the house, I just got lucky, right? Those things are as big as trucks," Owen said, starting to think this might not be the best plan anyone had ever come up with.

"Yes, but they're not very bright. You humans have odd expressions. I won't need much time. I'm sure you'll manage just fine." She wished she felt as sure as she sounded. Orla wasn't even sure she could get them back to her world. She had never attempted a portal conjuration before, and she hoped she could pull it off. "Okay, on the count of three: one, two."

"Three."

Owen and Orla each spun to see from where the voice had come. Standing about ten feet behind them was not another troll, but something not so unlike a troll that Owen could think they weren't in trouble. The being in front of them stood just less than seven feet tall, had short dark hair on his head, with a lighter, shorter coat of fur over his body, reminiscent of the troll's thick, hairy hide. The creature had longer, pointier ears than a troll, and lacked the large tusks. His body was knotted with muscles, and the armor he wore was of a finer quality than that of the troll troopers they had faced earlier. He held in his hand a long handled axe with two short swords sheathed about his waist.

"Now, ya lil faerie, yous given us a bit of a run, but it's time fer ya to come home now," his voice wasn't as harsh or as rough as the trolls'. As he spoke, he took slow, measured steps towards the companions.

"We've got company coming up from behind us as well," Orla whispered as the new threat approached them. "What are you to do with us?"

"I'm just t'bring you back is all. I've got no argument with either of yous; I'm just here fer the bounty. You knows the rules, no faeries belong here anymore."

"Owen, when I say "go", run for it. I'll try to hold them off and give you a head start," Orla whispered, still keeping her back to the approaching trolls.

Owen didn't like the plan much, but he honestly couldn't see anyway out of this. He wondered, as this new creature approached him, if he was the one who had turned his parents into statues. And in doing so, a small burning began to fill that aching void in his chest. He didn't know how, but he would get Orla and himself out of this and find a way to save his parents.

Just then, the trolls behind them rushed forward with growls and shouts, the creature in front of them yelled shouts in a language deep and guttural, and Orla leapt backwards over the heads of the charging trolls.

"Now, Owen, run!" she yelled as she flipped over the heads of the rushing trolls who collided into one another. The leader of this triad side stepped them both, remaining on his feet, while Owen was knocked to the ground as the trolls crashed past him. *They're as dumb as posts*, Owen thought as he scrambled back to his feet, ignoring the pain in his leg where they had banged into him.

Orla landed softly on her feet, and still in her hybrid form, sprang at the nearest troll on the ground. She grabbed him by the sides of his head, and with all of her strength drove his head into the rocky ground with a loud THUD. She didn't wait to see if the troll was conscious, which he wasn't; she sprang at the leader who crouched into a battle stance. With the blunt end of his axe, he caught Orla in the stomach, knocking her to the ground in the center of the hollow.

The second troll was trying to untangle himself from his unconscious partner when Owen grabbed the biggest stone he could find, lifted it, and drove it into the top of the troll's head. Again, with a painful THUD, the troll's head was driven into the ground, Owen wasn't as strong as Orla, however, and his troll was still conscious, albeit dazed. Owen looked up in time to duck below the shaft of the long handled axe that swung his way. He rolled down the slight depression towards Orla as the troll leader walked down the hill towards them.

As Owen got back to his feet, he could see that Orla was moving, and letting out a slight moan while holding her ribs. The smack she had taken had knocked the wind from her, but at least she was still awake, Owen thought. He started to get as much space between himself and Orla as possible. *If I can get this leader-guy to turn his back to her,* he thought, *maybe she can start the ceremony.* As he began to work his way back towards the trolls, he noticed the one he hit already getting to his feet. The beast didn't look too happy as he began running towards him. The troll commander again shouted orders, and the troll trooper again didn't heed them, just as the troll was about to smash into Owen, Orla leapt onto his face. Now in full leopard form, she raked her front and hind claws over the trolls eyes and head. The creature yowled in pain as Orla hissed and growled.

The troll stumbled backwards as Orla leapt off of him before hitting the ground. The huge troll whimpered and cursed as it rolled, holding its face in the reddening snow. As Orla moved around the troll commander, he turned his back to Owen. Owen didn't miss his opportunity; he grabbed the troll's hammer, barely able to lift it. He crept behind the leader, and lifted it has high as he could, but before he could attack, the commander turned and faced him. Surprised, Owen dropped the weapon square on the commander's foot resulting in a loud crunching. The commander backhanded Owen to the ground, grasping his now ruined foot. Orla, shifting to her mixed form, grabbed the unconscious troll's helmet and smashed it across the leader's jaw, rendering him unconscious with a loud THUNK.

Without wasting any time, Orla shifted to her *Fey* form, and centering herself in the hollow, began quietly to chant in a singsong voice that again reminded Owen of birdsong in the springtime. A soft blue glow began to surround her as her song intensified with the light, she took Owen's hand in hers, and they vanished from the enchanted hollow.

14

Brule woke to the frightful pain in his foot and ringing in his ears. *This is absolutely maddening*, he thought as he pushed himself into a sitting position. He winced from the pain in his foot, but was already focusing past the pain. *Bumbling fools, cousins or no, it's the last time I hire them as back up. Let the Troll Corps keep them. This is one of those times I'm thankful for my elven lineage more than my troll.* Using his axe as a crutch, he pushed himself onto his one good foot. *Well, this is going to bring me a bit of trouble I suppose; so much for an easy bounty on this one.*

The storm was still blowing the snow horizontal across the circle, so Brule held up one of his huge arms to shield his face from the snow and evaluated the scene: his two remaining men down, the quarry gone, himself injured. His employer would not be pleased. He flexed one massive paw in agitation. More dexterous than his troll cousins, his hand still possessed the thick, sharp, bear-like claws common to trolls while, possessing a nimbleness and agility akin to his *Fey* brethren.

Even in the blowing wind and muffled noise of the snow, he heard someone heavy approaching from the direction of the target house. Dropping his axe and unsheathing his swords, he lowered his foot into the snow. Taking most of the weight onto his good leg, he readied himself for whatever broke the lip of the circle. Before he made a visual on the intruder, he picked up the scent on the roaring wind: troll. *Must be Mentogg,* he thought, lowering his swords. *That blast kept him down longer than I would have thought.*

Brule watched as his cousin crested the hill. He carried two stone statues in either arm with ease. His face was still cut and bruised, but most of the swelling had gone down. Trolls heal quickly.

"Hey, whatcha doin' wit dose, aye?" Brule shouted above the wind. *Moron,* he thought.

Still nursing a broken jaw, the troll just nodded his head in the direction past Brule's left shoulder. Brule glanced over in the direction and saw the dark robed figure standing along the rim of the hollow. Juxtaposed with the snow, the dark figure slowly began descending into the circle. The slowness of his gate belied the fluid grace of the body beneath the robes.

Now, here's trouble, Brule thought as he turned to face the being that had hired him. Brule was almost a third taller than the dark robed figured, but all his years as a bounty hunter made him wary of this person. His instincts told him he was one not to be crossed, nor trusted.

"Greetin's sir, what brings yerself here?" Brule asked, facing the robed figure while sheathing his two swords.

"To clean up your mess, half-breed," the voice hissed from under the hood of the robe. Brule bristled, literally, the hair along the back of his neck and shoulders standing on end. He'd heard the insult often growing up, but had never gotten used to it. He had found that while *Fey* didn't want to have anything to do with him, or his mixed heritage, his troll relatives were a bit more accepting. As long as he could fight, they found him worthwhile enough to feed, but Brule had grown tired of the brutal lives of trolls eventually as well.

"Slight set back," was all Brule could manage to say.

"You were sent here for one simple reason. Catch the Sylvan realm-jumper and bring her back to me. You did not do that, though, did you? I do not appreciate failure, Brule," the voice hissed and was lost in the blowing of the storm.

"I unda estimated her is all," Brule started, his anger was cooled by the thought that he finally might have bitten off more than he could handle. "She got help, there was only one mark, you said nuthin about two, but I ain't finished yet," he added almost as an after thought. *Careful now, he wants something, and is positioning you into owing him for this complication,* Brule thought, as the robed figure looked from troll trooper to troll trooper.

"I still want the realm-jumper apprehended and brought to me, but now because you and your buffoons for henchmen have cost me more time, you will have to compensate me for that waste. You will need to find new troopers."

"Dat's alright, I waz gonna git new muscle fer the next job anyways. Whatta 'bout the second mark, I ain't gettin compensated for two," Brule added. "She took the kid, I think, wit her."

"You don't understand me; I am taking your trolls for my own compensation. You will have to deal with the Corps for their loss on your own, and how you deal with the second person is your problem." And with that the three trolls disappeared, leaving Brule, the two stone statues, and his employer standing in the hollow in the middle of the storm.

"But..." Brule stopped before going any further. *Careful. They brought that on themselves anyway, watch yourself.*

"Whatcha want wit the statues?"

"That's none of your concern, they are coming with me. Find me the Sylvan and bring her to me. Understood?" The robed figure walked to the statues, turned, and gave Brule one last look from beneath his hood and vanished.

"But, that's contraband. Now I've gone and done it. The holidays just won't be the same without my cousins around. Ah, who am I kidding, I never liked them anyway. At least now I won't have to pretend to be as dumb as them anymore."

Brule walked to the center of the hollow, kneeled on one knee, and touching an amulet around his neck, disappeared.

15

W ell, that wasn't too hard," Orla said as she collapsed unconscious next to Owen. She immediately changed from her snow leopard-elf form to her pure Sylvan one. Owen himself was feeling a bit woozy after being transported from his world to hers. He kneeled down next to the elf and rolled her over.

"C'mon, wait a second, you never even told where we were going," he said cradling her head in his lap. "Or was that another secret you couldn't tell me?" He looked around uneasily. *If we came back this way, the trolls won't be too long in coming either.* The circle they just appeared in was similar to the one they just left. The major difference was he could see this one without Orla's help. In Orla's world, no spells had been cast to keep humans from seeing the circle. The large stones were green with ivy crawling up their sides. The enormous trees surrounding this circle were quite dead, however, large hulking, hollow vestiges of the trees in Owen's world. This circle also seemed to be in the midst of an old ruined city. Large white stone buildings and pillars surrounded it. To Owen, it appeared that this location might once have been the central garden or green in the middle of a rather old city. *Wicked. It's just like out of one of Mom's books*, Owen thought.

Walls were crumbling down onto walkways while dark green ivy grew up and along everything. The circle was surrounded on four sides by four very ornate staircases, all of which descended down to the hollow. From Owen's vantage point, he couldn't make out much more of the immediate area, but it did feel like some sort of arboretum gone wild.

He knelt beside Orla, pushing her hair back from her face, and gently tried to wake her. When that didn't work, he tried to cradle her in his arms and stand up. She was much lighter than she looked, but he still didn't think he could carry her like this for an extended distance. He walked to the staircase that seemed to not have any buildings immediately adjacent to it. As he topped the last stair he could see why.

At the top of the stairs, Owen looked out over a field of sarcophaguses and tombstones. A vast field of grave markers, the largest cemetery Owen has ever seen, and beyond that, an open field of blue nothingness. The city in which he stood, and the cemetery adjacent, had been built on the edge of a freefall, overlooking a wide open sky of nothingness beyond. From this point, it looked to Owen that he could walk right into the sky.

"Geezum crow," Owen whispered. "Yeah right, next option?"

He turned and looked around the rest of the city. The three other stairwells led to three separate avenues that lead away from the sacred circle. Owen looked up at the Sun. To him it looked like each stairwell faced each compass direction: North, South, East, and West. He looked back at the girl in his arms.

"Any hint as to which way we should go?"

Owen began to have the feeling he was being watched. A slight tickle ran up his spine and neck into his hairline and scalp. It was not a good tickle. He quickly scanned the surrounding area, but there were so many doorways and windows someone could be anywhere. He decided he would just take the alley directly opposite from the grave yard. Seemed like a good choice to him. Get as far from the cemetery as possible.

Carrying his companion in his arms, Owen quickly stepped down into the circle and back up the opposite stair. The buildings on this side looked to be in varying states of disrepair. The bleached stone shone like albino veins in the morning sun beneath the dark green ivy that clung to it like skin.

Owen didn't like this city.

It could have been the whole experience up to now, or the proximity to the grave yard, but there was something about the city that gave him the creeps. A presence, or the pallor of the buildings themselves, clung to the city as apparent as a stench. And Owen didn't like the shadows. Every doorway and window cast one. Admittedly, many windows were shuttered closed, but many more were left open and the dark confines of the spaces beyond were left in thickening shadow.

The darkness watched him with hunger and malice, and Owen wished for nothing more than to be through this town. Staying to the center of the avenue, out of the grasp of the shadows, Owen hurried down the street. He could see forest beyond, and he dashed toward it, not daring any further looks into the buildings he passed for fear of what he might find.

16

Owen stopped once they reached the edge of the forest. He turned from the cobblestone road he'd been following and pushed into the dense mountain laurel that lined the roadside until he came to a large white oak, whose limbs bent low to the ground, creating a small bungalow of leaves and wood.

He sat, leaning his back to the great tree and realized that he was still cradling the young elf in his arms. Owen laid her down beside him, propping her head upon one of her arms and laid his jacket over her.

"That was freaky," Owen finally said with a shudder, breaking the silence.

"*Cer'Logg de Mortem*," Orla said in a whisper without opening her eyes, "the City of the Dead."

"Brilliant," Owen replied, sliding further down the tree trunk and trying to be as unseen as possible. He looked up through the branches and could see the sun approaching noon above them. His stomach gurgled and growled its hunger.

"I really don't want to be anywhere near this place when it gets dark," he said aloud hoping Orla would answer, but she lay still. Owen traced back over the events leading to this point. He was still having trouble grasping that all this was really happening.

Orla stirred.

"Oh, thank God," Owen said sitting up a bit straighter.

"Oh, ouch," Orla said trying to sit up, wincing in pain. Breathing in sharply, she grasped her ribs where the troll leader had struck her with his axe shaft. She wrapped her arm around where the shaft had made contact and pulled herself into a sitting position. She looked around and got her bearings before turning her attention on Owen.

Owen for his part was just too awestruck to do anything but stare. He still found himself unwilling, or unable, to believe everything that had happened thus far. And even with this girl beside him, it was still too inconceivable.

"You carried me all this way?" Orla asked looking back towards the city they had first appeared in. Before she collapsed, the stone buildings and the placement of the circle had reminded her of the stories she'd heard of the City of the Dead, but the stress of the enchantment had been too much for her to remain conscious. But the glimpse she had caught had been enough, that and the overwhelming feeling of foreboding the City seemed to admit.

"Yeah," Owen said, awkwardly digging small trenches in the duff with his feet.

"How'd you know to come this way?" Orla asked slightly bemused by the boy's unease.

Owen laughed a bit, "It was a guess. It was the first road that led directly away from the grave yard."

"Good choice," Orla said nodding her head in approval. "We need to keep going, though. We should be as far from *Cer 'Logg* as we can be by night fall."

"Who lives there?" Owen asked, partly not wanting to know, and partly not expecting Orla to tell him.

"Those that wake in the dark, death in the night, the *Vam-Pyr*," the girl said, quietly looking back towards the white stone city.

"Vampires!" Owen exclaimed.

"And their minions, yes," the girl said. She laid her hand upon her ribs and very quietly spoke words in a language Owen could not understand. Her hand glowed a faint blue at first, but the light flared brighter until it was finally, in an instant, gone. Orla stood up without any sign of pain.

"C'mon we need to move," she said holding her hand out for Owen.

"You don't need to tell me twice," Owen said hoisting himself up and brushing himself off.

17

Orla led Owen out of the thicket of mountain laurel and onto the main cobbled road Owen had detoured from when he first left the City. His shoulders and arms were still tired and a bit sore from carrying Orla all that way. He tried to chase the thought from his mind knowing that they needed to cover much ground before nightfall. He chanced a look back down the road towards the City. Its bright stone walls in the glowing noon sun offered no warmth. The still and quiet buildings presented only unspoken malignent intent.

It didn't take any further encouragement for the two young people to move quickly down the road, which soon turned to dirt and gravel and then finally dirt alone. It was obvious to Owen that this road no longer saw much traffic. It was easily wide enough for two cars to pass in opposite directions, but the lack of use had allowed weeds and other vegetation to begin creeping back up onto the road surface. The ground was still hard and solidly compacted, however, from its previous history.

Owen tried to divert himself as they moved into the forest. He identified the trees and small plants that he knew as he walked passed them: trout lilly, wintergreen, sugar maple, red maple, beech.

Orla had shifted to her hybrid form and was walking just slightly ahead of him as they traveled along the road. Owen could see her feline nose sniffing and her more feline like ears alert as the companions moved quickly down the road.

They hadn't been traveling long when her pace slowed slightly and the look on her furred face became a bit more concerned.

"What is it?" Owen whispered feeling her unease.

"I'm not sure yet. Strange scent from up ahead on the road. Lots of bird noise," Orla answered straining her acute senses for a clearer picture of what was happening, but a sharp bend in the road kept her from seeing what she was scenting and hearing.

"Careful now," she said as she stepped a bit more in front of Owen, who noticed and felt a bit foolish about the elf girl moving to protect him, but Owen realized that in her world he was more than a bit out of his league.

As they rounded the corner Owen could see a dark shape on the road before them. The dark mass seemed to undulate, moving to and fro and up and down as if a pile of black jelly had been spilled upon the lane. Then Owen heard the noise, the cawing of dozens of crows. The mass finally began to make sense and take proper shape.

Owen was watching a huge murder of crows hoping, walking, and flapping in a mass on the road. As Orla and he crept closer, the raucous birds quickly took notice of them and began to take roost in the elm trees over the road in which they'd gathered. Now Owen could see a much smaller, tattered shape on the road in which the birds had been so interested.

Orla turned her nose up at the smell now. The acrid scent of death, albeit freshly dead, clung to the back of her throat like cellophane.

"Should we get off the road?" Owen asked, a bit curious to see what was up ahead, but a bit more hesitant to find out.

"I don't think so," Orla answered, studying the sides of the road. "I'm still picking up a scent I can't place—that I've never smelled before. Let's just move through here quickly." The small *Fey* began to move a bit faster down the road, scanning from side to side, leery of any dangers that might be lurking in the shadows.

It quickly became apparent to Owen that what had been covered in crows a moment before was a person dressed in long robes. As he and Orla approached Owen could see the corpse was very much human looking, much more so than Orla. The crows had not been on the body very long, and it was still very much intact. One arm was draped across the face so Owen couldn't make out much detail, but from what he saw this person could have been human. From beneath the arm a long gray beard hung matched by long locks the same color that spilled upon the brown earth. The hand extending from the open sleeve had been mutilated by the feeding birds.

Owen stopped. Something deep inside him prompted him to move the arm from the man's face; a voice in the back of his mind goaded him to see if the corpse was human or not.

"Owen, c'mon," Orla hissed back at him. She was no more than ten feet in front of him, but the noise of her beckoning seemed very loud below the suddenly silent birds. Both Owen and Orla could sense the unease of the forest around them. Owen's curiosity suddenly gone, he began to turn from the corpse when he noticed the dead man's other hand, or lack there of. Where the second sleeve lay empty upon the ground there was a large dark stain in the dirt where a hand should have been. Owen noted then that the saturated sleeve was darker than the rest of the robes. That was when he noticed the small black ring laying just outside the stain on the hard, dry dirt road, its blackness standing out on the pale brown background.

Something tore his arm off, Owen thought, as he bent down with a deep sense of revulsion, unable to stop himself he picked up the ring. A memory flickered in the back of his mind: all those stories of magic rings, but the memories were squashed as the eerily silent forest suddenly came to life once more with a thunderous crash.

As Owen spun around, he saw two small trees snapped in half and a multitude of crows take off amongst the shards of wood. What materialized from behind the veil of corvids was larger than the trolls that had attacked him at his home, but its appendages seemed even more oversized and oddly out of proportion to its body and torso. The creature stood nearly ten feet tall, and its head seemed too large for its thin neck and thin shoulders. Its long thin arms hung nearly to its knees. The creature's torso was long, with a thin frame, but with a large pot belly. Its short legs were thick, but its knock knees thicker. When the creature bellowed, Owen noted, the few teeth it possessed were widely spaced, like stones in a grave yard—and not so unlike the color of them as well. Its yellow skin was spotted in large brown splotches.

It lumbered towards the boy, raising one thin gangly arm above its head. It held in its hand an awkward club Owen thought at first, until he recognized the soft pale arm, bite marks and all, for what it was. A sudden squeamishness wracked Owen's stomach. The next bellow from the creature, however, brought Owen to action once more.

"Ogre!" Orla shouted as she leapt towards the creature, but she had some ground to make up before she was on it.

Owen looked past the Ogre to a large tree just off the side of the road, a fat sugar maple with low limbs that hung over the roadway. *I wish I was standing there*, he thought, as he absentmindedly slid the ring upon his finger.

With a rush of wind and the sound of ruffling feathers suddenly filling his ears, Owen had a very different view of the Ogre. He was suddenly watching the Ogre's backside as it fell face first into the road next to the corpse where Owen had only a moment before been standing. Orla was suddenly leaping past him, quickly looking towards him with a startled expression on her face, the fierce growl abruptly silent.

Not good, Owen thought, quickly looking down at the ring now upon his index finger. A thin beam of sunlight penetrated the shade of the maple under which he stood illuminating the band on his finger. It was completely black, onyx or ebony, Owen thought, but then he noticed the fine detailing along it. It was etched to look as if it was crafted of tiny bound black feathers. The craftsmanship was so amazing, Owen found himself momentarily distracted from the danger at hand.

The Ogre stood just as Orla was landing upon his back. A startled groan escaped his throat as Orla's claws sank into his mottled flesh. The huge creature wheeled around wielding its macabre club. Orla's growls could be heard above the din of the Ogre's protests. Relocating Owen, the creature again charged, Orla suddenly forgotten by the sight of its intended victim.

Owen took a step backward, feeling the deep fissures of the tree trunk behind him. He saw the low hanging branches above him and thought they might offer some defense to the now trotting giant. Its strides were long and ungraceful, with huge feet slapping the ground more like flippers than feet.

If I can just time it right, Owen thought.

"Owen! Move!" Orla growled from the back of the ogre as she raked new gouges down its back.

The monster lumbered on two more steps, Owen closed his eyes and thought about the spot he had been once before, next to the dead man. Once more there was a whoosh of feathers in his ears and an instant of vertigo, which was suddenly gone with the sound of more breaking tree limbs.

Owen turned to see the ogre beneath several large tree branches which he had fallen amongst as he crashed into them. Orla was looking about trying to find Owen when, finally, her eyes settled on him. The look upon her half cat form was strange, but as she shifted forms in front of Owen he saw the look of distrust, caution, and fear appear momentarily upon her *Fey* face before disappearing. Orla looked at him blankly before turning her attention to the ogre once more.

"We should hurry before he wakes up," she said over her shoulder, not taking her eyes off the monster.

Owen looked down at the man dead in the dirt once more and fought the macabre urge to move his arm. He hurried after Orla, leaving the scene behind them to the gregarious crows once more.

18

As the sun slowly crept across the flagstone floor, the Queen stirred beneath her silk sheets. The thick drapes were pulled back from the window frames to allow the night sky to show its moon, stars, and planets while breathing cool night air into her chambers. As the rays crept ever closer to the slumbering figure under the silk sheets and exotic fur blankets, it seemed to hesitate. The beam of light considered the figure lying beneath the bedding; her slender, lithe form, skin the color of rich soil, face hidden beneath the cascading raven hair. The sun stopped short of touching the bedposts and seemed to retreat at the recognition of whose chamber it had entered. As the burning orb rose higher into the morning sky, the light faded from the bedroom and slowly meandered its way back to the open window facing east. It lingered at the sill, as if it considered approaching the still figure once more, tempted to bath her in light, but the figure stirred slightly and the last of the light leapt from her presence into the bright morning sky.

The body under the sheets and canopy bed moved again, and in the first moments of awakening she felt it, the presence of a human, a boy bordering on manhood to be exact. A feeling she hadn't felt in a very long time. Her eyes remained closed, but she rolled over in bed, her smooth skin sliding easily against the slick silk sheets. Her tongue flicked out like a serpent and tasted the power the child brought to her world, and a slow smile opened across her ageless face, still hidden behind her long, rich, black hair.

Slowly sitting up in bed, her hair fell away from her face, only to envelop her shoulders, back, and breasts to become a midnight shawl of hair. She opened coal colored eyes in the still dark room, and the smile played across her face.

"What a glorious morning," Lilith the Dark Queen of Illenduell said in her slightly raspy voice. She stepped from her bed, the cool morning air quickly turning her naked skin to goose flesh. Lilith approached the window sill facing East and the light seemed to shrink from her approach, the darkness enshrouded her; the light avoided her. She surveyed her Kingdom from her tower bed chamber, the highest peak in her castle, Dunkeln'Tocht in the Thorne Mountains.

"What a glorious mourning indeed..."

19

The two companions traveled cross country for the better part of the morning. Owen was pushing his limits as noon approached. He'd always thought himself a rather skilled hiker, with strength and endurance, but he was tapping into his reserves already, and they hadn't even hit lunch yet. For her part, Orla was doing fine. She knew she was pushing the human, but she wanted to get as much space between the City and them before nightfall as possible.

Neither of the companions mentioned the ogre or what had happened back along the road. For Owen's part, he wasn't sure he could really articulate what he had done or that had happened to him. Orla had found herself deep in thought. Everything she had ever been taught about humans had been called into question when the young man beside her had saved her from the Death Dogs and later the collar trapping her in her animal form, but now all the stories of deceit and mistrust were returning to her. Had she made a mistake bringing this boy into her world after all?

Owen had tried to preoccupy himself by studying the landscape of Orla's world as he traversed it. Brooding on the ring and what had happened didn't seem productive, and quite frankly, he was scared to think too much on the ring, or to even try to take it off. For now it fit nicely and peaceably upon his finger, and he figured to let it stay that way.

Orla's world was surprisingly similar to his own, albeit Owen hadn't been really sure what to expect. With the exception of mountain laurel in the understory and more oaks in the overstory, the two worlds seemed very much alike. The ground he covered in the morning had been hilly, foothills really, of a mountain range similar in size to Owen's Green Mountains, which Orla had called the Coimhno'ir Mountains. When Owen had asked her what that meant, she said it meant *guardian* in his tongue. He thought about asking her what they guarded them against, but then thought better of it. He spent the rest of the day concentrating on not letting anymore distance creep between him and Orla as she lead the way. The bells in her hair softly raining as she stepped over twigs that lay silent for her only to snap noisily under Owen's feet.

"I figured we'd stop for lunch on the top of that small knoll on the horizon," she said in her song bird voice.

"Sounds good," Owen responded trying not to sound too tired. He was really looking forward to the rest. When they had first set out he'd found himself recounting the previous day and morning's events, and as the morning passed his thoughts began to focus more and more on just keeping up with the faerie in front of him.

Orla stopped short and Owen nearly walked into her. He looked up to see where they were, he had been watching her feet, like he had for the last hour, and hadn't realized they'd reached the top of the knoll.

"Gypsylvanians," Orla said as if that should explain everything. Owen said nothing, waiting for her to explain. It took her a few seconds to remember he would have no idea who or what they were.

"Oh, sorry. They're sort of nomads, they travel around, tell people's fortunes, perform. Some people say they're thieves and can't be trusted," Orla said, looking at Owen as if he too was a Gypsylvanian.

Owen looked down over the knoll and was thankful to see the road leading away and around from the hill on which he stood. In a small field to the side of the road were five very colorful carts, and off to the side of the carts were ten mules, all hobbled and grazing on the bright green grass. He saw small cooking fires rising from amongst the carts and caught site of brightly dressed individuals. They all had very dark hair and none seemed to be as faerie-like as Orla. They reminded Owen that he had never asked Orla about the dead man in the road from this morning, and now these people seemed more like him than Orla herself did. *I thought there were no humans here*, he pondered.

"We might be able to buy some clothes off of them for you," she added, "You'd make a good Gypsylvanian, except your eyes are too light, too blue. Stay here and eat lunch. I'll go down, and see if we can get you some clothes. I don't have much money though," she said, handing him a small pouch in which she had been storing berries, nuts, and currants in as they hiked through the morning.

"I'll be back in a little bit, don't go anywhere," she said more harshly than she intended. She paused for a moment considering apologizing, but then thought better of it. "Don't vanish on me," she said instead as she walked down the hill to the wagons below.

Where would I go? Owen thought as he sat with his back to a large white oak and watched Orla work her way down the hillside. *She's fearless*, he thought as he pulled out some berries and began to eat them, savoring each one, trying to make his meager lunch last a little longer.

As she walked down the hillside toward the Gypsylvanian wagons she wondered if she was making the right decision. She was somewhat confident that if they did turn out to be thieves she could outrun them in her leopard form and get herself to safety, but what of Owen. Or, what if they had a *Draiodoir* with them? She would be able to enspell Orla before she knew what was happening. If she could get Owen clothes, though, they wouldn't have to worry so much about taking the road and could possibly make better time. He had faired better than she had expected, but they needed to make better time still and get as far from the City as possible before dark.

She stepped up to the first wagon and heard the laughter and giggling of young children and her tension eased some. She stepped around the wagon and saw a young family cooking their mid-day meal. A young, attractive woman was tending the fire, while a young, muscular man was wrestling with three children, two of whom had him by his legs, while the third he held upside down. It was the upside down child who first noticed Orla.

"Hiya Miss," the upside down boy said, with blood rushing to his face. His father quickly right-sided him and placed him on the ground. The two girls, now that Orla could see them from around their father's legs, came with their brother to investigate her. As Orla stepped into the opening and then into the shelter of the wagons, which had been parked in a horseshoe shape to allow for privacy from the road, she noticed the rest of the families around their own cooking fires. She counted two other families, both with older parents and older children. A single cooking fire stood alone and unattended at the moment.

"I'm so sorry to interrupt," she started as she stepped to the first family.

"My name is Orla and my companion and I have been traveling, but his clothing has become," she smiled, "un-wearable, and we were hoping you or one of the other families might have some to spare."

The father smiled and bowed, the mother smiled less and bowed more slightly, but Orla felt that she was welcomed none the less.

"I am Giovanni and this is my wife Olga, and these are our children. My two older brothers and their families are our companions along with my Mother and Grandmother." Orla noticed that neither of the older woman were anywhere to be seen.

"I'm sure we could find some clothing for you, but I hope you pardon if I might say, traveling and performing has not been very profitable for us this year, so we will have to charge a fair fee for the garments we sell you."

"I understand," Orla said with a curtsy and wondered whose idea of fair they would be using.

"Now, um, where is this friend?" Giovanni asked craning his neck around the wagon the way Orla had come.

"Oh, he stayed down the road a ways. He was embarrassed by the state of his clothing and wanted to stay out of sight."

"Ah," Giovanni's expression changed slightly, allowing Orla to glimpse a suspicious interior, but then reverted back to his polite, host exterior. "Well, then, how large of a person is he, is there someone here about his size that we might use as a judge of fit?"

Orla quickly scanned the families, who had now taken notice of her, and were watching her with a happy curiosity. Orla was beginning to feel that this outward jovial feel they exhibited was part of their performing personas.

"That boy there, he's about the same size as my friend."

"Ah, not a problem, let me see what I can come up with for you. Will you need shoes as well?"

"Oh, yes please, if you have any to spare."

Giovanni stepped over to his brother's family and after exchanging a quick explanation the two men climbed into the wagon closest to his brother's camp fire.

"Please sit," Olga motioned Orla to a small pillow on a blanket next to the fire.

"Thank you." Orla sat, knowing this moved her out of Owen's sight from atop the hill, but feeling to not do so would have been an insult.

"Tea?" Olga offered a small ceramic mug to Orla, still steaming in the noon day warmth.

"Hmmm, thank you."

"It is a special blend my family makes while traveling. It reinvigorates you while relaxing your weary muscles. Please drink. May I ask where you are traveling to and from?" Olga smiled sheepishly, but Orla knew the young woman was seeking information about the travelers, disguising it by simple politeness.

"We are heading back to my village in the Sylvanni Kingdom, and traveling back from a pilgrimage to the Caomhno'ir Mountains." Orla noticed Giovanni emerge from the wagon with a small bundle of clothes over one arm and a pair of black boots in his other hand.

"Ah, Madam, you are in luck, we had some clothes in the size you wish, but I'm afraid we do not have much to offer, and what we do have is of very fine quality, for which I'm hoping you have enough to compensate us for parting with such exquisite tailorship." He handed the clothes to Orla, and she had to admit to herself, they were fine garments. She looked back at Giovanni and she could tell he had recognized her admiration of the clothing.

"We also only have these fine doe skin boots, again of the highest quality. I had to convince my brother to part with them, he did not want to sell them at any price, but I convinced him that you would be a worthy owner of such exquisite boots and would be fair in your trade for them." He handed over the boots, and even though they had much wear, they were still in exceptional condition and would be more than adequate for Owen.

"How much?" Orla asked.

"Hmm, well, the clothes I would have to say we would need at least five silver, and the boots alone should bring another five, what you say?"

Orla knew that in her village she could have fetched a much better price, but under the circumstances this price was not out of the question. She pulled the small leather pouch from under her tunic and handed it to Giovanni. "There is fifteen silver in there, is there any chance we could purchase some food with the remaining five coins?"

Giovanni smiled widely and nodded his head in approval, "Of course, Madam."

He spoke quickly in the language of the Gypsylvanians and Olga moved quickly into their own wagon, only to reappear moments later with a small bundle wrapped in a brightly colored scarf and a small leather water skin. She handed the bundle and skin to Orla.

"It is not much, as my husband said, these have been lean times, but it should be enough for a week or so." Olga bowed again to Orla. As Orla stood up and began to make her farewells to Giovanni's family she noticed a woman walking over to her from the abandoned fire. She was Gypsylvanian without a doubt, but seemed different too. She still had long dark hair like the rest of the woman in the caravan, but hers was just starting to streak with gray. She still moved as one of the young woman, but as she stepped up alongside Giovanni, he bowed and addressed her as "Grand-mother."

"Ah, a young Sylvan, I thought I sensed a ripple in the power in my caravan. What brings you to our humble wagons?" She spoke slowly and articulately in Orla's native tongue.

"I was in need of clothing for my companion and food to help us finish our journey back to my homeland," Orla said with a bow of respect.

"No need to bow to me, Princess," the older woman said with a smile and a slight bow of her own. Orla's chin dropped slightly at being recognized, but *How?* she thought. "Ah, yes, forgive me; I am Madam Prushj'niev, the Matriarch of this clan. Now, this companion, I would like to meet him as well."

Orla had the feeling along her spine that Madam Prushj'niev already knew who and what Owen was. She wasn't sure if she should be bringing a human back to a Gypsylvanian Caravan when the older woman in front of her spoke again.

"Easy my good, Princess, I mean you and your friend no harm. It has been a very long time since a *Manslchich* has walked amongst us here, and I would like to meet him and *Read* for him, nothing more," Madam Prushj'niev said with a nod in the direction of the knoll where Owen was waiting for her. Orla curtsied, thanked her, and turned back to Owen. She was going to have to bring him back down to meet the woman.

Owen watched as Orla came back around from the corner of the wagon. He'd been a little concerned when she left his field of vision, but he also figured she could take better care of herself than he could, so he knew he shouldn't worry too much about her.

As she made her way up the hill, he noticed clothes and shoes under one arm and another bundle in her right. *Some food I hope.* The berries and nuts for lunch hadn't done much for him, and as she stepped into the little oak grove atop the hill his stomach groaned noticeably.

"Well, they didn't rob us too badly for the clothes, hopefully they're a good fit, and we were able to get some food as well. Not sure what they gave us, but you should probably eat some of it before we head out again. Oh, and their Matriarch would like to meet you."

"Uh, what? How? Meet me? Why?"

"She sensed you up here somehow, she's probably some sort of sorceress, and she could tell you were human, she wants to meet you. I'm not sure it's the best idea, but I also don't want to offend and insult a *Draiodoir*, they've hexed people for less.

"Go ahead and get dressed, and we can head down there."

She handed Owen his new clothes and turned her back to face the caravan again, giving Owen the most privacy he was going to get. He took the clothes and stepped back down the opposite side of the hill a little ways from the wagons before beginning to undress.

He laid out the clothes on an old downed tree. A pair of black wool pants, a thick, black, leather belt with silver, square buckle, a white, rough spun, cotton tunic undershirt, a black, wool vest with intricate red and orange embroidered runes and knot-work on the front, a knitted charcoal colored wool sweater, and a jacket that seemed to Owen to be a wizard's sleeve. It was long, down to his calves, with large cargo pockets on either side, sleeves that to Owen seemed short, ending just below his elbows, but with large gaping cuffs reminiscent to Owen of a Monks style of robe. It was a rich dark brown and waxed to repel to the weather. It was re-enforced and double thick across the shoulders to provide further rain protection. Owen put on everything but the sweater; he stored that in one of the large cargo pockets of his jacket. He slid on the boots. They were a well worn soft black leather. When he first pulled them on they came all the way up to his thigh, so he rolled them back down to just below his knee. In one of the pockets of his jacket were a pair of leather, doe-skin, black gloves. He stashed them back in the pocket in case he needed them later.

He stood up and looked down at his new attire. He looked like a character out of one of his mom's stories. At the thought Owen felt a pang in his heart and a renewed sense of urgency. He stashed the rest of his own clothes into his other pocket with his gloves and marveled at how much space they seemed to have.

Climbing back to the top of the hill, Orla turned to see how he looked.

"Well, you certainly look like a Gypsylvanian, except for your light eyes of course. But this will do, this will do very well compared to your old clothes. Most folks won't even look at you twice or mark you as a human now, although they'll probably check their purses two or three times while you're around," Orla said with more levity than she had used since their encounter with the ogre. It didn't go unnoticed by Owen, but he stayed his tongue in case of ruining the lighter atmosphere the remark had created.

She motioned him to where she was sitting and indicated the food she'd laid out for them. It wasn't much, but it seemed more substantial than the few berries he'd eaten before. They each had a small piece of hard bread, a wedge of cheese from a large waxed roll, and a small piece of dried and salted meat. Owen guessed venison, but wasn't sure.

"How far to your village?" Owen took a bite of the cheese without even noticing how it tasted. He had become fixed on finding a way to cure his parents. He figured there must be someone in Orla's village that could help them with this; Orla certainly seemed to harbor no love for trolls.

A little surprised by his sudden change in demeanor, Orla tried to remember her geography, "If we stay on this road we should be able to make it in a week or two, I think."

"A couple weeks? We're that far away? Is there any faster way? Horses?"

"We could try to find some steeds, but I just spent all my money buying clothes and food. We would have had to take the chance of going into a city to find someone with steeds for sale, though. And by doing that, we would raise the chances of being discovered. I'm not going to assume that those trolls have stopped pursuing us."

Owen nodded. She was right of course, he was an oddity here and to go into a city or village raised the chances of being discovered, and if the trolls caught them then there was no one to save his parents. Maybe there would be a farm or ranch along the way where they could buy horses, or even steal a couple, he mused.

They finished eating their improved lunch. Orla wrapped the scarf with their bundle of food around her waist, in an improvised fanny-pack Owen thought. Then they stood and headed down the hillside towards the Caravan to meet the *Draiodoir*.

20

The Matriarch of the Prushj-niev clan was sitting crossed legged by her youngest grandson's cooking fire. Her grandson sat to her left, his wife to her right. The three young children were no longer present. The other two families continued about their business as if nothing was different from their normal day to day affairs.

Owen noticed almost immediately that these people possessed none of the faerie-like traits that set Orla apart from him. They were similar in build and looks to him and the dead man along the road. It was true; Owen could almost pass for a Gypsylvanian, if not for his eyes. Their eyes had no discernable pupils or irises. They were solid black from what Owen could tell, very different from his own light blue eyes. However, with his eyes closed, his own black hair and coloring would be a match for anyone else in this family. Even his stature was similar to the young men at the other camp fires. Apart from their strange eyes, everyone here looked the same as the pictures of Gypsies Owen had seen in his own world. Were they the same or distant relatives?

Owen followed Orla to the fire; she knelt on a blanket across from the older woman. Now that Owen was closer he could see she was older than when he first saw her from a distance. Another woman exited the wagon beside them and came and took her place between the man and the first woman. She too looked older, but not as old as the first. *Mother to the man, daughter to the older woman*, Owen thought.

Owen knelt beside Orla on the blanket and the oldest woman in the center spoke.

"Welcome, *des Mesch*, it has been a long time since one of you has walked amongst us."

Owen nodded to her and smiled faintly, not knowing what else to do. He had no idea what he should say or do or what she was talking about. The old woman sat and studied him for a moment. She closed her eyes then, letting her head droop slightly, resting her chin upon her chest. To Owen it seemed an awkward and long time before she lifted her head and looked on him once more.

"You are the bringer of change, the uniter of worlds; it is my honor to meet you. You have a long road ahead of you, heavy burdens you will carry, with loss and sorrow as your guides. But, you will not walk alone. Remember, compassion is mightier than any magic. Go and may the light never leave you." At that the two older women stood and walked back into the wagon adjacent to them. Giovanni stood as did his wife and they both nodded to Orla and Owen and went back to preparing their noon day meal.

Orla took Owen by the wrist, turned, and stepped out onto the road, heading south towards Sylvan.

21

Night came silently. It whispered through the trees along the road, slowly stretching shadows until they were shadows no more and only evening remained. The sun sank in the West without a sound. By the time Owen and Orla realized how late it was getting they had few choices for a secure place to camp for the evening. They were preoccupied with this when they practically walked into the stranger walking down the road.

Both Owen and Orla stopped short; Owen's hand quickly went to the black feathered ring on the index finger of his opposite hand. He could feel the hairs on the back of his neck stand on end, and he knew that Orla was very close to changing form. She stood lightly on her toes, but every muscle was taught and ready to spring into action.

In the moment that followed, which to Owen seemed like many very long moments strung together, he looked at this fellow on the road. He was an extremely tall man, taller than any man that Owen had met before. He guessed he must be close to seven feet, shorter than the three trolls, but rivaling the troll leader. He had a very long white beard, which Owen noticed—even in the dim light—had food crumbs stuck in it. His clothes were old and travel stained. His dark gray cloak was tattered at the hem. His hood was up and pulled low over half his face. Owen was again feeling that he was in a dream, as if a character had stepped from one of his favorite books. Merlin, Gandalf, and

Dumbledore ran through his mind, but then he noticed the man's walking stick, or more correctly, walking spear. The pilgrim before him held an old worn spear, nearly as tall as the man himself, the shaft rough hewn, knotted and uneven, and the spear head nicked and pitted.

Owen stole a glance to Orla for an instant, but in that instant, in his peripheral vision, the man seemed to stand straighter, bolder, and his spear was solid and true, with glowing red runes down the shaft with a frighteningly strong and edged tip. Owen looked back to the ragged pilgrim before him. This man was much more than he seemed.

"Greetings little ones," the wanderer said, his voice a deep bass, like a drum reverberating in your stomach. It seemed to resonate in the air even after he had stopped speaking. It was not a frightening sound, however, one of deep comfort and warmth. Owen felt, however, under different circumstances, that drum could be a very frightening sound indeed.

"Evening," Owen said, inclining his head towards the stranger, but not taking his eyes from him. Orla took a step to the side separating herself some from Owen.

"Greetings," she answered, her voice on the verge of a growl, a soft warning to the stranger. Owen had never seen her react this way. Not even with the trolls, or ogre, and not when she first went to the Gypsylvanians was she this on edge.

"Easy, young miss, I mean neither you nor your traveling companion any harm. I am just a fellow traveler on this long road this night. It is getting late, however, so I must be passing by, I would suggest you do the same. Find yourself a secure place for the night. The road in the dark is not always a safe haven for young travelers like yourselves."

"Thank you," Owen answered. He felt drawn to the stranger, in a grandfatherly way.

"Thank you and good evening," Orla answered stepping to one side to allow the pilgrim to pass, but not turning her back on him.

In that moment, as the stranger passed, Owen again heard the flapping of wings, the sound of wind through feathers, and saw a glimpse of the pilgrim in another guise. He wore a large iron helm, his spear was straight and glowing, and he wore a great shirt of mail. Two large wolves stood by his side and two very large ravens circled his head. And when the pilgrim looked at him, Owen could see that one of his eyes was missing, leaving an empty socket seeing all.

The vision faded as the pilgrim passed, Owen shook his head slightly, trying to regain his focus. *What just happened?* he thought, as the wanderer inclined his head to them as he walked by, but never looked back.

"Sir?" Owen asked, causing Orla to start as she was just beginning to relax some.

"Yes?" the pilgrim paused, not completely turning back around.

"I believe I have something of yours," Owen said, stepping forward and sliding the Raven Ring from his finger. Owen held it out towards the pilgrim.

The pilgrim pulled his hand out from beneath his cloak. It was a huge paw of a hand, easily big enough to envelop Owen's whole head. Owen noticed white scars and calluses on the hand, *a hand used to work and battle*, he thought. Owen dropped the ring into the pilgrim's palm, thinking he heard wind and feathers once more. The pilgrim closed his hand around the ring and brought it back within the shadows of his cloak. Owen noticed the shadow of two great birds fly over head and into the forest beyond.

"It is indeed, and if we both weren't pressed for time I would like to ask how you came across it, but I fear we both must be on our ways before the night truly falls. Good evening, good master," the pilgrim said, turned, and walked down the road into the shadows of the forest.

22

Orion shown brightly overhead. It was his night with a bright full moon. A hunter's moon. The Pilgrim stood in a small glen a stone's throw from the road, now dark and empty. He watched the stars and thought of Orion, the Hunter, his friend, his brethren, his charge. The cool air of autumn had silenced the night. No more peepers, no more night birds, just quiet. Dead Quiet. His time. He looked to the small pile of twigs and dried wood he'd gathered, pointed the tip of his spear into the middle of it, and said "Kveikja" in his booming, otherworldly voice. His baritone traveled through the silent woods, and at the sound of his voice the twigs took light.

Sitting crossed legged before the fire, belying his age; he laid his spear down in front of him. Its runes glowed in the light of the fire. The spear told the tale of his people and their decent from the Creator to present day. It was a long tale, a powerful tale, a powerful spear. It was *Gungnir.*

The wanderer sat before his fire, his eye closed. He neither moved, nor did it seem that he even breathed, but he did, just seldom. He seemed to be waiting for someone.

His fire continued to burn, never growing or dwindling. He never added more fuel, nor did it spend what was already within. It just burned continually. As the fire burned, and the Pilgrim sat, his birds soared over the country side. At first they followed the two young travelers he'd met on the road, but once they had settled down for the evening he turned his ravens loose to bring him news, something he had not be able to do for a very long time.

As the man sat, lost in thought, another man stepped into the circle of light. He too was tall, almost as tall as the Pilgrim. He wore a long cloak as well, and in the fire light it was the color of a winter sky covered by storm clouds. He sat across the fire from the other man and said nothing. He laid his great bow before him, adjusted the quiver of arrows on his back, and waited.

After a while, the Pilgrim opened his eye and saw the Hunter sitting across from him.

"Ah, you made it," he said at long last.

"Of course, when my liege calls, I come," the Hunter said from beneath his cloak. His voice was quieter than the Pilgrim's, not so much like thunder, but like a whispering wind through a wood, the sound of a snow fall on a crisp morning, or the quiet stepping of a doe through a meadow.

"I am no more your liege than the river to its bank, it has been too long for such formalities," the Pilgrim said, sadness creeping into his voice. "There are too few of us left for it."

"We have dwindled, true. And yet you call, and I come. It has always been that way. I am, as always, your faithful servant."

A small smile creased the Pilgrim's lips beneath his beard. He rested his paw-like hands on his knees. In the recesses of his mind his ravens whispered their secrets to him, of deeds long done, and of ones to come. They opened a long since closed eye to the proceedings of the world, and his mind swam in a current of occurrences and possibilities. It had been a very long time, and his mind reeled at the task.

"I have need of your skills."

"I assumed as much."

"The *Maou'r* has stepped into our World." The Pilgrim leaned forward and pulled a branch from the fire. He prodded the fire with it even though it needed no assistance.

"So that's what I felt, he hasn't been here long."

"No. I met him on the road at dusk." The Pilgrim looked up at the

Hunter sitting across from him. Hidden beneath the cowl of his cloak, he knew the other man was studying him. It was his way. "I like him. It has been a long time since Man has been amongst us; I had forgotten what they can be like." The great man leaned back, as if slugging off a thousand years, "he returned Hugin and Munin to me." The Pilgrim couldn't see it in his face, but he thought he detected a tensing of the shoulders of the other man.

"You have your sight back?" the crisp hoar-frost breath whispered from beneath the hood.

"Aye, I do." The Pilgrim hesitated in telling his old friend that the sight was tainted. A thousand years of happenings and possibilities, a maze of confusion his atrophied mind struggled to wade through. The other man sensed the hesitation. *Damn him, even now his senses are as keen as on the day of Creation, and how mine become dull and impotent.*

"But, you don't see the true path, yet." This was said as a statement, the cold of a clear winter sky when the wind lifts to meet you head on.

"Aye."

"And your task for me?"

"I want you to escort the *Maou'r* and the Sylvan that accompanies him. I believe they're heading to her Kingdom. Your skills will be needed, and I fear tested, by several parties who will be seeking her and the boy. Not all have revealed themselves to me as of yet, but some may already be pursuing him. His presence alone in Parathas is a source of great power for some, and if he was to fall into their hands, he could create an unbalance. Just as we felt his presence, I am sure others have as well."

"I will go then, but wouldn't a guardian be more effective than a hunter?"

"Aye, at times maybe, but they will be hunting him, and you my friend, are the Lord of the Hunt. None match your skill, and before the end, the hunters may need to become the hunted."

The Hunter stood without effort, grasping his great bow as he did so. The Pilgrim stayed seated, staring into the fire. "Be safe and may the ground rise to meet you...."

"And the wind be always at your back," the Hunter finished the old farewell, turned and left the clearing.

Time passed as the Pilgrim sat still before his fire, again his breathing slowing. At a time before dawn a lithe shape emerged from the small conflagration. The flames flared, lengthening to the height of the woman just as she appearred, and then, just as quickly shrinking to their original size. She stepped from the fire, never making a sound; as if the flames were no more than any other doorway. She sat across the fire from her liege and waited patiently.

"You're late," the thunder boomed from the still, old man.

"I'm never late, my Lord, I came as soon as you beckoned." Her voice was the soft hiss of water on a hot frying pan. The light from the fire illuminated her bright, green eyes. The Pilgrim opened his eye and looked across the fire at another of his charges and again wondered where he would be leading her in this new affair.

"You have felt his presence?"

"Of course, my Lord," she replied. She shook her head slightly, shaking her long mane of auburn hair.

"Good. I want you to stay informed of their travels."

"As you wish," she said, absently reaching into and coressing the fire. "Anything else, my Lord?"

"Yes, you are to retrieve an...artifact for me. Your unique abilities make you the most suited for its retrieval," and with that the Pilgrim seemed to slip back into his meditative state once more. *Just don't fail me in this, there are too few of us left, I need you all to be forthright and faithful*, he added to himself.

23

Fire crackled and spit in the hearth of the dark room. A small, bent shape leaned over the glass orb on the dais before it. The dark robes hid the small, slim shape beneath, but power exuded from the robes in waves. The orb glowed slightly, pulsing with each noise transmitted from the other side.

"The Princess is heading back towards Quailan. I will have a surprise waiting at the Fall's Bridge for her."

"This mistake is unacceptable. Fix it. She should not have been allowed to live the first time. Finish this, now."

"Yes, M'Lord."

"I have sent the Houndsmen and his hounds after her again; he assures me he will not lose her trail again."

"Is that necessary, M'Lord?"

"Do you question me?"

"No, M'Lord."

"Good. If you had done your part originally, his services would not have been needed. And the statues?"

"On their way, sire."

"Good. Their acquisition was very fortunate for you. A, surprisingly, insightful thought on your part. However, when it comes to this girl, do not fail me again."

The orb crackled its transmission and then went silent. The figure stood from the stool it was sitting on and walked to the hearth. The fireplace was large; the figure could easily stand within it without slouching. It touched a brick along the wall and a silent and secret door opened beyond the fire. It stepped through the fire, without pause, the flames licking the dark robes as it did so, but leaving them un-scorched.

The corridor was dark and dank. Condensation dripped from the stone walls, mildew grew along the ceiling. Torches in sconces, hissing from the occasional drip, were placed every twenty feet along the hall as it descended downward. The only sound that could be heard through the thick walls was the dripping of water.

The figure slowly walked down the corridor, which meandered back and forth along itself, until it finally came to a large oaken door, barred and reinforced in iron. No lock or knob was visible. The robed figure placed a small delicate hand on the door, which glowed blue slightly, and then opened.

As the figure stepped into the room, lights illuminated the space before it. The room was large and circular. In the center of the room were large laboratory tables with a mahogany desk to one side of them. Two doors sat opposite each other in the room. The figure strode to the one on its right, opening this the same way as the previous. Once this door opened, the figure strode through.

Inside were Brule's three cousins.

They kneeled in a semicircle around a large box covered in a black tarpaulin. The three trolls were chained in place. Their necks held by huge iron collars bolted to the ground in front of them, forcing their foreheads to the floor. Their wrists were also manacled in the same manner, keeping them in a position of submission and obedience. As the robed figure entered the chamber the room lit to receive him while the trolls groaned in fear and pain.

A whinny came from the cloth covered box. The box was nearly seven feet tall and easily eight feet long. The figure stepped to the box and removed the sheet with a quick yank. The tarp covered four posts firmly sunk into the stone floor of the chamber. Not a box at all. Chained to the posts with iron shackles, stood a white horse, with silver mane and tail, and a single spiral horn growing from its forehead. One collar and chain was about its neck and chained to the two forward posts. Its two front legs were shackled together and then chained to the two posts as well; while the hind legs were bound the same way to the rear two posts. The unicorn stood about fourteen hands tall at the withers. Her coat was the white of newly fallen snow. Her mane and tail looked as if each hair was a single strand of silver. The single horn that grew from the center of her forehead was spiraled and came to a very fine point. The horn itself looked as if it was made from mercury. It seemed to move and ripple within the light, to be fluid and yet solid at the same time.

If the trolls had not been bound they would have been able to reach up and touch the magnificent animal in front of them. The three trolls could smell the animal and its fear from the moment they had been transported to this chamber and into their bonds. The unicorn bound and in the presence of these evil beings was in a state of panic. Its flanks were soaked with froth and sweat, while its eyes bulged with panic from its skull. Where the chains and shackles bound the animal, it had rubbed itself raw and bloody from trying to free itself. The iron in the manacles negated the animal's natural magical abilities, keeping it from breaking free of its bonds.

The robed figured approached the chained animal and ran its hand along her flank. The animal shivered from the touch and doubled its efforts at freeing itself. Another burst of adrenalin surged through its already panicked body to no avail. A small hiss of a chuckle escaped from the hood of the figure. The trolls growled and whimpered and the figure seemed to absorb the misery in the chamber and grow larger from it. He walked between the four bound beings and began to chant. As he did so markings on the chamber floor began to glow. They were letters from an ancient language spoken before man was created; they were letters of power, letters of creation, and letters of destruction. The chanting grew louder and the figure became more animated. The unicorn reeled in terror, digging great gouges into its flesh as it pulled on its bindings. Its horror grew with the impassioned chanting, both rising to crescendo. The robed figure drew a long, thin dagger, and before the unicorn could sound a response, the figure slit the animal's throat. The arterial blood from the dying animal showered the three trolls, which growled and shouted in a combination of excitement and concern. Blood lust overpowered their fear. The blood pooled in the center of the four creatures, pooling around the robed figure's boots. The chanting subsided, but still resonated in the chamber as if continuing the beating of the now still unicorn's heart while the trolls began to transform with screams of fear and agony.

24

Owen slept restlessly once he and Orla reached their stopping point for the night. She was still very upset with him after their encounter with the Pilgrim, but Owen couldn't explain to her how he knew the ring belonged to that man, or why he decided to give it to him. It just did, and he just did. It seemed like the right thing to do at the time.

He had asked why she was so anxious around the traveler and she had been her usual vague elf-self, he thought. She had mentioned something about not being sure, and she chastised him for talking to, not to mention giving magic rings to, complete strangers. She would think that someone who spent their whole life without Magick would have a little more care when dealing with it, or in this case, "dispensing" of it.

They had walked the rest of way to their camp in silence. They didn't even speak while eating their meager dinner and it wasn't until Owen lay awake, feeling the cold slipping in through his jacket and wool sweater that he felt Orla in her leopard form lay down next to him. He could feel her warmth through his jacket and sweater. *It would be amazing to have the powers she has, to never be cold, to be able to protect yourself, or your family*, he thought as he finally drifted off to sleep.

His whole body shuddered from the growling form next him in the morning. He woke with a start, but very slowly opened his eyes. He could feel Orla next to him, still in leopard form, growling loud and fiercely, but whatever she was growling at was on the far side of him, out of eyesight. He heard the soft crackling of a new fire, the snapping of pine and dry twigs, the rich scent of burning evergreen, and the aroma of roasting chicken.

Owen sat up slowly.

Orla continued to growl, but she moved with Owen, matching his sitting with her own crouching, rising into a position to leap if necessary.

Sitting across the small clearing they had found adjacent to a small cliff face surrounded by young cedars sat a cloaked man. The cloak was the color of snow clouds. His hood, cast off, revealed a bearded face. His trimmed beard and hair were once red, but now fading into white like a small desperate campfire in a blustering blizzard, only glimpses of flame were now visible through the sheets of snow. And even from across the fire, Owen could see his eyes. They penetrated into his heart; he felt the man across from him could read in his face his every thought, every feeling in his heart. The eyes were blue, the color of glacial ice.

As with the Pilgrim, Owen felt a connection to this person, something he couldn't describe or articulate, but an innate fellowship. Owen noticed Orla inch forward and realized too that whatever kindred connection he felt to these people, Orla innately felt something drastically different.

"Easy, young Sylvan, the Pilgrim you met on the road the previous evening simply asked that I act as your guide and guardian on your journey back to your homeland."

Her growling eased some. Orla sensed truth in his words. The *Aingeal* were spoken of often, but their intentions and actions were always their own. She had just assumed they too were stories, and now she'd met two in as many days. *They are drawn to him*, she thought, *like moths to a flame.* Her *Fey* cousins the *Sidhe* had more to do with their kind than the Sylvans. *I will watch you Aingeal, Owen does not know what your presence here means, and maybe I don't understand the full extent either, but I know you do, and because of that, I will not trust you.*

"I've brought you grouse this morning, break your fast and then we must be on our way." His voice was crisp like a cold winter's day.

Grouse not chicken, Stupid. "Who are you?" Owen asked. So far he'd been stuck taking everything on faith, from both Orla and everyone else. He wanted more answers.

"I have many names. To my people I am the Hunter. I am the son who walks in the cold."

"*Geimhreidh*," Orla growled from her hybrid form. She had shifted and Owen had not even noticed. Owen noticed the man's bow lying on the ground beside him. A huge weapon almost six feet in length and Owen imagined the draw on it greatly beyond what he was capable of. Alongside the great bow also lay a great two-handed sword. Its pommel wrapped in blue leather.

"That is one of my names, the one given to me by the *Fey.*"

"Uller," Owen whispered. Again, the name came to him from the recesses of his mind. He had heard of the Norse god before, one of the ski resorts back home had a festival every year in name of the old deity. But why would he think of it now?

"Yes, and others called me by that name."

"What does the *Fey* name mean?" Owen asked, looking to Orla for a translation.

"Winter," she answered, the tension easing some from her voice. And Owen thought it fitting. Everything about this man reminded him of the season, from his voice and appearance to his very clothes, and just the feeling in general. But Owen was having a difficult time grasping the fact that a deity from ancient mythology was alive and well, cooking breakfast for him.

"But how? In my world people worshipped you as a god over a thousand years ago." Owen looked to Orla, but he read in her expression her reluctance to explain.

"Not again Orla, I need some answers. Elves? Vampires? Gypsy fortune tellers? And now gods? This may be normal for you, but where I come from you're all faerie tales."

"These days have been anything but normal." Orla turned and even in her hybrid form Owen could see her stubborn look.

Orla watched Owen for a second, turned to stare back at the *Aingeal*, and then looked back to the human. "And here, you are the same. I grew up hearing scary stories of your people before bed each night. *Be a good girl, Orla, or the humans under your bed will get you!*" she said with slight scorn to her voice, but also the hint of concession. She knew this was hard for the human, and not fair to expect him to take everything at face value. "He is no god. I don't know everything about them. I don't know much to be honest. I grew up hearing stories about them, along with humans, and how they are not to be trusted. How they had brought many wars and battles across our world, and how once, a long time ago, they were worshipped by humans. He and his people are the *Aingeal*, the First Men." She turned her attention back to *Geimhreidh.*

Owen looked back to the man across from him, who seemed to be studying them.

"She is not too far off the mark. We are not gods, but we were worshipped for a time and many of my people began to believe they were divine. That was our lowest hour, before the Great Schism between our worlds. For my part, I am but a hunter, I am the steward of the time of cold dormancy. I do not come to cause hardship, but try and do what I can to help. And in this, I was simply asked to act as guide." Winter pulled the grouse from the fire, and used a hunting knife from his belt—that caused Orla to tense all over again—to split it in two. He handed one half to Owen and the other to Orla, using the spit he used to cook it on to serve them.

"We don't need a guide. We can follow the road back to my home," Orla said, unveiled threat hanging in her voice.

"Ah, but the road is not safe. I will lead you across country."

"The road is safe enough; the woods hold worse dangers than the road by day."

"Ah, but I will guide you past those dangers, and please believe me, young Sylvan, what pursues you is quite as dangerous as what you would find in the Wilds."

Orla digested this for a time and then looked back to Owen who had been watching her. He was feeling quite overwhelmed at this point.

"If he is right, and it seems that certain beings here have sensed you crossing over into my world, than there may be people besides the trolls following us." She looked back to the First Man. "You may lead us as far as the Falls Bridge, and know that I can sense my homeland and will know if you try and lead us astray."

"Aye, and I'm sure you will tell me if I do," Winter said standing. Owen saw now that the man was nearly as tall as the Pilgrim, but thinner in build, possessing an inner strength that seemed to seep from beneath his cloak. Remembering his visions of the Pilgrim when he did not look straight at him, Owen turned his head slightly and looked at the man from the corner of his eye. He did not change; to Owen he appeared to be a well traveled woodsman, a hunter, nothing more and nothing less.

25

After breakfast the trio turned from the road as Winter had promised and began to work their way deep into the Wilds. The Hunter took the lead with Owen following and Orla bringing up the rear. Owen didn't particularly like the order, but he admitted it made sense. He knew he was the weakest link of the three of them, and the way they'd been acting made him think that more than just the trolls would be after them, and in particular, Orla.

Owen also missed talking to Orla. On their first day they had walked next to each other for most of the journey, and even though they didn't talk constantly, they spoke more than now. Orla had tended to avoid discussing many of the subjects Owen brought up in regard to her Realm, but in many other ways she was very forthcoming. However, just walking along beside her was more enjoyable than this. Winter didn't stop as much, he pushed hard to get away from the City, covering more ground by doing so. He didn't slow his pace for their shorter legs either. Owen found himself again focusing on just keeping pace with the bigger man.

Orla had reverted back to her Sylvan form and found herself with plenty of time to ponder *Aingeals* and why they might be interested in Owen. She would have to look into it more once they reached Quailan. And the idea of reaching Quailan itself made her worry about Owen and what would become of him there. She was also worried for Quailan itself. She knew she had left her village for a reason she now couldn't remember, before appearing alone in Owen's Realm wearing that magical collar that wouldn't let her shift forms. Someone or something had sent her there, and had wiped her memory clean, and had sent Death Dogs there to deal with her. Maybe having this hunter with them wasn't such a bad idea after all. She and Owen had been lucky up until now. She had a bad feeling things were going to get worse before they got any better. All the thoughts and concerns made her head hurt, and made her long for the simpler time before she awoke in Owen's world.

They walked all morning. Owen had decided they were heading south, possibly a little southeast. The ground they were covering was getting more hilly, but never seemed like it was becoming mountainous. He had lost sight of the range they had been traveling alongside.

The trees also changed as they headed south and with the elevation of the hills. The upland tops of the knobs grew into dark shaded hemlock groves. As he climbed down these knobs, the hillsides of the uplands facing south were covered in white oaks, while the north sides were yellow birches and beeches. The lowland mini-valleys they went through were filled with maples and willows. Sometimes in these valleys between the knobs small, fast moving creeks bore through them. The creeks were never more than a leap across, but sometimes looked as if they were one or two feet deep, with small rock cobble bottoms. On more than one occasion while leaping over these brooks Owen saw what looked like trout, in small clusters, all of a size that would have set records back home.

As they pushed through the morning he noticed that Winter never seemed to alter his pace except if he was waiting for Owen or Orla. He never broke a sweat or even seemed fazed by the effort, but then Owen thought, *if he is Uller like he said, then he's been alive for more than a thousand years, he's been doing this for that long or longer.*

They stopped for a short break at noon. They ate dried venison, cheese, what was left of their hard bread, and refilled their water skin at one of the many creeks they crossed at a spot where the water ran quickly and white over a section of large rocks just before dropping from a small fall. Winter never ate any of their food; he drank from his own skin and chewed some dried meat from a pouch. He seemed impatient and was anxious to go again once they had finished their lunch.

Once they were on the move again, Owen felt better for the rest and food and had a renewed vigor to his step. He was still feeling alone, though. None of them had spoken during lunch and whenever he tried to make eye contact or look over at Orla, she was always looking somewhere else. He was wondering if she was mad at him still for giving the ring to the traveler.

He got his mind off it by looking over all of Winter's gear and weapons. He carried a small pack, which seemed to be mostly empty at this point, and slung over his back was his great sword, sheathed in faded blue leather. Alongside the pack and sword was a great quiver of arrows. Owen couldn't see exactly how many shafts were in it, but he guessed more than two-dozen arrows, every one longer than his arm, and of many different colors of fletching and wood. The quiver itself was again made from dried, dyed, and hardened blue leather. He carried his great bow with him. He wore calf high, soft, nut-brown, leather boots and faded, patched, and worn wool pants. Under his cloak he wore a rough spun, blue tunic buckled at the waist by a brown leather belt with a round silver buckle. Off this belt were several leather pouches, and one small bag, and his hunting knife was sheathed and tucked through the belt.

As the day wore on and they made progress through the hills, the terrain began to level until Owen could see a broad plain before him. As the hills ended so did the forest, giving way to grassland that stretched as far as Owen could see. Along the border of this edge habitat ran a much larger river. This river was easily five times as wide as any of the others, reaching close to twenty feet across. It too ran quickly, but from Owen's vantage point on this last hill, it seemed to be shallower in places, making it a little more fjordable.

Winter turned and looked back the way they had come as if measuring the distance. He looked back for a while and then down at his two companions, then he looked out over the expanse before them.

"The plains aren't as flat as they appear from here, it is deceiving. We will find small knolls and valleys, but we will be more exposed. I'm afraid we might not have distanced ourselves as much as I would have liked today from the circle you passed through. I would prefer to camp near the edge of the woods for cover and not to venture so far from this quick moving current."

Owen understood the idea of camping near cover, didn't follow what the man meant about the river, but was at a point of exhaustion where he no longer cared. He would wonder about it later. He hoped the next quarter mile to the river would be a quick one. Orla also remained quiet, but Owen wasn't so sure it was because of exhaustion.

They traveled the last little bit quickly, picking up the pace in anticipation of stopping for the night. Winter questioned whether they should try pushing through the night, but after evaluating his wards he decided against it. As they found a spot for camp Winter drew an arrow from his quiver and let it fly before Owen even realized what he was doing, he followed the arrow as it struck home in a snow goose just lifting off from the river. Winter, retrieved, dressed, and skinned the goose in a matter of minutes.

"Dinner," was all he said when he was done. He quickly struck up a fire with his flint, dried leaves, and moss. Slid the goose along a spit he had cut from a branch and then settled himself by the fire. He slid his pack and sword from his back, laying them along with his quiver next to his great bow. By the time the goose was done the sun had already set.

Owen and Orla had collapsed by the fire, Owen realizing for the first time she seemed as tired as he. He looked to her when they were just finishing their dinner and for an instant their eyes met, she had been watching him too; she smiled quickly and looked away. *Maybe she's not still mad at me,* he thought to himself.

"I'll take the watch tonight. I don't like our proximity still to the City. You two sleep, we need to cover more ground tomorrow, and we do not want to tarry in the plains." He pulled his hood up over his head, hiding his face from the other two at the fire.

"You'll need to rest also," Orla stated.

"I'll be fine, young Sylvan, the *Aingeal* are a hardy stock," Winter said and even though they couldn't see a smile, Owen thought he heard one in his voice.

"I'll stay in my leopard form then, to lessen the chances of being taken unawares." The hooded man nodded in response.

Owen and Orla turned in for the night where they had seated themselves by the fire. Owen had simply lain down where he sat, using his sweater for a pillow. Orla shifted to her full snow leopard form. Owen again marveled at her ability to do it and then at the animal itself. He always had to remind himself that this amazing cat was Orla. She curled up in a ball and closed her eyes. Owen pulled his hands up under his head to sleep, but noticed something odd about the finger that had worn the Pilgrim's ring. He brought his hand closer to his face, but even in the dim light of the fire, he could clearly see a pale scar around his finger. The skin that had been in contact with the ring was older, whiter, and thinner looking. He couldn't be sure because of the bad lighting, but it looked as if the scar made small feather marks all along his finger.

He was inspecting the scar when he began to hear high pitched squeaks and what sounded like hundreds of small wings beating.

26

The town wasn't very much of a town. Most maps didn't show it, and the ones that did belonged to the outlaws and brigands that called the small village home. The town of Stormhollow was just that, a hole in which to hide from the storm. Located just east of the mill town Brawn, Stormhollow was a haven for anyone who didn't want or couldn't belong anywhere else. And for those few who did reside there personally, it wasn't entirely safe.

It consisted of a saloon, a general store, a hotel, and an armorer. A few owned houses outside the village proper, and most of these kept their homes to themselves.

Brule owned one of these houses. It was his safe house. He knew that he wouldn't always be welcome amongst his troll brethren or within the Troll Corps, so once he had built himself a little nest egg from his bounties, he built himself this place outside of Stormhollow. It was a refuge for him for just such a time as this.

He wasn't sure what had become of his cousins, but he knew it couldn't be good, and he knew that the Corps would start to look for their missing troopers soon enough. Once word got back that they were gone, it wouldn't take the Troll Corps long to dispatch a unit to come after him. Then the chase would be on.

Even though his employer put him in what seemed like an impossible situation, he figured there would be a way out of it. His work ethic and pride wouldn't let him give up on the bounty and the Realmjumper, but he wasn't even sure he would still get paid once he got his mark now anyway. *This whole job has gone to Hades*, he thought as he walked into the saloon. *What am I going to do about the Corps?*

It was a slow night for the Flayed Fey saloon, there was a small table in the corner occupied by a trio of goblins, and another with a few gnomes, but otherwise the place was empty except for the barkeep, Keller, and his waitress and wife, Cleo. Both were from a small tribe of *Herpastians* that lived in the Deep South. They were both tall and thin. Both bald from head and to toe and covered in smooth soft scales. Their skin was that of serpents, Cleo being lavender with deep blood red diamond patterns over her whole body. Keller was black with yellow and red bands running from head to heel along his back, four large bands that started at his brow line and ran over his skull, down between his shoulders, and then splitting and running two each down either leg. Their eyes were like pieces of coal, with no visible pupils.

Brule sat with his back to the wall at a table on the far side of the saloon. He grabbed a chair and propped up his foot. Cleo approached, she knew Brule, he wasn't in often, but he was the only half-troll that she had ever met, so he was easy to remember.

"Evening," she said with a slight hiss and lisp. She and Keller also possessed forked tongues that slithered between their fangs when they spoke.

"Hey Cleo, any dinner tonight?"

"Yesssssss, we sssstill have sssssome roassst pork and potatoessssssss."

"Great, and a pint of ale, too."

Cleo returned to the bar and went into the kitchen. Brule watched her to the door and nodded a greeting to Keller who began pouring his pint for him after his wife placed the order. Brule turned his attention back to the other guests in the room. The gnomes were in the midst of telling long and exaggerated stories; they all had long white beards which came to a point just above their round bellies. They dressed in bright reds, greens and blues, and all had large, bulbous noses.

The three goblins all spoke in quiet, hushed tones, and occasionally would steal a glance over at Brule. They made him uncomfortable. He loosened his short swords and boot dagger in their sheathes when no one was watching. He had enough trouble, he wanted none here, but he would be ready if trouble was coming. *The Corps can't know by now can they? They can't be sending people after me this soon, besides no one in the clan should know about my house here?*

He was in the middle of that thought when Cleo returned with his meal and drink. He ate it quickly, not realizing how hungry he was. Gulping down the last of his ale, he stood, dropped a few coins on the table and left the saloon. He walked down the road, pausing just outside the armorer's building and watching the entrance of the saloon to see if anyone followed him. When no one came, he left the center of Stormhollow and entered the wood outside of town. There was no path to his place, he never took the same way twice, and when he came closer to his house, he moved carefully amongst the few traps he had set around the border of his stronghold. As he stepped into the small clearing and stood before the small building, he became overwhelmed by a sudden weariness. He unlocked his door and entered.

The room was dark with a faint musty smell to it. He lit an oil lamp by the door and crossed the room, lighting candles as he did so. In the hearth were logs and kindling ready to be lit. He struck his tinderbox and got the fire going. Above the fireplace hung a large hand and a half sword, the only possession passed on to him by his elven father, which Brule touched gently in greeting. He went back to his door, it was a thick door, made from white oak, and braced with iron and silver. He locked and latched it. His windows were shuttered with the same combination of materials, and his chimney had silver and iron grates placed at the top of the flue. The building itself was made of stone, heavy granite that Brule had hauled to this location himself over the course of three years.

He walked to the bed in the corner of the small, one room building. He took off his axe, standing it along the side of the bed; unbuckled his sword belt and placed the short swords on the floor along the side of the bed, and pulled the dagger from his boot and placed it beneath his pillow. His pack, armor, and clothes he left where they fell, and then he climbed into bed. The wool blankets smelled slightly of mildew, and strangely the smell eased some of his tension. He lay in bed and stared at the ceiling.

Why take the statues? It had been eating at him since his employer had left the circle. No humans were allowed into the Realm. Everyone knew that. *Hell, I was hired to grab one of our own jumpers, so what's with them taking two back.* The troll rubbed his eyes with the heels of his huge paws. *And the kid with the jumper? I'm no expert on humans, but I'd bet my bounty, he's no fey. What I'd get myself into…*

It was long into the wee hours of the morning before Brule's mind stopped asking questions and he finally drifted off to sleep.

27

Sunrise brought little light to the small stone house Brule had built. He had slept restlessly through the night, with occasional dreams of his cousins being tortured. At one point during the night he thought he heard sniffing and snuffling coming from his door, but exhaustion kept him from fully coming to consciousness. He also knew his house, and anything less than a dragon would have a very difficult time getting into it.

In the morning he took from his pack the rest of the hard tack provisions he had taken on the trip and finished them off. Some dried beef, salt pork, smoked cheese, smoked trout, flat bread, dried dates, and beech and pine nuts. He drank the rest of the wine from his skin and downed the remaining water in his gourd. Brule had some extra provisions in his house, but he always tried to leave that for emergencies. He'd have to get some supplies from the general store today before leaving.

He would also need to find himself a steed as well. He could take an extra day here and make straight for the Sylvan's Falls Bridge if he could find a horse. That would be the best place to try and cut off his mark, it was the only pinch point between the City and the Sylvan Kingdom. He was sure he'd be able find one, even one large enough for him; but it would cost him he was sure.

As for the bridge, he couldn't imagine where else she would

head. It was a hunch admittedly, but usually his hunches worked for him.

After breakfast he evaluated his gear. For the most part he hadn't damaged or lost much of his equipment or armor. His armor received mostly minor scratches, a few nice gouges from the cat-girl, but nothing worth repairing or replacing. He acknowledged if he had worn the hard shod iron boots that some races preferred he'd have to be replacing them after what that *human* had done to his foot with that hammer, not to mention having to probably bury a few toes as well.

Overall, with the exception of his cousins and his pride, it hadn't cost him much. He was more disappointed about losing his pride, although the fall out from his cousins' disappearance could be a bother. He walked over to the planks by his bed and lifted a false one. He pulled out a small chest, retrieved one leather pouch and replaced the box and board. At his wardrobe he pulled out fresh breeches, tunic, and socks and dressed, leaving his dirty clothes in a laundry basket for washing later that day.

He placed his axe along the mantel, below the sword already hanging there, strapped his belt and short swords to his waist, slid the dagger back home in his boot, and walked over to his weapons chest. He undid the lock and opened it. The chest held enough weapons to arm a small garrison. He pulled out a large morning star, its head intersecting plates making a six pointed star, made of iron inlaid with silver, with a two foot steel handle wrapped in leather. The weapon had a sling and sheath that allowed it to be worn over the back. He placed the weapon on his back and turned to the chest. He pulled out a throwing dagger and slid it into a sheath in his belt. He removed another dagger with a wrist sheath and strapped it into place. Lastly he pulled a hand axe, balanced for throwing, with a long ash handle. The weapon looked like a tomahawk, but with a stouter, iron blade and head. The hand axe he slid into his belt at the small of his back. He grabbed his empty leather pack and slung it over his shoulder.

He gently undid the bolts, trying to make as little noise as possible. Once the bolts were pulled he quickly opened the door and strode out into the morning. It was a bright glorious morning and in complete contrast to how Brule was feeling about his day ahead of him. His stomach grumbled, and Brule turned towards town figuring to fill his belly and pack before taking care of his other errands for the day.

Brule left his small clearing and headed back into the town. After a quick, but large breakfast at the Flayed Fey of griddlecakes, sausages, bacon, eggs, toast with fresh butter, and goat's milk Brule made his way to the general store. He purchased more traveling rations and supplies and got a lead on a local who might have horses for sale. After filling his pack with the new supplies, he checked his equipment. He decided he didn't need to make a stop at the armorer's for any last minute repairs and left town headed for the horse breeder's home.

28

Up Owen, get UP!" Winter yelled as a swarm of bats came pouring forth from the forest edge. The *Aingeal* had stepped closer to the fire, sticking his great sword into the earth before him and knocked an arrow, waiting for a target. Orla was already up and by Owen's side, still in leopard form.

As the bats swarmed around the three companions, Owen could see their red eyes and sensed their unnatural forms, a feeling he never got when Orla shifted to her animal self. A few of the bats peeled off from the main swarm and shifted to an in-between hybrid form, half-man and half-bat. They had huge heads with large ears. Their faces were partly elongated revealing sharp teeth in the pugged-muzzle. Their hands were two fingered with a thumb while the remaining two fingers were still a part of the skeletal support of their large bat wings, now folded back as they stood on the ground. Their whole bodies were covered in light brown fur, and their legs were short and bow-legged with long grasping toes ending in sharp claws.

They hopped and leapt towards Owen and Orla, Owen thinking them reminiscent of large African vultures he'd seen in documentaries. They got to within about ten feet when two arrows partially erupted through their sternums. Owen saw Winter quickly knock another arrow. The two werebats in front of him fell to the ground reverting to their true humanoid forms, dead from the silver tipped arrows.

Owen squinted in the dim light, trying to make out the flying shapes by the low glow of the campfire; the moon was still low in the sky, and not providing much light yet. Orla seemed to see the small shapes fine and would occasionally leap into the air swiping at the bats. Winter had become swarmed by the small shapes, dozens circled his head, not allowing a clear shot while several shifted into the hybrid form and closed on the archer. Others shifted and came towards Owen and Orla.

Owen felt helpless. He wished now he hadn't given away the black ring. He waited for the man-bats to come closer; Orla protectively stepped in front of him. More bats flew down on them, forcing him to raise his hands over his head. The man-bats hissed and rushed towards them, but Orla cut them off, tackling one to the ground. Raking it with her claws and biting it violently.

The other two closed on Owen. He raised his hands menacingly. As the lycanthropes came within reach one let out a horrifying scream and, again, Owen saw an arrowhead extend from the werebat's chest before it toppled over. A quick look at Winter revealed the Hunter still swarmed in small bats and surrounded by three hybrids. How he got the shot off, Owen couldn't tell, but he knew no more would be coming; the First Man dropped his bow for his great sword.

The lycanthrope took a swing at Owen, but missed as the boy ducked under it. Owen took a step back as the animal lunged at him, only to be knocked off course and driven to the ground by a tawny blur of fur. Hisses and growls erupted from Orla's feline throat, and Owen could see that her fur was blood streaked. He hoped it wasn't hers. The creature she had attacked earlier was still on the ground and back in human form, a young girl from what Owen could see.

The campsite was pandemonium. Orla was completely entwined with the lycanthrope on the ground, and Winter was surrounded and engaged with easily half of the brood, most still in bat form, content to blind and distract the man. Two more human forms lay at the Hunter's feet.

Owen focused back on Orla, looking for an opening where he could help her, when he heard a soft chuckle behind him.

He quickly turned and could barely make out a human-ish shape in the darkness beyond the campfire. Yellow eyes glowed brightly while a slit beneath them, devoid of light, darker than the shadows themselves twisted into a grin. A silver rapier was held in its left hand. The shadow was suddenly before him, moving through the darkness like an eel through water. Its dark hand reached for Owen, who instinctively pulled away while trying to step back. The shadow laughed harder.

"You're my prize for tonight," it laughed again and lunged forward, stepping out of the darkness and into the dim light of the campfire. It seemed to lose some substance in the light, but the night was dark enough for the being to remain solid and reach out again for Owen.

Owen attacked, punching quickly with his right and left. As his hands connected they passed harmlessly through the shadow deymon, slowing slightly, but slipping through the creature and leaving it unscathed.

"You're bolder than I would have thought," the deymon said as it lunged again with the rapier, driving the blade deep into Owen's shoulder, just above his collar bone. He screamed and fell backwards, sliding off the blade.

The shadow stepped forward, looming over Owen, his blade dripping Owen's blood.

Orla tackled the man-bat to the ground. Instinct, fear, and anger had taken over. She had rarely ever released her consciousness in cat form, but instinctively she had loosened the reins this time. She had to, holding back might get her or Owen killed. She lost large patches of memory, things became a blur, and there was so much pain, anger, hurting, screaming, and blood.

She was very thankful for the memory loss later.

Orla did remember the first bat going still beneath her, however, and turning to see another reaching out for Owen; she leapt from the still form, tackling the second in one effortless leap. It screamed and clawed under her, raking her sides and stomach with its own hind claws. She found the soft tender neck and squeezed, feeling the creature go still below her. She felt no pain, she had a single thought in her feline form, protect Owen, at all costs. She turned and saw a shadow pierce Owen through his shoulder with its sword, Owen falling backwards and the being closing on the fallen boy.

Winter swung his great sword and cleaved the man-bat's head from its shoulders. It didn't have time to scream, a soft gurgling was the last noise it made in this world as it met the ground. He pivoted, spinning to meet his new threat. Two more werebats leapt at Winter, opening their great wing membranes, using them to help lift and propel them towards their target. He brought his great sword around dispatching both with one mighty swing. He swung in a huge arc, cleaving a swath through the bats that littered the sky. Deep in the back of his mind he felt the presence of a greater evil, this one from the Abyss. He reached out with his mind and senses as he continued to hue through the swarming bats and found the shadow deymon standing over his charge.

Winter breathed deeply, tasting and feeling in his lungs the crisp autumn night. *Winter is coming*, he thought.

"Owen and Orla, into the Silvermoor, make for the river. Fjord the river!" he shouted, looking in the direction of his two young charges. Orla was on top of a werebat and the shadow was standing over Owen. The young man was gripping his shoulder while the shadow's sword was dripping the boy's blood menacingly over his stomach.

Owen felt the temperature drop several degrees; the cool evening became crisp in a matter of seconds. He looked to Winter just as he swung his two-handed sword in a large arc over his head, literally swatting bats from the sky. He then heard the man shouting to them about crossing the river and making for the other side. He looked up and the shadow was grinning its unholy smile.

The pain in his shoulder suddenly seemed trivial. He thought this was the end; he wished he could have done more to help Orla and Winter, to have saved his mom and dad. The shadow leaned forward with his free hand to grab Owen. Owen kicked out, but the deymon didn't flinch. It grabbed Owen, easily lifting him into the air.

"Once my Mistress finishes with you, I will take great pleasure in tormenting your soul in this world and mine," it hissed through what passed for its mouth.

Owen caught movement out of the corner of his eye and turned to see Orla leaping from the body of the fallen lycanthrope she'd been battling. She leapt toward the two of them, shifting shape in mid-leap from her leopard form to her full Sylvan. Orla had one thought, protect Owen at all costs, and keep him safe from the evil that pursued them. That one notion prevailed over all other leopard thoughts that drove her. As she transformed back into her *Fey* shape, she quickly took in the scene. A shadow deymon had Owen and immediately a conjuration came to mind. She cupped her hands in front of her, forming a bright globe, and shouting *Illuminos* as she did so. The shadow dropped Owen and brought its arm around to shield itself to no avail. The creature shrieked in pain. The globe was as bright as the noon day sun and just as deadly to the shadow. The shadow deymon dissipated into nothingness just as any other shadow exposed to the midday sun.

Orla crashed through the quickly fading form of the deymon. Owen dropped to the ground; the arm and hand once holding him were now too intangible to support him. With a THUMP, and loud groan, Orla hit the ground next to him without her usual grace.

Owen heard Winter shouting something about crossing the river again and could see the Hunter still surrounded by bats. Owen crawled to Orla's side and rolled her over. The color had drained from her face, much like when she had transported them between the realms. He lifted the young *Fey* from the ground, ignoring the pain in his shoulder. Chancing a quick look towards Winter, he could see the *Aingeal* working his way towards them and the river. The majority of lycanthropes were concentrating on the archer. Owen made a break for the river.

A score of bats rained down on him as he did so. Cutting Owen's face with their small claws and entangling themselves in his hair, pulling locks of it out with them as they flew off. Blood began to flow freely into his eyes. Owen, however, pushed on, driving the pain and fear from his mind; he had one goal, get Orla across the river.

Before reaching the water, however, he felt a tug on his mind, a sweet seduction of thought. Somewhere far off someone was calling him, tempting him to turn back towards the City. The cold tingle that ran down his spine snapped his mind back to reality. The metallic taste in the back of his throat, the feeling of small insects crawling across the inside of his skull, and the cold, prickling feeling down his neck and spine lingered from his first introduction to the Death in the Night, the Vam-Pyr.

He didn't stop moving towards the river, the fear pushed him harder, but he felt the pull on his mind to stop, and turn back. He could hear voices in his inner ears whispering to him to stay, sweet voices, attractive voices, offering him whatever his heart desired to only stay but a moment more. Owen's pace slackened.

"Owen MOVE!" Winter yelled from behind him. The First Man's ice cold voice broke through the sweet enticement of the Vam-Pyr's, fueling Owen for a re-newed surge towards the river.

He stepped into the quick moving water and immediately felt the cold bite through his pants. The river was bone-achingly cold, causing cramps to travel up his shins, through his knees, cramping his thighs. The bed of the creek was loose cobble, making his footing troublesome at best as he tried to wade across.

Owen worked his way, as quickly, but as carefully as he could. As he reached the center of the river, the water was reaching his thighs; it was much deeper than he had originally thought from the bank. The river dragged on his legs, trying to pull him into its depths. Each step was harder than the last, stepping further and deeper into the loose cobble bed with Orla dipping deeper in the water with every minute. He had lost the sound of battle by the rushing river; the water had drowned out any other noise. Owen just hoped Winter was okay and fjording the river close behind him.

The wind was stronger out in the middle of the creek as well, and as Owen took his next step a sudden gust caught him, making him stumble. The river, as if sensing his instability and weakness, pulled on him dragging him beneath its surface.

Winter felt the un-natural chill of the Vam-Pyr pulling on his charges. He was immune to the effects of their seduction, but their thoughts on the wind caused his skin to turn to goose flesh and made his breath show in the cool night air.

He had waded through the throng of werebats as they swarmed him and tried to slow his progress to the river. He followed as closely behind the *Maou'r* as possible and was impressed at the heart the young human showed. He fought his way through his own share of lycanthropes, carrying the Sylvan the whole way to reach the river.

Once the boy was safely in the Silvermoor, Winter turned to finish off the threat, now less worried for his charges' safety. The number of werebats was severely depleted, but their masters' desires for the boy urged them onward. Winter braced himself as the bats again tried to overwhelm him with their numbers, but the First Man carved a swath through their ranks just as the Hunter's Moon broke from the tree line to illuminate the Silvermoor and the plains beyond.

Winter is coming, Winter thought as the chill in the air turned to bitter cold. Only a few lycanthropes were lucky enough to escape the cold which froze their brethren in mid flight. Small dark shapes rained down around the Hunter as he slowly cleaned his blade and sheathed it once more. A moment of doubt troubled the archer as he considered whether the Vam-Pyr themselves would venture this far away from their City, so close to the rapid current of the Silvermoor, but he no longer felt their foul souls upon the air, and the moment of pause quickly passed.

With the departures of the remaining lycanthropes the forest was again surprisingly silent. The soft roar of the river behind him was the only noise the Hunter could hear. He turned to see his charges on the opposite shore, but when he looked across the expanse the bank was empty. There was no sign of Orla or Owen.

The cold of the river slammed into Owen's chest like a sledgehammer, driving the air from his lungs. His chest ached from the cold and lack of oxygen, and his temples felt like they were going to explode. Owen almost lost his grip on Orla, but was able to grab her wrist in his left hand before she was swept down stream.

The river drove him into its bed, however, slamming his back, shoulders, and head into the stones that comprised the river bottom. Even in the fast moving blackness of the torrent, Owen knew his vision was blurred from the blow to his head, his consciousness balanced on the edge of a knife as he and the Sylvan were swept downstream.

Bounced against the floor once more, Owen's lungs screamed for air, but he was suddenly, jarringly stopped. Something had snagged his clothing and was holding him in place feet below the surface without any hope of a quick breath as the river rolled over him. He was trapped at the bottom of the bed, and he felt his grip on Orla slipping as the river continued to buffet him, anchored to its bottom.

Owen fumbled trying to break himself free of whatever held him. After years of canoeing and kayaking with his father, with repeated drills and reminders to always carry a knife on his vest in case of such an accident, Owen was quick to reach for a blade, but found none. He quickly tried rolling his body, turning it against the current of the river, and suddenly whatever was holding him gave way. Without another second to spare he ballooned to the surface for a quick and brief breath of air, while again being washed down the Silvermoor.

The river swept them farther downstream until finally coming to an oxbow that pushed them to the bank where Owen, exhausted, was only partially able to drag Orla and himself from the water. He wasn't sure if Orla was safe from the edge, but exhaustion overtook him and he passed into darkness.

29

The rest of the night for Owen was a blur as he passed in and out of consciousness. The rushing river down past the oxbow was constant noise, just a steady buzzing of sound, drowning out any other. The cold numbed him, and even when he was awake, the world seemed fuzzy about its edges.

He came to in the still of the night when his shivering seemed to wake him. He floated on the edge of consciousness, just beyond the veil. What had awoken him was the sound of snuffling around his face. The night was still too dark for him to see anything, but he distinctly heard sniffing and what sounded like the breaking of twigs and branches.

Owen drifted off into the dark once more.

Owen dreamed, or thought he dreamed, of a large wolf or dog pulling them from the creek, dragging each of them by their clothes and laying them under a canopy of evergreen branches. And while they were lying there, still shivering from the cold, the animal brought hemlock branches and laid them over Owen and Orla, blanketing them with the bows.

He drifted off to sleep once more.

When Owen woke again it was still dark, but the moon was now visible in the western horizon. The cold was gone from his arms and legs and the fuzziness in his mind had faded. He was incredibly tired still, but lingering dreams of a wild dog, and the thought that someone had helped them from the creek stirred him.

He suddenly remembered Orla and sat up fully, knocking his hemlock blanket from him only to see her lying next to him, still sound asleep. He noted, however, that the color had returned to her cheeks and lips, and her expression was one of pleasant, deep slumber and no longer the drained expression of exhaustion as before.

Sleep, a deep rumbling voice told him.

Owen suddenly began to feel tired again and his eyelids refused to remain open, as he began to fall back to sleep he thought he heard that same voice trailing off into the woods once more, as he caught the quick glimpse of a bushy, plume of a tail.

Sleep well, my Maou'r.

Owen slept.

When he woke he remembered little of the dreams he dreamt the night before. He remembered vaguely something of a dog. He felt as if he had dreamed quite a bit, but nothing came to him, he had no recollection of the journeys and adventures his subconscious had been privy to.

It was the early gray of dawn and reassuring himself that Orla was still fine, he drifted back to sleep under his blanket of hemlock.

30

Malek walked softly through the undergrowth of mountain laurel; he could tell by the baying of his hounds that they had picked up the realm-jumper's scent. The crescendo had changed in pitch and intensity. He knew the sounds and vocalizations of his Death Dogs the way a parent recognizes his child's cries, coos, and laughs. Malek knew each bark, growl, whine and howl of his beasts. The dissonance rang through the chill autumn air.

The deymon stepped into a clearing beneath a large white oak tree. The canopy of the laurel was only slightly taller than Malek; he stooped instinctively beneath its branches. It was apparent that his hounds had spent a lot of time here; the duff was torn and tilled under the paws of his animals. *The girl must have rested here for a time*, he thought to himself. *Now that my dogs have your scent, I will have my prize shortly.* With that thought he turned his attention to the sky. Morning was not far off, after all these centuries of being bound by the darkness, the creature of the Abyss sensed when the light was approaching. *We will not reach them this evening, but on the morrow my hounds will pick up their trail once more and we will have them by the mid-dark.*

The Hunter's Moon illuminated the deymon, which was slight of build, typical of his breed and clan, with pale luminescent skin that seemed to reflect the moon's light. His eyes were large under a protruding brow that sported two curved horns that curled back over his skull to bend back along his jaw line. He wore hardened scale armor, with high leather boots. Around his chest he wore a bandolier of supplies for his hounds, consisting of whistles, leads, collars, muzzles, meat, and a short, stout club. At his waist he wore two short, sharply curved scimitars.

Malek took in the moon one last time and then hurried after his hounds. He was glad they were finally moving away from the City. He had no love of the Vam-Pyr and they would not think twice about dining on him, nor trying to enslave him as one of their servants.

31

Brule never felt comfortable on horseback. It was possibly his large stature that made him feel this way. Most horses were far too small, and the few that he could ride, the large dressier, or war horses, were themselves mighty intimidating. Put a sword in his hand and pit him against a unit of goblins and he wouldn't break a sweat, but put Brule on horseback, and he felt very out of sorts.

The horse Brule was riding was a large roan dressier. Fit and sound, from what Brule knew about horses, with an easy temperament as dressiers went. It had a calm personality and slow pace. For most horsemen the horse would have been considered slow and too mellow, but Brule was comfortable with the beast.

They clip-clopped along, the great stallion occasionally dipping his head and taking a bite of grass, as they walked. Brule let the horse lead for the most part, picking its path through the woods, only occasionally giving gentle guidance with the reins.

Brule had bought the horse from a *Fey* the day before. He was a large man with a great mane of hair which reached down his back and accentuated the two horse ears that poked from the top of his head. He had a small log cabin near Stormhollow which was surrounded by huge meadows where his horses roamed. He didn't often part with his animals, but he would make an exception for Brule. He felt that there was something more to the bounty hunter. He had invited Brule to sit on his large front porch and enjoy the morning while his wife, a slender and pretty Dryad, with hair the color of ferns and eyes that sparkled like a woodland stream, brought him coffee, fresh bread and smooth butter for his third breakfast. Brule sat impatiently waiting for the man to return, but thoroughly enjoyed the simple fare offered him. The herder's wife offered him no conversation, only smiling politely as she served him.

When the man finally returned he walked beside the large horse that would become Brule's steed. It was the largest horse Brule had ever seen, and it was the only horse Brule had ever sat upon that didn't feel too small for him. Even the smallest of ponies made him uneasy, however, and this monster of an animal frightened him more than any danger he had yet to face. The animal was large even for a dressier. Its soft red coat was full and healthy. The animal looked to be incredibly fit, and Brule began to realize its size and presence were misleading when it came to the animal's disposition. It was a shy, timid animal. When dressiers were meant for war and fighting, for intimidation and combat, this animal seemed more at home on a canter through a wood than on a battle field. The horse obviously would never have made it as a knight's mount. But then Brule was no knight, nor would he ever be one, and he had no intention of ever riding into battle as cavalry.

It seemed the Herder had indeed found Brule's horse.

When Brule had inquired about the animal's name, the Herder responded by telling him, "He'll tell you when you're ready." Brule left it at that, the price of the horse was fair, and even if the Herder seemed a bit of a fruitcake, why should it matter to Brule? Brule never truly felt too comfortable around those crunchy, tree-hugging, druid types anyway.

As they rode through the forest, Brule's mind wandered. He continually returned to the loss of his cousins and of their fortune at the hand of his employer, and even though he felt no love for them, they were after all, family, and he wished no harm to them. Which he feared, was exactly what had happened.

His mind would then wander to the job at hand. He wondered if indeed he captured the realm-jumper, if his employer would then release his cousins, which might, in turn, be enough to appease the Troll Corps and get him off the hook with them. But then he thought of the girl he chased. She didn't fit the typical profile of a jumper. Brule had never met a Sylvan who had jumped before.

And then there was the issue with the second one, the *non*-Sylvan. Brule still wasn't convinced he had been a jumper to begin with, and his gut kept telling him the kid was a human, which made him a jumper *now*, but how had he and the Sylvan teamed up in the first place? His physical features could place him in several of the tribes and races in this world, but his behavior didn't fit with theirs. He certainly wielded no magic like one of the wizarding or witch covens, and why the partnership with the young Sylvan? Most folks who jumped the realm were either looking to escape someone or something here, in this world, or were working the human's world and bringing contraband back to this one. They were typical crooks, smugglers, and thieves. These two seemed like kids. They seemed too young to be jumpers already, unless they'd happened upon some old relic that had sent them over. So why then was there all this cloak and dagger stuff with his employer about her return?

All this wondering was beginning to make his head hurt.

His mount had paused by a small creek to take a drink, and Brule unsaddled himself to do the same. The saddle, a gift from the Herder, was a beautifully crafted piece. He said it had come with the horse and should then leave with the horse. When Brule inquired of the horse's past, the Herder again said he would tell him in time. The horse stopped drinking as Brule knelt beside him, cupping his hands, and bringing cup fulls to his mouth. The animal watched him out of the corner of his eye. Brule never noticed before, not that he ever paid much attention to, or ever got this close to, the intelligence in the eye of a horse. When Brule had finished drinking, he stood; the horse took another drink while Brule hoisted himself back into the saddle. And when the troll had righted himself, the horse again began his slow journey towards the Sylvan Kingdom.

They traveled thus for much of their journey. As Brule became more comfortable with his horsemanship, the horse instinctively picked up his pace and began to make up the lost time that had begun to worry Brule. Again, most of the traveling was done without much guidance, the animal picking the best path through the wood while Brule only occasionally corrected their course.

Over the course of their journey Brule began to become very found of his companion and began to look forward to taking the saddle in the morning and to brushing the animal down at the end of the day. It didn't take long for a bound to form between the two giants.

32

O wen, it's time to wake." The voice was the sudden chill of snow spilling from a pine bow and slipping down your collar. It was sudden, shocking, and immediately woke Owen up. He sat quickly, brushing his hemlock blanket aside one last time.

Orla was already awake and sitting by the fire, she still looked as if she had a chill, and was lost somewhere deep in thought, some place other. She didn't even look away from the fire at him when he sat up, he might not have been there from her reaction.

Owen turned his attention to the Hunter tending the fire. As was becoming his custom, he had procured breakfast for the small party. The Hunter looked little the worse for wear, with the exception of a small scar above his left eyebrow, a slight purple line that seemed much older than a wound that had only been suffered the night before. His clothes were a bit more ripped, worn, and blood stained, but otherwise, he looked none the worse.

As Owen sat up, he realized his own injuries weren't as quickly healed. He could feel the tightness of the scabs on his face and along his scalp, and the deep wound to his shoulder brought a gasp to his throat, which he stifled into a cough. The wound hadn't stopped weeping yet, but as Owen looked at it, the injury did seem to have some sort of poultice spread over it. The wound throbbed, a constant pounding. Owen wondered how he ever carried Orla so far with the injury. He looked back to the girl across from him.

"Orla? Are you alright?" He knew it was a dumb question as soon as he'd asked it.

Orla slowly turned her attention from the fire to him. She didn't answer right away. A small, sad, smile creased her lips, and her eyes became glassy from the tears that welled in them.

"No, I don't think I am. I know you are new here, Owen, but in all my life I have never been hunted like this. My home was always a magical place, a *peaceful* place. I don't know what world this is!" She took a deep breath, trying to quell the panic and fear rising in her throat like bile. "I've never known fear like this! As far as I can tell, someone captured me, magicked away my memory, trapped me in my leopard form, and sent those evil creatures to kill me. So, no, I'm not alright!" Only one tear escaped her eye as she turned her attention back to the fire.

"I'm sorry, I know it was a stupid question, I'm sorry I've caused…."

"You have nothing to be sorry for; I'm the one who's gotten you involved…." Orla cut him off, she pushed her face into her crossed arms that were draped over her bent legs. *I will not cry before Owen and the Aingeal*, she thought.

"No, it wasn't you; it was those who sent you there," Winter interjected, his voice crisp in the morning.

There was silence for a moment while Orla dared not speak; she calmed herself, took deep breaths until she knew she could talk without her emotions betraying her, until she knew her eyes were dry enough not to spill anymore tears.

"If you hadn't saved me from them, then your parents wouldn't have been put in danger, and then I wouldn't have had to bring you here, and everything that's happened since."

"I didn't save you, it's been luck. If anything, if it wasn't for me, you'd be able to do a better job keeping yourself safe," Owen said, although what she said made his heart race and his insides warm.

"Not to interrupt, but maybe it's time the two of you fill me in as to what *has* been happening since you crossed paths," Winter said as he handed the two young travelers their breakfasts and sat down on a log with his own.

Owen looked to Orla and she just shrugged.

"Okay, well, I guess it started when I first saw Orla in leopard form," Owen replied, picking up a rabbit leg and tearing a piece of meat off it.

After relating their whole story, he found it hard to believe how much had happened in such a short time. Winter didn't respond at first, he sat across from them, studying them, stroking the beard on his chin.

Orla had stared into the fire for the whole story as if in the flames she could see the events happening all over again.

"I have to find out why I was sent to your world, I can't imagine why," Orla said as much to herself than to the two men with her.

"What about the collar, could someone tell from that?" Owen asked.

"Possibly, let me see it," Winter interjected.

Owen instinctively reached for his jacket pocket, but he now wore the Gypsylvanian coat. He stuffed his hands into its deep pockets looking for his old clothes only to realize his pockets were empty, his mouth slightly parted. He couldn't find the words to say it. The collar was gone. *The one thing that could have made a difference.*

"My clothes must have come loose in the river," he said feeling miserable, he couldn't keep the sound of loss from his voice.

"That's okay, the one who had wrought the magic would have most likely guarded it against scrying and detection anyway," Winter offered, trying to assuage the young man's pain.

"It seems the two of you have been through quite a bit." The Hunter eyed the two young people before him. He could almost see the bond that now tied these two lives together. In the short time he had traveled with them, he'd seen each risk their life for the other. But did they realize it yet, had they noticed it yet?

He abruptly turned his attention to Orla, "Will Quailan be safe?"

It was a thought she had considered already. She couldn't remember who, where, of how she had been captured. She remembered wanting to leave her city to go and see her father at the capital, but she couldn't remember why, or if she had indeed left.

"I...I do not know." So much was happening she hadn't had time to even consider what else to do or where else to go. Quailan had always been home. Quailan had always been safe.

"What about for him?" Winter already knew the answer, or rather, had a strong suspicion.

"I…don't know that either."

"They may want to question him, and there are forces within this world, some of whom we've already felt, that will want to get hold of him." Winter didn't want to scare the boy, but thought he should be made aware of the danger he was in just being here. He leaned over and picked up the stick he'd been widdling before the two had awoken. A long piece, approximately four feet long, tapered on both ends. He began to carve and shape the wood again using his hunting knife.

"Why?" Owen asked.

The Hunter turned his attention back to the boy and studied him again for a few moments. He considered him, his mirth, his weight, his character. He weighed the importance for him to know, to understand all that had happened in his race's prehistory. Was it time for the *Maou'r* to remember?

He decided it was.

"Long before man can recall, the worlds were joined; and then they were not. The Great Schism we call it. Man was a superstitious species with no magical nature, and they feared and were jealous of all things magical. In the beginning it did not matter, like the rest of us, men were few, but they began to reproduce in increasing numbers, overcrowding the world, invading other's territories, chasing them out, or just killing them in some cases. Man had an affinity for technology and invention, and it was not long before their weapons and armor and tools began to rival some of the minor magics. And it wasn't long before some of us began to take advantage of that. But man had another nature that appealed to some of us. They had faith. A faith that was so powerful, it rivaled some of the greatest magics, and when that faith was placed in some of the beings of our world, they became powerful. The belief men put into them actually made them stronger, and it wasn't long before man began to worship some of us as gods."

Winter paused, breathing in the cool morning air, and wondered if he ventured too far in telling the *Maou'r* all of this.

"When the worlds were split, those beings were bound to our world, to prevent them from crossing over. Others from our Realm were not so bound, they were not affected by the humans, and so there was no need for such safeguards, and over the many millennia some of those beings have crossed over. But never since the Schism has a human crossed back. Until now. Those beings bound here, can feel your presence, they can feel the power which you bring, and they will seek you out for it."

Owen was speechless. Things just kept getting worse and worse.

"What do you mean split?" he finally asked.

Winter held out his hands, one on top of the other—palm to palm, splayed his fingers, and then turned them, so the fingers were no longer aligned, but his palms were still joined. "One once overlapped the other, as one world, but with the Great Schism the two were twisted out of sync. Our two worlds are still joined, anchored together; one cannot be without the other. More closely linked than those who separated the two originally thought.

"There are still points, anchors, where our worlds overlap and are still bound to each other, like the Sacred Circle you passed through, and other holy sites."

Owen looked to Orla for confirmation. She simply nodded and looked back into the fire. The color was coming back to her face; the purple tinge to her lips had faded.

"He'll be safe there," she said more to herself than to the men with her. They both turned their attention to her. "I'll make sure of it," she said, looking back at them.

Owen believed her, more than anything else because he was having a lot of trouble believing the rest of it at the moment, he believed her.

"I don't doubt that," Winter replied, still carving the stick, "For whoever was involved in your abduction and banishment, you will have many more very concerned about your safe return, and they will not be so easily caught off guard again."

Orla nodded in agreement.

"Winter?" Owen began, suddenly remembering some of the previous night. "You didn't pull us from the river, did you?"

"No, I assumed you had done it yourselves." The Hunter surveyed his immediate surrounding. "I could sense your presence down river once the battle was over and followed you here, but you were already clear of the river."

"I may be confused, but I think a dog may have done it," Owen suggested.

"It was," Winter said taking in the tracks left about the campfire and the river bank. "A big one."

"Another Sylvan?" Orla asked surprised.

"No, I think not," Winter surmised.

"But then, who, or what?" Owen asked.

"That's a good question," Winter admitted, with what to Owen seemed a bit of a smile beneath his beard.

"So, what's our plan now, then?" Owen asked, needing to move on from this conversation. His mind was overflowing with too much information; he needed something immediate and tangible to occupy it.

"We still get you to Quailan; I believe it will be the safest place for you for the time being," Winter said standing. He pulled a long piece of thick string from a pouch on his belt. He secured the string to one end of the stick he'd been carving, and bending the stick, bowing it, he tied it to the opposite end. He then held the bow in his left hand and drew it back with his right. The bow bent easily and straight. He eased the string back, releasing the tension gradually.

Winter gave the bow to Owen.

Owen took the bow; he couldn't believe it. He stood up, thinking the pull would be too great for him, but tried anyway. The bow drew easily, like the pull was mere ounces. Owen knew better, he knew this bow could put down a moose. Owen didn't recognize the wood, and as if reading his mind the Hunter answered.

"Yew. The string is venison gut. I have another for you, but you shouldn't need ever replace it." He handed him the extra string and a thin dried leather quiver with a shoulder strap. The quiver held no arrows.

"Thank you," Owen said.

"You did well last night, considering you were not armed. This will serve you better." Winter took an arrow from his quiver. It was shorter than all his others, about the length of Owen's arm. "And it will feed you in need as well. You will fletch all of your own arrows but this one. This arrow will bring you the feathers to fletch your others."

Owen took the arrow and slid it into his quiver.

"Have you used a bow before?"

"A little, my dad got me one, for hunting."

"Well, we'll practice every day from here to Quailan, and I'll instruct you on how to fletch your own arrows," the God of the Hunt told the young *Maou'r*.

"And you, my little Sylvan, I have not seen one of your kind wield magicks like that in a very, very long time," Winter said. Orla looked up and met his gaze, *he misses nothing*, she thought, *he is studying me even now*.

"I've always had an interest in it, and have studied very hard," she said defensively.

"Aye, it is apparent, I do not doubt your dedication or commitment to the art. It is the fact that the Sylvans gave up their affinity for more complicated magicks in pursuit of their shapeshifting talents a very long time ago that I was curious about. I have not known a Sylvan in a very long time who could wield the magicks you did."

Orla didn't answer at first, she looked to Owen and then back to the fire, she began to speak, but hesitated.

"At an early age I realized I had more…. adeptness…I guess…is what they called it…so I found a teacher…or, rather, I guess he found me. I have been trying to focus my talents since," Orla spoke quietly as if embarrassed by her powers.

"Does your family know?" Winter asked his voice cool and distant.

"No."

"There is no shame in it."

"I know," she said defensively. "I…just…Sylvans gave up this way, and there are many who would be suspicious, or fear me, or distrust my family. Many would try and use this politically against my father," she said the last quietly as if not wanting to give anyone ideas, but Owen realized this was her true rational, she feared the fallout against her family.

"Fair enough," Winter conceded.

Orla looked back at Owen, first into his eyes, and Owen wondered what she was thinking as he stared back into the green orbs, but then her own eyes drifted across his face, and along his hairline.

"Those cuts and scratches, they're from last night?" she asked.

Owen instinctively brought his hand up to his face to hide and inspect the damage. "Yes," he said awkwardly.

"He got those carrying you to the Silvermoor, to get you away before the Vam-Pyr arrived. Their underlings were trying to stop him. Here, rub this into those scratches and drink this tea." Winter pulled a small kettle off his side of the fire which Owen had not seen, and handed him a basswood leaf with more poultice on it, a thick, clumpy green mixture. He then took the kettle and poured it into a small gourd cup, and handed the cup with the steaming liquid to Owen.

Owen took the cup and placed it on the ground beside him; he then looked around for something he could look into to apply the poultice to his wounds.

"Here, let me help," Orla said standing in one swift motion. She slid over next to him, kneeling before him, and took the leaf from his hand. She dipped her left index and middle finger into the ointment and turned her attention back to his face.

"It's a mixture of wolvesbane and some other herbs. While you were sleeping I examined you for any bites, and found none, but the poultice and the tea are just to make certain you weren't infected by the bats. You cannot contract lycanthropy through scratches, only bites, but better to err on the side of caution," Winter said this as he turned his attention to the campfire and began to spread the ashes and extinguish it.

The ointment was cool and soothing on the scratches, immediately taking the fire out of them. The fact that Orla was applying it, however, was making his skin burn and his face turn red. She seemed not to notice, but she was awfully close, and the soft touch and soothing feeling of the poultice was making Owen feel a little dizzy. He'd never experienced anything like this before.

"Next time, just leave me," she said teasingly. It was the first time she'd teased him since they'd come to her world, and it felt good to have that lightness between them again. She smiled slightly, and dabbed a great gob of ointment on the tip of his nose before she leapt backward landing exactly where she had been sitting previously.

"All done!" she exclaimed as she did so.

"Would you have left me?"

"No," she said looking him in the eye.

"Then you shouldn't expect me to leave you," he said standing. Owen rubbed the gob of poultice off his nose, wiping it onto his pants. He picked up the gourd and looked inside. The tea seemed to have cooled enough, so he drank it in one giant gulp. Expecting it to taste wretched, but it was only slightly bitter with a slight aftertaste. He slid the cup into his jacket pocket.

"Tastes better hot," Winter said as he finished dashing the fire. He slung his great sword across his back and lifted his bow. He needed to get them across the plains as quickly as possible. The river would hold the Vam-Pyr at bay only for a short time, unless he and the children had inflicted more damage to their familiars than he thought. He held no doubt that they would be pursued, if not by the night-stalkers then by others within the realm who would want the *Maou'r*.

They began their trek across the plains immediately after breaking their fast. Winter quickly found a game trial that they used instead of pushing their own way through the waist high grass. The trail was easier and helped disguise their direction. They pushed hard through the day, resting at noon for a brief lunch, but even then Owen received little rest.

Winter, immediately on finishing his light meal, began instructing Owen on the use of his bow. Drilling him on hand placement and finding the right anchor along his cheek. The first few practice sessions didn't even have Owen handling an arrow, only his bow, with repeated drawing, anchoring, holding the mark, and then gradually relaxing the draw. They continued this even as they began their march again after lunch. Winter repeatedly drilling Owen as they made their way across the plains, picking a target and having Owen un-sling his bow, draw, aim, and hold, sometimes to Owen for what seemed agonizing minutes. By the end of the day he had blisters along his right hand from drawing the bowstring back.

When they stopped for dinner that evening, Winter worked on a piece of leather through the evening and by the time they were settling into their bed spots for the night, he tossed it to Owen. It was an archer's glove for his right hand and a leather bracer for his left forearm.

"Those should cut down on the blisters and welts. Don't worry about the blisters, they'll be calluses soon enough. G'night now the two of you," he said as he took up his usual watch. It seemed that the *Aingeal* never slept.

Again Owen fell fast asleep. He was exhausted after the long day of hiking, but felt as if he'd done better this day than the last. He wasn't quite sure if it was because the landscape was flatter or because he was beginning to build some stamina. He hoped for the latter but assumed it was the former. His muscles and joints held a dull ache that once he was still whispered their discomfort to him.

During the evening Owen began to dream. In his dream he heard the soft sound of fluttering feathers and saw the Sacred Circle across from his home and the troll leader who had been following them. He was speaking to a small, black hooded figure in the clearing, and then one of the larger, more grotesque trolls appeared, carrying Owen's parents under each arm; hefting the stone statues as if they didn't weigh more than a pair of grocery bags. Then the robed figure vanished in the circle, taking the three larger trolls and his parents, leaving the leader behind. The feathers sounded again, faint in the night as if at a far off distance, and were slowly replaced by the baying of hounds. Owen recognized the sound immediately. It was the sound of the Death Dogs that were chasing Orla the first day he'd seen her in leopard form. He could see the dogs now, running through tall grass, leaping above, showing their large heads, green eyes, and slovenly jowls. They were far off, but coming. And then he was looking at a large head in shadow through thick grass, with only its eyes visible—deep brown eyes. The feathers grew loud in his head waking him.

Owen woke with a start. The night was quiet around them. A westerly breeze swayed the high grass, leaning it east. He could make out Winter's silhouette from the moon, facing into the breeze, head slightly upraised, as if scenting the wind.

"What wakes you, Owen?" he asked, never turning his face from the wind.

"The wing beats, did you hear them? They were so loud, or was that part of my dream?" Owen sat up, drawing his jacket more closely around himself, fending off the chill wind.

Winter quickly stepped to Owen's side. "Wing beats? Did you wear the Raven Ring you told me of?"

"Y…yes," Owen stammered, not knowing if he had done something to anger the *Aingeal*.

"And they still visit you? Interesting. Quickly, what did you see?"

"My parents, they're here!" Owen said trying to calm himself.

"Here? Certainly not. Really? But I haven't felt their presence. Are they still stone?" The Hunter asked, trying to focus, to find the trail in the story, to learn who was behind this.

"Yes. They were taken right after Orla and I left, it looked like."

"I think they're still statues, or I would feel them. Anything else?"

Owen heard the soft sound of rain on leaves and realized Orla was now sitting beside him. "Yes, the Death Dogs, I saw them on the plains."

"That is not good news. Up now you two, we must be on our way," he said standing from Owen's side.

"Do you think they're really on the plains, do you think he has the sight?" Orla asked surprised at Winter's conviction in Owen's vision.

"He's worn the Ring of the Ravens, he still bears its mark," Winter said, pointing to the scar on Owen's finger, "and I smelled decay on the wind just now and was wondering from whence it came. This explains it. Now up you two!" Winter quickly cleared their camp, packing anything they needed and dashing the small remains of their cook fire.

Orla and Owen stood at the same time. She took his hand in hers and looked him in the eye. "I'm sorry about before, I shouldn't have let my emotions get the better of me."

"Don't worry about it," Owen shrugged, keenly aware of the young *Fey's* hand in his.

"I wish I hadn't gotten you involved, because of the danger to you and your family, but right now, I'm very glad you are here with me," she said quickly letting go of his hand and turning to gather her own things.

"Me too," Owen said to himself as he watched her gather her belongings.

They left at a fast pace, close to a jog, when they broke camp after Owen's vision. He'd found the dreams troubling at the least, but had quickly become pre-occupied when Orla and Winter had informed him they could hear the first telltale sounds of their pursuers, the long baleful sound of the hounds. It wasn't much longer after that Owen heard terrible outbursts from the undead animals himself.

"They've reached our camp," Winter stated flatly as he changed his order in the procession. "Orla take point and keep us heading toward Quailan, as direct a route as you can. Owen stay between us, as close to Orla as possible."

"I wish we'd been practicing with arrows today," Owen said as the tall man slowed his pace to allow them to pass him.

"Nay, you two are not to tarry in this battle, Owen. Do not stop to fight, either of you. If I fall behind, leave me, I will find you, but do not stay to help." Winter was now behind them, pushing the pace harder than when he led. Owen could hear the soft steps of his boots in the tall grass. In the dark, and in the need for speed, they no longer kept to the game trail. "These foes are beyond you, they will tear you to pieces. The Vam-Pyr and their ilk wanted you alive. If the hounds can't tree their quarry, they fall upon them, tearing them apart. They have no other thought, just an overwhelming desire to pursue and destroy their prey," the *Aingeal* whispered to Owen from the darkness behind him.

"Great," Owen said.

"Hold that arrow until you have no other course, *Maou'r*."

Owen walked faster, stepping closer to Orla, her soft bells guiding him in the night. *This will have to end,* he thought. *I will find who's doing this, who has mom and dad, and make them pay. I won't let them hurt her.*

The trio pushed themselves at a dangerous pace, all the while aware of their pursuers gaining on them with every step. The howls and baying were unceasing. The crescendo sent chills down Owen's spine, turned his stomach dangerously to the verge of vomiting, and caused uncontrollable shivers at every outburst.

When it sounded like the animals were finally upon them, Orla shifted to her hybrid form. Owen reassured himself by grasping his bow more tightly, and finally Winter broke the cacophony of the hounds with his gelid voice.

"Keep moving, I will deal with them and meet you during the daylight, do not tarry on the plains," and with that the Hunter vanished into the darkness of the night, dropping from sight into the high grass and darkness.

"He will slow them, but he will not be able to take them all," Orla growled in her semi-feline form. "He is not their prey, we are. They will not stop for him; some will break past to keep pursuit."

Any reassurance he had felt when Winter had turned to fight for them was gone, replaced by the chilling knowledge they would be facing their own number of Death Dogs this night.

"Keep moving Owen! The longer we can keep out distancing them, the closer we get to dawn, the safer we are."

Owen remembered that Orla had been pursued by these hunters before, this wasn't the first time she'd been the Death Dog's quarry, and she had survived. They would get through this, they had to, his parents were depending on him.

That was when he heard the first scream and whine from the animals behind them. Owen could see the Hunter in his mind, hidden amongst the grass, laying in wait for the pack to over take him. When they were unaware, consumed by their obsession to pursue their prey, he would attack. Letting arrows fly with lightning speed, dropping dog after dog in their tracks. The whining continued. Owen tried to turn the outbursts into numbers, counting dogs felled by the archer, but the noise was too great and too confused, and then he heard the soft undercurrent he hoped he wouldn't; the sound of dogs still on their trail, the howling and baying of pursuing Death Dogs.

"Push yourself Owen! Those are the ones we need to outrun!" Orla growled from in front of him. He pushed harder, but he could already feel the burning in his thighs and calves. He would begin to slow soon, he wished she would keep on; she could outrun them in leopard form.

"Orla shift! You can outrun them!" he rasped between ragged breaths. He knew she would refuse, but he didn't want her hurt for his weakness.

"No," was all she growled in front of him.

The dogs sounded as if they were right behind him now. He was thankful for the full moon, without it he wouldn't be able to see anything. He could make out Orla's slight form in front of him, breaking trail and guiding him in the darkness. He again tried to count the animals from the noise behind him, but couldn't discern individuals from the growls and howls. He was concentrating on that when, all of a sudden, Orla disappeared from in front of him with a scream.

Winter had stopped pushing the two young people in front of him, turned, and knelt on the trail they had made. He bent to the ground, leaning his ear on the soft soil and listened. He could hear the tread of the animals behind him and then the slow methodical pace farther behind them of the Packmaster. *In time, you're mine,* he thought.

How many? he asked. There were so many Death Dogs pursuing them it was difficult to separate all the footsteps. Two dozen at least, he thought as he sat back up. *Too many, damn them, too many.*

He pulled his great sword from his back and planted it blade down into the earth until the hilt was below the grass line, pulled out a dozen arrows and planted them head first into the ground in the same manner. He knocked one and waited. *Soon,* he thought.

It was not long before he saw the soft green of their eyes pushing through the grass in front of them, he again tried to get a head count, but the onslaught of them was too great, too confusing, one mass of eyes, jowls, and spit. Their scent and sound were overpowering now, but still he waited, *not yet, no, not yet.*

The Hunter waited until the beasts were nearly upon him.

Now! he thought and fired. The first arrow found its mark, so did the next dozen, all sinking and downing the already dead beasts in cries and screams of agony. When he'd loosed his last arrow, they were already on him, he dropped his bow and drew his sword from the earth and began hewing through the mass of Death Dogs, sending them back to the Abyss that birthed them. But still he thought *too many, still too many, some slip past!*

But he cut through them, there were more than he had counted, and still they poured over him, trying to get past and again after their quarry. They tore into limb and body, but he did not fall, he slew them in great numbers, piling their bodies about him. But still they came, and some, a scant few, passed.

Before Owen could slow his momentum, he too was falling after Orla. The plains had given way to a short earthen ledge that dropped to a small watering hole. What Owen's dad would have called a duck puddle. But there were no ducks at this pool. Owen stopped rolling at the bottom of the puddle just before actually crashing into the water. Orla was beside him, already kneeling and checking back up the short drop for their pursuers.

Owen began to stand, but then he saw a large shape across from them on the other shore. It was the large shape of a dog, different somehow than the ones chasing them, though, Owen thought. Then, in the starlight, he recognized the deep brown eyes from his dream.

The moon broke the lip of the water hole, illuminating the animal across from them. Orla finally noticed it. It was the largest dog Owen had ever seen. It was easily a meter and half tall at the shoulders with an enormous head, which held the two penetrating eyes. It looked like a large wolf to Owen at first, but then he recognized the differing characteristics his father had taught him to search for.

It wasn't uncommon for Vermonters to call his dad and inform him of wolves in the state. His father investigated every one, most were simply coyote sightings, others were dogs, occasionally he'd get a hybrid, but never did he find sign of wolves. He had always told Owen how to distinguish the two, just in case. And with this animal, Owen knew what his dad had been talking about.

The coloring was that of a wolf, white undercoat and legs, with gray fur down the shoulders and back, gray beneath the eyes and down the bridge, to the tip of the black nose, large head with pointed ears, edged in black, with black guard hairs down its length.

It had huge paws that even from across the pond Owen knew would dwarf his own fist. But the similarities ended there. Whereas wolves have skinny, keel shaped, chests, this animal had a large, muscled, broad one with thick powerful legs, a robust neck, and a curled tail that bent back over the animal plumed with white fur. It looked to Owen like a wolf on steroids.

"Oh boy," he said. Orla stood still, saying nothing. The sound of the Death Dogs was still behind them, but the earthen bank had muffled their noise somewhat. They had not been as close as Owen had thought.

Do not fret Maou'r. I am not of the stock hunting you.

"Can you hear that?" Owen asked, hoping he wasn't finally losing it.

"Yes," was all Orla said. She seemed to be at just as great a loss as Owen.

She can hear me as well; it would be rude to speak to one and not the other.

"You're talking, how?" Owen asked.

In a manner of speaking, yes. I do not possess the same vocal arrangement as hominids, so I must project my thoughts into your minds instead.

"It was you, last night?" Owen realized.

Yes.

The sound of the hounds was drawing closer, Owen began to stand up, but a great rumbling of a growl erupted from the animal across from them. Owen not only heard it, but felt it in his stomach, reverberating off his diaphragm.

"Easy," he said.

I growl not at you Maou'r, but at those that follow you. We haven't much time. I am Duine Madra, in your tongue, the First Dog. The last in my line, the last of the first, King of Dogs.

"But I thought dogs came from wolves?" Owen asked, increasingly aware of the Death Dogs closing in on them, and realizing this might not be the best time for such a question.

And where did they come from? We were created to guard and protect the Maou'r.

"And when the Schism happened, you were sent here?"

Yes. Our nature is magical and the Maou'r's not. Many of our lineage were left in your world, with you, their blood thin enough, their magic weak enough, to escape banishment to this Realm. It has pained us to be without the Maou'r, but the prophets foretold the coming of the Maou'r again, and the reuniting of the Maou'r with his Duine Madra.

A great growling and howling erupted from the top of the embankment. Dirt and earth crumbled down onto Owen and Orla. A growl escaped her throat and she prepared for the onslaught of the Death Dogs. Green eyes appeared at the top of the ledge, and then there was a great howling. Very unlike the unearthly baying of the Death Dogs, this howling brought courage and hope into Owen's heart, and a strange feeling, deep in the recesses of his mind, of dejavue.

The *Duine Madra* leapt across the small pool, clearing it easily with one mighty bound, just as the pack of undead hounds descended from the ledge, clashing with them head on. Growls and whines erupted from the tumult of bodies and dirt that then rolled back towards Owen and Orla to crash into the pond. Owen tackled Orla out of the way as the animals tumbled passed. He stood quickly, drawing his bow and knocking his one arrow; standing side by side with the Sylvan who was already on her feet.

The pond splashed and sloshed, great beasts leapt and cried, and Owen could see the water darkening under the moon. Much blood had been spilt. And suddenly, as quickly as it had started, the fight was over. The water stilled, and a single shape emerged from the water's edge. The large dog slowly approached the two companions, water dripped from its dense coat while the smell of decay hung in the air.

The *Duine Madra* approached Owen and bowed its great head to him.

The Death Dogs have been dealt with. Long has their kind been an abomination to mine, this reckoning has long been coming.

The great dog lay down at Owen's feet with a great sigh and slowly began licking his wounds.

Owen looked at Orla who had shifted back into her Sylvan form, and the *Fey* simply shrugged, sitting down beside the animal.

"What's your name?" Owen finally asked.

The Duine Madra stopped nursing his wounds and looked back at the *Maou'r*.

Just as your language is not pronounceable by my tongue, mine is not by yours, it has always been the custom of our two species that the Maou'r name his Duine Madra in his own language.

Owen thought for a moment. He and his father had often talked about getting a hunting dog that they would train to hunt upland birds with them. His father always wanted to name the dog Boone, but this animal was so much more than any hunting dog. This animal was beyond any dog Owen had ever known before, but he could think of no other name. And the idea of his father and the name they had once decided upon for their own dog seemed like the only choice at the moment.

"Would Boone be okay?" Owen asked awkwardly.

It will do well. I am Boone of the Duine Madra, last of the First, and King to all dogs.

33

Boone licked and cleaned his wounds while Owen and Orla waited before heading towards Quailan once more. The *Duine Madra* had licked his pelt clean, and Owen could see in the moonlight, how the once stained fur was white once more. Even in the pale light, he had been able to make out dark spots that seemed to be more than just blood smears, deep punctures and tears. Boone had saved them from the Death Dogs, but at what cost, Owen thought. Now there seemed to be not only no more blood, but no more wounds.

The three traveled quickly by the light of the moon. Boone took the back of the line and Orla again led. None of them spoke as they moved silently through the night. Owen felt better having the *Duine Madra* with them, and it seemed that even Orla had relaxed some. As first light began to dawn and the world slid from blackness to mundane gray, they stopped their journey. They made no campfire, but instead ate their dried provisions and the leftovers from Winter's previous meals. Owen hoped the Hunter would find them before they left again on their journey.

When they stopped for the morning Boone settled himself beside Owen. The great animal acted as if he'd known the boy his whole life. He made no qualms about rubbing alongside him, or bringing his head up and from below Owen's hand to leave it resting on his massive skull.

As Boone sat beside him, Owen noticed that all the animal's wounds from the night before were gone. His coat was as clean and solid as before his meeting with the Death Dogs.

Orla sat down along Owen and shifted into her hybrid form.

"I guess you don't need me for warmth anymore," she teased as she shifted.

"Sorry," Owen said, but still lay down so his back touched hers as she curled next to him. He thought he heard her purr as he did so.

I sense that you have some injuries that are not yet healed.

Owen still wasn't used to the soft voice that sounded like a low rumble of thunder in his mind. It did not feel wrong or intrusive, just surprising every time it happened.

"No," Owen said instinctively flexing his shoulder and feeling the sting of the wound.

I can help you, as I cleaned my own wounds, if you'll let me.

The great beast stood. He moved in front of Owen and nudged his nose against his injured shoulder. Reluctantly, Owen opened his tunic to the dog. He turned his head, thinking at first this would make him queasy, but as the dog began to lick and clean his wound, a warm tingling began to grow from within his shoulder and work out towards the surface. Owen looked down at his shoulder as Boone pulled his massive head away and saw the fresh pinkness of the scar left on his skin.

Sorry that I was unable to mend the wound completely. It had already begun to heal on its own, and the weapon used to inflict it was touched by darkness, making my healing difficult.

"Don't apologize, its fine, its perfect, thank you," Owen said, feeling much better about the injury. The great dog picked its head up and looked into Owen's eyes. Owen was comforted by the large brown orbs and saw an intelligence and loyalty in them he had never encountered in an animal before. It was like looking into Orla's eyes before he knew she was truly an elf when she was in leopard form. The depth of intelligence and soul seemed bottomless. The dog leaned forward and licked Owen's face, immediately making all the small scratches warm with healing.

When he had finished cleaning the wounds on Owen's face he curled up and lay next Owen once more.

G'night Maou'r, the dog said as he lay down next to Owen.

The Hunter swayed in the waning moonlight. The bodies of the Death Dogs would soon dissipate in the morning light, but still he waited for the PackMaster. He too would have to retreat from the sun, but Winter was certain the deymon would arrive before sunrise to enact his revenge for the slaughter of his pack. Or so Winter hoped.

The wind had shifted and was now blowing southwesterly, leaning Winter along with the tall grass in that direction. Winter had lost the PackMaster's scent with the changing of the wind. But he could still feel the deymon coming. The hatred it held for the person who killed his hounds would push him, drive him till dawn forced him back to the Abyss. It wouldn't be long now, the Hunter mused, as the deymon came into his view.

To its credit, the deymon had kept itself hidden from the Hunter until it was only ten meters distant. Still an easy shot for the archer and with plenty of time to draw and shoot, but the *Aingeal* gave no indication that he had detected the creature.

The PackMaster was using a minor invisibility spell, and his own practiced stealth of movement to close on his quarry. He'd known the moment his pack had been ambushed and felt it as they began to die. Malek knew that their killer would be formidable, but a PackMaster is nothing without a pack. Malek would kill his pack's slayer or die trying.

As night began to fade into morning, he felt the familiar pull of the Abyss, but he fought its calling. He knew that once daylight broke upon the landscape he would have no choice but to retreat or burn in the morning light, but he would risk that to take this soul with him this morning.

He saw the Hunter now, unawares of his approaching enemy. He slowly unsheathed his scimitars, twin sickle blades. He smiled a grotesque grimace of a smile. His lips peeled away from wickedly sharp fangs and his tongue licked out over their tips, tasting the air. He tasted no fear, or anxiety. The Hunter was completely unaware of his approach, Malek thought, as he closed to within two meters.

He sprang from the grass; both scimitars slicing through the air, but the Hunter brought up his great sword and parried both attacks easily, gracefully. Malek was dumbstruck. He had been certain he had gone un-noticed. This creature was cleverer than he had thought. He attacked again, twin blades lightning fast through the air. The Hunter blocked one, but had to dodge the following barrage of slices and cleaves. Malek smiled his sneer once more, baring his teeth at Winter as he drove the man back, but then Winter took to the offensive after a quick parry and joust of his own blade. His reach, and the length of his own weapon, was enough to keep the smaller deymon at bay as he forced his attack upon the PackMaster. Without his hounds he was little threat to the *Aingeal*.

Winter knew that dawn was close at hand and that he must end this duel before the deymon gated itself back to the Abyss, fleeing from the morning's light. Winter feigned an attack low, and when Malek brought his scimitars down to block the great sword, he drove the blade deep into the deymon's chest. Malek dropped his blades, which hissed as they touched the prairie grasses.

"Shadow will consume you, *Aingeal*. Hellfire will taste your soul," Malek rasped as his immortal life dwindled on the blade of the Hunter.

When the life had finally faded from the deymon, Winter slid the dried husk of the creature from his blade. He cleaned the weapon in the rich prairie soil. By the time he had finished, light had broken upon the horizon and the Death Dogs were dissipating into the morning. The archer slid his sword back into its sheath and turned his attention back to his companions' trail. He found it quickly and began to trot as he headed after his young charges. He picked up his pace; over the trail of Owen and Orla were the frantic tracks of Death Dogs that had escaped him the night before.

Owen woke to the gentle prodding of a very large muzzle. He opened his eyes to see Boone's large black nose and further past it his two large brown eyes.

Someone approaches. They move quickly and quietly.

"Winter?" Owen asked and hoped. He leaned over and gently touched Orla's furry shoulder. "Orla? Someone's coming."

The Sylvan was awake immediately; she rolled slightly and looked back at Owen and Boone. The dog was still lying down, but looked like one taught muscle, ready to spring. His ears were up and forward, his nose slightly raised into the wind. She shifted into her full leopard form to have the full senses of the leopard and raised her own nose in the same fashion. The dog's sense of smell would be better than the cat's, but there was the slightest hint of Winter on the air.

"It's Winter," she said once she'd reverted back to her Sylvan form.

Is he pack?

Owen hesitated, he hadn't ever thought of it like that before, but then answered, "Yes," and wondered what Boone would have done had he said no.

"He said he would find us by morning," Orla whispered.

"Why are we still hiding?" Owen asked smiling.

Just because one sense tells one thing, doesn't mean it's true, Maou'r.

Owen could see the muscles tensing beneath the dense fur. The great dog was ready to defend the two of them again; he'd already risked his life once for two complete strangers, Owen thought. There was so much more to this animal than someone would first think.

His pace slows. This one is well in-tune with his surroundings.

"He's the Hunter," Owen whispered to the *Duine Madra.*

He is Aingeal?

"Yes," Owen said and could see the dog visibly relax before him.

"I can see him now," Orla said, still staying below the grass line. He looks battle worn and weary, but it is him I believe." She looked to Owen, "There are many things in this world that can appear as one thing, but be another, but few can master it below the light of day," she said inclining her head towards the sun.

"You're all well concealed, but I can hear you," Winter said, the relief palpable in his voice. The three companions all stood from the grass. The grass easily came up to Owen's waist, Orla's chest, and on

Boone it came up to his shoulder leaving only his tail, neck and head visible above the grass.

"And I was curious as to the third set of tracks that seemed to have joined your small group," Winter said stepping over to their small camp and seating himself.

His cloak and tunic were torn and blood stained. He had noticeably fewer arrows in his quiver. And he seemed more tired and weary than Owen had ever seen him. He pulled a piece of dried meat from a pouch on his belt and began to chew absently. He undid a wineskin and took long draws on it. After a few moments he turned to the *Duine Madra*.

"It is an honor to meet you, *Duine Madra*, I thought your line long since past, but after seeing the tracks along the river, I wondered, and hoped," Winter said bowing his head to the massive dog that stood sentry next to Owen, who had seated himself across from Winter and had patiently waited for the man to refresh himself. Orla had seated herself on the other side of Owen, not wanting to come between the dog and his *Maou'r*.

Boone bowed his massive head to Winter.

And it is good to make the acquaintance of an Aingeal. I have heard many stories of your People.

Owen heard the low rumble of the voice and figured Boone must be projecting his thoughts for all three of them to hear again.

"What have you named your new Guardian?" Winter asked.

"Boone," Owen replied awkwardly. He wasn't sure the name was quite right in this new world. He always thought it a great name for the dog he and his father had talked about getting.

Winter seemed to weigh the name and then said, "A good name, strong and simple, too often in our history we have created names that were too long winded."

He turned back to his meager breakfast and drank more from the skin. He seemed to be more refreshed and in better spirits than when he first arrived. He looked at the three individuals across from him and measured them each in turn. He finally settled on Owen.

"It has been a long while since a *Maou'r* has found himself in the company of a *Duine Madra*. And I do not believe a Sylvan and Human have ever traveled together." Winter crossed his legs, leaned his head back, and let the wind blow lightly on his face.

"And an *Aingeal*?" Owen asked.

"A very long time indeed," Winter answered without looking at him. "How did you come across our friends?" Winter asked Boone, lowering his head once more and looking to the dog.

I sensed his presence the moment he arrived in our Realm. The bond of the Madra to the Maou'r is strong. The bond guided me to him.

"And it seems both your arrivals were timely. I am in your debt for your assistance in keeping my two charges safe."

It is my Wyrde to protect the Maou'r, no gratitude is needed.

"I saw him in my dream last night too, well, just his eyes on the plains," Owen said. He'd recognized the brown eyes immediately. The idea that he was now dreaming about things which happened was disconcerting. He looked at the scar on his index finger and made a mental note not to try on any more abandoned rings.

"Have you all rested some this morning?" Winter asked, returning his wine skin to his belt and standing.

The three companions in turn all nodded, none wanting to admit that more rest would be welcome.

"Good, then I think we should continue on, the sooner we are off the plains and back to the forest the better," Winter said, as he adjusted his gear and headed off in the direction of Quailan. Owen and Orla followed, walking side by side for the first time since they'd left the City together, with Boone following behind.

34

The fire crackled while the wind blew down the flue, sending sparks dancing across the cold flagstone floor. The Dark Queen watched this from her place by the window. She looked out across the barren, jagged landscape that was her home. Her army was strong, her Mountain Trolls and the *BeljAhri* that lived deep within the mountains were without equal in the Realm, but she would not have time to draw them all out before Winter set in. She must act quickly, decisively, and draw forth an agent she could dispatch quickly on her errand. The Thorne's would soon be blocked by ice and snow, further separating Lilith from the Kingdom to the East.

The Dark Queen stepped from the window and walked to the center of her room; she faced her fireplace, and closed her eyes. A slight wind blew from the hearth, sparks drifted out from it, lightly falling to the stones. Lilith's long hair stirred, the light crème colored shrift she wore blew back against her slender form. The silk dress was cut low, revealing her bosom. The back, beneath her long hair, was also cut low, revealing to the small of her back. The sandals she wore matched her shrift, and were tied to mid-calf.

The Dark Queen turned and left her bed chamber. She stepped quickly and lightly down the stone stairs that led to the rest of her Keep.

Dark things in dark places along the corridors felt the wave of power that flowed before her and knew to be away when she passed their dark crevices on her way to the bottom of her fortress. The things in the dark, both large and small, scampered, ran, crawled, and hopped to avoid their Queen. They could feel her mood, and it was not a time to dawdle; she would not treat them kindly if they crossed her path.

Lilith stepped down the stairs and was lost in her own thoughts. Her walking took her down into her Keep as she descended into the bowels of her domain.

Brooding on the assured interference of the *Aingeal* did not do much to improve her mood, and as she turned a bend in one stairwell one of the wretched dark creatures of her Kingdom scurried for its hole too late. Purple fire blazed from Lilith's finger tips as her eyes glowed the same, sickening shade of lavender.

The small deymon was about the size of a house cat. But similarities ended there. Its face was long and bald, with the flat snout of a crocodile and many sharp pointed teeth. Its body was covered in a thin gray fur, while its hands and feet were also hairless, with dexterous little toes and fingers. It had a long prehensile tail that at the moment slapped and thrashed, as the fire licked across its body.

The scorching of the small deymon did little to improve the Dark Queen's mood as she stepped over the smoldering corpse of the unfortunate creature. As the Queen turned the corner of the corridor many more of the same type of deymon came out of their own dark retreats and fought and squabbled over the charred remains, tearing and ripping it into unequal shares.

The Witch Queen continued on her journey until she reached the very bottom of her Keep. The walls were no longer smooth, chiseled and polished, but instead were rough hewn stone. Few sconces lit the way anymore. When she finally stopped, the room was cavernous and filled with steam. Large chasms spit and spewed smoke and other gasses into the air.

Lilith walked to the center of the room, threw back her head and raised her arms. She began to chant, a language not heard or spoken for many a millennia. At first her pace was slow and meticulous, but slowly it began to intensify and quicken. Sweat began to glisten across her brow and bosom, the heat and steam seemed to be increasing as well. Great boughts of flame spurted like geysers from the fissures in the ground before her. Her thin shrift began to cling to her as she perspired. Her breathing quickened, but still she chanted, stronger, harder, louder, and the ground beneath her began to shake.

What she had been calling had heard her and was coming. But it was not bound to her yet, and it did not want to be bound.

The greater deymon was coming quickly.

Lilith focused on the incantation, she must speak it without mistake to fully bind the deymon to her, she did not want to draw it forth only to have it come unbound and try to destroy her. She had no time for such nonsense.

A great column of fire erupted before her, lighting her shrift and sandals a fire, but still the Witch Queen continued her conjuration. The fire seemed to dance along her skin, never burning her. The flame enveloped her, burning her garments until they fell to the rock below. She took no heed; the beast was almost upon her. She could feel its essence in the ground beneath her, pushing forth, striving to be released. Lilith called the words and bound it to her and to this earth until her spoken charge was completed.

The deymon was hers to command, bound to her flesh and black spirit.

A great divide opened in the rock, belching fire and steam, spewing gasses and noxious fumes. Lilith lowered her arms, her hair was plastered to her body with sweat, her skin turned to gooseflesh even in the humid, rank atmosphere of the bowels of her castle.

Two great scaled hands lifted from the chasm, grasping the ruptured floor. Huge black eagle's talons ending in long hooked claws reached from the Abyss and began to hoist an enormous form from the dark.

The Vrok had come.

35

Hellfire gushed forth as the Vrok hefted itself from the fissure in the rock. Its enormous head followed the wicked taloned hands and sinewy arms. The Vrok's head looked like a large bear skull, stretched with thin, petrified flesh, turned a mummified black. Its eye sockets were empty, with only a dull reddish glow from deep within, while its nose and lips were long since gone, leaving a grim snarling visage of the animal it resembled. From the top of its head grew two large, curving horns that wrapped around to end next to the deymon's eye sockets.

Its neck, like its arms, was long and snake-like, stretching from a dark carapace that was its torso. The shell looked like some sort of insect's exoskeleton. As the deymon stepped from the crater from which it was spawned, its long legs, ending again in eagle's talons, took purchase on the rock. A long, thick, muscled tail lashed unhappily behind it. The tail was scaled like the beast's hands and feet, with small vertical plates down the length of it until it vanished within the carapace. Darkness and shadows clung to it like unholy black wings.

The beast stood nearly eight meters tall and towered over Lilith. It exhaled loudly through its nose, blowing her hair back from her face and shoulders, its hollowed eyes looking the woman over.

The Dark Queen lowered her arms to her sides. She knew the dark beast was now hers. It had been a long while since she had summoned one of the Lords of the Dark. She could feel its animosity towards her, but she was unconcerned. Now that it was bound to her it would carry out her wishes; it was an extension of her own will and hate.

The deymon leaned closer to the woman before it. Its thoughts were old and angry, it had not been disturbed in millennia, and it did not appreciate being awakened, but the woman had spoken the words of commanding and calling true. It was bound to her now, her will was its. The Vrok stood up and threw back its head, bellowing into the dark chamber, disturbing dark things in dark places. The cavern shook from the intensity of the noise.

A slight smile played across Lilith's face. *The Aingeal will not be expecting one of the Great Deymon to be called forth. One of its kind has not been seen from Illenduell in a very long while.* The dark woman smiled more broadly and strode from the chamber, the dark beast trailing behind her like an obedient dog.

36

Winter's attention was drawn to the West, toward the Thorne Mountain Range. The dawn had not yet broken, the world still consisted of shades of blues and grays. Owen and Orla still slept soundly with the great dog, Boone, lying between them, keeping them warm and comforted against the coming winter.

Winter scratched his beard and considered what it was he had felt. The sudden, thrusting of power into the Realm, not so unfamiliar than when the *Maou'r* had entered the Realm, but there was a lingering feeling, an aftertaste of sorts. He looked to his charges. They hadn't budged, hadn't seemed to notice the tremor, but if he wasn't mistaken, he had noticed the *Duine Madra's* ear twitch the instant of the surge in energy.

Winter stood from his sentry post and walked to the trio sleeping. Boone raised his head as the man approached.

"We should get going early today. I felt something strange just now, and want to pick up our pace to Quailan," Winter said to the animal lying between the two young friends. The great dog nodded his head in understanding, stood, and stretched—arching his back like a cat and then stepping from between the two bodies.

Orla woke first, shifting from her hybrid form to her Sylvan shape. She stood and stretched herself. "Bit early, isn't it?" she asked, stifling a yawn.

"Yes," Winter said, prodding Owen with the end of his bow. "Owen, time to wake."

Owen rolled over and looked up at his three companions standing above him.

"Did I oversleep?" he asked getting up quickly.

"No," Winter said, "we must be away early this morning. I think it dire we reach Quailan as quickly as possible."

The small company picked up their belongings and broke camp quickly, Winter again taking the lead with Boone bringing up the rear guard. Owen and Orla found themselves walking next to each other and only falling to single file when the trail narrowed so much that they had no other choice.

Owen continued his training with his bow along the way. Winter was a persistent, but patient teacher. Owen was now able to begin to acquire feathers to fletch his own arrows, and after three misses, one grouse and two snow geese, he finally took down a tom turkey. The companions feasted on it for dinner, stuffing it with wild onions and mushrooms, and then cooking it over birch wood and under a birch bark oven Winter had fashioned. When they were finished eating that evening, Winter began teaching Owen how to fletch his own arrows. He first took him out from camp, and along the forest edge they had finally reached, until they found suitable branches from which to carve arrows, and then returned to camp. Winter set Owen working on whittling down the arrows; he had already plucked the turkey before dinner and therefore had his feathers for fletching. Once Owen had a few shafts straight and true enough to make into arrows, Winter produced from his belt a pouch that he again gave to Owen. The pouch was full of broad heads of different metals and shapes. Winter told Owen to start with the small silver tipped ones. Also in the pouch was more string with which to tie the heads and feathers to the shaft. Owen tied the silver tips to the cedar shaft and then tied the feathers on as Winter instructed. Owen handed the arrows over to Winter for inspection. After looking them over carefully, holding them at arms length and looking down them, gently testing their weight and balance, he handed the three shafts back to Owen.

"Well done, very well done for your first arrows. Add them to your quiver along with the arrow I gave you. Keep the heads and feathers and we will collect more shafts as we travel tomorrow. Always keep an eye for future arrows as you travel, you will never have too many for that quiver."

With that Winter resumed his nightly watch and Owen settled down along side Boone and Orla, both of whom had already settled in for the evening. Owen was quickly asleep. The traveling was becoming easier for him, and in just the few days of being in this Realm, there was a distinct change in his body. Muscles were forming, defining, under his Gypsylvanian clothing.

And while the others slept, the Hunter again turned his attention West, and he again could feel the unease that had been haunting him all day long. Something had entered their world, just as Owen had, but something old, and something greatly evil. It was moving towards them, but not as quickly as they were moving. It was limited in its movement, Winter could feel. It traveled at night, restricted by the sun maybe, and did not push as hard as the small party while doing so. He would investigate this new development as soon as he could, but he would first need to get the *Maou'r* and the Sylvan to her Kingdom. Then he could back track to this presence he was feeling.

Winter again roused the companions before dawn, having a small breakfast of hare and freshly picked apples waiting for them. There were no complaints, they could all feel the unease in the archer, and they could tell some new threat was weighing on him. They broke their fast in silence and were again traveling towards Quailan before light. Along the way, Winter continued Owen's instruction on the use and art of the bow.

Orla had taken to practicing and reciting her own studies. She did not actually perform any spells in front of her companions, but she kept a watchful eye for needed materials for her incantations as well as quietly reviewing the words to her spells and summonses.

Boone quietly and happily kept watch at the end of the company. He was content just to be in the company of his *Maou'r*, as if a piece of him had finally been restored after long ago being severed.

Winter continued to move quickly, feeling the presence behind them as a growing threat. He helped distract himself with the tutelage of the *Maou'r*. He was a quick leaner and a good student, unafraid to ask questions and to try what he was asked; he practiced even when the lessons for the day were over, and the archer had to admit that the boy seemed to have an affinity for the bow.

As they stopped for the night, they again feasted on the results of Owen's practice, two small snowshoe hares, still in their brown summer pelts. After dinner Owen again fletched arrows for his quiver while Winter looked on. Orla sat by him, absently scratching Boone's head, and wondering what everyone would say in Quailan when she returned, and with a human.

Winter finally broke the silence when it was near the time to turn in for the night.

"Once we are in sight of the Falls Bridge I'm going to leave you and head West," the Hunter said. "There is something I want to investigate in that area of the Realm. Once I am convinced it is nothing of concern, I will come back to Quailan to see how you are faring."

Owen and Orla exchanged glances.

They will be fine, Boone said in his low booming voice. *I will see them to Quailan.*

The *Aingeal* nodded his appreciation.

"Once we pass the bridge, we'll be in the Sylvan Kingdom anyway, we should be more than safe then," Orla added.

"You should be safer, but I would like you all to stay alert. Remember, Orla, we still don't know who or what sent you to the Human's Realm," Winter replied. The young Sylvan slowly nodded her understanding; resigning herself to the fact that her abductor may have been one of her own people.

"You'll come back though, right?" Owen asked.

"Yes Owen, I will be gone but a short while on this errand, and then will meet with you three in Quailan in no time," Winter smiled at this, he had become found of the young *Maou'r* and Sylvan, and was glad to hear in the boy's voice the same feelings.

"But now, I fear you must turn in, I will be waking you all early again on the morrow."

37

Elcin sat quietly in the watchtower. He had drawn evening sentry duty three nights in as many days. He was not pleased. The thought that he deserved a respite from the watch was not far from his thoughts, but right now the cold night was making his warm bed seem that much further away than next evening.

He stood and walked about the small square structure. The tower consisted of four five meter posts with cross supports topped by a two meter by two meter square hut. A low, meter tall wall surrounded the hut while a sparse thatched roof covered it. Hanging from the roof in the middle of the tower was a large brass bell. The structure gave the appearance of shelter, but didn't do much to keep out the weather, or on this particular evening, the wind.

He pulled his cloak closer about his shoulder, leaning his spear between the crook of his neck and his shoulder, as he wrapped his arms about him. He'd been a part of the watch since his fifteenth birthday, and in the two years he'd been reporting to duty he had never seen anything to sound the alarm over.

His village was one of many of the Lost Tribe that inhabited the North West stretches of the Thorne Mountains. They were the first Kingdom east of Illenduell. But in all the time he'd been on the watch, and for as long as most could remember, nothing from that dark region had ever ventured this far east.

Elcin concentrated and scanned the forest before him as he did every half hour. The Tribe was always on the lookout for any intruders from the Thorne Mountains, prepared for any incursion from the Witch Queen. The Lost Tribe had minimal psychic abilities or magick adeptness; it was why when the Great Schism occurred they were banished to this world. Other than their heightened sensitivity and empathy, they appeared completely human. Elcin used his own psychic ability to sense for any thoughts or feelings of dread within the forest beyond the Village.

At the very edge of his scan, Elcin thought he sensed something, taking him completely by surprise. It was a bounce of sorts, almost a ripple within his scan. He focused and scanned again, but now it was clear, no ripple this time.

Odd, it was like my scan hit a bump the first time, he thought to himself as he paced the tower once more. His feet were still cold, but the pacing was starting to get his blood pumping again. He looked to the corner of the tower where he stored his dinner. He knew that within one gourd was warm soup, and spiced wine within the other. Both would warm him well, but if he ate and drank them this early in his shift, he knew he'd fall asleep long before dawn. He couldn't afford to have that happen, again. The Chief Warden still wasn't pleased with him because of the two other times he'd been discovered sleeping while on watch.

As the dark beast approached the tower, it felt the young man's attempt at detecting him. He had almost been taken unawares and had just raised his shields in time before the boy's senses washed over him. His shield and concealment charm had worked fine, and the sentry had returned to his pacing, completely unaware of the deymon's presence. The dark creature was amused at the thought of the destruction that lay before it.

At first angered by its awakening, the deymon soon realized the pain, strife, and fear it could wreak on the Realm as it was forced to hunt its quarry. Its master had simply commanded it to hunt, to find the *Maou'r* and any who accompanied it. "Kill its companions and return with the *Maou'r*, for the most part, unharmed." She didn't specify that it could not enjoy its journey along the way.

When the deymon, who had once had a name, as all deymon's do, but which had long since been forgotten by all but the Horde themselves, had sensed the village at the base of the mountains, it knew it would feast on fear and flesh this night.

The greater deymon, shrouded in darkness and shadow, crept through the tall Dawn Redwoods that grew along this portion of the Thorne's, stalking the first of its prey for the night. Moving on all fours, grasping both ground and tree trunk alike, leaping from tree to giant tree and crawling in between, the dark beast closed silently. The soft glow from within its eye sockets deepened from a bright burning ember red, to a deep arterial blood crimson. It had been too long since the deymon had feasted on living flesh.

Elcin looked back to his dinner. His mouth watered thinking of the venison and barley soup. His fingers and toes were still cold, his nose cold and dribbley. *Maybe just a portion of it*, he thought as he stopped pacing and began to walk to his dinner. But then he felt something. A tingle in the back of his mind, he sensed something else out there. He was being watched, stalked, he could feel the otherworldliness of the creature. It was close and trying to hide itself from him, but he could feel it.

His dinner forgotten, Elcin turned and reached for the bell that was suspended from the center of the thatched roof, hanging on a stout cross beam. That was when he saw the deymon. It was perched on a tree, directly level with the tower's shack. It was enormous.

Elcin slowly reached for the bell.

And the beast let out an unholy growl and hiss that caused Elcin's bowels to release. The deymon leapt from the tree, grabbing a hold of the tower as it landed. The structure shuddered under the weight of the creature. The legs and supports groaned and bent as the tower began to lean to its side.

The sudden movement and peril shocked Elcin to his senses. Forgetting his ruined breeches, he hefted his spear and drove it towards the abdomen of the beast. The weapon shattered on impact with the deymon's armored torso. Elcin stepped back from the creature. He reached out with his mind, trying to notify his village of the danger just beyond the town limits. The deymon reached for him as the tower toppled over, throwing Elcin clear as it fell.

The deymon leapt from the structure, landing gracefully on the ground beside it, opposite where Elcin landed. He stood quickly all too aware of the pain in his wrist and ankle. He saw the bell lying amongst the debris, and knew that it rang only slightly as the tower had tumbled. Elcin hoped the village had heard the faint noise or his desperate psychic warning. As he turned to run for the forest, the beast leapt across the broken structure knocking Elcin to the ground. The deymon had swiped at him with its enormous talons, and he could feel the wounds across his back begin to open and leak beneath his ruined cloak. The wound to his back was beyond pain. He was aware of it, and was sure that it was serious, but he couldn't register the pain at the moment. He rolled over and looked up at the deymon above him. It stood watching him with its hollow eyes like a cat teasing its prey.

The great deymon drank in the fear that rolled off the young man lying on the ground before ending his turmoil. One last taste before leaning forward and ending the man's life, devouring his soul in one massive attack. The deymon fed, feeling stronger and more alive than it had felt in a very long time. *Yes, the awakening had not been a bad thing after all,* the dark beast thought as it fed and anticipated the rest of the night's hunting.

38

All was quiet save the roaring of the deymon. The beast had ravaged the village, but many of the residents had hidden themselves away in catacombs beneath their homes, sealing the doors with holy and magicked wards. The sentries had not been allowed to sound any bells; they were each stalked and killed in turn. Some of the Lost Tribe had felt Elcin's warning, sensed the death approaching, and sought shelter.

The Vrok had still eaten its fill, however, and was now feasting on the fear of the villagers, drinking in the palpable excretions, almost as rich as the blood of innocents. It screamed into the night once more, a sickly, gut wrenching noise that killed animals of weaker heart and caused stronger animals to flee at the sound.

The beast stood atop a small stone house, one of the few left standing and not burning, rearing its great macabre head while sounding its call. Many for miles around, that didn't hear the scream out right, were still struck with a chill causing the hairs on the backs of their necks to stand on end and their scalps to tingle. The fear from the town exuded like sweat from a pig and the Vrok drank it down like water from a spring, filling its lifeless chest.

But there was the dull ache of its charge still to be carried out, the annoying urging at the back of its mind, clawing at its unholy essence to carry out its task, that kept the beast from the complete enjoyment of its meal. Its Mistress's will was his, for the most part, and the wretched beast leapt from the roof and continued on its way, following the pull of the *Maou'r*. Once more on its appointed task, the ache eased, and the deymon moved at its own pace again. Being awoken was more rewarding than it had originally anticipated.

39

The creature cried again, shattering the quiet of the night. The wind howled while sleet and snow pelted Owen's face. The sword shattered against the Vrok. The broken sword lay in pieces on the ground. Feathers and wings beat in Owen's ears and he saw a wooden bridge across a water fall, huge, hideous, monstrous creatures blocked one end juxtaposed to the pretty autumn colors of the leaves behind them. Suddenly, he was standing in a stone hallway watching a small, dark robed being slip into a small passageway in a stone wall. Feelings of dread and foreboding overwhelmed him. The feathers sounded again, loud and raucous.

Owen woke.

Winter stood sentry on the edge of the small clearing where they had spent the night, the ever vigilant *Aingeal*. Boone lay next to Owen. He looked asleep as well, but Owen noticed the dog's ears, flinching and turning, listening to his breathing, he was sure the dog was well aware of his dreaming and now awake state. He looked to the other side of Boone to see if Orla was still asleep, but the young *Fey* was nowhere to be seen. Owen sat up a little more to get a better look.

She is not gone, just in the wood, south of the camp, in the direction of her Kingdom, came the deep soothing voice into Owen's mind. He had quickly come to find the voice in his mind a comfort, a calming, soothing, hum of a voice.

"Thanks," Owen said quietly. "She been up long?"

No.

"You can tell if she's alright, right, from here?" Owen asked.

For the most part. She is communing with her deity from what I can tell.

"Oh," Owen said. He looked in the direction Boone had indicated.

Go Maou'r, your restlessness is apparent. She won't mind.

Owen blushed some, but in the dull light of the pre-morning it wasn't obvious. He rose to his feet. Looking in the direction of Winter, who was now looking back at him, and nodded a greeting. The archer returned the gesture and began walking towards camp. He settled himself at the remains of the small camp fire, and began to stoke life into it once more.

Owen stood and slowly walked to the edge of the clearing, feeling, and knowing, the *Duine Madra's* eyes were on him the whole time.

Owen stepped into the wood and immediately found Orla kneeling before a great yellow birch. The tree was the largest one of its kind that Owen had ever seen. It had always been his father's favorite tree, and Owen remembered with a clenching of his throat, how his father lightly touched and dragged his hand gently along them when he found them in the forest.

The small elf had her back to Owen, but he saw her make the same sign she had made on the day he had first met her. She lightly touched her forehead, heart, and then the ground with her hand, and bowed her head reverently. Owen took another step forward and a twig snapped beneath his foot. He cursed under his breath.

He heard a quiet giggle escape Orla. "I'm not sure what that meant, but I'm willing to bet you wouldn't say it in front of polite company."

She stayed kneeling, but turned and inclined her head to look at him. He smiled sheepishly at her and continued to her side.

"What ya doin?" he asked, trying to sound casual as he sat down next to her.

"Just grounding myself again, since we have been back in my world, I have not given thanks to Gaia," she said, looking back to the large tree.

"Who's Gaia?" Owen asked a little self consciously, he didn't want to offend his friend, but he was curious.

Orla looked over at Owen for a second. She wasn't surprised that he didn't understand or know of her belief, but she wanted to make sure he was being sincere. She had grown up hearing stories of how humans cared nothing for their world or more specifically, nature, and how they made great machines and contraptions to tear down their forests and belch smoke and pollutants into their air and water. It was one of the greatest arguments of her father's opponents within the senate. The humans had poisoned their world, which in turn was killing theirs. Her father's adversaries wanted to reclaim, reunify, the two realms, and in the process wrestle control of the human world from them.

"Gaia is everything around us, the air, the soil, this magnificent tree. I see her in all of nature."

Owen looked back at the tree. "Is she your God?" he asked, looking back to her, trying to make sense of what she said.

"Gaia is what she is. She provides us with our world; I was simply thanking her for it. She is our host here, it is only right to thank her for what she provides," Orla said. It was difficult for her to put into words what Gaia was to her. She had grown up with the knowledge that she was everywhere, and that without her, there would be no food, shelter, water, air. It seemed like a simple concept to her.

"In my world, people go to church, or temples, and pray to God. Some religions have lots of Gods. I just thought that's what you were doing," he said, his voice drifting off as he looked back to the tree. "Maybe folks in my world would be better off just saying thanks once in a while too."

"My people believe in a Creator as well, but Gaia is the essence of everything that sustains our life, the Creator gave us life…and she created Gaia as well…she created everything," Orla said, thinking she understood more of Owen's religion. She leaned forward, bowing to the tree once more, touching her forehead, heart, and ground again, and then stood.

Owen inclined his head towards the tree and stood. He could hear the soft crackle of the fire behind them, and the surprising smell of what reminded him of bacon coming from it. He and Orla left the yellow birch and returned to their camp.

Winter and Boone were waiting for them. Boone had seated himself next to the fire and was quickly eating the breakfast Winter had given him. Winter served Owen and Orla their breakfast before begining to eat his own, his attention drawn back west after doing so.

40

As the small group traveled through the morning, Winter continued Owen's training with the bow. The archer also instructed the young *Maou'r* on animal tracks and sign, as they came across it along the way, in addition to the many plant species they encountered. Owen was used to traveling through the wood with his dad and being subjected to the same types of lessons, but the information that came from the *Aingeal* seemed more easily absorbed for him, and there seemed to be something more to it, something arcane.

Owen noticed that the Hunter's attention was constantly drawn West and behind them, something weighed heavily on the man, but he didn't share it with the group. He kept the party moving at a good pace, but not as desperately as previously. They seemed to have settled into a rhythm each day and evening. Between lessons Owen and Orla would walk and talk alongside each other, Orla becoming freer with her explanations of her Realm and some of the history and stories of her people. There were often times when Owen felt she was leaving pieces out as before, but he didn't push as hard as he had. He was content with the pace at which they were moving as well.

Boone continued to act as rear guard for the party and would walk behind the two young people, rarely partaking in the conversations during the day. Many times Owen began to forget that the dog that traveled with them was so much more than any dog he'd known before.

And apart from his lessons, Winter was more solemn and quiet. He seemed to be concentrating on other thoughts when they were not practicing the bow or explaining some natural oddity.

They were moving more deeply into the Wood, and Owen began to notice an incline to the march. They were entering a more mountainous area which again slowed their pace. Owen wondered if he was the only one who could feel the change in aspect in his leg muscles.

The woods were dark and damp. Deep green moss grew over every exposed rock and boulder. Large coniferous trees Owen had never seen before grew throughout the forest. Winter called it the Sentinel Wood and said long ago the trees themselves had been charged in guarding the lands to the south. Many of the trees of that time had long since passed, but many were still inhabited by the spirits with which they had been imbued long ago. Some of the spirits were still good and content, but others had turned to malice and animosity.

The boulders the group passed amongst became larger, like giant stone blocks dumped from their container, Owen thought. The deep green mosses and lichens grew along the boulders, covering them with a blanket of varying greens. Many of the large trees had toppled and uprooted, leaving huge root masses splaying like fingers in the air.

As Owen passed one such stump, he thought it an oddly humanoid shape. Looking more like a hunched old man made of tree roots and limbs than flesh. Owen looked at the shape with some interest and mirth, but as he began to turn his attention back to the road the stump blinked at him.

Owen stopped abruptly in his tracks, Boone quickly coming to a stop behind him, always alert and ready. The *Duine Madra* was well aware of all living creatures in the presence of the *Maou'r*. Orla stopped as well. Owen grabbed her arm and watched the mass of roots very slowly begin walking through the woods.

"Wassat?" Owen asked.

"Oh," Orla giggled, "Sorry, shoulda warned you," she laughed again. "That's a Shambling Stump. Pretty common in these parts."

Winter had stopped walking as well and had returned to the others.

He also watched the Shambling Stump begin its slow shuffle away from the small group.

"A fair bit surly, though," Winter added as he again turned his attention from the stump to look West, then check the position of the sun, and then back in the direction they were heading.

"And rightly so, I'd say," Orla added. "Not all, but most are a bit grumpy, but if you had termites and slugs crawling up in you, I bet you wouldn't be none too pleased either," she said smiling, giving Owen a nudge. He was still a bit dumbfounded by his newest discovery. Even after everything that had happened over the course of the past week, there still seemed to be things in this world to amaze him.

The Shambling Stump looked like a blown down tree, all roots at odd angles, but enough of them in proper arrangement to give the creature the appearance of a person. Long green lichen grew like a beard from its long tree root chin. Two yellow eyes blinked beneath heavy bark lids. It ambled at its own pace, moving through the wood without much care or concern for anyone or anything else.

After the stump had vanished from view, the party began moving again, falling into single file order. They marched into the evening until just before dusk, when the sun was a bright red orb in the Western sky. The clouds in the West seemed to be a fire from the glow of the sun, a deep burning orange and pink. Owen caught Winter on many occasions, while preparing the evening fire and meal, stealing a glance in that direction. Boone busied himself by patrolling the area and then coming back to rest and lay beside Owen, eating his dinner from his reclined state.

As they finished dinner and began to turn in, Winter came and knelt beside Owen and Orla. Boone was lying between them which had become his custom, giving himself up as a pillow to his two companions.

"As Orla can tell you, we are very close now to her Kingdom, by this time tomorrow you will have reached and crossed the Fall's Bridge, which is the border to her country. Once across, the road to Quailan is a quick one. On the morrow, I will bid you farewell. I have errands I need run that I feel pressing against me, but once conducted, I will return and meet you in Quailan."

"But I thought you were coming with us to the bridge," Owen began.

"And so did I, but I fear something has come up that I need investigate. As well, I feel, there is another matter I must attend quickly. With Boone in our company now, I feel much more at ease letting you finish this last part of your journey on your own. You will be safe in his care."

The great dog looked to Winter, nodded, and then rested his massive head on Owen's leg, agreeing with the archer's assessment.

"Stay in Quailan until I return to you. I feel you will be safer within its borders than anywhere else. Orla's people will take care of you well. Now get some rest, we will make our goodbyes on the morrow." The Hunter rose from his crouch and walked to the outer ring of their small clearing, as was his custom, and took up watch.

He would not leave prematurely unless he felt he must. He has been much distracted by happenings in the West. It is best for him to see to them, I will make sure we make it to the Sylvan city.

"I know you will," Owen said, stroking the coarse fur on the large dog's head, "I will just miss him when he's gone."

41

So how long do you think you'll be?" Owen asked, as he sat across from Winter while they ate breakfast. Winter was again pensive and restless, seeming eager to be on his way, but anxious about the safety of his charges. His attention was divided this morning between the West, which had been drawing it the past few days, and between the *Duine Madra* eating his own breakfast by Owen's side.

The Hunter turned his attention back to his young charge. He didn't want to leave the young man anymore than the *Maou'r* wanted him to leave, but the growing dread within him and the shadow that he felt in the West were forcing him to leave Owen's side. Besides, there was the other matter to attend to, one he felt pressed to do, as if time was of the essence. Something that he had never felt in all the centuries he had walked amongst and apart from Man.

He was fairly confident that the presence of the *Duine Madra* was a good omen. Between the Sylvan and the First Dog, Owen was well protected, not to mention that the youth had shown a certain adeptness at preserving himself.

Winter considered Owen a moment longer before answering, maybe it was being in the presence of the *Maou'r* after so long, or maybe it was this particular boy himself, but the Hunter knew he had a growing fondness for the young man.

"Soon Owen. As quickly as I can manage," Winter said, his voice holding none of the coolness it originally had. His voice was the warmth of a late winter day when the snow pack becomes heavy with moisture, when jackets, scarves, and mittens are abandoned for thick sweaters under the warming sun.

"But don't neglect your practicing," he added with a smile. "I expect to see much improvement with your bow on my return."

"I will," Owen answered glumly. He had begun to think of Winter as the answer to his parents' imprisonment, a key to their rescue. Now he wasn't so sure. He was feeling desperate for their safety again.

As if sensing his thoughts, Winter added, "Quailan might be a good place for you to start seeking information and aid in finding your family. There are many powerful and influential people within the Sylvan government, and Orla may be able to provide some help in arranging meetings with them."

"I can, Owen," she added trying to cheer his mood. She hadn't been completely honest yet with him about her family, and she wasn't sure how he was going to take it when she was.

"Okay, and when you return, we can try and put it all together, and find them?" Owen said, looking up and meeting the First Man's eyes.

"Yes," he said without losing the young man's gaze.

"Okay then, we'll wait for you, and in the mean time, I'll find out where they are and who has them," Owen said.

The small party quickly broke camp and made plans for separating. Orla, Owen, and Boone would continue to head south towards the Fall's Bridge and Quailan while Winter would strike out West. When they had all gathered their belongings and were ready to break camp, they met once more by the now extinguished cook fire.

Winter held out his hand to Owen, "It has been good traveling with you Owen; we will see each other again shortly."

Owen took his hand and smiled at the much taller man. His hands were large and calloused. Owen felt a pang in his heart similar to what he felt the moment he first saw his parents as statues. But he trusted Winter, and knew that he would return to Quailan for him as soon as he was able.

Winter looked to the Sylvan and dog standing beside Owen. He nodded to them, "Again, it's been my privilege being in your company."

The great dog inclined his massive head to the *Aingeal*.

"May Gaia hold you in the palm of her hand and hold you close while on your travels," Orla said, her voice reminding Owen of the first time she spoke to him, sounding like warblers in spring.

"Thank you. Be safe now, all of you, there are villains at work here, and until we know who they are, and what they're up to, we must be wary." The tall man bowed once more to the companions and then turned. Pausing, he lifted his face to the light breeze as if scenting the wind, or testing the air, and said almost to himself, "The seasons are changing; winter is coming and will be close at hand." He didn't turn back then, but continued on his way. He covered much ground in a short time and Owen realized for the first time that the Hunter must have felt like he was crawling while traveling with him. In no time he lost the *Aingeal* within the wood.

The remaining companions turned and went their own way, Orla now in the lead, and Boone following behind. Owen found himself once more sheltered in the middle of the order. Whenever possible, as they marched through the day, he and Orla walked abreast and chatted about the events of the past few days that seemed to have happened a lifetime ago. She spoke of her family for the first time and how she hoped her father would be in Quailan—and not in the capital—and how she looked forward to seeing her little sister. She wondered out loud if they thought she was a captive of someone, or if they believed her dead at this point, and how they would react when she all of sudden stepped from the wood.

Boone followed behind alert as ever, always on guard, and protective of his *Maou'r*.

As the day lengthened, their climb became steeper and rockier. Ledge outcrops became common, herding the party along high drops and climbs through the ridges. The forest composition changed as well. They left the open forest floor of the high canopy Sentinel Trees and entered a dense forest of firs, spruce, and cedars that grew from the cracks and fissures of the rocks.

They stopped for a brief mid-day meal, resting for a short period, and then were off again. Orla was hopeful to reach Quailan before nightfall. As the rumbling in Owen's stomach began to remind him it was approaching dinner time, he could hear the roaring of a nearby river and falls.

"We're close now," Orla said, beaming at him. She could barely contain her excitement at the prospect of being home once more. Her pace had quickened without her noticing it, and the trio continued on their way to the Fall's Bridge.

As they grew closer, Owen noticed an interesting change in the landscape. The path they were on stayed flat and relatively unchanged while above and below them the hillside began to resemble giant rock stairs. To the uphill side of him was almost a sheer climb that leveled off a hundred feet above his head, while on the down side it looked to be a fifty foot drop. The pathway they walked along looked like it was about twenty feet across, large enough, barely, for two cars to pass, Owen thought.

The wind is not in our favor. It blows at our backs. The deep low boom of the *Duine Madra's* voice echoed in Owen's mind interrupting his thoughts. *But something is still foul in the air. I can't scent it, but there is something close that I can sense.*

Owen looked to Orla who looked back at him.

"Any other way across?" Owen asked.

"No," Orla answered, fighting a feeling of dread at the thought of something preventing her from making it home.

"This bridge sounds like a good place for an ambush," Owen added, picking up a stone from the trail, and absently rubbing it between his thumb and forefingers.

"Well, it is, it's one of the reasons we built it on the edge of our Kingdom."

Owen turned to Boone, "It's our only way across. Keep alert; we'll be careful, okay?"

Okay.

Owen took his bow from his back and knocked an arrow, and Orla shifted into her hybrid form. Boone stayed in the back of the order, but stayed much closer to the other two.

"How much farther to the bridge?" Owen asked.

"Not far, another hundred feet, the path bends once more and then opens onto the bridge," Orla answered in her soft hybrid growl.

The three made their way around the last bend, where the wind picked up off of the fall, swirling around them and spraying them with the mist from the torrent of water cascading over the ledge above them.

The water crashed off the edge of the stair above their heads and fell straight along side of the wooden bridge that Owen could now see. The water came to no more than 30 feet within the bridge, but still surprisingly close, Owen thought. *I wonder how many times they've had to fix that after a flood*, he mused.

The bridge was made from stout timbers which anchored it on either side of the expanse to stone foundations, while the bridge itself was rigid and large enough across for a car or wagon more likely, Owen thought.

The sides of the ledge and pathway not in direct line with the falls were wet and covered in moss in many places from the spray. Owen approached the bridge very carefully and looked over the edge. It dropped for another fifty feet into a large pool, and then slowly meandered downstream and back into the forest out of view. At any other time it would be a wonderfully beautiful and magical place. Owen realized why Orla had spoken so fondly of the bridge in their previous conversations, but now there was only apprehension.

The air is foul.

"I agree," Orla growled.

The scent of evil is strong here, but the wind blows such that I cannot pinpoint it.

"Then be ready, we must cross the bridge, so we'll do it carefully, and as quickly as possible."

Owen stepped onto the wooden structure, arrow pointed at the far end. Orla stepped up beside him.

"There will be Sylvan sentries on the far side; they may be concealing themselves in the wood now, waiting for us to cross. We don't look like the friendliest travelers right now."

"True enough," Owen answered, but didn't bother lowering his bow.

"Now, when'd you find the time to find yerself a doggie?" Owen recognized the brutish voice immediately. He spun, and found his target, as the Hunter had instructed him, in one fluid motion. His fingers tensed ready to loose the arrow into Brule's heart.

Boone stepped between Orla and Owen, squaring off on Brule. The large Trollbjorn seemed unfazed by the large dog. He held no weapons. Owen scanned the terrain quickly and couldn't tell from where he had stepped, the wall behind him was almost a sheer cliff with no purchase to be seen, unless *he had come from under the bridge*, Owen thought. A deep guttural growl emitted from Boone's chest. The great dog's hackles were raised, he stood proud chested, with his head up, and ears forward. He didn't bare his teeth or snarl; *he didn't need to*, Owen thought. *How can he just stand there and not be scared of him*, Owen thought again.

Onto the bridge the pair of you. I will deal with him. But be wary, he is not what is fouling the air; there is evil here, and close by.

"No," Owen said. "He's the one who took my parents, I want answers." Owen raised his bow, the tension on the string causing his arm to cramp, but he focused past it. Winter had made him hold it steady for longer than this, but his adrenalin was never this high before.

Owen.

"Hey now, I never took yer folks kid," Brule said, holding up his hands in defense. He stepped close, rounding a little to try and get Boone from between them. "C'mon, call off your pooch, woulda? Let's talk, waddoya say?"

The growl that came next silenced them all and gave Brule his answer, Boone would not relinquish.

"I'd stay where you are," Owen said. "He doesn't like Bounty Hunters much."

"Aw, you still sore about that, c'mon kid, it was just a job. You two have cost me no limit of trouble, ya know?" Brule said, standing still and holding his ground. *What am I doing,* he thought. *Why ya talking to them, just do the job, get the bounty, and get outta town. Too many unhappy as it is.*

"Where are my parents?"

"Dunno." Brule shrugged, it was an awkward gesture for the giant half-troll, trolls don't have to shrug that often.

"Owen, let's just get across the bridge, once we get to Quailan we can send guards to bring him back," Orla said, her voice still a growl.

"No," Owen said flatly. "He answers me now, here, or I put an arrow in his chest."

"Wow, ain't someone gotten a bit bitter since we last met. That bow's a grown-ups' toy, mate, I'd be careful wit it if I was you. Listen, girlie, you're coming with me. You're a realm-jumper, and it's my job to bring you in."

Owen felt the bridge move and heard a low grunt and growl from behind him above the din of the falls. The bridge groaned under the extra weight as one of Brule's cousins stepped onto the structure. Owen didn't turn to see this new danger, neither did Boone take his eyes off of Brule, but Orla did.

And what she saw were still recognizable as trolls, but they were unlike any troll before them. They each had huge horns that now grew spiraling out from the sides of their heads. The two spikes were more than a foot long and grew from just above the creatures' temples, splaying slightly to the sides as they did. They had long serpent tales that thrashed about anxiously behind them. Their tusks were huge, almost too large for their mouths now; they dripped with drool and blood in the mouths from which they sprouted. Faint green glows emitted from their sunken eyes. They were almost twice their original size and only one could fit upon the bridge at a time. The first cousin to step onto the bridge held the lifeless remains of one of the Sylvan sentries in his *Fey* form. The other two cousins pushed and shoved to see who would step onto the structure next, Orla wondered how many more of them the bridge could hold.

The first monster troll on the bridge held a huge spiked club in its right clawed hand, the sentry in his left. He tossed the sentry over the bridge without a second thought and grabbed the railing to sturdy himself as he crossed. Spittle dripped from his tusks, mixing with the spray from the falls, its grunts, wheezes, and growls were drowned out by the roaring of the water. The bridge shuddered under its weight.

"Um, Owen, we got trouble," Orla said, stepping back to be able to see Owen and the troll at the same time, completely turning her back on Brule, the lesser threat at this point. She was fairly certain; these creatures weren't working for him anymore. She could feel the magical corruption that had caused them to mutate.

"Oh cousins, what did he do to you?" Brule cried. He started to reach for his hand axe when a growl erupted from Boone. The great dog closed the distance between them, Brule holding up his hands in submission was the only thing that kept the animal from going for his throat.

"Listen girlie, they're coming for both of us now, and they ain't gunna take you alive if ya know what I mean!" Brule yelled over Boone and the din of the falls. Owen chanced a looked over his shoulder and saw the monstrosity coming their way; turning completely around, he let loose the arrow, taking the troll in the knee, dropping it to the floor of the bridge.

"That should buy us some time," he said while knocking another shaft. "Boone, he's right. Are these what you sensed?" Owen shouted back to his dog. This was getting out of control fast, and he wasn't sure what he should be doing. *I wish Winter was here*, he thought.

Yes.

"Then they're our priority, not the bounty hunter…for now."

The great dog growled as he leapt up onto the bridge in front of Owen and Orla.

Behind me!

The force of the thought staggered Owen for a second as the *Duine Madra* leapt beside and past him placing himself between the danger and his human.

"We're not done here Bounty Hunter, I still want answers about my parents," Owen shouted over his shoulder as Brule charged past him.

"Yeah, yeah, yeah, got it, I'll pencil ya in, now stay back and let someone who knows what they're doin' deal with this," Brule shouted as he ran by Owen and Orla and took a position next to, and just in front of Boone, giving the dog as much room as he could on the narrow bridge.

The injured troll began to stand, ripping the shaft from his injured knee. Roaring as he did so, his two siblings behind him had sorted things out and the victor took his first step onto the bridge. As the first troll stood, Brule let loose his throwing axe, hitting the troll square between his eyes. It swayed for a moment and then fell off the bridge on the side of the falls, taking the railing, and a good portion of the structural integrity of the bridge with it. Even over the sound of the falls, Owen could hear the *Kla-dunk* of it hitting the pool below.

"Sorry cousin," Brule shouted after his fallen relative. *Never liked him much any how*, he thought as the next troll stepped up before him.

Brule pulled out his morning star from its place on his back.

"We should get outta here," Orla said next to Owen. "Let the bounty hunter deal with these things while we lose him."

"I thought there was no other way across the falls?" Owen asked, taking aim on the next misshapen troll.

Do not engage them, leave them to me.

"Not a chance, you think I'm leaving you here alone with them," Owen shouted back.

That's the idea.

"No way!"

"Owen, these things are corrupt with magic, they reek of evil. We should get out of here!" Orla shouted again, but staying between Owen and the approaching trolls. Owen had to side step her to keep his target in sight.

"I'm not leaving Boone," he said grimly and fired his arrow. It glanced off the side of the troll's face, just below the eye he'd been aiming for, opening a long painful gash along its cheek. The creature yowled in pain and hatred, slamming its club down where Boone had been standing a moment before, crushing and splintering cross beams of the bridge.

"I don't know how long the bridge will be able to take this kind of abuse," Orla said.

Boone latched onto the club wrist of the troll, the evil creature howled, and lifted his arm, pulling the dog completely off the ground. The troll began to violently thrash its arm, trying to shake the dog loose.

Owen let lose another arrow, catching the troll just below its right armpit, but still it shook the dog. Boone could be heard growling above the falls, as he tried to regain his footing. Brule closed on the monster, swinging his vicious looking morning star and catching his cousin along the side of its head. The monster shook its head dumbly, and then bellowed a challenge in their native tongue.

"He's going to throw Boone off the bridge unless I can put him down," Owen shouted desperately to Orla, letting fly a fourth arrow. This one caught the troll in the stomach, just missing Brule as it zipped past him.

"Hey!" the trollbjorn shouted as he ducked beneath a back hand from his cousin. Boone had regained his footing following the distraction by Brule and was savagely tearing at the monster's wrist trying to free his hand of the club.

"No he won't," Orla said as she leapt over Brule and landed on his cousin's shoulders and neck with her usual feline grace. She raked her claws over its face, hissing while doing so.

The second troll on the bridge closed in and took a mighty swing at Orla while she was still on his comrade's back. She easily leapt away from the swing, letting the troll slam its club into its brother's back, driving the injured troll to his knees with a grunt.

Boone released his grip of its wrist and retreated to Owen. Brule tried stepping back from his cousin, but not before the kneeling troll was able to plant a hefty punch in the bounty hunter's midsection, dropping him onto his back with a groan.

Orla leapt from the bridge decking to a railing to avoid another swing from the uninjured troll's club. It splintered another section of the bridge that groaned in protest under the combined weight of its occupants. The troll swung again, knocking the railing on which Orla had just been perched flying into the falls. Orla landed right in front of the kneeling troll, who snatched at her with his free hand, grabbing her about the waist.

She hissed, growled, and yowled at him, clawing his hand, ripping and rending great pieces of flesh from it, but the monster was unfazed. He just tightened his grip. Orla screamed.

Owen let loose three quick arrows in succession, all on the beast's right side, far from Orla, but even though they each found their home, none seemed to faze the troll. Orla struggled against the grip as the creature hefted her up above its head.

"Put 'er down, ya great big dolt," Brule shouted as he got back to his feet and closed on his cousin, raising his morning star and quickly bringing it down on the arm that held Orla. "She's not worth a penny to me dead!" The arm gave an enormous crack, followed by an anguished scream from the monster. Orla fell to the bridge and dragged herself to her knees, before ducking again as the enraged troll swung its club, still from its kneeling position, striking Brule across his chest, sending him crashing into the far railing, seemingly, the only railing still intact. It began to lean dangerously under his weight.

"Get her and that dog outta here," Brule shouted at Owen. "Whoever hired me to come git her, also did that to me cousins, and he's the one wit yer parents, not me." Brule looked for his morning star, which he'd dropped when he hit the railing. It was lying in front of the injured cousin, who was now just getting to his feet with Orla still on the ground in front of him.

"Boone! Orla! Help her!" Owen shouted knocking another arrow.

You are the Maou'r, my place is defending you, came the calm booming reply.

"No, help her, I'm fine, she needs help!"

Is she pack then?

It took Owen only a second to process the question, although it struck him as odd to think of her that way. "Yes!" he shouted, and in that instant Boone again charged into the fray with the trolls, stepping between Orla and the creature in front of her.

The troll began to swing again at Boone, who held his ground between the troll and the still dazed Orla, but Brule stepped in and took the hit. He brought his own attack up to meet his cousin's, swinging his newly unsheathed short sword to deflect the blow. The club and mutated troll were stronger, the blow smashed down into Brule's shoulder resulting in a loud crunch, driving the joint from its socket. The bounty hunter grunted, but gritted his teeth through the pain.

Brule switched hands with his sword and drove the blade deeply into the troll's neck, until flesh met hilt, and drove the creature back with all his might, pushing it free of the railing and bridge, allowing the troll's weight to pull it free from his sword as it fell to the pool below. The force of the attack had driven him to his knees as his opponent fell from the structure. He turned to see his last cousin storming towards him.

Boone dragged Orla back to Owen.

We need to leave. We need to flee. I am near spent.

"No!" Owen said in shock. "He just risked his life for you two, and you want to leave him?" Owen fired two more arrows into the approaching troll, it barely noticed them. Brule looked to where his morning star was laying, but it was well out of reach, he resigned himself to his sword again.

It is the only way; I must get you two to safety.

Owen turned and met the *Duine Madra's* eyes. "No," he said. As he turned back to Brule, he saw his last cousin back-hand him across the bridge. He skidded across the structure, digging in with his bear-like claws, but his momentum was too great and he began to slide off the bridge.

Owen didn't hesitate; he dropped his bow and ran for the bounty hunter. Sliding across the bridge, he grabbed the man's arm as he began to lose his grip with his one good hand, the arm from the injured shoulder hanging limply. Owen grabbed his wrist and tuffs of hair with both hands, but the weight of the trollbjorn pulled him towards the edge of the bridge until he felt the clamp of Boone's jaws on his ankle.

"Ow!" he yelled.

Let him go! He will be the death of us all!

"No!" Owen grunted back.

"Lemme go, boy," Brule wheezed up at him.

"You can't hoist me up, and my cousin's coming for you, now."

As if on cue, a yowl and hiss erupted from Orla behind them as she savagely clawed and attacked the troll, driving him back from her defenseless friends.

"That's one special lady ya got yerself there, lad," Brule joked as he coughed, bloodied spittle appearing on his lips. Owen was losing his grip.

"Grab my arm, Boone can pull us up," he grunted as the troll dangled beneath him.

"No, lemme go, it's my fault yer here anyways," Brule looked below and was surprised to think his life might end this way. "C'mon kid, I'm slipping anyway."

"No!"

"Good luck finding your parents, kid. Honestly, I never had nothing to do with that business. Not sure what you done to these people, but I hope you find yer folks."

Owen, I can't hold you any longer without breaking and biting through your leg! Drop him!

Brule's wrist slipped from Owen's grasp, but he still held onto clumps of the troll's dense fur, preventing him from falling a moment more.

"Help me then," Owen said through gritted teeth, the pain in his arms was causing spots in his vision, and sweat was dripping into his eyes.

"Don't think that's quite an option anymore kid...," Brule said as the tuffs of fur pulled free from Owen's hands and the bounty hunter plummeted into the pool below the falls.

"NO!" Owen screamed, frustration and anger over taking him. Without Brule's added weight, Boone was finally able to pull Owen back, away from the edge.

Orla dodged the attacks of the troll at the far end of the bridge. She had succeeded in pushing the monster to the end of the ruined bridge on the Quailan side. The creature had great gashes across its face, arms, and chest. Orla's white and gray fur was blood stained. Owen had never seen her so possessed before. She moved fluidly, with grace, and fierce poise. She was more a leopard now than he'd ever seen her before. He raced across the bridge to his fallen bow, ignoring the pain in his ankle and shin, pulling an arrow from his quiver as he did so; he was down to only a few. Boone had raced across the bridge to engage the troll again and help Orla the best he could.

Owen knocked the arrow, pulled the bowstring back to his anchor point along his cheek, aimed and fired in one liquid motion. He never felt more at peace or one with his bow before, it was as if Winter were there with him.

He let the arrow fly and it flew straight and true. It took the troll in his right eye and sank up to the fletching. The troll let out a bellow of pain and surprise that turned to a soft moan as it fell forward onto the bridge. The structure shuddered under the sudden crashing of the giant troll. It creaked and swayed slightly.

"Run for it!" Owen shouted as the bridge began to give way. Boone and Orla were already on the far side near Quailan. They both leapt off the bridge in plenty of time. The bridge began to buckle in the middle where most of the fighting and damage had occurred. Owen was across it by the time it started to slide towards the river below. He was running up hill as it began to fall. He made one mighty leap, stretching as he did so, and tumbled onto the ground of the far side. He landed hard and without any grace, but was safe. Boone and Orla both ran to him, Boone immediately inspecting him for injury and sniffing and licking his face. Orla sat beside him, laying her arm around his neck, and her head on his shoulder. She seemed exhausted.

She shifted to her Sylvan form, and Owen immediately noticed the deep bruises she had suffered from all the debris that had been crashing about her and from her combat with the trolls.

"We need to get her somewhere safe and take care of these," Owen said, standing and helping Orla to her feet. "We won't be making Quailan tonight."

I'll find us a safe place to rest for the night.

The companions moved away from the falls and deeper into the woods, Owen helping Orla walk as they did so. Boone found a sheltered grove for them to rest for the night. Owen knelt beside Orla and made her comfortable, left Boone to guard her, and went out after some herbs Winter had taught him could sooth contusions and bruises. He wasn't gone long and was back before night. He made Orla a poultice for her injuries and a spicy tea to drink that helped her sleep. He and Boone, much to Boone's distress, split the watches.

The night passed without further incident in the Kingdom of the Sylvanni.

42

A giant roan dressier stood in the middle of the slow meandering current of the river. It was waiting for someone. Its rider had left it on the bank below as he scaled the cliff wall to the bridge above. He had stroked the horse's neck and spoken reassuringly to him that he wouldn't be long and would be back shortly. But the horse had known better, as most horses do.

When his rider had reached the top of his climb, the horse had walked downstream and then entered the cool refreshing water to wait. It hadn't been long. He was able to hear the fighting at the bridge and occasionally caught glimpses of the fighting above. Twice he watched as his rider's enemies fell from the bridge only to sink down within the deep reaches of the pool below the falls.

The horse was grateful his rider had opted not to wear his armor for the climb he had to make, telling the horse while he spoke that he felt it would be too cumbersome. The horse had agreed.

When he saw his rider dangle from the bridge, and then fall, he felt slight trepidation, but assured himself that his rider would be fine. That was why he had entered the middle of the stream and had waited there in the first place.

The dressier bent and plunged his huge head into the cool water, and pulled out, within his teeth, the back of his rider's tunic. The horse dragged the trollbjorn to the shore where he rolled the man onto his back. He pushed down onto the man's stomach with his mouth and nose until the man retched and spat up river water, and then the horse rolled him onto his side.

The horse then went and munched on the grass growing along the bank and waited. He had done all he could do for the troll, now he must wait for the quick healing and fast metabolism of the species to take care of the rest.

He looked back once to the bridge as it crumbled into the river, and washed past them on the bank. After watching it float past, he went back to eating the grass. As night came, the horse pulled his rider further from the bank, and back under the cover of the wood's edge.

He stood by his rider during the night, occasionally dozing, but then waking to the sudden nearby night noises that always startle horses in the dark.

43

Hey, it's time to wake up," Owen said gently rubbing Orla's shoulder. She rolled over to look up at him, and he was thankful to see that the swelling and bruises had gone down and lessened. She smiled at him as she wiped the sleep from her eyes.

"And I thought yesterday you looked and sounded just like Winter, now you won't even let me sleep like him too," she teased as she sat up. "Where's Boone?"

"He said he was gunna find some breakfast," Owen said standing and going back to caring for his fire. "I can't make a fire like him, though, that's for sure."

She smiled as she sat down next to him. He bent over and blew gently on the small ember glowing beneath the dry grass and pine needles. Smoke lazily floated up from a brighter ember.

"Want some help?" she asked smiling.

"Yeah, go ahead, nuke it," he said sitting back.

"Nuke it?" she laughed.

"Yeah, torch it already; my pride can't take anymore of this."

"Tine'," she said in her native tongue, as sweet as songbirds in the forest. The kindling burst into flames. Owen quickly added wood to the now roaring conflagration.

"Yeah, nuke it," he said laughing.

Boone came back with a rabbit in his mouth and laid it at Owen's feet.

"Anything else in there?" Owen teased; Boone just tilted his head at his *Maou'r* and then went and lay down with a great *huff*.

"Winter used to clean it," he teased again; Boone got up and turned his back to the two laughing friends and laid back down, sighing loudly again. Owen pulled out his hunting knife and began cleaning the rabbit while Orla stretched and yawned.

"I heard a small creek last night, is there a spring nearby?" she asked. "I'd like to wash and freshen up some."

"Yeah, down the trail a bit," Owen said still skinning the rabbit the way Winter had shown him.

Boone got up and slowly started walking in the direction of the trail and spring.

"I guess he'll show you."

"Why is he in a mood this morning?" she asked quietly as she walked by Owen.

"Oh, I think it's because of the ambush yesterday, and my taking watch last night. I think he's upset because he didn't protect us enough or something," Owen said looking down the trail after his dog. He didn't bother mentioning that one of the reasons he wanted watch was because he wasn't sure how well he'd have slept last night anyway. He'd gone hunting with his dad since he was twelve. And even though he'd shot grouse and rabbit, yesterday was different. He'd killed in self defense, not for food, but to end a life, albeit an evil life, and to preserve his own. He knew it was in self defense, but he still wasn't sure how he felt about it.

"Well, that's rubbish," she said. "If it wasn't for him we both would have been troll food."

"You know that, and I know that, but he won't hear it."

"Well, I hope he cheers up, he's so sad when he's grumpy," she said with a giggle making Owen smile again. She quickly followed Boone down the trail and Owen watched them both until they were out of sight. He finished cleaning and dressing the rabbit and stuck it upon a spit and placed it over their fire.

When Orla and Boone returned from the spring she whispered something in her tongue to the fire and it roared to life once more, quickly cooking the rabbit roasting above it.

Once they had finished breaking their fast, they packed up their things and headed down the trail to Quailan. By midmorning Orla was already telling them they were on the outskirts of the town even though Owen saw no signs of it.

In that case I think I should be less seen.

"What?" they both said at the same time. "Why?" they did it again.

I feel it best if the Maou'r is seen without his Duine Madra. Most people believe my kind to be extinct, and I feel that is for the best, for now. By himself he may be able to pass for someone other than the Maou'r, but with me by his side, some may recognize him as for who he is. Also, we still do not know who was behind your abduction, Princess.

"Princess?" Owen said surprised. Orla ignored him.

"But what will you do, where will you go?" Orla asked.

"You're not going to leave too?" Owen added, already feeling the tightness in his chest, and the lump growing in his throat.

No, I am not leaving. I will be close, closer than you realize, all you need do is call me and I will come, but I believe it better if we keep my presence secret…for now. Alright?

Owen and Orla begrudgingly nodded in unison. Boone walked up to them, Orla first, who he was closer to in height, when looking up, his nose almost came even to her chin. He pushed his head into her stomach, rubbing it on her, and then looked up and gave her a quick lick on her chin. He looked her in the eyes and then turned to Owen. He approached his *Maou'r* and met his eyes and held them for a moment before leaning his head into Owen's torso. Owen scratched the great dog on his head and behind his ears, before the dog looked back up at him. Owen leaned over and kissed him once on his forehead, just between his eyes, where his two white eyebrows almost met. Boone nodded once and turned into the wood. As the King of Dogs slowly began to move out of sight he said, *I will be close, all you need do is call.* And then he was gone, lost in the wood.

Owen again felt abandoned. He turned to Orla and her expression was just as he felt. They both turned and headed towards Quailan not as happy to be going there as they had been a moment previously.

Not long after Boone had left, the two companions came to a small clearing. The grass freshly cut and bailed. On the far side of the clearing a snowshoe hare, just beginning to whiten to its winter coat, sat nibbling on shoots along the forest edge. Without a moment's hesitation, Orla shifted to full leopard form and went chasing the hare about the glen.

Owen stood fast, dumbfounded, he certainly wasn't hungry yet, and he figured this close to Quailan Orla wouldn't have stopped for anything. Just then Orla leapt at the hare, shifting to her hybrid form in mid leap, reaching for the hare with her humanoid paws. The hare leapt away, just out of reach, and shifted form as well. Before Owen's eyes he watched the large rabbit change to that of a combination of a female Sylvan and a snowshoe hare. And then he heard giggling, uncontrollable giggling, coming from both Sylvans in a strange mix of feline growl and lagomorph squeaks.

Owen approached the two girls lying in the grass and stood over them with his arms akimbo waiting for an introduction.

Orla looked up, saw Owen, and shifted back to her Sylvan form, standing up as she did so. Before Orla could say a word, the hare-girl reached for her and hugged her tightly.

"Orla, where have you been? We feared the worst; father has ordered search parties through the entire Kingdom." Owen looked upon the girl with the same amazement as when he had first looked at Orla. The girl was shorter than Orla, but just barely. Her body was completely covered in mostly white fur that Owen knew would be completely snow white by the first snowfall. Her face, apart from the fur, was more human looking than Orla's in her hybrid form, with the exception of having extremely large blue eyes, and the ears of a hare. Her hare ears, at the moment, were laid flat down her back, clasped by a silver hoop, reminding Owen of a girl with her hair in a ponytail. The girl's upper body was very much that of a *Fey* girl, Owen was thankful she too was fur covered there as well; her hands were a combination of fingers and rabbit's toes. They were long like a finger, but ended in a rougher pad with long black lagomorph nails. Her waist and upper legs again were *Fey*, but from her knees down resembled a giant hare's.

Owen had no doubt she could leap great distances or deliver a wicked kick to someone.

Owen cleared his throat.

"Oh, sorry. Owen, this is my little sister, Maya," Orla returned the hug and turned to her sister who eyed Owen suspiciously.

"Hi," Owen said with an awkward wave.

"Who's he?" Maya asked Orla, not taking her eyes off of Owen.

"A friend, the person who actually found me and brought me back home, now don't be rude!" Orla chastised her sister, smiling apologetically at Owen. He returned the smile.

"Oh, sorry, nice to meet you," the young Sylvan said, bowing slightly to Owen.

"Nice to meet you too," he said.

"Now, about father, is he here? In Quailan?"

"No, he is still in Narsus; the Re-unifiers have kept them all in session," Maya answered, twitching her nose like a rabbit.

"Stop that," Orla chastised her for the unconscious twitch of her nose. "He was there when I left, I'm certain. Well, I'm almost certain." Orla looked at Owen. "I really think I was leaving to tell him something, and then POOF, nothing, until you found me."

"It's alright, it will come back, give it time," Owen said. "Do you think we should continue?" he said, filling the sudden awkward silence.

"Yeah, good idea, Maya will fill me in on what's been happening while I was gone," Orla said taking her sister's hand and turning back to the city.

Owen followed as Orla returned to Quailan.

44

M om would love this!" Owen said as he, Orla, and Maya walked into Quailan. They hadn't entered the city proper yet, but the outlying, country-folk homes, amazed Owen. There was a very neighborly way about them that reminded him of his own village in Vermont.

The homes were logical now that he thought about it, but until seeing them he had just expected homes of any normal town like his own world. But things were different in Quailan because these were Sylvan homes. And Sylvan homes meant variety.

There were homes in the tops of the Sentinel trees that grew around the village for Sylvans that morphed into birds and other flying animals that Owen could see zooming from tree to tree and home to home. They passed homes that burrowed down into the earth for Sylvans who were more comfortable below ground, and then there were the types of homes Owen expected, above ground wooden and stone structures that began to form streets and roads that led into the village proper.

Orla and Maya kept a quick pace, Orla had said she wanted to make it home before too many people recognized her and word reached the homestead before she did. She had also wanted Owen moved through town quickly as well. No one would be expecting a human in their world, so that would work to their favor, but on close examination someone might be able to deduce what and who he really was.

Owen tried to keep his eye on the road or on the two Sylvan sisters in front of him and not look like a tourist, but he found the village to be amazing. The younger sister quickly filled in the older in their native tongue, which Orla had slowly been trying to teach to Owen, but who was having difficulty grasping the rich language.

Sylvans in every animal and hybrid form were everywhere: goats, horses, deer, frogs, mice, birds, even a polecat. Well, Owen wasn't certain they were all Sylvan, he wasn't sure if Sylvans themselves could distinquish between one of their own and a natural animal. Some may have been the actual animals, but who could tell? Homes of every type that would be homey and welcoming to every imaginable animal ranged through the town. Owen was just beginning to wonder what type of home a snow leopard and snowshoe hare would have when he spotted it. Knowing right away it was theirs, and finally having an idea as to who he had truly befriended.

On the outside of the town, along the rock ledges that acted as the city limit, was a stone house. It was not an elaborate or exquisite home, but it was one of the largest homes in Quailan and set apart from the rest. It had a stone wall that surrounded the home, with a large iron-gate set in the front of it; if Owen was going to pick the home for a *Princess* it would have been that home. The building looked as if it was a part of the cliff face it was built along. It also looked like it was in a place of respect and authority upon the hill, a home for royalty or nobility. As they weaved through the village streets, they kept heading towards the stone home.

The rocks were hewn from a soft looking white stone that gleamed in the midday light. The house's roof was a reddish colored slate shingle, with large brick fireplaces sprouting up throughout the home.

As they neared the building Owen was also taken aback at the cleanliness of the village. The homes were clean and neat, and overall the village was pleasantly scented—unlike many cities he'd been to in his own world. The streets were cobblestone with wrought iron light posts. In the glass globes atop the posts small glowing spheres raced about, as if enormous lightning bugs had been caught and left in the street lamps to shed their light.

They made it to the iron gate in front of Orla's home without being stopped or recognized from what they could tell. Orla stepped forward and gently placed her hand on the lock of the gate, there was a quiet *click* and the large door swung open. The three young people quickly entered and closed the door behind them.

"Who's home?" Orla asked looking up at the house before her.

"Hmm, well, Urma and Nem will be here certainly, and Chamberlain of course, and I believe that Phan and Jain are here as well. Not to mention some of the old guards, the ones not out looking for you, obviously. Oh, and there are a couple of *Sidhe* here!" Maya said quickly, now in her *Fey* form Owen could truly see the family resemblance. Her skin tone and hair were almost identical to Orla's, except that Orla's hair seemed to be a bit lighter at this moment of the season and her skin a bit darker, but Owen figured that may have been due to the last week or so of traveling all day under the sun. *How long had it been?* he wondered. *Let's see it was a...*

The door to the house opened emitting a rather portly woman who came bustling down to the two girls.

"ORLA!" she bellowed and grabbed the *Fey* in an enormous hug lifting her clear off the ground and twirling her about as if she weighed nothing. "EVERYONE COME QUICKLY, ORLA'S BACK!" she boomed again. Maya jumped excitedly up and down clapping her hands while an enormous number of Sylvans came running from the building. Owen also made note of two other people who leaned from one of the second floor windows and peered down at the scene below. They both seemed to notice him standing away from the mass of people around Orla and paid special attention to him.

Owen noticed they both were female, approximately the same age, one with very blond hair, almost white in its pigment and the other black, almost void of any color, just a negative space, a shadow within a shadow, it was so dark. Both women had very fair skin with thin, fine, features. They also seemed to be much taller than the throng of Sylvans gathering below with him.

The two women backed away from the window and Owen turned his attention back to the crowd before him. Several Sylvans in what

Owen took as uniforms stood around the crowd and seemed to be paying particular attention to him. They wore leather jerkins and burgundy cloaks, over black suede breeches and boots. None seemed to be armed. An older Sylvan stood on the steps and watched him as well. Even though he wore a smile, and occasionally looked down on the returning Princess, his eyes held no mirth and they looked at him quizzically. He was tall for a Sylvan, taller than most of the others around save a guard or two, but he was thin and given his age, Owen guessed, frail as well. He wore a black cloak and charcoal gray robes beneath; his hair was silver with lingering streaks of black in it.

The two women that still lifted and spun Orla were as different as the moon and sun. One was plump, with graying hair, and deep wrinkles set into her eyes and mouth that seemed to have been etched there by much joy and gaiety. She truly seemed a jovial sort of person. The other woman, even though she was beside herself with glee it seemed, was more stand-offish and taciturn; she was tall and thin, seemingly much younger than the first. Her hair was pulled back in a tight bun, and was the color of wet straw.

As the cheering and laughing began to subside there began an uncomfortable silence that seemed to be focused on Owen. Many of the gathered Sylvans had begun to notice him. It didn't take long for Orla to notice it and immediately step to Owen's side.

"And who have you brought back home with you from your journey, Princess Orla," the older Sylvan on the stairs asked, eyeing Owen intently.

"Oh, er, ah…" Orla stammered. "This is Owen McInish, my rescuer and friend," Orla said, sliding her arm through Owen's and squeezing lightly. Owen blushed slightly as the women rushed forward and began squeezing and patting his shoulders while thanking him profusely for returning their Princess to them. Several of the guards and the older Sylvan just eyed him that much more intently.

45

O wen sat in a large receiving room. He knew there were two guards behind the doors to his back, and that Orla and the older Sylvan, named Chamberlain he'd learned, were in the room behind the door closed in front of him. The chair he sat in was hard and uncomfortable by design. This was where they brought people before their liege to be tried, judged, or any other reason the Lord of the House would want someone uncomfortable and waiting for him.

He turned his attention to the scar on his finger. It was tough to see under all the dirt and grime from the road and his travels, but he could tell it was there. The skin was much paler, and it actually looked withered where the ring had touched him, as if the band of skin was that of a hundred year old man's instead of a fourteen year old boy. *Well, almost fifteen, two more days? Was it two, three? Or was it yesterday?* Owen thought. While stuck in the room waiting for Orla, he had been given enough time to try and recount their journey and travels to Quailan. *Not that it will make any difference here.*

Owen heard Orla's voice behind the door, but couldn't make out what she was saying. It made him think of everyone's reaction outside. Most of the folks took it at face value. It wasn't their place to investigate the matter, that was Chamberlain's role in her father's absence. He had asked them to come inside and had invited Owen to this room, posted the guards, and then asked Orla to come with him.

Presumably to fill him in, but Owen had no idea how much she was going to tell him.

Owen had been surprised by everyone's reaction outside. He thought for a second someone was going to ask not only who he was, but what. The Gypsylvanians were close in appearance and maybe there were other races in Orla's world that he could also pass for? The *Aingeals* were human looking too, for the most part, except for their exceptional height.

Just then the door opened and Orla came out with Chamberlain following her. He didn't seem pleased, and Orla seemed somewhat flushed as well. She stood next to Owen as he stood up.

"Well, it seems we owe you a great debt of thanks," Chamberlain said, as he stepped forward and bowed awkwardly, he was not a man who bowed often, Owen thought.

"Um, no problem," Owen offered uncomfortably.

"Indeed. I'm sure you are weary from your journey, and like the Princess, wish only to refreshen yourself and rest. I will have Nem prepare a guest suite for you. I will also send word immediately of the Princess's return and of your heroism in the matter, to her father. However, until he sends word back, or returns himself, I must ask that both of you remain in the house and do not go into town until we find out who was behind the abduction. Yes?" Chamberlain spoke well, clearly, articulately, he was a man who liked to speak, and especially, to be heard. He was accustomed to being listened to and expected to be understood.

"Yes," both Owen and Orla answered. Chamberlain then motioned for them to leave the room. At the door he asked the guards to escort the two of them first to the Princess's room and then to the guest's quarters. He made no specific mention of the guards staying at Owen's door and therefore, Owen thought that would most definitely be the case.

The guards wound the two friends through Orla's home and eventually found her room. She smiled at Owen as she stepped into her chambers while the guards closed the door behind her.

He wondered, now that Orla was home, and had turned out to be some sort of royalty, if he would ever get to see her, or see her without a chaperone, again. The guards brought Owen to his room, opened the door for him, and then departed down the hall without a second look over their shoulders. So, Owen guessed wrong. He was a guest after all. Now if he could only remember how to get back to Orla's room.

He entered his room and was surprised at how quickly the servants had been to it and prepared it for him. There was a large copper tub filled with steaming water, a bar of cream colored soap, and a scrub brush on a long wooden handle. Two towels were draped over a stand next to the tub and a large reed matt was placed between the two. His large bed, placed by the window overlooking a terrace, was already pulled down; the bed looked to be goose down, Owen thought. There was a pitcher of water by the bed stand and fresh clothes placed on the edge of the bed. Owen stepped over and inspected the clothes. They looked to be a combination of attire. The black suede boots looked like guard issue, but the fine midnight blue cloak, edged in forest green runes, spoke of much wealth and craftsmanship. The pants were soft buckskin leather, supple and as soft as brushed cotton. His tunic was unbleached cotton with dark blue and green piping along the neck and sleeves that matched his cloak. A thick black belt that matched the guard boots completed the outfit. He wondered whose clothes he was borrowing.

Owen tuned back to the bath, stripped down, and climbed in. He almost fell asleep in it, it was so relaxing. He couldn't remember the last time he'd had one, and he couldn't remember the last time cleaning himself felt so good. Once he had finished the water was a wretched brown color with silt resting on the bottom of the tub. There was a stopper in the bottom of the bath that he unplugged which allowed the tub to empty into a drain in the floor. He hoped he hadn't just let his bath out on the person in the room below him.

Owen towel dried and then dressed into the clothes provided with the exception of the boots and belt. He wore his own Gypsylvanian pair and belt. He slipped his gloves through the belt in the front. In the corner of the room he noticed a long mirror and approached it.

"Like a character out of one of mom's stories," he said with a smile that slowly slipped away. *Mom, dad,* he thought.

"I'll figure something out, I promise."

He stepped out onto the terrace that opened into a courtyard on the back of the house. The yard was as long as the estate, but the wall that surrounded the small home ran along the sides of the property and back into the rock ledge behind the home that towered hundreds of feet above it. There was a large tree in the center of the yard with dark burgundy leaves and a metallic looking bark that reminded Owen of some sort of birch, one he had never seen before.

He looked from one end of the courtyard to the other and gauged the distance. It wouldn't make too poor of an archery lane, he'd have to ask Orla if it would be okay for him to practice. Now that he was feeling confident with the bow, he didn't want to pause in his practicing. He looked up at the sky, *close to evening. We'd be looking for a place to stop for the night by now. I hope Boone and Winter are okay out there.*

He looked back into his room at the large bed. He felt a twinge of guilt at the thought of his friends spending another night on the hard ground and he having a bed, but it looked so inviting and he was so tired. He walked towards the bed as if a spell had been cast on him. His eyelids grew heavy, his limbs drooped. He shed his clothes as he approached, *how long has it been since I slept in a bed,* he pondered. He made sure he left the door open onto the courtyard and night beyond. He'd grown fond of the night air after spending so many evenings under the stars since coming to this world, *but then again, I always left the window open back home too.*

He laid down into bed, barely pulling the sheets over his shoulders before falling soundly asleep.

46

Owen dreamed.

A snow leopard landed softly, almost silently outside on his terrace. It crept into his room, circled his bed, and sniffed along the door. It then walked over to his night stand, and dropped something from its mouth there; it then slowly walked over to his bedside and watched him sleeping for a time. After a short while it silently padded to the terrace and leapt off the railing into the night.

In the distance he could hear the chortle and faint quorking of ravens. Wings and feathers rustled, perching themselves on the terrace railing, tipping their black heads from side to side watching him with black pearl eyes.

Hugin and Munin brought news.

Owen saw a man draped in a storm-cloud gray cloak walking through the snow; he was in a small village. Stone houses burnt, corpses strewn along the streets. He bent to the ground and inspected a track. Standing again he began walking with the wind and snow at his back, his great bow held lightly in his hand.

Feathers rustled.

A large dog stalked quietly through a village, following a scent trail it came to an iron gate, peering through up at the dark windows of the house beyond. It padded down the street, steering into the woods, coming to rest on a small knoll. It tilted back its large head and howled a song of sadness and loneliness.

Wings beat.

A dark robed figure bent over a blue sphere, images flashed before it. It spoke animatedly to the orb, finally covering it with a black velvet cloth. The figure turned and walked into its fireplace vanishing from view.

A tall bearded man beneath a dark cowl stood in a gray forest. Snow covered the ground; it came to his knees. He held a spear that in the night glowed red. From the woods another man emerged, silent and swift. He held a great bow and was hooded and gray cloaked. The first man handed the second a long sword and scabbard. Wrapping it in a blanket the man with the bow strapped it to his pack, nodding to the other man; he vanished back into the woods and night.

Owen woke.

It was well into the morning and the sun shown through the open terrace doors spilling across his bed, warming and waking him. He yawned and stretched, he hadn't slept this late since before finding tracks of a snow leopard in the snow just beyond his backyard.

He stood from bed and washed in the basin on the dressing table. A saucer held a mint smelling paste which he scooped onto what he thought must be a tooth brush and cleaned his teeth. It had been a while since he'd been able to brush his teeth and he was amazed at how nice it felt. His teeth had felt as if a forest had been growing over them they were beginning to feel so fuzzy.

He dressed quickly in the clothes left him, the way he had the previous evening, including his own boots and belt. He undid his bowstring after making his bed and laid his relaxed bow on it. He left his almost empty quiver next to it and made a mental note to fletch more arrows as soon as possible. He was about to leave when he noticed something on his night stand. There was a silver metal cloak pin in the shape of a cat's head. Owen picked it up and inspected it. On closer examination, a leopard's head, he realized. He pinned it to his cloak and absently looked back down at the scar on his finger, more obvious now that it was free from the dirt of his traveling.

Turning, he left his room and found himself in an empty corridor. He thought for a moment and decided to try and retrace his steps and find Orla's quarters. The walls were mortar and stone, with granite slab stairwells. Sconces were placed every twenty feet or so he guessed. Tapestries hung along the corridors and depicted many different scenes from Sylvan life and, from what Owen could tell, recounted families and lineages of those who had occupied the house previously.

At no time did he meet anyone in the halls, which he found to be quite strange. At one stairwell he paused only briefly and heard voices and banging that to Owen sounded like pots and pans. He concluded those stairs must lead to the kitchen and continued on. Time to time he had to pause and try to remember which way they had come, he had been so exhausted after finally reaching Quailan that the evening's events seemed to blur and fade. He vaguely remembered something being said about food being brought to them if they wished, but he had fallen asleep long before he ever considered eating. Now, however, he was famished.

He finally came to what he thought was the door to which the guards had escorted Orla. Owen was surprised to see no security or anyone about. She had, after all, just been returned from having been abducted, and yet, the house was silent and still.

He knocked on the door, but no answer came, so he tried it, and was surprised when it swung open.

He looked both ways down the hall and then entered, closing the door behind him. The room was larger and much more extravagant than his. She too had a balcony, and terrace, and large fireplace. Orla's bed was of a large canopy sort. She also had a large mirror in her room, along with a dressing table and large closet behind. He also noted she did not have a copper tub like he had in his room.

He had only walked in a little further when he heard trilling and buzzing come from the top of the canopy bed. He looked up just in time to avoid the diving bird that dove at his head. The bird swished past, made one more attempt, driving him to his knees. *Beeer Beeer Beeeee* the black throated blue warbler trilled at Owen before it flew to the far side of the room, pulled up to a quick hover for a moment, and shifted into the form of the younger of the two women who had greeted Orla yesterday.

"What are you doing in the Princess's room?" she trilled in her own voice, not much different, Owen thought, than the rattling warning of the warbler. "No men are allowed without a chaperone in the Princess's presence!"

Owen quickly turned to see who else had come, what men were here, and then realized she meant him. *Man? Ha, nice, that's right, no boys here.*

"I…was…just…" Owen stammered.

"I don't care what you just, you may not come here looking for the Princess, let alone let yourself into her room uninvited. Besides, she is not here; she is at the reception for her homecoming. Why are you here anyway? You should be down there."

"I didn't know about it, I couldn't find anyone else, so I just came looking for Orla," Owen said, causing the Sylvan to flinch by calling the Princess by her name only.

"Well, if no one came to collect you for the reception then I presume you were not invited, in which case, you should make yourself scarce while the other quests are here. You may eat afterward with the other servants in the kitchen, after lunch is served. Now, I have work to do, so leave these quarters at once, and do not come back unless invited and escorted by myself or another of the Princess's house." With that the woman shifted back to her warbler form and continued to fly and trill around Owen's head until he left the room and closed the door.

"Sonofa…" Owen said as the door closed behind him. *Not invited? Fine*, he thought and stormed off back towards his room. Again the halls were empty.

When he reached his room he collected his bow and quiver and left again. He worked his way down to the courtyard below. Along the way he found an empty apple crate which he took to use as a makeshift target. There were a few rotten apples in the crate still, so he took them as well.

The court yard was a long rectangle the entire length of the estate. One side of the rectangle was the main house, the other the cliff edge, both ends were the high stone wall that surrounded the home. Ivy grew along either wall, while the ledge supported a few cedars and purple vetch that found purchase amongst the rock. Along the side of the home were various plantings of all sorts, roses, lilies, columbine, and irises. The yard itself was well kept and had many different types of plants and trees Owen didn't recognize along with the various flowering dogwoods and cherries that he knew. One great tree grew in the center of the yard, the one he had seen the previous night from his terrace.

The tree appeared to Owen to be some great species of birch tree he had never seen before. Its bark looked almost as if made from a silvery liquid metal, reminding Owen of mercury, it seemed to shimmer and move when looked at. It was a remarkable tree with dark burgundy foliage and violet catkins. It was also enormous, easily taller than the estate.

After walking the yard and inspecting some of the stranger plants, Owen set his crate up on the far end and paced off thirty meters to the other side. There was still ample room in the yard, but finding a straight path beyond that distance was difficult because of the landscaping. He pulled two of his three arrows out. The third being the one Winter had given him to collect his fletching feathers with, which he wouldn't use for practice shooting. He stuck one arrow in the ground in front of him and knocked the other.

Drawing back the string he let the arrow fly, taking the first of two apples he had placed on top of the crate. The arrow pierced the fruit and then thunked harmlessly into the ground behind it. Owen fired the second arrow with the same result. On his walk down to the arrows he walked along the rock wall and collected a few branches of cedar to make into arrow shafts later that night. He collected his two arrows and returned to his practice spot. He stuffed the cedar branches into his quiver and repeated his practicing. With each arrow his anger and feelings of rejection lessened. *Maybe she hadn't forgotten, or maybe she told someone to tell me and they forgot, or maybe there was a mix up*, he thought, letting his anger go and focusing on the arrow the way Winter had taught him. He fired four more volleys and collected more cedar branches before he heard applause from behind him.

He turned to see two Sylvans about his and Orla's age watching him. One was a bit taller than the other, with long snow white hair past his shoulders. Even at a distance Owen could make out that he also had penetrating sky blue eyes. His skin was fair, much fairer than Owen's, and much, much fairer than Orla's. He wore leather armor dyed gray, with matching thigh high gray boots. His tunic under the armor was white, matching his cloak. He wore midnight blue breaches, a long sword on his hip, and a bow and quiver along his back. He watched Owen intensely and Owen wondered how long they'd been watching him practice.

The other Sylvan, the shorter one, was the one clapping. He had short, reddish hair, cropped about his head. He wore no armor, but instead a black tunic that matched his boots and cloak. He wore leather breeches similar to Owen's, and he too was wearing a long sword in a scabbard at his waist. Another sword was planted into the ground in front of him blade first. He had a mocking grin on his face as he clapped.

"Well, well, the hero needs to practice. I figured someone who rescued the *Princess* was probably some famed warrior, not some boy still learning the craft," the shorter boy said, mocking Owen.

"You're not bad with the bow, but can you fight hand to hand," the Sylvan said yanking the sword from the ground. The white haired Sylvan said something quietly to the other, but was ignored it seemed, as the red haired one approached Owen. He tossed the sword, hilt first, to him, which Owen caught at the expense of dropping his bow. The sword was heavy and awkward, and Owen could now see it was a well used practice blade.

"Haven't had much practice with a sword," Owen said, sounding meeker than he wanted to.

"Oh, well, in that case, let me give you a lesson," the Sylvan said unsheathing his own blade. He took a few practice swings, slicing the air, and intimidating Owen while he stepped forward.

"Um, isn't it a lil dangerous to be practicing with real swords?" Owen asked quickly raising his own blade as the young Sylvan engaged him. Owen quickly blocked the first two attacks, stepping and stumbling backwards.

"Ha, scared of getting a little dirty, or maybe a scratch?" the Sylvan mocked.

"Jain, I don't think this is appropriate," the white haired Sylvan said, as the other ignored him and continued to assault Owen. He had the distinct feeling the boy was simply playing with him, and mocking him all the while.

"Not as easy as a bow, eh? Much harder when someone is upon you?" he asked between lunges and slashes.

Owen parried, he was getting angry again. Why did he deserve this? What had he done to them? All he'd done is come back with Orla. *I was minding my own business!*

"Archers make me sick, they'd rather stick an arrow in your back than fight you face to face," Jain said, pushing Owen further back.

"Shut up!" Owen said, attacking for the first time. The sudden lunge and swing took Jain by surprise, his Sylvan speed helped him bring his blade up in time, but the surprising speed and strength with which Owen had countered disarmed Jain, sending his own blade point first into the ground, shaking from the impact as it did so.

Owen was just as surprised as anyone. Jain blushed, his cheeks turning an angry scarlet; he looked to his sword and then menacingly at Owen.

"Maybe I'm not the one who needs a lesson," Owen quipped, unable to keep the anger from his voice. Jain began to reach for his hilt, but Owen stopped him, tapping the hilt with his sword blade.

"I think I'm done for the day, thanks…," but before he could finish the smaller Sylvan morphed in front of him.

His features melted into a hydrid feline form somewhat similar to Orla's, but with just as many differences. His coloring was much different, more grays, browns, russets, and reds, with black spots. His clothing remained as he changed into his hydrid shape unlike Orla. His ears were larger than hers, a bit more pointed as well, with noticeable fur tufts on their tips. To Owen he seemed to resemble a bobcat, but then again, he wasn't allowed much time to take it all in.

Jain leapt at him, clawing and attacking. Taking large swipes at Owen's face close enough for Owen to feel the wind of the attack, but not actually striking him. Owen raised his arms in defense as he fell backwards, dropping his sword while Jain shredded the sleeve of his new tunic. The Sylvan growled and yowled as he did so. Once Owen fell, covering his face with his arms, the growling turned to laughing. Owen put his arms down and realized the Sylvan was back to his *Fey* shape sheathing his sword.

"WHAT IS THE MEANING OF THIS?"

Owen stood quickly to see Chamberlain stepping into the court yard, looking none too pleased. The taller of the Sylvan boys gave Jain a glair.

"Jain? Phan? An explanation please," Chamberlain said not even bothering to look at Owen.

"We saw the Princess's friend here in the courtyard and thought we'd welcome him. He seemed interested in practicing his swordsmanship, but I'm afraid he wasn't very good," Jain said, stifling a smirk.

"Indeed," Chamberlain answered, finally looking at Owen, who looked all the worse for wear.

"McInish, I'm not sure I feel very good about you being armed while you are a guest in my, our, home," Chamberlain said.

"And why is that, Lord Steward?" a voice asked from behind the Steward. Owen thought the voice sounded like it would come from a rose if one could speak. Rich, luscious, sweet, and beautiful, but if you weren't careful, it could bleed you like a thorn as well.

Owen looked past Chamberlain to see the two women he had seen in the window the previous day approaching him and the three Sylvans. These two women were much taller than the other *Fey*, and even Owen, for that matter. Both women approached Owen's dad's height, close to six feet, he thought.

They were both amazingly, strikingly, beautiful as well; tall and thin, but both very different in appearance than the other. The woman whom Owen thought had spoken was fair and blonde with pale green eyes the color of jade. Her hair was long, well past her waist, almost to the backs of her knees. She had sharp, angled features, with high arching brows. And because she had her hair pulled back and pinned behind her head, Owen could see she had pointed ears as well. She seemed to glow from within, illuminating her pale skin, giving it warmth that the white haired Sylvan lacked in his pallor.

She was dressed in a long white gown edged in a deep green, covered by a forest green cloak. Owen could see that she wore deep forest green leather boots beneath the gown. The dress was tied at her waist with a matching leather belt where a sheathed dagger was secured.

The second woman had dark midnight black hair and eyes that seemed to have no pupils, just large onyx orbs. Her features were angled as well, but she wore her hair loose and Owen could not see her ears. She wore a silver shirt of thin, linked rings, the craftsmanship of which seemed more ornate than practical, but Owen had little doubt the armor was of the highest quality. She had belted at her waist a long, curving, sheathed sword and a bow across her back. She too wore the green cloak and boots, but she wore sapphire colored pants and tunic beneath her armor with matching leather gloves tucked into her sword belt. She also had a similar dagger and sheath belted at her waist. The woman looked at Owen curiously, as if appraising him.

"You are at peace with my sister and I carrying our weapons, and seeing how we invited your other guest here to tutor him in the Sidhe ways of the sword and bow, we hope you won't inhibit us in thanking your guest in the rescuing of your Princess," the blonde Sidhe spoke again. Her voice was light and airy, but beneath it there was power and control.

"Of course not, *Senira*. If the boy is under your charge then I have no worries for his well being. I trust that you and your sister will care for him well. A weapon such as these in the wrong hands can be most dangerous, and I would not want to see him come to any harm.

"As for you two," Chamberlain said, turning his attention to the other two Sylvans. "Come with me, if you cannot be productive with your time, then I will find useful tasks to occupy you."

The three Sylvans left the courtyard, and the two Sidhe waited for them to leave, studying Owen intently as they did so. He shuffled his weight back and forth from foot to foot, and was wondering if he'd just fallen from the frying pan and into the fire when the lighter sister finally spoke.

"Owen McInish, I am Silan of the Sidhe, and this is my sister, Aiya. We are ambassadors from our Kingdom, sent here to speak with your Princess's father, the Lord of Quailan, Senator Negu. However, when we reached Quailan he had been recalled to the capital and away from his search for his daughter. We have decided to wait for his return, and we are pleased we did so." The lighter sister looked to the other.

"Yes, we are very pleased. If we had not, then we would not have had the opportunity to meet the *Maou'r*," Aiya replied.

47

"Y our secret is safe with us, Owen," Silan said as the two Sidhe followed him into their chambers. After the elf Aiya had revealed to Owen they were fully aware of who and what he was, they suggested they retire to their rooms so they could speak more freely with less chance of being observed or overheard. Owen had followed them dumbfounded through the house until they brought him into their rooms.

I should know better than to be surprised by anything anymore, he thought as they offered him a chair.

"You are surprised we know who you are," Silan said, sitting on the edge of her bed, while Aiya locked the door and then walked to the doors by their balcony.

"Well, yeah," Owen said, looking up at her. "I know I shouldn't be surprised anymore by what happens here, but how'd you know?"

She smiled at him then, the first real emotion her porcelain features had revealed since he'd met her.

She looked a knowing glance to her sister and then back to Owen. "Many of the races here in Parathas have foretold your coming for a very long time Owen, the *Maou'r* has been anticipated longer than you realized. And, as for how we knew, well the Sidhe have been known to be very perceptive. A very long time ago the Sylvan and Sidhe were more closely related than we are now, but while our cousins began a

1

more physical and natural magical approach, the Sidhe continued to follow a more cerebral approach to our magick.

"Don't worry Owen, most Sylvans should not recognize you for who you are, and we will not tell anyone. On the contrary, we will make sure that while you are here you are safe from any outside threats, for it has been foretold that one of the Sidhe would become an ally of the *Maou'r* on his return to our world."

Owen just looked at the elf blankly. *She must be joking*, he thought. "Um, you know that I ended up here by mistake, right?" Owen asked.

Silan smiled again. "Many times what seems to be happenstance in our lives has more purpose than we are initially privy too."

Owen smiled too, what the Sidhe had said was similar to what his mom would often tell him: "Everything happens for a reason," she used to tell him.

"Yes, often times it does," Silan said, and again smiled at her sister who returned the expression.

"I do think it best if we continue your training. We were watching you practice, you are an exceptional archer. May I ask where you acquired your bow?" Aiya finally asked after being silent since the courtyard. She was much quieter than her sister and seemed very comfortable letting her do most of the speaking for them.

Owen considered this a moment and then figured if they already knew who he was, than there couldn't be any harm in them knowing about Winter too. "It was given to me by the *Aingeal*, Winter," Owen said.

The two elves again exchanged looks, this time of surprise. "*Geimhreidh*? He has traveled with you, but where is he now? Why did he leave you?" Silan asked quickly, concern clouding her face.

"He said he had errands to do, and left us just before the Falls Bridge. He had become really anxious the last couple days, always looking behind us and towards the West," Owen said sparking another knowing look between the two sisters.

"He said he would come back to Quailan once he had done what he needed to do," he added.

"Then we will wait here with you for his return," Silan added, standing from the edge of her bed.

"And in the meantime you and I will begin your training, if you like?" Aiya asked with Owen nodding his enthusiastic response. "If you have learned the bow from *Geimhreidh*, than there is nothing else for me to teach you. Continue practicing on your own. However, every morning you and I will work on your swordsmanship," Aiya said standing and walking to the door.

"Now, Owen, if you'll excuse my sister and me, we have much to discuss. We will come for you shortly, would you be willing to have your noonday meal with us?" Silan asked, as she escorted him to the door of their chambers.

"Um, yeah, sure, okay," he said as he walked into the hall. "And thanks, for before, with those other guys," Owen said almost apologetically.

"Think nothing of it," Silan said as she closed the door to their room.

Owen now stood in the hallway and tried to remember how to get back to his own guest suite. He looked down one of the corridors and then the other. He opted for leaving the way they had come in from the courtyard. Once there, he quickly retreated to his room the way he had come out into the yard from his own quarters. No one else was in the yard at the moment, but he wanted to get back to his own apartment. He missed being in the woods with his three companions. Ever since coming to Quailan, everything had been different, he hadn't seen Orla since they'd reached her home, and he wasn't even sure if that was by her choosing or not.

Once back to his room, he closed the door, and walked over to his bed. He realized that the copper tub was no longer in his room and that his quarters had been straightened and cleaned. He quickly inspected and inventoried his belongs, feeling guilty after doing so, to make sure all was in place. The only thing missing in the room was the large tub that had sat in the middle of the room.

He then inspected the damage to his new tunic, which seemed ruined in his opinion, and decided he would change it for his old one. He walked to the wardrobe where he had hung his old clothes to retrieve his other shirt. All his old clothing had already been washed, dried, and returned to the piece of furniture. He took the shirt out and changed, hanging the ripped tunic back in the wardrobe.

He walked back to his bed and pulled out the pieces of cedar he had taken from the yard. None of them were particularly good pieces of wood for an arrow, but it was the best he had at the moment, and he would just be making them for practice anyway. He got to work on the arrows with nothing else to do until lunch.

48

The rumbling in Owen's stomach had long since reminded him it was past noontime when the knock finally came. He had finished fletching his new practice arrows, and was just sitting, watching the songbirds in the courtyard from his terrace when the wrap on his door sounded.

He stood and walked to the door, opened it but a crack, and seeing Aiya, opened it further to allow her in. She entered, and he closed the door behind her. She slowly walked around his room, taking in everything. Once she had finished, she turned and faced him. She watched him a moment before saying anything. Owen was growing increasingly impatient.

"I apologize for being late for our meal," she said inclining her head slightly.

Owen noticed that the elf always seemed to be fully armed and armored. The few times he'd seen her in the house, she was always in her armor and wearing her weapons, where as her sister only wore the dagger and robes. He also noted her posture, she was always in a battle stance, even when she seemed at ease, she was like a coiled spring, he thought.

"Why are you always in your armor and ready for combat, but your sister isn't?" Owen asked. He was beginning to get tired of always being the one getting questioned, and summoned when others wanted him, or not summoned at all and forgotten about, for that matter.

"I'm a Sidhe Sword Maiden, my sister is not," Aiya answered, a sly smile playing across her lips. Her black eyes sparkled in the afternoon sun shining through the terrace doors. "But don't consider her unarmed; on the contrary, she has a larger arsenal than I."

Owen thought for a moment, she was playing with him, seemed to him like most people were thinking him a simpleton and he was getting tired of that too. "She's a mage then."

"Yes. And no. All Sidhe are spellcasters to an extent, even the Sword Maidens. My sister, however, has been trained in the art of the mind; she can cast her thoughts and wishes into other's minds, as well as, other not so pleasant things," Aiya said, and Owen suddenly realized that this elf was more forthcoming with him than anyone else had been, more so than even Winter and Orla.

"Why are you telling me all this?"

"You are the *Maou'r*, we are here to aid you, deceiving you would not be doing so," Aiya answered. "But I did come here to dine our noon meal, are you not hungry? I for one am famished."

"Me too," Owen answered and opened the door. "Isn't Silan coming?"

"I am afraid not. I've already gathered our meal; I figured we would eat while we train. The food and weapons are downstairs," Aiya said, walking past Owen and into the hall. She moved fleetly, like a deer, he thought. Her movements were quick, swift, and graceful. She seemed to glide across the floor, even the wind seemed to part around her.

Owen followed her quickly down the stairs and then out into the courtyard, it was already passed midday and the sun was already passing beyond the rooftop of the great house.

They sat and ate quickly; the meal was grapes, cheese, sweet unleavened bread, and small tomatoes. Aiya spoke seldom, but when she did, it was succinct and to the point. She did not waste her breath or thoughts on wordy replies or small talk, and even though the silence at first made Owen uncomfortable, he soon learned to like it, and found it comforting.

After the meal, they stood, and Aiya stepped to the weapons and equipment she had brought with her. "We will start with the *clai'omh*,"

Aiya said, tossing him a wooden sword. "It is the traditional practice weapon of my people; I was pleasantly surprised to find them in the Sylvan armory, although it did take some rearranging to reach them." Owen caught the weapon, it was much lighter than the practice sword he'd held before, and significantly more balanced. Aiya laid her bow down and undid her quiver from her back, laying it beside the bow. She picked up a *clai'omh* of her own.

"Spells and a bow are much more efficient, and are preferred methods of combat when they can be employed, but sometimes your enemies are too close for those types of fighting. Too much bravado has killed more warriors than it has saved. There is nothing courageous about choosing to use your sword over your bow, remember that, but sometimes you have no choice. We are learning the art of sword fighting for those times; let us hope you never need it." Aiya held her *clai'omh* up vertically before her, Owen imitated the gesture, and then the woman put the weapon down and stepped into a fighting stance that Owen tried to mimic.

She began slowly, letting Owen build his confidence, trying to imitate her fighting technique and stances. They sparred for an hour straight, at the end of which Owen was saturated with sweat. He had shed his cloak, rolled up his sleeves, and opened the tie on his tunic, but was still sweaty and exhausted by the time they had finished their first session, not too mention, bruised and sore.

Aiya was a persistent, but compassionate teacher. Even though she wasn't vicious with her blows; she also made a point, the *clai'omh* may sting now, but a sword would be deadly later. Owen sat down on the lawn and wiped the sweat from his forehead. Aiya immediately picked up her bow and arrows; she didn't seem tired at all.

"Tomorrow, we will start earlier, first light, to avoid the audience we drew today. I think it better you practice in private," Aiya said indicating the terraces. "Hold onto the *clai'omh*, and practice in your room, when you have time."

Owen looked up and saw Orla watching from her balcony. He waved to her, and she hesitantly waved back, before walking back into her room. Aiya grabbed the rest of her things and left, leaving Owen to gather his own belongings. He had just fastened his cloak, when he heard bells that sounded like rain on leaves.

"I was surprised you never came to the reception," Orla said quietly from behind him. Owen whirled ready to snap at her that he hadn't even been invited, but then he saw her.

Orla wore a light, white, cotton dress drawn at the waist by a loose silver belt. She had an unbleached wool shawl about her shoulders. Her hair had two small braids, one above each temple, while the sides and top of her hair was pulled back by a clip that resembled Owen's cloak clasp. The rest of her hair fell loosely about her shoulders.

"I didn't know about it," Owen said instead, without any fire in his voice at all. On the contrary, it was actually hard for him to speak.

"I specifically asked Chamberlain if he'd sent someone for you, and he told me he did," Orla explained.

"Nope. Never knew about it. I went looking for you and was attacked by some insane bird-lady."

Orla covered her mouth to stifle a giggle. "Nem, she's my...she's my attendant," Orla said awkwardly and somewhat embarrassed. "She's very protective, especially after what's happened."

"Well, she was pretty mean about it. I mean, it's not like we haven't been hanging out together, every day, for like, the last week. And then I come looking for you, and she tells me I can't see you anymore unless you're escorted by her," Owen explained, a little angry, and more than a little unnerved.

"She said that?" Orla asked a little more annoyed now. "I'll talk to her, sorry for that, like I said, she's protective. I saw you practicing."

"Yeah? Aiya said we had watchers, for how long?"

"A while. I wasn't the only one, my cousins were watching, and I saw Chamberlain too."

"Ah, great, everyone saw me getting thwapped then. Cousins?"

"Yes, Phen and Jain."

"They're your cousins? Great, just great," Owen said exasperated.

"Why, what happened?" Orla asked, concern breaking her voice.

"Nothin', not a big deal," Owen said, "What are you doing, now?

Tonight?" Quickly, Owen tried to change the subject before she asked anymore about what had happened.

Orla took the hint and let it slide, but she wasn't happy about it, she decided she would look into what had happened on her own.

"Chamberlain asked that I see him tonight, he wants to fill me in on everything that's been happening while I was gone. I guess I've been gone longer than we thought, and a lot of things have changed. Maybe I can come see you after him," she said, trying to change Owen's disappointed look.

"Sure, no problem, whatever," Owen said, trying to sound indifferent. "I should probably go clean up."

"Oh, has anyone shown you where the baths are?" Orla asked, happy for another change of subject to finally have something she might be helpful with.

"No, there was a tub in my room when we first got here, but then someone came back and took it away while I was out."

"Well, we normally only use the tubs like that when a guest first arrives. The house is built above hot springs and downstairs we have two bath rooms, one for the men and one for women. If you just take the stairs, directly below your room, you'll find it. They're wonderful, especially after training.

"You were quite good, you know? Especially for someone who's never used a sword before," she added quickly.

"Yeah, thanks. I don't feel like I did that well, and these lumps seem to contradict your opinion." Owen was still feeling sullen and not willing to give Orla an inch.

"Well, I thought you did well, and I bet your *Sidhe* instructor was pleased with your performance," Orla couldn't help keeping a jealous twinge from her voice. She hoped Owen hadn't caught it, and for the most part, he didn't. He thought she was jealous of him being trained by the Sidhe Sword Maiden because she wanted to, not because she would rather be spending the time with him.

However, at that moment, Owen looked up at the sound of flapping wings and the unmistakable trilling that was coming straight for him. He fell over backward, just in time, to avoid a strafing from a very agitated black throated blue warbler.

BEEER BEEER BEEEEEEE!

Orla stifled a laugh again by covering her mouth, she was in enough trouble with Owen already to be caught laughing now. "NEM! Now stop that, he was doing nothing wrong, Owen is a perfect Gentle… er…Gentle*Fey*. Now leave him be!" The warbler strafed Owen one more time, causing him to duck and drop his things to cover his head, before flying next to Orla and morphing back to her *Fey* shape.

"Sorry Ma'lady, but no man should be out cavorting with you un-chaperoned, and this bloke has been warned once already!" she said, pointing accusingly at Owen.

"Bloke?" Owen said indignantly.

"Nem! Owen is a friend of mine, keep in mind. He's the one who saved me and brought me back home. I expect you to treat him better than this!" Orla said trying to sound stern in front of Owen, but touched by the woman's concern.

"Bloke!" Owen said again.

"Yes, Ma'am," Nem said un-abashedly.

Owen stood and dusted himself off, picked up his things, and began to walk away, "I'll see ya later, Orla," he said, without even acknowledging Nem as he stormed off.

Orla sighed and turned to her maid, "Nem, Owen is a good friend; you need to treat him better. He wasn't the one who kidnapped me remember, he's on our side."

"Yes, Ma'lady," the nurse said as she glared at Owen's back as he walked away.

49

So it must had been you that done it," Brule said to the large horse grazing in the high, bank grass across the campfire from him. "No one else around, really." The horse didn't answer, he kept biting and chewing, biting and chewing.

"Well, I don't suppose you'll ever tell me," Brule added, poking his fire with a long stick he'd used to roast the trout he'd pulled from the river. The horse paused chewing for a moment, considered the question, and then went back to grazing.

"Naw, no way I'll ever know, really."

The large trollbjorn was doing much better. His quick healing was more than capable of healing the wounds he had received at the claws of his cousins, even though, admittedly, his shoulder and sword arm were still a might sore, swollen, and stiff. But considering the battle and fall, he was doing remarkably well.

When the large man had come to, he'd been lying under a large hemlock, and considering his clothes were dry, had been out of the water for a while. But Brule didn't know he had been laid in the sun to dry, and then moved beneath the branches afterward and back and forth once more, before coming around. Brule guessed he'd been unconscious for at least a day, but who really knew? The horse maybe, but he wasn't talking.

He must have been conscious enough to crawl up onto the bank, come to, and crawl under the trees. It was the only explanation. He paused and looked at his horse again; he could have sworn the animal had just been watching him out of the corner of his eye.

"Naw, just yer imagination," he said and went back to poking the fire. Another day and his body should be good enough to travel. *And then what?* the large man thought as he considered all that had happened upon the bridge, and the choices laid out before him, *and then what?*

50

Owen leaned his head back against the cool stone as he soaked in the steaming bath. The room was built of smoothly hewn rock, located in the basement of the great house, and unlike any basement Owen had ever been in before. It was warm and steamy; the stone walls were completely smooth, free of any mold. The ceiling was low, but rougher, and perfectly clean. The rock floor was smooth, but held more traction than the walls, like walking on sandpaper, Owen thought.

He had been a bit hesitant, at first, about using the large bath; he preferred the privacy of his own tub, in his own room. But it looked as if he had no choice, and he desperately needed a cleaning. When he had first entered the room, the warmth and steam made it easy for him to shed his already damp clothes. There were two adjoining rooms, one was a changing room, warm, but dryer than the second. The second room, was large and rectangular, with a square pool in the center. The small pool seemed to be fed by an underground spring that pushed clean, fresh water in while a channel in the floor allowed for the continual movement of the water out of the bath and into an unseen aqueduct away from the room.

The changing room had fresh towels and a basket of some sort of dried plant, similar to a loofa, Owen thought, for scrubbing. The plant was perfume scented. He'd grabbed one along with a towel, before slipping into the pool.

Both rooms were lit by small glowing globes in the corners. Owen had undressed in the changing room, leaving his clothes in sight from the bath. Inside the large pool was an inner bench that ringed the inside edge of the walls of the bath, acting as a chair for anyone soaking. Owen's skin was a little pink from the scrubbing he'd given himself with the plant-brush, but he felt clean, and the water was soothing on his tight, sore muscles. Large purple welts had begun to appear along his arms, legs, chest, and shoulders. He smiled despite them, who would have ever thought Owen would be in a place like this, learning to sword fight? Certainly not Owen, nor anyone at school, nor his parents. The thought of them quickly brought back the familiar ache in his heart and tightening of his stomach.

His muscles hurt in a much different way than when he'd been trekking across the countryside. But he didn't want to lose the stamina he'd gained on the long hikes. He'd been devising a way to try and keep his legs under him for when Winter returned. He couldn't leave the grounds by order of Chamberlain, but the house seemed to be rather large itself, with at least three floors, and a basement with many different staircases. There seemed to be a rather low number of guards within the house. From what Owen could tell, most of the guards were posted outside the house in the front courtyard, and on the wall itself, which seemed strange to Owen. He made a mental note to ask Aiya if she thought it strange as well.

He leaned his head back, and enjoyed the warm water. It had been a while since he felt this relaxed. It was then, when his muscles and focus were at their most at ease, that he saw the enormous spider crawl across the ceiling of the bath. It was easily the size of a soccer ball, and even in the dim light of the room, Owen could see it was black with bright red tiger stripes across its abdomen and legs. It crawled quickly along the ceiling and then slid down a web; moving quickly along the floor and out the bath drain in the wall. Owen gave an involuntary shiver at the thought of the spider. He looked around apprehensively for any others in the room, and then checked for any webs in the corners or along the ceiling, but the room was absolutely clean.

Even still, Owen climbed from the bath, quickly toweled dried, got dressed, and hurried from the two rooms. He felt foolish to leave because of a spider, albeit a very large spider, especially after being hunted by Death Dogs, bounty hunters, and giant trolls. *But, it was a really BIG spider,* he reassured himself as he took the stairs two at a time back to his room.

He went back to his quarters and wondered how much more time he had until dinner. He resigned himself to exploring the house in the meantime. He put on his torn tunic and his old Gypsylvanian breeches and vest, and headed out of the small room. He stopped in the hallway, and made a conscious decision to head in the opposite direction of Orla's suite.

51

Ah, c'mon in Orla, c'mon now," Urma said as Orla poked her head around the corner of the kitchen. "Oh me, oh my, it's good to have ye back 'ere wit us, it is," the portly *Fey* said as she worked some dough with a rolling pin on a butcher's block table. Her apron, hair, and dress were covered in flour, with a large smear across her forehead.

"Thanks Urma, it's good to be back, I just wish father was here," Orla said, pulling a stool to the table at which Urma was working.

"I know ye do, Sweetheart, I know ye do, but being a S*eanado'ir* is very important, and he has responsibilities to all the citizens of Quailan," she said, in between thumping the dough with her large, meaty fists.

"I know, I know, still…I was just hoping he'd be here," Orla said.

"I know ye do, tsk, tsk, poor thing, but he'll be back soon, I'm sure of it, Love. You just go ahead and count on it," Urma said, now back to rolling the dough flat with her roller. She rolled it until it was almost paper thin and then took out a large, sharp knife, and started cutting the dough into small triangles with lightning speed, causing Orla to sit back to be well clear of the slashing blade.

"Now, where's that hero of yours gotten himself to?" Urma asked teasingly with a mischievous smile.

"Dunno. Nem, scared him off pretty good, twice now. She's been even worse since I've been back, she barely let me breath before. Now she's being mean to my friends the moment she sees me with them," Orla sighed again. Things were easier when she was being chased by deymon dogs and trolls, at least then she could do and be with who she wanted. *Argh!* she thought. *Why couldn't I be from a normal family, why'd my dad have to be in the Senate?*

"Now, now, Love, ye know as well as I do, that Nem means no harm, she loves you as much as any of us here, ya know, but she just shows it differently is all. Especially after you goin' missin' an all, ye really can't blame her now, can ye?"

"No, but, I just…I just wanted Owen to like it here, and everyone has been so mean to him,"

"Everyone? Excuse me, Miss, not everyone. Just tell that friend of yours to come down here, I'll take good care of him, okay?"

"Okay, sorry, not everyone, but close, and something happened between him and Phan and Jain, but he wouldn't tell me what. And Chamberlain was, well, Chamberlain. But if you're not used to him, then, well, you know how he can be."

"Ah, yeah, I know, well, I do."

"And well, I just wanted him to like it here," Orla said again, feeling so much lonelier being back home than she had before.

"Well, he will, Love, he will, he just needs to get used to it here."

Orla smiled weakly at Urma, snitched a piece of dough and headed for the door; it was getting close to the time she was supposed to be meeting Chamberlain anyhow.

52

Winter had come to the Thorne Mountains and Illenduell with a vengeance. Lilith had not seen hoarfrost this vicious and drifts this size in centuries. The blizzards had arrived shortly after her Vrok had made its way from the mountain range entering into Parathas, and they had not ceased since their first flakes. Every passage in and out of Dunkeln'Tocht was cut off and would be until spring. But Lilith was not angry; she knew this would happen, which is why she had sent her dark agent out of her Keep when she had. The *Aingeal* would try and contain her, but her dark will was already loose upon the land.

The Dark Queen stepped from her windowsill and approached her bed; the sheets were pulled down and rumpled. There was nothing to do but wait. She hated waiting, but she had learned that this game she played was one of patience and cunning. To move too quickly meant defeat.

The Witch Queen slipped from her gown and crawled back beneath her silk sheets. She smiled despite the cold fabric at the thought of the havoc and destruction her servant would soon be evoking.

53

When Owen made it back to his room, he still involuntarily shivered every time he thought about the spider. *After all we've been through, and a big, red and black spider gives me the willies*, he thought. *I'm glad no one was there to see me*. He had dressed quickly, bolting from the bath, and was half way back to his room before he had slowed down to a walk. He didn't think he'd ever get to sleep that night.

Once back in his room, he paced about with boredom. Owen finally walked onto his balcony and decided he would set up targets below and practice with his bow from the terrace. He grabbed his apple crate, and went down to the kitchen, where everyone was busy prepping for dinner. It was easy enough to sneak in and grab a few more crates and some old potato sacks without being noticed. As he was leaving a mourning dove perched above the doorway cooed at him, but otherwise he went unnoticed. Once outside, he found the gardener's pile of mulch and filled the sacks, and then stuffed each sack into a crate. Owen stood the crates with the sack side facing his terrace. He spread the crates out amongst the courtyard's shrubs and trees. The young archer then quickly walked along the rock ledge and found himself some more cedar limbs to make into arrow shafts. As he was heading back to his room, he walked past the great silver birch tree in the center of the yard.

Owen stopped. Sprouting just off to the side of its roots was one lone root sapling that hadn't been there earlier in the day. It stood about four feet tall, was perfectly straight, and just the right width. He stole a quick look around, and when he was contented that no one was watching, he pulled out the carving knife he used to whittle his arrows and cut the sapling from the ground. He packed the earth back down to hide where he'd removed the young tree, and then, grabbing the rest of his cedar pieces, rushed back to his room. He stowed the new material for his arrows under his bed and went out onto his balcony.

After firing and retrieving his arrows from his targets five times, he was winded enough to take a break after returning to his chambers. Evening was quickly approaching, turning the sky to deep shades of purples and pinks, accenting the clouds that drifted past the cliff beyond his terrace.

Owen laid his bow along the foot of his bed and sat down. He was just about to pull out his fletching materials when he heard a distant howl. It filled his heart with sorrow to hear the call, the feeling that a piece of him was missing struck him deep within his chest. He walked to his balcony and could tell that the voice came from the woods just beyond the wall to the East. The deep baying was un-mistakably Boone's howl. It still filled Owen's heart with courage and bravery, but he could feel the dog's saddness at being separated from his *Maou'r*. The strong emotion was on the verge of bringing Owen to tears when the howling abruptly stopped.

Owen slumped down on the floor of the terrace and felt emotionally drained. He realized then how badly he missed Boone, and how quickly the large dog had become so important to him.

He stood and rushed down to the kitchen. Most of the serving staff was now out in the dining room, and Owen noted with some resentment that he had not been called for dinner. The only other creature in the kitchen with him was the mourning dove which had flown over to sit on a stool next to the butcher block.

Owen began looking for scraps around the kitchen, meat, vegetables, anything really, when a voice behind him made him jump straight in the air with fright.

"Something I can help ye with, young master?" Owen turned to see sitting on the stool, the older, and more portly of the two women who had greeted Orla the previous night. Urma, he thought her name was.

"Um, er, well, I was just looking for some scraps really," he said, embarrassed.

"Well now, me oh my, we can do better than that for the hero of my Princess!" the woman said, standing up quickly. She spun back around to Owen. "Why aren't you at dinner with everyone else now, anyway?"

"I wasn't invited, didn't know," Owen said glumly. "But the scraps aren't for me, if that's okay, they're for my...I mean, there for a stray dog I saw on the other side of the wall, if that's okay?"

"Ha! A stray now, is it? Ah, I bet it's 'ol Duncan Riddle it is, skulking about, looking for hand outs, but we're all entitled to a meal I suppose. It'll be just between you and me, how's that?" she asked, beaming at Owen conspiratorly.

"That's great! Thanks!" Owen said, feeling like this was the best of both worlds; food for Boone, and no one knowing about the *Duine Madra*.

"Now, once you've fed that stray, you come back here and get yerself a proper dinner yerself, you hear?" the plump woman commanded.

"Yes Ma'am," Owen answered. Urma handed him a towel filled with food for the dog, including a piece of mutton, a knuckle joint of left over roast beef, along with some dried fish, potatoes, squash, and apples.

Owen took the bundle, and raced to the courtyard. If he wasn't mistaken, when he had snooped around in the gardener's shed for the mulch, he'd seen a door that exited through the side wall that was, at the time, unguarded. He slipped through the yard to the gate and found it still unoccupied, which Owen again found curious. *Doesn't anyone care that someone nabbed Orla once already?*

He pulled back the two locks on the inside of the reinforced oaken door, one at the midsection where the door ring was, and one about a foot above the ground. The door was heavily reinforced with large iron plates and bars across its thick wooden planks. He slid the bolts back after checking to make sure no one was around. Owen pulled on the ring and the door slowly, hesitantly, inched its way open. It was incredibly heavy. He finally opened it just enough to squeeze through.

"Hope this works," he said to himself as he emptied the contents of the towel on the cobblestone walk just outside the gate. He looked around again. The door opened onto a small alley way that led down to the main road that then ran in front of Orla's house. The road was lined with smaller, but just as affluent and well kept homes. He looked up at the sky and the first stars were beginning to come out, revealing the constellation Orion on the horizon. A pang touched his heart and he hoped his new friend was well. Checking the wall once more to make sure he was alone, Owen whistled. It was just three loud blasts before stepping back behind the door, closing and bolting it behind him, and then heading back to the kitchen. His own stomach already grumbling.

Orla sat at the dining room table and continued to look at the empty seat. Owen hadn't come to this meal either, *is he really that mad at me?* Chamberlain sat at the head of the table, usually reserved for her father. Her cousins, Phan and Jain sat on either side of him, while Orla sat on the opposite side of Chamberlain, Maya to her left. Silan and Aiya, the two Sidhe, sat to her right with Silan sitting next to her and Aiya sitting next to Phan. Owen's place had been set between Maya and Jain.

Three servers brought them their meal and waited on them throughout. Orla didn't recognize any of them. Within the weeks she was gone, the serving staff she had known since she was a little girl had been let go, Chamberlain had explained that there had been some suspicion of them having a connection to her abduction, but no *solid* evidence to charge them with anything. He felt a change was *refreshing* for the household. Many of the guards that Orla had known were no longer here as well and she wondered if they were out searching the countryside for her still, or if they'd just been sacked also.

She wished she could be in the kitchen, eating with Urma like she used to when she was younger. However, with guests in the house, and she being the oldest heir and representative of the Senator, she had to be at dinner, *it would have been better, though, if Owen had come.*

Boone sat upon a wooded hillside not far from the estate that Owen and Orla had entered. The house was built into the cliffside abutting the township. The rest of the town sprawled below the main house. Boone had already investigated the town, crossing its roads and streets during the dark of night, sticking to the shadows.

After he had left Owen on the road to Quailan he had come across the trail of the three trolls. They had traveled through the woods not far from the main road Owen and Orla had taken into the village. He back tracked them to the town, and eventually found what he thought was their origin, a sewer tunnel that ran under Quailan out into the forest. He had been unable to access the tunnel due to the large iron gate that secured the opening.

Other than the trail, he found nothing useful to them, and the separation from his *Maou'r* had been a bitter hardship. He spent long hours traveling through the countryside trying to find things to occupy his time, but instead he found himself howling mournfully out of loneliness.

The great dog sat with his massive head tipped backwards and howled at the night sky. He hoped Owen could hear him, could feel his distress. Maybe the boy felt it too, he wondered.

He hadn't been howling long when a broken twig caught his attention. A bull elk appeared in the valley below, between him and Quailan. Maybe there would be something to preoccupy him this evening, he mused, as he began to stalk the unawares animal.

He stalked the huge stag until it scented him about twenty meters off; when it bolted, Boone gave chase, great lopping strides with his tongue lolling out the corner of his mouth. He felt like a puppy as he crashed through the underbrush, pushing the stag to limits it had not needed before this night. No cougar had ever driven it so hard; no wolf had the stamina of the *Duine Madra*.

Boone broke off his chase before he and the bull had depleted their energy and reserves. Boone felt better for the chase. The great dog began to trot back to the hill when he heard a familiar whistle call from Quailan, three quick bursts and then nothing.

It was already dark, so he quickly worked his way into the town from where the whistle had come. When he was closer, he picked up Owen's scent, but then he also caught the scent of fresh food as well. His mouth watered as he picked up the pace.

Once he reached the gate door, he already knew what was waiting for him. Owen had brought him dinner, which meant Owen had been thinking of him. He sat by the gate and looked up at the part of the house that shown over the wall. He could not see nor sense any sign of Owen in any of those windows, but his scent was strong on the door, he hadn't been gone long from this spot.

Boone ate the food Owen had left while sitting at the gate. The moon had just broken from above the cliff face spilling a moonbeam next to the great dog. Boone held his paw just above the ray of light before it touched the ground. He then dipped the huge appendage into the light as if it were a puddle. The great dog withdrew his paw and pressed it to the huge oaken gate. His paw glowed silver in the moonlight and when he took his foot away a great silver paw print was left branded into the wood. He looked once more at the building and then trotted back into the woods to continue patrolling the forests around Quailan.

54

When Owen returned to the scullery, he was greeted by Urma and a large mug of spiced tea. She had also begun preparing him dinner. He had thick corn chowder with large pieces of red potato and bacon. The *Fey* also had waiting for him a roasted chicken stuffed with wild mushrooms and rosemary, and a loaf of thick dark bread with a hard crust, which Owen dunked into his chowder. She pulled a stool next to his and shared the meal with him. He wondered if this was her dinner she was splitting with him as he sipped his tea that seemed to sooth and ease some of his heartache.

They ate quietly, Urma didn't press Owen for any information or question him while they chewed and drank their meal, but when they were finished and she produced a thick, golden brown, blueberry pie and a mug of hot chocolate she became a bit more talkative.

"Now, how was it you came across our Princess then, Master Owen?" she asked innocently while forking a piece of pie into her mouth.

"She was being chased by three Death Dogs, still in her leopard form," Owen offered, blowing on his chocolate and trying to cool it. He wasn't sure how much of their story was common knowledge now in the household, and didn't want to be caught in a lie. He figured if he steered clear of any part of his world, or being human, he would be okay.

"Really now, and you saved her from them?" The older Sylvan was sitting on the edge of her seat, stuffing the last of her pie into her mouth.

"Well, it was close to dawn, I distracted them long enough until daybreak," Owen admitted, thinking he sounded much less of a hero with that telling.

"Well done!" Urma exclaimed, "Brains over brawn, my dear Owen, brains over brawn!" she cheered, clapping her hands and teetering on her stool.

Owen smiled in spite of himself; he liked Urma much more than any of the other household servants he'd met thus far. She asked him a few more non consequential details, which Owen answered honestly, again not wanting to contradict anything Orla might have already told Chamberlain or anyone else. He was sure she would try and be as honest as possible and only change or leave off the parts about his true origins.

"Oh, we are all so grateful to you for bringing our Princess home to us!" the portly Sylvan said, refilling Owen's chocolate and sliding another piece of pie before him. Owen smiled and accepted the dessert, but wasn't so sure everyone in the household felt that way.

"Thanks," he said.

"And with you here to protect Orla in the future, we'll all rest easier at night, we will," she said, beginning to busy herself with cleaning and straightening. Owen nearly drowned himself with a sip of hot chocolate at this. He coughed and sputtered chocolate as he tried to collect himself. Once he had finished coughing he concentrated on eating his pie before anything else of that subject could be broached.

He was down to his last bite of pie when Orla walked into the kitchen, to a whoop of glee from Urma, and an enormous hug as well. Her eyes opened wide in surprise as she saw Owen eating his dessert followed by a slight smile. Once Urma had replaced Orla to the ground, she walked over to Owen.

"I missed you at dinner," she said, sitting across from him.

"Yeah? It's tough to make it on time when you're not invited," Owen replied, averting his gaze, finishing the last of the chocolate from his mug.

"What? But I told…" Orla stopped. She would get to the bottom of this, but not here. Owen would have come if he'd been asked, she was sure of it. "I'm sorry, I asked that you be invited. There must have been a mistake."

"Yeah, like every other meal," Owen said, lowering his voice, so Urma wouldn't hear the angry tone. He felt guilty being angry with Orla in front of the kindly cook.

"I'm sorry. You were better off though, I always took my meals in here, with Urma, when I could. It's much less formal and Urma is much better company," Urma smiled at this, and playfully bumped into Orla as she walked by the two young people carrying dishes and utensils back to their cubbards.

"Yeah, she's really nice, she even gave me some food for a *stray* dog I saw on the other side of the wall," Owen said.

"Oh, great, I was wondering about that stray, how was he?"

"Didn't see him, but I left the food, hope he's okay," Owen said, the anger and tension leaving his voice.

"Me too."

"Are you busy tonight? Do you have time to hang out, or is Nem going to try and peck my eyes out again?" Owen looked around while saying this, making sure no angry warblers were nearby. Urma let out a slight chuckle.

"No, she's not around, but I have to go and meet with Chamberlain now. I was just coming through to see Urma and ask her to send some food to your room." Orla stood from the stool and shrugged. "I'm really sorry Owen; I'll make it up to you, I promise."

"S'okay," he said, feeling more depressed than angry. At least she hadn't forgotten about him, he could understand her being busy in her own home, especially being a Princess and all.

"But guess what? That Sidhe, Silan, she said she can help me get my memory back and find out who kidnapped me!" Orla said with a gasp of surprise and delight from Urma behind them, which the Sylvan quickly covered up by coughing. Orla smiled at the woman and turned back to Owen. "Isn't that great?"

"Yeah, that's awesome. When?"

"She said tomorrow morning. Do you want to come?" Orla asked looking away.

"Yeah, that'd be great," Owen said a little relieved to be able to spend some time with his friend. "Thanks."

"Don't thank me, silly, but I gotta run. Chamberlain is very unpleasant when I'm late. I'll come get you on my way to see Silan," Orla said hurrying from the kitchen.

Owen saw Urma smiling at him with a knowing expression, so he finished his pie and excused himself from the kitchen. He headed back to his room feeling less lonely and a little better about things with Orla.

55

As Orla stepped in front of the large door to Chamberlain's study she hesitated before knocking. A thought came to her, well almost came to her, in the presence of the massive door. There was something at the back of her mind, like an itch, that she couldn't seem to reach. It lingered there, irritating her at its consistency, but wouldn't reveal itself to her. She tried to push the out-of-reach thought further from her mind and knocked on the large door.

After a moment a muffled "Come in" could be heard as the door released from its latch and parted slightly from the doorframe. Faint light peaked through the crack into the hall. The smell of incense, sulfur, and other odious smells drifted from the tight confines.

She lightly pushed open the door and stepped into the gloomy room, closing the door behind her. Chamberlain sat behind his large and overcrowded desk. It was covered in books, parchment, scrolls, maps, skulls, bones, feathers, stones, crystals, and any number of odd components one might use in a conjuration. He sat in a high backed leather chair with large arms and cushions to keep the Sylvan from disappearing within its deep recesses. He wore his same dining clothes, but with a thick dark robe over them, one, Orla remembered, he normally reserved for her lessons.

He did not look pleased.

She stepped in and sat opposite him in a wooden chair that was neither as ornate nor as comfortable as his. She, however, had learned long ago that there was no way of making it comfortable, and so she sat and didn't bother trying to find the best position. There wasn't one. She simply waited to find out why her tutor was in this mood this evening. She sat for what seemed a very long time while the steward considered her.

She contented herself with looking around his study and then looking over the steward himself. He seemed older. *Strange*, she thought, *I wasn't gone that long.* Chamberlain tapped his fingers on the desk in front of him. His eyes looked Orla up and down, analyzing her, as if trying to solve some equation from which all her parts provided the variables.

"What were you thinking?" he said venomously after the long pause. "Accepting an offer from a Sidhe mind-witch to read your thoughts and meddle in your mind!"

Orla was taken aback, never had Chamberlain spoken to her this way before. He was a strict teacher, especially when it came to using magick, but never had he taken such a tone with her. Wide eyed, she looked back to the man who'd always seemed more an uncle than a teacher and couldn't bring herself to answer, she started, stammered, and stopped, looking down at her hands.

"What would they look for while in your mind? What thoughts? Secrets? They could use against the Sylvans or your father. Or worse, what if they discovered your using magick, what would happen if they told your father, or his enemies within the senate? What if it came to light and the citizens of Quailan learned of your enchantments? Did you ever consider any of these things, *Princess*?" Chamberlain was livid, spittle spotted his lips, his left eye twitched, his ear lobes turned puce. Orla had never seen the man like this; she had never feared him before tonight, not in the way she did now.

"What do you have to say for yourself?" Chamberlain asked, finally stopping his rant, and folding his hands in his lap, stopping them from flailing about as he berated Orla.

"I...I'm sorry," she whispered. She looked up at her teacher, "I didn't think..."

"No, you certainly did not," Chamberlain interrupted, slamming his fist down on his desk. Orla dropped her head again, not meeting the angry Sylvan's eyes. "For all we know the Sidhe were behind your abduction, did you ever consider that?" his voice flared in anger. Orla couldn't bring herself to look at him, tears welled in her eyes.

"N…No," she stammered.

"Well you should have. You are a Sylvan Princess and I would have expected better judgment from you, especially in your father's absence. Obviously, you are not ready to govern in your father's place while he is away; it is a good thing that I am here to make sure things are still conducted in an appropriate manner." The Sylvan finished in a calmer tone. "Orla, look at me." The Princess did as she was instructed, hesitantly. "I am sorry if you feel I am being harsh, but you need to think this way if you are to ever rule this household, or if are to take your father's seat in the senate, you cannot remain so naïve your whole life."

Orla nodded in sad agreement, wiping the tears bulging from her eyes.

"Go then, that is all I have for you this evening. On the morrow we will begin your lessons anew, and I expect you to be in a clearer state of mind than you were this evening."

Orla stood and left the room feeling summarily dismissed; something she had never felt before, something—being a Princess— she never expected to feel. Once in the hall she headed back to her quarters, quickly, and with her head down. She was currently not in the mood to converse with anyone she might meet in the halls.

After dinner Owen retired to his room, possibly, even more confused regarding Orla than before. He found himself wanting to be angry, but feeling troubled and guilty for being so. He had never been so confounded before. On his way back to his room, he had run into Orla's cousins in the hall, and had to listen to some heckling from Jain about his sword fighting skills, or rather, lack thereof. He had noticed that Orla's cousin, Phan, had remained mostly quiet during the exchange with Jain, once actually suggesting to the other Sylvan that they move along and act more appropriately towards a guest in their uncle's home, but without any conviction to actually change the behavior of the other.

Once back to his room Owen paced about, something he had begun to do more often. He was annoyed and frustrated with the two young Sylvans, who were making him feel like he was back at school, being bullied all over again. *Some things are the same in both worlds*, he mused while pacing, but then finally broke from his brooding and went to work on fletching new arrows.

He pulled from under his bed the potential shafts he had taken from the courtyard, starting with the piece of silver birch. He worked it down to the right length, smoothing the shaft to a perfect finish. He took the last of his snow goose feathers and fletched it, two white, and one black, while fitting the front of the arrow with a silver broad head worked with veins of iron throughout. He wrapped the arrow head to the shaft with thin silver and copper wire that Winter had provided. Once finished, he was immensely pleased with the arrow and felt it was his best work yet. He slid it home into his quiver and got to work on the rest of the cedar pieces he had collected, working most of them into practice arrows while reserving some better shafts for hunting.

He had just finished his last arrow and was standing his quiver next to the foot of his bed when he heard a light thump on his veranda. Turning quickly and instinctively reaching for his bow, he saw the familiar form of a snow leopard in the shadows of the balcony. The cat slowly stepped into his room and shifted form.

Orla was wearing a dark black cloak, and holding another just like it over her arm. She smiled meekly at Owen as she handed him the garment. "Quickly, put it on," she said, blowing out the lamp and candles Owen had lit to light his room to work by. "The guards are making their rounds, and we only have a small window of time to sneak over the wall," she added, as she stepped back to the balcony. She pulled a small piece of rope from under her own cloak.

"What?" Owen asked startled.

"I need to get out of here for a while, clear my head," she replied as she shifted to her hybrid form. Turning back to Owen she asked, "Wanna come? I figured you'd be itching to get outta here too."

"Sure," Owen said, throwing the cloak about his shoulders; he didn't need much encouragement to want a break from the house either.

Orla leapt to the roof above Owen's terrace and then lowered the rope back down to him. She wrapped it about the chimney on the roof to help brace it as Owen took hold, and slowly pulled himself up. He was pretty impressed with himself once he reached the roof; he would never have thought he could have done that two weeks ago. Once on the roof, Orla recoiled the rope and headed to the West side of the compound, down onto the gardener's shed, and onto the wall. She lowered the rope again and Owen used it to climb down into the alleyway he had visited earlier that night.

Something on the large oaken door caught his eye, making him investigate what it was, while Orla hopped from the wall. He saw in the moonlight a large dog's paw print, branded into the wood. He had no doubt as to whose paw it belonged to. It was the largest dog track he'd ever seen.

"Is this where you left his dinner?" Orla whispered next to him. Owen nodded. "I guess that's his way of saying thanks."

Owen touched the track with his hand, and felt that increasingly familiar pang in his heart for his absent friend. Orla tugged on his arm, and the two quickly disappeared into the shadows of the alley as the guards appeared along the wall making their rounds.

56

Quailan at night was a very different experience for Owen. More townsfolk were out and about than Owen would have first thought. Many of whom were quick with a "G'evening" and a nod. He and Orla stuck to the shadows and alleyways, the less traveled routes through the city, of which, Orla seemed to be more than familiar. They worked their way to, what to Owen felt like, the center of the town and stopped outside two large wooden doors that had once been painted a pale yellow, but now appeared as whitewashed and tattered. There was a sign above the door that Owen couldn't read, but which Orla translated for him.

"The Grumbling Goblin," she said, as Owen looked at the worn, wooden sign of a frowning goblin.

"Kinda sketchy, ain't it?" he asked, as he pulled his hood down a bit, and wrapped his cloak tighter about him, fending off the cool autumn breeze. Orla had suggested he keep his hood up and low across his brow, hiding his ears and a good portion of his head and face in the process, making it more difficult to mark him as human or anything other than Sylvan.

"Yeah, that's the point," she said with a grin, and pulled on the old door, which opened more easily than Owen would have guessed. They entered the establishment, and Owen found it brighter and much cheerier inside than out. Warm, sweet scented air met them as they crossed the threshold as well as the sound of gaiety and laughter.

A fire roared in a large stone hearth along the middle wall of the building, separating the two main rooms. A long counter and bar ran the length of the wall to his left while tables filled the floor and booths ran along the wall to his right and to either side of the fire. The room beyond the hearth and fire was too dimly lit for him to make out any discernable details.

The room was filled with many Sylvans of differing age. Most were neatly dressed and flushed in the face from laughter and spirits. Many of the booths were taken up with younger Sylvans while the tables were overcrowded with older ones. Owen found it interesting to see so many generations mixing in the same place.

"Oi!" an extremely large Sylvan from behind the bar bellowed at them standing just inside the doorway. "Pounce? That you? C'mon and git yerself in here now!" she yelled down the length of the bar, as she quickly made her way down to their end. Orla took Owen by his hand and dragged him to two stools on the far side of the bar. He was glad to see she kept her hood up as well, if not quite as far down her brow as his. Owen scanned the mass of people and realized a fair number of the folk had hoods and cowls on as well. Maybe they weren't the only two in here that didn't want to be recognized.

"Hey now, Pounce, that is you! Where ye been ye rogue scoundrel?" the beefy woman said, slamming her large ham-like hands onto the bar top. She smiled broadly and eyed Owen suspiciously. "Who's dis?"

"Yeah, I've been away. This? He's a friend, call him….," she paused, hesitating only momentarily, "Archer."

"Yeah? Well, any friend of Pounce's is welcome 'ere." She smiled at Owen making him truly feel instantaneously welcome. "The usual?"

"Yeah, make it two," Orla said.

"Yer friends are in back, bin 'ere 'bout a half hour. Go ahead, I'll bring the drinks back to ye's," she said turning her back to Owen and Orla and going back about her work.

Orla grabbed Owen's arm and began working her way through the crowd to the back room. "Archer?" Owen asked.

"Yeah, that okay? I thought it was a good one," she said, smiling back at him, her face barely visible beneath the hood in the dim light as they entered the back room. The atmosphere in this part of the establishment was much more subdued. The lights were dimmer, the tables fewer. The few people at tables or booths were much more quiet and reserved. Orla took in the room in a moment and quickly headed to a booth in a corner where two more black cloaked and hooded figures sat.

Owen followed in toe. He was feeling that overwhelming sense of spinning again, when too much was happening too quickly to process it all. Orla stopped at the booth in the corner, sliding in along the seat, pulling Owen in behind her. Two young Sylvans, Owen assumed because they still had their hoods up as well, sat across from them. From their noses and chins, Owen guessed one was male and the other female, and he reassured himself that they were about his and Orla's age. He could feel them eyeing him as he slid in the booth next to Orla.

"Thanks for coming," she said.

"No problem," the boy said. "Where've you been?" the girl followed. "We got your note, but then nothing."

"Note?" Owen and Orla both said at once, causing the two Sylvans to eye him even more suspiciously. "Sorry. Luna, Fawn, this is Archer, a friend, you can trust him, I do," Orla continued, which seemed to ease the nerves of the two others at the table.

"Now, about that note?" Orla asked.

"You sent us each a note before you disappeared, it said you had to leave Quailan immediately, head to the capital, and that you would send more word once you arrived, but then no word ever came," Luna, the male Sylvan, said. They had both pulled their hoods back some when Orla introduced them, just enough for Owen to make out their faces. "And then we heard through town that you'd vanished, been abducted, or something."

"Narsus? Why would I head to Narsus?" Orla asked.

"Your father," Owen answered quietly, as if just to her alone. She looked at him, and at this proximity he could see her eyes beneath her cloak. He could see she agreed. She had left the household to head, alone, to see her father, but why?

"That's what we assumed as well, but then we were terrified for you," Fawn added. "We didn't come forward, I hope that was the right thing to do, and then we'd heard you'd returned. We were so relieved to get your bird today," the young Sylvan said with a smile.

"I never made it," Orla said, after a moments silence while she and Owen digested the new information. "Sorry for frightening you so. I can't remember anything about wanting to, or even leaving, I remember waking up, in my *other* form, and being chased by Death Dogs." Luna and Fawn both sat back and looked at each other in surprise, and then back to Orla. "But Archer was there and chased them off, saving me. I came back to him later, and he unlatched a collar that had kept me from changing." Both Sylvans exchanged gasps of surprise. Owen sat back, *wow, does she really think that?* he wondered. *Makes me sound like a hero*, he mused.

"Are you sure? Do you know what you're saying?" Fawn whispered across the table. "Someone tried to kill you," she added with palpable doubt still in her voice.

"Besides the two of us, who else knew you were leaving?" Luna asked.

"I don't know. No one? At least, I would think I would tell no one else," Orla offered. She looked at Fawn. "I know the way it sounds, but Archer has the scars to prove it, we were hunted the whole way back to Quailan. I know it sounds crazy, but you have to believe me."

"So, no one else in the house knew who may have said something to someone else, letting it get out some how?" Owen asked, again feeling the eyes of Orla's two friends turn to him. "Not even Chamberlain," he said quietly, lowering his voice.

"Well, I can't remember! I wouldn't do it now, so I don't think I would have then, but I don't know, maybe I did…" Owen could hear the tension and frustration creeping into her voice; it caused a slight clenching of his own stomach to hear her feel that way. "If I did, though, who? How do I know who I can trust?" she asked.

"You can trust me," Owen stated flatly. Orla turned, smiling, she squeezed his hand, and let go just as quickly. Owen's heart began to race.

"And us too, Pounce," Luna added with a decisive nod of his cloaked head. Fawn smiled encouragingly at her too.

"Well, we're not going to find out anything more now….why don't you guys tell me how you all met," Owen said, hoping to change the subject for a while and therefore lifting Orla's spirits. Just as he had said it, the big, burly Sylvan from the front room plopped down a tray filled with four great mugs and all sorts of decedent desserts.

"And here ye go!" she announced as she began to pass around the mugs. They were thick, heavy pottery, filled with steaming chocolate with the slightest hint of raspberries. Fawn actually "ooooooed" out loud when the mug was put in front of her, and Orla and Luna wasted no time in pulling the drinks closer to them, breathing in the rich aroma. Owen, even though mightily impressed with the chocolate, was more impressed with the snacks and pastries being unloaded onto the table.

"Ye haven't been around enough lately, Pounce, maybe some a deeze will convince ye to come back more often," she said, smiling broadly, picking up her tray, and heading back into the front room.

There was a bowl, matching the mugs, filled with round chocolate balls, a tray of steaming mini-pies, a plate of fudge sticks, and another plate of thick cookies with large chunks of white chocolate and nuts in them. Owen's mouth began watering.

"Goblin eyes!" Luna exclaimed, and took one of the balls from the bowl, biting it in half. Blue crème stretched onto his lip and chin as he announced, "Blueberry!"

Owen looked hesitantly at Orla who smiled, laughed, and bumped shoulders with him. "Crème filled chocolates. Each one has a different fruit crème filling; Madam Duffell has always called them *Goblin eyes.*"

"Oh," Owen answered and reached for one. Fawn had dropped one in her mouth and smiled, "Orange, my favorite."

Owen bit into his as Orla chomped hers. His mouth puckered and his eyes watered. "Lemon," he announced. It tasted better than he would have thought, but *wicked* tart, he thought.

Orla laughed and smiled, a bit of the crème still on her lips, "Mmmmm, raspberry," she teased.

Owen finished his, his face puckering up once more for the group's amusement, which he joined in, and then took a sip of his hot chocolate.

All three Sylvans stopped what they were doing and waited expectantly for his reaction.

The warm liquid slid into his mouth and down his throat, rich warm chocolate with the hint of fresh raspberries. The feeling it gave him as it reached his belly was not so unlike Boone's howl. It was beyond refreshing, rejuvenating was more like it. Owen thought if he could have had this on their trek to Quailan, he wouldn't have needed to rest each night, they could have continued on every evening. It made his thoughts sure and clear, any doubt he'd had of Orla's loyalty or affection were cast away, the chocolate was the best thing he'd ever drank before. The three Sylvans giggled at the expression on Owen's face.

"Good, eh?" Luna asked with a smirk.

"Wow, that's the best thing I've ever tasted, what is it?" Owen asked.

"Chocolate," Orla answered.

"I've had hot chocolate before, and that's not it."

"It is, you've never had *real* chocolate before," Orla answered with a grin. "It's *magical!*" She took a sip of her own.

Owen took another sip and enjoyed the rich flavor. *She's right, though,* he thought, *it is just chocolate, or maybe this is the way chocolate is supposed to be,* he reflected, as he and the others began devouring the sweets before them.

It wasn't long before Fawn said she had to get going, and Luna agreed that he needed to go as well. They both slid from their side of the booth and stood next to the table.

"Tomorrow night then?" Fawn asked.

"'Fraid not," Orla answered, "I took a huge chance sneaking out tonight, if I get caught, they'll post a guard at my door after what happened."

"Alright, well, send a note again when you can get away, we'll meet you back here," Luna said, pulling his hood a bit more forward on his brow.

"And next time you plan on running off to Narsus," Fawn added, "don't plan on going alone." Orla smiled, and nodded at her friend's concern. The two left while Owen turned to Orla.

"I think I could be sick," he said, feeling like he would burst.

"Well, you certainly ate enough to be," she smiled. He slid out of the booth, adjusted his own hood, and the two left the Grumbling Goblin, waving to Madam Duffell as they did so.

They worked their way home through the streets the way they had come, Owen aware of every shadow, wishing desperately he had thought to bring his bow. He felt very vulnerable without it in the streets at night. They made it back to the alley gate without incident, however. Orla, shifting to her hybrid form, leapt to the top of the wall and threw the rope back over for Owen.

Late night?

The familiar voice rumbled in Owen's mind, he whirled around to see Boone standing behind him, just inside one of the shadows in the alley.

"Boone!" Owen exclaimed to a "Shush!" from Orla. Boone leapt across the alley and bumped his huge body and shoulder into Owen's legs, almost knocking him over. If dogs could smile, then Boone smiled. He pressed his great, massive head to Owen's chest, his tongue lolling out, his plume of a tail wagging in greeting.

"How ya been?" Owen asked.

Alright, yourself? Boone asked.

"Okay, miss ya, though."

And me you, but it is not safe for the two of you to be out in the city un-escorted, and looking at Owen, *and un-armed.* Boone looked up at Orla, wagged his tail, and nodded his enormous head in greeting.

"Hello Boone. I've missed you too!" she whispered from atop the roof. "But Owen, we need to get inside, quickly, the guards will be back shortly!"

She's right, but first. It's not safe, especially because I tracked the trolls we faced on the bridge back to the city, they came from a sewer tunnel on the outskirts of town.

"That can't be!" Orla exclaimed louder than she intended. She instinctively ducked and looked to see of anyone had heard. No one had.

I'm afraid it is, Princess. You both need to be very careful. I have been picking up strange and unholy scents around the city. You both must be cautious. And you both must get over the wall; the guards will be here soon. The great dog shouldered

Owen once more in farewell and then sprinted down the alley, back into the shadows and from sight.

Owen watched him go and then, reluctantly, grabbed the rope and climbed the wall. They both made it across the roof top and to his terrace without being noticed. Orla coiled the rope back up and shifted into her hybrid form to make the leap back to the courtyard.

"Orla wait," Owen blurted, "thanks for coming and getting me tonight. It was fun, your friends are cool, I mean, nice, I mean…" Orla smiled, her feline canines catching the moonlight.

"Don't thank me; I've been missing spending time with you. I'll see you tomorrow, okay?" Owen nodded, and Orla leapt over the terrace railing into the courtyard and out of view, thankful her fur hid her blushing cheeks.

Owen turned and went into his room. He first noticed his bed sheets pulled back, and his wardrobe doors open. A few other items were moved, but nothing looked missing from his room. His quiver and bow were still in the corner by the head of his bed. He went to his door, but it was still locked from the inside, he was just heading back over to his bow when he heard a frightening scream from across the courtyard in the direction of the Sidhe's chambers. The scream was filled with fright, sorrow, and rage; the pitch of which made Owen instinctively take a step back from his terrace.

57

Owen rushed for his bow and quiver, grabbing both; he sped to his terrace. He reached the railing just as Aiya leapt from her own, flipping backward off the iron grating to land in the courtyard. Four shadowy shapes trailed her, leaping from the balcony with the same fluid grace. Two landed in front of her, two behind, all armed with black bladed short swords, and long, thin daggers.

Owen instinctively brought his hand back to his quiver, and without conscious thought, almost as if the arrow placed itself into his hand, drew the silver birch arrow with its snow goose fletching. He knocked it, memory bringing his hand back to its anchoring point just below his chin, aimed, and fired. Without waiting to see the first arrow home, he reached and fired two more, both cedar shafted and turkey fletched.

On releasing his third arrow, he noticed an interesting thing regarding the first. As the silver birch arrow raced in on its target, it seemed to hesitate, pausing momentarily in the air just in front of its victim. The air around the dark clad creature shimmered, like heat off an asphalt road in the middle of August. It was for the briefest of seconds, but then the arrow passed through the shimmering air as if it had never paused. The two arrows following in the wake of the first sailed off in opposite directions.

The first arrow, however, found its target. A sudden surprised cry escaped the creature, but was cut short, as the arrow passed through its mark and sank into the ground behind Aiya. The creature dropped to its knees and its dark clothing fell empty to the ground. Aiya caught the briefest of movements as the creature vanished, but was preoccupied with her own assailants. Owen noticed in that split second, as the moonlight reflected off her face, gleaming wet tears stained her cheeks. Aiya was crying while she fought. She continued battling the two in front of her as the third turned and looked directly at Owen.

He fired two more cedar arrows, the only type he had left besides the arrow Winter had given him. Both arrows suddenly raced in different directions at odd angles to the creature as they neared their target. A quick glance back to Aiya in the throes of battle, and Owen's resolve was solidified. He would not leave her alone. The creature began moving towards him while Owen looked for an alternative weapon.

His *clai'omh* leaned against the corner wall of his terrace; it was his only other option, and the intruder was closing quickly. He grabbed the practice sword in one hand, and grabbing the railing in his other, he vaulted over it. The terrace was ten feet above the courtyard, and as Owen fell the distance he realized he shouldn't have made the jump. He held the railing for as long as he could, but still fell freefall more than six feet. As he landed, a shooting twinge of pain rose up his lower right leg into his knee. It took all his strength and determination not to fall over from the pain. He adjusted his weight onto his good leg, and moved into the fighting stance Aiya had showed him.

The creature that approached him was dressed all in black. Thigh high, black boots, folded over to its knees, leather jerkin and breeches, forearm high gloves, and a flowing black cloak, hood thrown up. Even the blades it wielded were black.

Owen expected to feel that startling unease of evil as it closed on him, but the feeling never came; instead there was an unnerving nothingness to its presence. The creature didn't stop to engage Owen, it just continued walking towards him, never pausing as it began its assault. Owen parried with his practice sword, as the creature tore huge chunks from it. Owen was very aware of the slim dagger it held in check, waiting for an opening to thrust it into Owen. The intruder pushed Owen backwards, keeping him on the defensive as he whittled the *clai'omh* away.

As they fought, Owen caught glimpses of the creature battling him. Its skin was as black as the garb it wore; smooth and perfect in its complexion. It had a hooked nose, reminiscent of a bird of prey, with penetrating black orbs for eyes, lid-less, with small horns protruding from its forehead, just above its brow. Its build was slight, almost feminine, and of medium height, close to Owen's. The creature never breathed heavily or seemed to be exerting itself. While Owen, in his own fatigue, began to become frustrated by the thought that it was toying with him.

These thoughts almost cost Owen his life. While becoming frustrated, he left himself open after one quick parry and the hand holding the dagger darted into the space. Owen twisted, bringing his own left hand to meet the dagger, but too slowly. The blade nicked his ribs, glancing off just below his left armpit. The resulting shift in position threw too much weight onto his already injured leg, causing him to stumble. The creature was about to bring his short sword down with a fatal blow when Owen made contact with his practice sword.

The creature hissed in anger, shoving Owen back with the forearm of his sword hand. Owen recoiled, quickly getting his weight back to his uninjured leg while positioning himself again in his fighting stance. He wasn't sure how much longer he could last against such a foe. The dark creature pressed the fight, closing the slight distance between them. Engaging Owen again, just as a silver crescent appeared above the creature's head before disappearing behind it, smiting it in one mighty blow.

The creature crumpled in upon itself, dissolving into nothingness, and leaving only its garb and weapons behind. Standing in its place was Aiya; sweaty and bloodstained, but whole. Her eyes were vacant, however, with a look of desperation. She looked at Owen with slight recognition and uttered one word, almost unintelligible.

"Silan."

58

"S ilan is dead."

Aiya spoke these words detached, removed from her body, as if on some ethereal plane, but still speaking through her physical self. Owen stood dumbfounded; the pain in his leg and side momentarily forgotten. *How could this happen? Do they really think they're keeping Orla safe?* His bewilderment turned to anger, not only at the assassins, but at Chamberlain and the household guards as well. *Where had the guards been?*

"HOLD FAST!" the voices broke from above and around them. "Intruders disarm at once!" Owen could tell they were surrounded, but after what Aiya accomplished against the real intruders, Owen felt these simpleton guards would be no match for her.

"We are guests in your house," Aiya said wearily, "the intruders have been dealt with, come see for yourself." After a moment's hesitation, four guards entered the courtyard and approached Owen and Aiya slowly. Once they reached the two, they inspected the remains on the ground while Aiya directed them to the three at the bottom of her terrace. She sheathed her sword, turned, and began heading back to her chambers.

"I said HOLD!" the voice came from a guard on the rooftop. Aiya stopped, and turned, slowly, easily finding the man in the night sky along the roofline with her keen Sidhe eyes.

"And I said I am a guest in this house. Where were your guards when they slew my sister?" she demanded, bowing her head for a moment, physically trying to regain control of her emotions. "I am heading to my chambers to be with her and prepare her for her final journey. If anyone should fire upon me, I shall take that as an act of aggression by all, and deal accordingly."

Aiya turned and left. No one said anything further to her. Owen stood where he was and became much more aware of the wound along his ribs and the pain in his leg, he wobbled slightly. A familiar voice broke into the courtyard from the west side.

"I said let me pass!"

"But, Princess, it is not safe!" came the weak protest.

"Move or I will have you discharged this evening!" Orla replied coolly, confidently, sounding very much like a Senator's daughter.

"Yes, My Lady," the humbled guard replied.

A moment later and Orla was by Owen's side. Her eyes quickly took in the damage and carnage. They went to the cloak and clothing on the ground and then to the cleaved *clai'omh* still in Owen's hand. The sharp Sylvan eyes that allowed her to see in night as effortlessly as her cat form looked over Owen. She quickly saw the growing dark spot beneath his left arm, and that he was putting most of his weight on his left leg.

"You're hurt." It was a statement, not a question.

"Heh, just a scratch," Owen said, trying to feign a British accent.

"In that case walk with me," she said, and began to turn away.

"Um, well, I'd rather not," he said weakly.

"I thought so," Orla countered, coming to him, "Where and how?" Orla took his right arm and wrapped it about her shoulder and began walking him towards the door beneath his terrace.

"Git yer arm off her this minute, boy!" a rough voice came from behind them. A gruff looking Sylvan in a guard's uniform emerged from the same door Orla had exited. Buzzing by his ear, and making a line straight for Owen, was a small bird. Owen had no doubt what kind of bird it was.

"He is wounded, Tolland. Doing your and your men's job for you!

Do not speak to him that way again," Orla said, physically jarring the sergeant with her words. The warbler closed in on Owen's head; he began to duck as Orla spoke again. "Nem! If you so much as touch a hair on his head I will have you in the scullery scrubbing pans for the rest of your stay in this house! Now fetch clean linen, hot water, and medicinal herbs and ointments to tend his wounds. Bring them to his room immediately." There was no doubt in her words. These words were coming from the Princess of the House, the head of the household in her father's absence. The warbler pulled up short, hovered for a second in front of the young Sylvan, and then shot passed both Owen and Orla and through the doors below Owen's room. The sergeant at arms stood motionless, never had the Princess spoken to him this way before, and he was shocked into inaction. Orla turned, and the pair began heading towards the door again.

"Thanks," Owen said.

"Shush," Orla hissed, with more sadness in her voice than he had ever heard before.

"What is it?" he asked, concern for his friend overcoming the pain in his side and leg.

"I heard the scream, and was on my way, but the guards had blocked the passage to the yard," she spoke quietly, barely audible for Owen, right next to her.

"I told them I heard a scream and they said they couldn't let me pass because it wasn't safe for me. When I asked what they were going to do about the scream; they said their orders were not to let anyone in or out of the courtyard."

"Orla, are you saying the guards knew these things were here, and left Aiya and me to face them alone?" Owen asked.

"You and Aiya? The guards said the Sidhe were fighting, they didn't mention you, but I assumed that both of the sisters were fighting," she answered, a bit confused.

"Silan is dead, I just saw Aiya fighting them, I think by that time they had already killed Silan. And the assassins had already ransacked my room; at least someone had gone through everything while we were out."

The two entered the hall and stairwell to Owen's chambers, quieting their tone even further.

"Owen, I'm scared, I don't know who to trust," Orla confided on the stairs.

"I know, me too, I don't think we can trust anyone but ourselves, and maybe Aiya," he said between gritted teeth, the stairs were making the pain in his leg excruciating.

The rest of the walk to his room and onto his bed was a blur. The pain was getting rather intense and he was having trouble concentrating on anything else. He did notice when they entered his room that Nem and Urma were already present. A vague, unconscious sense of relief hit him when he realized that Chamberlain wasn't there.

Nem had brought all the supplies Orla had ordered. Once the Princess had entered, and seen Urma, had dismissed Nem to help Aiya in the Sidhe chambers, instructing her to do and get anything that the Sword Maiden requested. With the door closed, Owen began to fade. He remembered Orla instructing Urma to not repeat anything she was about to see to anyone, and then as Owen slipped into unconsciousness he remembered a familiar bluish glow and warmth in his side and leg.

59

The world came slowly back into focus. First, Owen's hearing, fuzzy and muffled, came back to him. He could hear voices a little distance from him, or close by but speaking quietly, too quietly for him to hear anything definitive. Then his sense of smell awakened and he could smell fresh cut lawn, and the cool smell of autumn on the air, and what smelled like breakfast: fresh muffins and fruit, bacon and eggs, maple syrup and pancakes. He briefly wondered if he were home and if everything that had happened had been a dream. Thirdly, his sense of touch came back to him. There was an ache in his right leg, just above his ankle and to the outside of the extremity. There was also a tightness and itchiness just below his left arm, along his ribs. The feeling one has when a particularly thick scab is almost ready to fall off, when the skin is pulled taut and the scab has no give or flex to it. With the sudden aches, awareness returned, and Owen remembered the battle he fought with Aiya the night before. The dagger wound to his side, and the excruciating pain in his leg. Neither injury was as painful as he remembered them when he was last conscious. Finally, he opened his eyes.

Sitting at the foot of his bed were Orla and Aiya, both speaking quietly to one another. A tray of food sat between them, but neither ate from it. Orla sat on the bed, on his left side, while Aiya had pulled a chair up along next to her. Both looked tired and drained, physically and emotionally. Orla had changed to clothes similar to what Owen had first met her in. A simple cotton tunic, belted at her waist with a silver chain, and brown leather breeches, calf length. Her hair was loose and Owen could see the small silver bells braided into its mane. She, again, was barefoot.

Aiya was dressed for battle. She had changed her pants and under tunic, and now wore her mail shirt and bracers over the new dressings. Her gloves were tucked beneath her brown leather sword belt. The gloves matched her thigh high deer skin boots. She had also changed her cloak to one of a soft sea green, the color of the ocean on a cool winter's day, which matched her pants. Her hair had been pulled back, the sides tied behind her head in a long thin braid while the back remained loose. Her sword, bow, and quivers leaned against the wall, within easy reach.

Owen hadn't thought he moved at all, but both *Fey* immediately turned to him on his waking. Aiya stood and approached his bed, and Orla leaned closer, careful not to lean on him.

"How're you feeling?" she asked, concern etched all over her face.

"Fine," Owen croaked, not realizing how thirsty he was. Orla smiled, leaning back to the tray of food and retrieving a glass of juice, apple, by the color.

"Here, drink," she said, handing him the glass. He drained the apple juice in one gulp, the juice tasted crisp and felt wonderful. He was amazed at how thirsty he was. Both *Fey* smiled at him.

"You had us a little worried last night," Orla started, "you were hurt worse than you were letting on."

"Seem okay now, though," he said placing the glass down. "Thanks," he said smiling at Orla, but then the reality of what happened settled on him. "What were those things?" he asked, a slow burning kindling in his belly.

"*Ain'griefer*," Aiya answered, the word coldly slipping from her lips. "Assassins, deymons, from the Abyss."

Owen nodded, not knowing how else to reply to the information. *Just another evil creature trying to kill me or my friends.*

"Since when did you think you could leap from balconies?" Aiya asked, trying to lighten the mood of the room.

"Hmm, saw that, huh?" Owen blushed slightly, looking down at his leg that seemed to be wholly better, minus the slight ache.

"You did what?" Orla asked, a combination of anger and admiration appearing on her face. A warm buzz stirred in Owen's chest at the look, and he felt as if he would leap from a hundred more balconies if she would continue looking at him that way.

"He fired his arrows from the balcony, killing one of the *Ain'griefer*, but drawing the attention of a second. I retrieved that arrow for you, along with others, by the way, and put them back in your quiver. One that can slay a *'Griefer* is one worth saving. You can explain to me later how you came by it," she nodded her head indicating his quiver against the wall.

"When his other arrows had no effect, he took his *clai'omh* and leapt over the railing to meet the deymon." There was an edge of sadness, but one of great respect as well in her voice. "I have fought alongside some of the greatest warriors of the Sidhe, ones my people sing about in many ballads, and I fear none of them would have engaged such a foe using only a practice sword."

"It was all I had," Owen shrugged, feeling stupid for doing such a thing.

"And most, given the same circumstance, would have chosen to flee, rather than fight," Aiya added, looking out onto the balcony. "You owed no allegiance to me or my sister."

"I couldn't, wouldn't, have left you alone," he said, looking down at his hands, wishing he could have done more, maybe have come to help sooner, and saved Silan. Orla put her hand on Aiya's arm, comforting the Sidhe, while looking to Owen and smiling sadly.

"You did all you could," Orla said, "and sadly, more than anyone else. If you had not come to Aiya's aid, we might be mourning her as well." Again the young *Fey* sounded much like a Princess, Owen thought.

Aiya looked back at Owen and he could see the tears wanting to spill from her eyes, but she willed them to stay in place, and kept them in check. She leaned forward and gently kissed Owen on his cheek. "You owed me nothing, and yet risked all for me and Silan, I will not forget that, Owen McInish. My soul and my sword are yours. Your quest is mine," she said, and stood up from the bed, secured her sword and quiver, and picked up her bow. "Today I will prepare and tonight I will send my sister into the next world. On the morrow, I will help prepare you for your own quest. And once you are physically fit, will continue your training. However, after what you achieved last night, I think it is time to make your lessons a bit more difficult," the Sidhe smiled and began to leave Owen's room, she paused once more at the door before opening it.

"Princess, I fear your home is no longer safe for you and the *Maou'r*, it is my suggestion that we prepare to move on from here as soon as Owen is able."

Orla wasn't surprised by the statement; on the contrary, she had been considering it all night herself. At the moment, however, she could not find the words to express what she felt, her home had turned against her, it was no longer safe for her or her friends. All Orla could do was simply nod her agreement.

"But now is not the time to discuss this, we can speak further on it on the morrow," the Sidhe Sword Maiden said, as she opened and then closed the door behind her.

Orla turned back to Owen. "You JUMPED off the terrace?"

60

It probably wasn't one of the brightest things I've ever done," Owen said sheepishly. Orla smiled, and then laughed, the second time Owen could remember her really laughing since their return to Quailan. Owen laughed too. He really couldn't believe he'd done it either. And he was sure no one back home would have ever considered him doing something like that. *That was pretty crazy*, he thought.

"No, but maybe the bravest," Orla said, "and that's saying something." Owen stopped laughing and looked at her. She wasn't kidding, he realized. She was being completely serious.

"I haven't done all that much," he mumbled, but he was having trouble hiding his elation at her compliment. He could feel the blood rushing into his cheeks.

"But what were you thinking? A *clai'omh?*" she started laughing, and Owen, blushing slightly more, smiled too. It felt like forever since they'd joked and laughed, even though they'd done so last night with Fawn and Luna, it still seemed so much had happened since last night, so much time had passed. *I'm sure Aiya feels the same way, yesterday probably seems like an eternity ago*, he considered as Orla grabbed the breakfast tray and sat it in front of him.

"You need to eat something," she said. "I did the best I could last night, but you need to keep your strength up, you're not completely healed."

"So, you healed me? I was wondering who did after I passed out."

"Yeah, me and Urma, I made her swear not to tell anyone about me using magick." Orla looked pensive for a moment, worry played across her face.

"I doubt Urma is the one behind all this, I'm sure you can trust her," Owen said, he left out that he would trust her cousins only about as far as he could throw them, though.

"I guess, but you have to realize I grew up with all of them. My mother died shortly after Maya was born, and the memories I have of her are vague. Nem and Urma were my mothers, Chamberlain my surrogate father while my dad was away at the Senate." Orla took a piece of bacon from Owen's plate and ate it absently. Owen realized in an instant how hungry he really was, he dug into the pancakes.

When he had finished eating, Orla's mood had lightened some; she seemed to have shifted her thoughts. She stood and walked over to where Aiya had laid his weapons and came back to bed with his *clai'omh* in hand. It was about a foot shorter, with large wedges cut from the remaining length.

"I can't believe you challenged an *Ain'griefer* with this," she said in awe and mirth. Orla smiled at him again.

"Got lucky, is all." The boy had a sudden wish that Boone was here as well. He wondered if he'd be scolded for not calling the dog, and then was certain of it.

"Thanks. Boone ever show up?" Owen asked, both hoping he had and that he had not blown his cover.

"No, I was here the whole time, but I'm sure I would have heard some commotion if he had. It's probably for the best that he didn't come afterward," after a moments thought, "but if something like this ever happens again, you should call him to you."

"Yeah," Owen laughed, "I wouldn't be so banged up now if I had."

She smiled at him again. Orla stood and walked around his room. She opened his wardrobe, looked at his clothes, walked out to his balcony, and came back in. A silent pause enveloped them, and Owen felt a little uncomfortable.

"Is Aiya going to have a funeral or something for her sister?" he finally asked. Orla stopped her pacing.

"Well, I'm not sure of the exact custom of her people, their kingdom is pretty far from here, and they believe it is best to release the soul of the dead as quickly as possible. I think she's sending her on her next journey tonight. I think that's why she left this morning, to go and build her pyre. Before coming here last night she had prepared her sister for the journey."

Owen thought their customs and beliefs here were so different than back home. Even the way they spoke about death and dying and the next world. His parents believed in an afterlife, Heaven and all, but the people here just talked about death as if they were out taking a walk. It was natural to them; he'd known so many adults that acted so funny about it when he'd seen them at wakes or funerals back in his world.

"Should we go?" he asked.

"No. I think Aiya is expecting to do this alone, besides you're in no shape to travel. I think she's going to build the pyre on top of the cliff." She nodded her head in the direction of the high stone cliff along the back of the courtyard. Owen had to admit to himself he was in no condition to climb or hike to the top of that. He still felt horrible for Aiya though, first having lost her sister, now having to say goodbye to her and do this all alone, but then a sudden thought occurred to him.

"Orla, how much have you told people here about me?"

"Nothing really, I mean, I haven't told them *who* you are, except for Chamberlain. I had to tell him everything, but everyone else knows most of what's happened since we've been back to my world, but not about where we came from." He could tell, though, she was beginning to wonder if she'd said too much.

"Did you notice my room had been sacked when you brought me up here?" Looking around now, he noticed everything was in place.

"No. It was in perfect order," she said skeptically, "why?"

"It was?" Owen asked, getting a little nervous. "Right before I heard the scream last night, I stepped in off the balcony and my room had been trashed. My bed was undone, my wardrobe opened and gone through," he said, looking around again more carefully.

"It wasn't when we came in, Owen," she said, becoming more concerned, "I've been here all night, much to Nem's dislike, and no one's straightened anything, no one's had to."

Nem! Owen thought. *Can't be, she's been like a mom to Orla.*

"I know what I saw, Orla," Owen said. He knew he hadn't seen things. The deymons had come to his room too, but why would they come after him and the Sidhe? *And who would have cleaned up after them?*

"I believe you, but why would someone come in and clean your room?"

"Because they didn't want me or anyone else to know that those things were here last night for me too," Owen said, worried he might be sounding a little full of himself, or even a tad paranoid. *Really,* he thought, *an assassination plot, for me?* He wasn't really sure he bought it himself.

"Why would they have come for Silan and Aiya anyway? Why would someone want them dead?" Owen asked, although he was already suspecting the truth, he hoped Orla was too.

"Because she was going to read my mind and find out who abducted me," Orla said vacantly. Her thoughts were elsewhere. "Chamberlain had really berated me last night about agreeing to let her do it; he really didn't want her to."

"Why? What's he got to hide, unless…" Owen started and stopped. "Orla have you noticed how lame the security is here, I mean I don't know what it was like before, but it's like, nonexistent. I mean we came and went and no one even knew," Owen was stopped short by a knock on his door. Without waiting for a reply Chamberlain let himself into the room.

"Ah, good, Master McInish is awake, and doing well, I see," he gave Orla an inquisitive look, but continued to the bedside.

"From what my guards tell me, we are again in your debt for helping squelch a small disturbance last night," Chamberlain said, as he stepped to the side of Owen's bed and looked him up and down. *Small?* Owen wondered how much the Sylvan was told of his injuries and if Orla would get in trouble for helping heal him.

"But it seems you are not much the worse for wear, some of my guards were incorrect in the estimate of your injuries." He again looked at Orla and back to Owen.

Well, he knows then, Owen thought.

"I guess it looked worse than it really was," Owen said, returning the Sylvan's stare.

"Good then, it is unfortunate about the Sidhe, however, I fear that this may reflect badly upon our household and Quailan itself." He turned to Orla, "I hope you do not mind my speaking of this in front of our guest, my Princess, I assumed you would not mind?" Chamberlain asked, with more respect than either Orla or Owen would have expected.

"Not at all," she answered, surprised at Chamberlain's behavior.

"I have already dispatched an emissary to their Lord, with our condolences, in hopes of extinguishing any trouble this might cause; after all, they were guests here in our household."

"Thank you," Orla said, still taken aback.

"I met with the other Sidhe last night and expressed our sympathies, but she was otherwise engaged in the funeral rites of her sister. I noticed she retired to this room last evening afterwards, I trust that you were able to express our deepest feelings for her loss."

"Yes, Aiya and I spoke for a very long time, she does not hold our household responsible," Orla answered, hoping she was correct; Aiya had not spoken much about that particular topic. And honestly, Orla herself was questioning how much her household had to do with the presence of the *Ain'griefer* within their walls.

"Good," Chamberlain looked back to Owen, with a glimmer of something Owen saw in his eye, but couldn't place, "Very good indeed. Well, I'll leave you two young people alone again. I just wanted to check on our young guest," the steward said as he made his exit from the room.

After he had left, Owen and Orla sat quietly for a few moments not saying anything, afraid that Chamberlain might still be on the other side of the door and not wanting him to overhear. Orla quietly shifted to her leopard form and stealthily padded to the door, sniffing along the bottom edge. She didn't pick up any scent of anyone outside and so she padded back to Owen, shifting to her Sylvan form and sitting on the side of the bed.

"He's gone," she said.

"Good," Owen said, and then feeling awkward added, "I gotta be honest; the guy gives me the creeps."

"Yeah, I know," Orla paused, looking back towards the door, "he seems different to me, like he's changed, or maybe I've changed, I don't know...I used to get along a lot better with him, but now...it's just...he's been strange," she said. Orla just couldn't put her finger on it, but Owen was right, there was something going on with Chamberlain, and possibly even more of the servants. She certainly would have expected the guards to react a little differently if her father had been home. *Maybe that's the problem,* she thought, *dad's been gone too much.*

"Well, I think, maybe tomorrow, when Aiya is finished, we should all sit down and figure out what's going on. Because after your kidnapping and what happened last night, I don't think any of us are safe," Owen said. Orla just nodded her agreement. She had been certain they would be safe here in Quailan, she had promised Winter they would, but now she wasn't so sure. Now she wasn't sure of very much of anything.

61

Rocks broke and slid away as Aiya climbed the narrow single track up the steep slope on the west side of the cliff. The sheer cliff side that comprised the back wall of the estate faced southwest; however, the North, East, and West sides were also treacherous climbs. There was one trail to the pinnacle, long since abandoned by the Sylvan family below. In years past the trail led to a small keep and fortress, both a sentry post to defend the household from attack from the North, and also a fortified retreat if the estate was attacked from below.

The trail was comprised of loose rock and chaparral, causing even a sure footed Sidhe to stumble and lose her balance, especially while pulling the traditional funeral hand cart of her people. The *kla'airt* was a two wheeled wagon with long polls designed to be pulled by the kin of the deceased on their way to the freeing ceremony. The *kla'airt* was usually hand painted and inlaid with gold illustrating the accomplishments and deeds of the dead Sidhe, but Silan's *kla'airt* was blank. Aiya had had no time to paint, nor did she have with her the traditional paints or brush with which to anoint the wagon. Aiya had decided that her sister would be delivered to her pyre in the same way she had exited this world, quietly and without any sign. Death came to her quickly and quietly in the night, and that was the way Aiya intended to bring her sister into the next world.

This was the second time that day she'd made the trek. She had followed the trail to the summit earlier that morning, with the materials in tow for the pyre she had built. Again, following the custom of her people, not letting the deceased stay trapped in their body during the night. Her time was falling short, night was approaching, but she was confident she would make it in time. It wasn't much farther.

She knew too, that she was being followed, but she didn't fear her pursuer. She couldn't tell for sure what or who was following her, but she was aware that it bore no malice toward her, and could tell that it was escorting her on her task. In a strange way the creature's presence did reassure and comfort her.

The grade of the climb became steeper and she had to adjust her grip on the cart behind her. She could feel the blisters forming beneath her gloves from the climb, and that too, reassured her. *Small price I pay for you Silan*, she thought. The tears began to stream down her face and she welcomed them. Sidhe were creatures of the air, of spirit and wind, of fire and water. Their emotions could be just as volatile, or as calm as a smooth reflective lake. *I'm sorry I failed you Silan, I was the Sword Maiden, your guardian and escort, it should be I in the kla'airt. I will make a reckoning sister, this I promise.*

Aiya pushed forward, her resolve to seek those who sent the *Ain'griefers* burning deeply in her bosom. She felt that her pledge to the *Maou'r* would bring her to them. They were most assuredly after him as much as they were after her sister.

Upon reaching the summit, she made her way to the edge of the cliff to where she had built the pyre. The structure overlooked all of Quailan and the Sylvan Kingdom to the South. It also looked upon her own kingdom, in the deep forest and hills the Sidhe had claimed at the beginning of time, before the Schism, the *Smarigeld Coill*, or in the common tongue, the Emerald Forest. The luscious vegetation did look like a precious jewel, its color rich and deep. Thinking of her homeland caused a knot to form in Aiya's throat. She was homesick, especially now—but now—when she returned, it would be alone, without Silan.

She put the hand rails down on the hard granite peak, and stepped to the rear of the cart. Her sister was wrapped in fine linen, the finest she could find in all of Quailan. It was the white of snow. She leaned into the cart and lifted her sister, cradling her in her arms. She stood, paused for a moment, and held her sister to her, holding her the way Silan had once held Aiya as a baby. *I'm so sorry, sister*, she thought.

The presence of her follower on the peak brought her back from her thoughts. She still felt no threat, nor did she feel its presence as an intrusion, somehow she knew it was here to pay its respects. This creature had sent many of its own to the next world.

She walked Silan to the pyre and gently laid the Sidhe onto the platform. The sticks and wood that comprised the structure were dry and brittle, ready to burn with great intensity.

There were not many words of farewell in the Sidhe ritual of release. Aiya bowed her head, thanked Gaia for bringing Silan into life, and giving them so much time together. Aiya asked Gaia to send Silan onto the next world quickly, and on an Easterly wind. She leaned into the pyre once more and kissed the linen that wrapped her sister's forehead, wishing her safe journey.

She stepped away from the pyre, looked into the sky which was beginning to turn orange and pink. Not night yet, she had completed her task in time. Thick clouds were moving in from the west and on them she sensed a dark foreboding. She turned back to the pyre and with a word, *tine'*, the pyre took flame. The wood caught instantly and grew into a blazing conflagration in seconds, the smoke swept eastward, off the Cliffs of Quailan and into the next world.

Aiya wasn't sure how long she watched the fire, time and space seemed to blend into mere seconds, but she had a feeling that she had stood for some time. The sky was now dark, her sister gone; only embers of the pyre remained. The clouds in the west were now upon her and the wind blew in great gusts. She turned from the cliff and smoldering pyre and with her keen Sidhe eyes saw the large shape of a dog standing along the tree line. It had stood there watching her since she arrived. It had paid its respects; she was sure, in its own way and then patiently waited for her to pay hers.

Aiya returned to the trail and continued her way down to the household once more, Boone following at a distance behind her.

62

Owen couldn't sleep. After Orla had left for the night, he'd finally gotten out of bed and tried his leg. She hadn't let him up, and had gotten him everything he'd needed, so it was the first time since she'd healed him that he could try walking on it. It hadn't even been a day, and he was still sore from the fight and fall, but now after being in bed for the whole day his muscles were really beginning to tighten. Besides, he really needed to go to the bathroom. He had found them his first day in the home; the one he knew of was down by the baths.

He climbed from bed and changed into his original Gypsylvanian clothes, except for the coat and vest. After he'd passed out, he'd been changed into some kind of oversized tunic and pajama like pants. He'd wondered who'd changed him, but hadn't the nerve to ask Orla about it, she had never mentioned it either.

After walking about his room, and putting on the new clothes, he was pleased to feel the dull ache in his leg start to subside. The tightness in his ribs was gone as well. He wondered what would have happened to him if Orla hadn't been around, or if she couldn't have healed him. He pushed the thoughts aside; he really needed to get downstairs.

He opened the door to the hall and stepped out. It was night now, and the estate seemed, for the most part, empty, if not asleep. The thought that the home was less than secure still bothered Owen, how many intruders do they need before they put more guards in the halls and on the walls? Something wasn't right here, and he was going to find out what.

Owen turned and began walking down the hall towards the main stairs that led to the baths and toilets below when he saw a dark robed, hooded figure, taking the stairs to the level above his room. He quickly stepped to the wall, melding with the shadows as best he could. *Damn, I should have worn my jacket*, he thought. But he was sure the figure hadn't seen him. It had been moving quickly, and with its hood up, had little or no peripheral vision.

He left the cover of the wall and quietly continued down the hall, the figure was just reaching the top step of the third floor. It quickly moved through the opening and into the hall above. Owen quickly and quietly followed up the stairs. His soft leather boots were almost silent on the stone steps. Once he reached the doorway of the third floor hall, he again placed himself against the wall and leaned into the hall. The light was dim; there were fewer lanterns along the walls on this floor, with large hanging tapestries between the lights. Owen caught a glimpse of movement and a dark shape at the end of the west hall before it slipped from view. He quickly stepped into the hallway and walked down the long corridor to where he thought he lost sight of the figure. There were no doors or windows along this section of the hall, just two huge, ornate tapestries.

Owen looked back and forth along the hallway, but there was no sign of the figure. *Had I really seen someone?* he thought as he again realized he really needed to pee. He turned and headed towards the stairs, taking them quickly on the way down, three at a time.

Once he was on the first floor, he turned into the lavatory. The room was similar in construction to the baths the floor below. Sculpted stone sinks lined one wall which a small current of running warm water ran through, while a series of stone toilets were enclosed in wooden privacy stalls along the back. Very similar to what Owen was used to back home, but everything looked to be carved, or magically hewn in stone. And from what Orla told him, the warm and hot water was produced naturally from hot springs below the town. The water did have a mild sulfur smell to it, but it was quite faint.

He stepped from the bathroom and considered heading back up to the third floor to further inspect the hallway where the robed figure had disappeared, but considered heading down to the baths for a quick dip to clean up some. He hadn't washed himself since the day before and even though Urma, he hoped it had been Urma, had cleaned off much of the blood and dirt from the battle, he still felt dirty and wanted to wash. He figured it was more psychological than anything else, but it still would be nice to soak some. He just hoped he didn't see any more spiders while he was there.

The room was as he remembered it. It was dark, warm, and moist. The steam poured from the bath. Owen didn't go into the changing room; he stripped next to the bath and slid in. No one would be down here at this time of night, he figured. The hot water felt wonderful along his aches and pains, the tight sore muscles, and the magically mended bones. He was surprised at how good it felt and how weary his body had been. *I still can't believe I jumped off the balcony, what was I thinking?*

He scrubbed the remaining grime from his body and had just dunked himself one final time, when he saw movement down at the drain. He hesitated, sinking into the water to just below his nose, leaving only the top half of his head above the water line. The movement headed his way and it didn't take long to make out the stepping of eight black and red legs along the ceiling. He shivered involuntarily as it moved his way. He tipped his head back, so only the tip of his nose and his eyes were above the water and watched as the spider walked along the ceiling above him. It stopped directly above, and if an insect can consider, it considered him, hanging by its four back legs while dangling the four foremost at Owen. He thought he could see its mandibles opening and closing as well.

He shuddered beneath the water, causing a slight ripple along its surface and gulped bath water involuntarily. The spider returned its legs to the surface of the ceiling and continued its journey from the bath, exiting out into the changing rooms and main hallway.

Owen scrambled from the bath, dressed quickly, and raced from the room, almost in a duck, with a cautious eye on the ceiling the whole way to his room. He stopped, and leaning on his door, caught his breath. *Okay, that thing freaks me out*, he thought. *There has got to be something with that spider.* He'd never been scared of spiders before, he had never much *liked* them, but they had never caused him such trepidation before.

After catching his breath he considered going into his room and trying to get some sleep, but he still wasn't tired. He couldn't make any more arrows because he didn't have any new shafts, *besides*, he thought, *I'm not sure I want to be back out there, especially at night, right now.* He concluded he'd head back up to the third floor, and seeing how there weren't any guards walking the halls or securing the building, he'd make it his own responsibility. He slipped into his room, extracted his bow and quiver from their resting place, and headed from the room.

Owen took the stairs slowly and cautiously, he was scared he might run into the robed figure coming down as he was heading up. He made it to the tapestries without incident. He was trying to remember the layout of the house again, but he couldn't remember what rooms were up along this hall. He was certain, though, this was the last place he'd seen the figure. The floor was well worn and the stones smooth and free of dirt or dust, so there was no chance of finding any tracks. He looked at the large tapestries. They both were easily ten feet high and close to fifteen feet across. They looked incredibly heavy. A thought came to him; he looked along the edges of the tapestries. They too were clean of any dust and were well cared for by the household staff. He walked to the point where he thought he last saw the robed person. It was right at the edge of the furthest tapestry from the stairs. Owen took the edge and pulled it from the wall. The lighting in the hall was too dim to see behind the thick matt. He let the wall hanging go, retreated down the hall, removed a lantern from the wall, and returned to the tapestry. He again pulled it away from the wall and lit the area with the lantern. There was indeed a small door behind the tapestry. *Alright!*

Owen considered going and waking Orla and Aiya, but wasn't sure if Nem would be about Orla's room, and he wasn't even sure if Aiya was back from her sister's funeral yet. He also thought that maybe he should go back and wait until morning to investigate the door, but by then there would be much more traffic in the hall. Then again, if he went now, there was a good chance he'd run into the person he was following.

He decided to chance it. If the door was unlocked then he would go, if it was locked, he'd wait to show Orla and Aiya. He stepped fully behind the tapestry and into the little alcove of the recessed door. He tried the pull ring but the door wouldn't budge. It was locked. He looked for a key hole, but didn't see one, but the door was indeed closed off. Maybe it was locked from the inside, or by magic. He would definitely have to wait for Orla now. *So much for getting some sleep tonight*, he thought as he stepped from behind the wall hanging, *I'll never be able to sleep now.*

As he began walking down the stairs a large clap of thunder made him jump slightly, while shaking several of the lanterns in the stairwell. With the clap of thunder the rain began, and in earnest. It was a torrent, pouring steadily with interspersed loud thunder and flashes of lightning. Owen thought it a little late in the season for a thunder storm, but then realized that things might be different in this world.

He reached his room without incident, realized once inside that he'd forgotten to replace the lantern, but figured it would be fine until morning. The rain was coming down so heavily that it was splashing in from his balcony. He closed one of the doors completely, but only closed the other partially. He liked the sound of the rain and wanted to continue to watch the storm and listen to the thunder. He pulled his chair over and used it as a door stop to keep the open door from swinging open any further. Having the one closed reduced the amount of rain coming in almost completely. He'd mop up the rest in the morning.

He thought of Boone and Winter, hoping both had found shelter to avoid the weather. It was not a good night to be out in the elements. He stripped down and climbed into bed. The weather was a good distraction; it helped take his mind off the tapestry and hidden door, and the rain eventually lulled him to sleep.

63

It's time to wake, Princess," Nem's voice whispered as she gently touched Orla's shoulder. She woke with a start. She'd been dreaming, but now the image was lost. The servant had begun to draw back the sheets and blanket, but stopped at the gasp from the startled Sylvan. Orla drew the blanket back up to her chin while she gathered her bearings.

"I'm terribly sorry, Ma'lady," Nem said, releasing the sheets and taking a step back, "didn't mean to startle you." The maid looked hurt.

"No, it's all right," I was just in the middle of a dream when you woke me," Orla pushed back her own sheets and climbed from bed before the servant could help her.

She still treats me like a child, as if I can't wake myself or get dressed on my own, Orla thought as she stepped to the end of her bed and pulled a robe from the corner post. When Orla turned, Nem had already laid out an outfit for her on her dressing table. Orla sighed.

"You were gone late last night, Princess," Nem said innocently.

"Was I?"

"Yes, and in that man's room, and un-chaperoned for most of it," the servent added quickly, less innocently.

"I was caring to his wounds," Orla began.

"But, Ma'lady, that's what the servants are for, it's very inappropriate for a lady such as yourself," Nem started, but was interrupted.

"That man is a friend, who was injured protecting our house because our own guards failed to do so," Orla said harshly, taking some of the fire from Nem's own argument, but the servant didn't relent.

"Ma'lady, from what I hear, those attackers were here for the strangers, no one else, and our guards had done such a fine job of containing the intruders to the courtyard."

"They cut off Owen and Aiya from any aid, condemning them to death," Orla hissed through clenched teeth. Nem was really starting to make her angry when it came to Owen, *what does she have against him anyway, he saved me for Gaia's sake?*

"Orla," Nem began, reserving calling her by name only when she truly felt the Princess was missing a point she was trying to make, growing up it was when Orla had truly gotten herself into trouble. "We've had nothing but trouble since that McInish arrived."

"He brought me back! He saved me more than once from creatures and people who wanted me dead!" Orla shouted, finally beyond angry. "And my abduction wasn't any trouble? That was before Owen was here!"

"Something he probably had everything to do with," Nem added under her breath as she lowered her head in submission and defeat. "I'm sorry, Ma'lady, I'm only trying to look out for your best interest."

"Well, I'm not a child anymore, and you're not my mother. I can look after myself. I had to when I ended up on the other side of Parathas." Nem's hurt expression from Orla's words made her feel guilty for a moment, but it was past time she reminded Nem of her place. She was not her mom, nor would she ever be, and Orla was the Princess of this house, and almost an adult who could make her own decisions.

"You might as well put those away," Orla said indicating the clothes Nem had prepared. "I have something else in mind for today." She stepped out onto the balcony with the intention of staying there until Nem left, but a knock on the door drew her attention back through the terrace doors.

"The Princess is not yet proper, you'll have to," Orla could hear Nem saying.

"Who is it Nem?"

"Master McInish and the Sidhe Sword Mistress," Nem said with an acid tone that Orla thought inappropriate, but she let it go.

"Show them in, and thank you, you may go," Orla said, dismissing the woman.

"But, Princess, I haven't finished making the bed," Nem said indignantly.

"I'm perfectly capable of making it myself; thank you, Nem, that is all." The woman shrank to her warbler form and shot from the room like a bolt of lightning. Owen and Aiya entered, both dressed as if ready for adventure.

"Give me a minute to dress, then we can go where we may talk freely," Orla said, stepping back into her room. She stepped into her closet and drew out several items in which to change. She looked to Owen and Aiya who were watching her. She smiled at Owen.

"Just because Nem isn't here doesn't mean you still don't have to turn around." Owen blushed to Orla's amusement and turned around immediately. She even saw a smile from Aiya at the embarrassment she'd caused the young man, but then immediately felt guilty for joking during an obvious time of mourning for the Sidhe.

"I'm sorry for your loss, Aiya, and for my behavior, I should…"

Aiya stopped her with her hand, smiling sadly at the young Princess. "Not at all, Princess. Humor is one of Gaia's remedies for healing our most grievous wounds of the heart. You don't need to apologize; Silan would not want any of us to be sad about her journey. She would want us to rejoice at her departure to the next world," Aiya said stoically. If she believed the words she spoke, she was having difficulty saying them convincingly. It was still too close, the pain still too much on the surface. Orla nodded her understanding and dressed quickly.

Once finished, she told Owen he could turn around, the redness had faded from his cheeks, but he still looked embarrassed.

"I think it best if we leave the house to discuss what we need to," Orla said, with nods of agreement from her two companions. The three left her room, and exited the house through the main gate, quickly heading out of the city and west, not speaking, and traveling in silence.

64

The companions came to a small clearing within the wood which suited their needs. The three sat and waited quietly for their fourth. It wasn't long before Boone entered the clearing and again excitedly greeted Owen by bumping his shoulder into the boy's stomach and hips, while lifting his great head in greeting. Owen was as excited to see Boone again.

Orla watched and smiled in wonder at how quickly the two had become so close. The link between the *Maou'r* and his *Duine Madra* was something of great magick for certain, she mused, as Boone took in the other attendants of their gathering. Orla smiled at him, and he greeted her in similair fashion to Owen with only slightly less enthusiasm, but then he turned and looked at Aiya.

The otherwise stoic elf was in awe of the dog before her. She had seen the animal the night before, but not this closely. She had wondered if the beast had come with the *Maou'r*, but hadn't known for sure.

"*Duine Madra*? But we believed you extinct," she stammered quietly.

I am the last. The companions all heard, Owen's heart warming at the soft rumbling in his head once more, like warm cocoa on a cold winter day.

Aiya turned her attention back to Owen and looked at him in further admiration and appreciation. "If I had any doubts of your true origins, they are now gone," the Sidhe said to him. She looked back at the great dog, "It is an honor to meet you, and to hopefully travel in your presence…again," Aiya said, bowing her head reverently.

Boone nodded his appreciation.

Owen looked at his dog that sat by his side.

I am sorry for your loss. I should have been there.

It was Aiya's turn to nod. "It was the right thing to do; no one suspects the *Maou'r* is in Quailan. Most don't even consider the possibility."

Boone looked to Owen, *you look fit considering the attack, I am grateful for that.*

"Thanks to Orla," Owen said, smiling at the *Fey* across from him.

Then I am indebted to you, Princess.

Orla smiled, and blushed slightly at the praise from both Owen and the *Madra.*

"You should be proud of your charge, he fought bravely, and without his aid, two Sidhe maidens would have made the journey last night. It *was* you who followed me in the wood?" Aiya asked, letting her gaze drift back to the summit of the cliff face.

Yes. Boone rumbled in all their minds. They all knew the great dog regretted not being there the previous night, and knew that he must have grieved for the Sidhe lost. They also knew that while in the wood that night, he would have let no harm come to Aiya during her time of grief.

"I found a secret door behind a tapestry on the floor above my room," Owen broke the silence.

To where?

"Dunno, the door was locked," Owen offered, slightly deflated at not having more information. "But I saw a dark robed figure enter it, he might have been the one in my dreams. It was tough to tell."

"I didn't know of a passage there," Orla said dumbfounded. An embarrassed look crossed her face quickly replaced by anger. "I am the head of that house, steward or no. With my father gone, I'm old enough now to be in charge, and they're keeping hidden passages from me?" Owen could see how enraged she was. The betrayal of her home kept getting worse.

"I don't like this, we should leave at once," Aiya added. She was standing somewhat apart from the other three in attendance, unsure of her place amongst the three friends.

"But Winter said to wait," Owen added.

The Aingeal did say to wait, but I don't think he foresaw the events unfolding within Quailan.

"They're right, Owen," Orla said, sounding defeated. "I told Winter you'd be safe, and right now, that's anything but the truth. You should go."

"What?" Owen couldn't believe it. "No way, you think you're any safer?"

"Well, but," Orla started, realization coming slowly to her. *No, I'm not safe. He's right. Whoever banished me may be a part of the household, may still be there!*

"If I leave, we all leave," Owen concluded for everyone, "but we would need a way to get word to Winter." The others nodded their agreement. The Hunter would be arriving, soon possibly, and they would want him to be able to follow them quickly and easily. "But where do we head?"

"Narsus," Orla said, matter of factly. "It was where I was headed last time, and I don't know for sure, but I don't think I ever got there. I think whoever abducted me didn't want me to get there and that's why they got rid of me," *and they couldn't kill me themselves. For whatever reason, they couldn't do it, so they gave others the means and reason to do it*, she thought to herself.

"It's a logical place to head," Aiya added. "The Sylvan council is still meeting to decide their position on Reunification before the Kingdom's officials meet to debate the issue. All of the Kingdom will be within the walls of Narsus in less than one moon's time."

"All of the Kingdom?" Owen asked. Even he thought the idea sounded like a bad one. Everyone in one place, at once.

"Ambassadors from all of the Treaty Kingdoms will meet in Narsus to discuss the matter. Narsus has always been the central point, neutral ground for most countries to meet like this," Orla explained.

Owen and Aiya made eye contact, she didn't like it either. It was the place to start. Whoever was behind this didn't want Orla there, and Owen hoped he could find a lead to his parents there.

"Okay, the where is settled, now the when," he said, looking to Boone to see if the big dog felt the same as he did. He nodded his massive head.

"Tonight," Aiya said.

"Too soon, I need to settle some affairs, make arrangements to get word to Winter," Orla said, surprised at the speed with which the group wanted to leave.

Too soon, Owen also thought.

"Is that what cost you your plan last time?" Aiya asked, not cruelly, but simply asking a question. It was a good point, Owen thought.

"Maybe she's right," Owen offered. "I know you can't remember, but maybe it was someone you told, or left a note for last time that aided, if not committed your abduction," Owen saw the pain in her eyes and wished he could comfort her, but it was beginning to look more and more like someone close to her had been involved.

"Or maybe not," Owen offered. "We won't know until you get your memory back, so we should be careful who we contact."

Orla nodded, a resolve taking shape in her eyes as they teared up slightly. "I have two people whom I know I can trust and with whom we can leave word for Winter. They are not of the household, Owen has met them. I feel they're our best chance of leaving and getting word to him." Orla looked at the three others facing her, Aiya still seemed skeptical, Owen and Boone both nodded their agreement.

"How long to leave them word?" Aiya asked finally.

"I can get word to them tonight; we can leave late tonight, early tomorrow," Orla suggested. A firmness taking hold of her voice, the more the plans solidified, the better she was with them. She had promised Winter Owen would be safe, and Quailan was proving her wrong, it was time to move from here. She was becoming more resolved to solve the mystery of her own disappearance. She had expected more of an investigation and more concern over her abduction when she returned home; instead, most of the house had reacted to her vanishing as if she had run away like a silly, spoiled, little girl.

Enough time, Owen thought. *I can do it by then.*

As if reading his mind, Boone asked, *and the passage?*

"I suggest we leave it, too dangerous to bother with now, we need to move, and quickly," Aiya suggested.

I agree, the great dog added, bumping his head into Owen's side as if to emphasize his point with the boy.

"I don't like to leave without knowing what is behind that door, but I think you're right, it's too dangerous to investigate now. We need to get clear of Quailan." Orla looked at Owen, made eye contact, and looked away.

I hope she knows what I'm thinking, Owen thought to himself. *Or, I'll be waiting alone at the door for her.*

I'll meet the three of you by the garden gate at midnight, if there's trouble Owen, whistle. With that the large dog trotted back the way he'd come into the clearing, his tail raised and arched over his back, his ears forward and alert, his head lowered to the trail.

The three other companions returned to the trail they had come by and returned in silence to Orla's family estate. At the front gate, before entering, they stopped and in hushed voices agreed to meet at a quarter to midnight in the courtyard. They were to travel light, Aiya and Orla would collect what extra food they could from the scullery. Their capability for stealth outweighed Owen's willingness to help. All other supplies would be their own personal packs and traveling gear.

They entered the household and went their three separate ways, Owen and Orla stealing glances at one another as they went.

65

A cool autumn breeze blew Orla's hair slightly as she sat with her legs crossed on her bed. Her terrace doors were swung open, letting in the cool crisp air, and letting out Orla's soft chanting. Her eyes closed, her hands resting lightly on her knees, two black-capped chickadees entered her bed chamber, answering her call.

The two birds rested themselves on her outstretched fingers, one in either hand. At their slightest touch the Sylvan opened her eyes and smiled down at the two birds. She was pleased with her achievement. They tilted their heads this way and that and chipped at the young girl. One letting out a *phoebe* while the other a *chic-a-dee-dee-dee* waiting impatiently for their instructions.

"Okay, okay, geez," she said. "I need you," she looked at the bird in her left hand, "to find Fawn, and you," indicating the bird in her right, "to find Luna, and give them this message:" The two birds stood a bit straighter and prepared themselves for their charge, for chickadees are very responsible birds. "I, Orla, am leaving again. You must wait and seek the *Aingeal*, *Geimhreidh*, when he comes to Quailan and before coming to my household. He will most likely come quietly and unseen, but my two friends (you two) will watch for him and alert you of his presence. They will also tell him to seek you out as well. Tell him of the note from before and of my disappearance, and tell him we have headed again towards Narsus. Be safe. And lastly, but most importantly, I am sending Maya to your care. Watch her for me," she lifted her hands up off her knees, and after considering the Princess one last time, the two birds took flight and left her room.

Orla turned her attention to her closet and began pulling out clothes and supplies to bring with her when she left this evening. She needed everything ready long before midnight, because she was certain Owen would be expecting her at the tapestry before they met with Aiya.

66

Owen stepped behind the tapestry. He lit the door with the lantern he'd brought and waited in the alcove of the locked door. The tapestry behind him completely absorbed and blocked the light from escaping into the hallway beyond the hanging. He wasn't certain the look he and Orla had exchanged meant she'd meet him here. He just hoped he'd explained the door well enough in the clearing with everyone else that she'd be able to find it.

It seemed like an hour passed before there was movement on the edge of the wall hanging and Orla's soft songbird voice whispered from the gloom of the hall, "Owen?"

"In here, quickly, before someone sees you," he whispered back, glad that she had come. His heart raced and only partly for the adventure waiting beyond the locked door.

"I thought I'd find you here," she said, as she stepped into the alcove with him. Owen immediately became aware of how small a space it was.

"It's locked, I think magically, from the inside, I needed help getting in," he explained, using the lantern to light the door and show the Sylvan what he'd found.

"Sorry I didn't get hear sooner, I had to convince Maya to go with Luna and Fawn. She didn't want me leaving again, and wasn't too keen on going with them."

Owen frowned slightly, "You think they'll stay quiet about all this until we slip out tonight?"

"Yes," Orla answered without question. "They may be the only people I'm sure about anymore," she said meekly.

Owen nodded his understanding and turned his attention back to the door.

"Hmm, not sure if I can crack it, I'll have a try, but what if someone comes while we're in there?" Orla said, while running her hands along the edge of the door and frame.

"Yeah, I was thinking of that," Owen said, he knew she wouldn't be happy with his plan, "That's why I think it best you wait here."

"*What?*"

"Listen a sec," Owen added quickly. "You wait outside in the hall. That way if the person in the robe comes, or anyone else who knows about this door, you can stall them or, if we're really lucky, whoever it is will just keep walking down the hall, and not even bother stopping for fear of you finding out about the door," Owen said trying to finish before Orla could cut him off.

"I don't like it."

"Yeah, I knew you wouldn't, but you have enough pull to keep anyone from following me. If we both go, we could get cornered down there, where no one will be able to help or find us."

Orla thought for a moment, she knew he was right. Whoever abducted her wouldn't have done it in the open; they would have done it in secret. Someone in the household might be against her and her family, but certainly not everyone. And if the person did happen by while she was there, chances are they would just keep going rather than chance stopping.

"What do I say I'm doing if someone comes by?" she asked, and Owen knew then that she'd agreed to his plan.

"Dunno. You'll have to come up with something. Sleepwalking maybe?" Owen smirked.

"What if they're already down there?"

"Then I'll have to be extra quiet," Owen said, feeling more confident about going down the hall.

"I'm quieter," Orla said, still not wanting to concede completely.

"I know, but I couldn't stop anyone in the hall, besides most guards would jump at the chance to lock me up for acting funny or being awake and about at this hour," Owen said, and remembered they had a schedule to keep. "Speaking of late, we only have about an hour to go before we need to meet Aiya; you better give this a shot."

Orla leaned against the door, placing both her splayed hands around the door ring. She slowed her breathing, concentrated on the complex incantation in her mind, and slowly let the words and energy escape her mouth, pushing the magick energies through her fingertips into the door and into the lock on the other side.

Owen had been right, there was no mechanism. It had been a magick lock. A tough one too, but Orla had been strong enough to break it. Whoever had cast it hadn't thought their work would have been challenged magically, or else they would have placed protective charms over the spell and wards upon the door. The door opened slightly on well oiled hinges, not making a sound.

"Okay, be back in a jiff," Owen said, trying to sound braver than he felt at the moment.

"Be safe," Orla said, as she stepped back and let him pass into the doorway. She fought and won the sudden urge to give him a kiss on his cheek for luck, and before she knew it, thankfully, the moment had passed.

She closed the door slightly behind Owen, and stepped out from behind the tapestry. She had no idea what she would say if someone came down the hallway.

Owen stepped into the dark corridor, his lantern the only light. The beam from it shown weakly down the hall, fading into darkness only ten meters from the entrance. Owen slowly began walking down the hall until it abruptly stopped at a spiral staircase heading down. He considered going back and telling Orla what he had found, but decided he needed to move quickly, he could give her a full report once he came back. He quickly and quietly started down the stairs that were hewn from a type of granite, Owen concluded. As he traveled down the stairwell it soon became warmer and more humid, he suddenly realized he must be close to the baths and hot springs.

The stairs ended in a damp and moss covered half moon tunnel. The walls and ceiling were completely rounded and covered in a thick green moss. The floor was clear of the vegetation, but slick to walk on. There was a worn path in the center of the tunnel. Owen began following the passageway. As he walked, he could hear the hot streams moving along the walls around him. At one junction he actually came to the exit drain in the floor of the men's bath room. Bending over, he could look through, under the stone wall where the bath water passed into the tunnel. He stood up; this was the tunnel the spider used. He gulped, holding the lantern up to light the ceiling over his head and the walls closest to him.

The tunnel continued away from him. He walked farther, trying to remember all the bends and turns. He came to a T intersection and chose the tunnel to his left. Owen walked another few minutes and came to the tunnel exit that looked and smelled like they joined the main sewer system for Quailan. Owen began back tracking the way he'd come. Disappointment bombarded him and brought down his already somber mood. He'd hoped this corridor would bring some clues as to who had abducted Orla.

As Owen followed the tunnel back, he stopped at the intersection. Bending to the floor, he brought the lantern down to the stone, and then held it up in front of him in the direction of the new tunnel. The floor had that same, similar wear to it down the middle. He didn't hesitate; he took the new way, hoping he wouldn't get himself too lost in the process and not be late to meet Aiya.

The floor had a gradual incline to it, which offered some hope to Owen that he was at least heading back towards Orla, one of the general directions he needed to head at least. The tunnel bent slightly, and as Owen and the beam of light came around the corner he illuminated two large, reinforced, double doors.

He stepped up to them and was disappointed to find them locked.

Cursing under his breath, he was startled by the quiet giggle behind him. He nearly jumped into the ceiling. He spun around to find himself face to face with Orla.

"What are you doing here?" he whispered, as he caught his breath.

"Looking for you," she answered. "It's getting late, and besides, standing in the hall was dull."

"No one came by?"

"No, not a soul," she said, looking up at the enormous doors. "I've lived here my whole life and never knew these tunnels existed." The tone of her of voice was far away, disillusioned, the tone of a child discovering the truth about some long thought belief.

"Locked?" she asked.

"Locked."

Orla leaned her hands against the doors, again in the same fashion as upstairs, and with the same slight blue glow pushing from her fingers, opened the two giant doors.

The smell of old, coagulated, spoiled, and fermenting blood escaped the room from behind the doors, making both Owen and Orla cover their mouths and noses and fight against vomiting. The stench made their eyes water, and clung to the backs of their throats.

Owen held up the lantern and forced himself into the room.

As they entered it lit of its own accord, causing the two friends to pause momentarily in fright, thinking themselves discovered. The room was gigantic. In the middle of the room were four posts with something lying still amongst them. As they approached they realized this was the source of the stench. Owen at first thought the dead animal was a horse, a dead horse, once white, but covered in dried blood. Then he saw the large wound to the animal's forehead and had another thought. Orla voiced his guess.

"Unicorn. Someone killed a unicorn in my home," she choked. Tears streamed down her cheeks and her shoulders shook. "How could someone do this? How could someone kill a unicorn?" She bent low to the dead animal, wanting to touch it, to make sure what she was seeing was real. She stopped just short of touching it, the realization just too horrifying.

"They're sacred animals, pure, as innocent as a child," she whispered. The beast's horn had been dug from its skull.

Owen looked about the chamber and saw three sets of manacles on the floor of the chamber. Something else had been bound here. He saw the splash marks from the unicorn's blood and saw how it would have splashed and covered the other captives.

"Orla look," he said, pulling her attention away from the animal.

She looked at the floor and back to the dead animal. "This is where the trolls were changed, where they came from, how they got into the sewers," she whispered the words, as if saying it any louder would make even more true.

"How could anyone do this?" she asked again.

Owen looked around the room and saw another door on the far side, a smaller, people sized door. He touched Orla's shoulder gently and pointed towards the door. They both slowly walked towards it, knowing that it would bring them closer to the person who had been hunting Orla since they met.

67

Unlocking the next door was as simple as the first two for Orla. She smiled despite herself. The growing concern that she knew only one other person in the house that could wield magick was weighing heavily on her, but every time she broke through another of her adversary's lock spells provided her with a boost to her pride and ego. However, she always came back to the thought that the person setting these locks was also the same person that probably banished her to Owen's realm, and in doing so, intended her to die there.

Chamberlain.

The door opened as quietly as the others, swinging lightly on its hinges. The two friends stepped into the hallway. It was dank and damp, and immediately started to climb upward on a steep angle, switch backing on itself on each end. They began to climb.

"Any idea how long we've been in here?" Owen asked, becoming worried they were going to miss their meeting with Aiya.

"We still have some time, depending on where this comes out. We'll be on schedule," Orla said, preoccupied with where this tunnel would exit. She was trying to form the layout of the labyrinth, mapping it as she'd been walking through it, and coming to the conclusion this would lead beneath the upper floors of her home.

They finally came to another wooden door, unremarkable like the others. Door ring, no lock, but magically secured none the less. Orla placed her hand to it and willed it to open, speaking the incantation to unlock it.

It unlocked without a sound, opening slightly. They stood in the back of a large fireplace. Thankfully, the fire was small and the heat being thrown by it was not overwhelming. The slight crackling and spitting of the blaze was enough to disguise the slight noise of their stepping through into the hearth from the hooded figure with its back to them. The cloaked individual was bent over a desk, intent on what it was doing.

The hallway caused a slight draft, pulling the flames towards them and increasing the height and intensity of the fire. They stepped out of the doorway and closed the door behind them; automatically sealing itself on closing, a function of the charm.

Owen could slightly, but Orla more clearly with her *Fey* hearing, hear the conversation. The bent figure seemed to be talking to something or someone in front of him, beyond Owen and Orla's view.

"Now that I have the statues, deal with the boy. He's been nothing but trouble, and he is no longer a commodity," a voice crackled over static, the sound of glass breaking during an electrical storm.

"Yes, Master," the bent figure answered with a slight, quiet voice. Owen and Orla both looked at one another. They recognized that voice, there was no doubt. Chamberlain.

"And deal with the girl. Enough of your pititful attempts, do it and be done with it. I am growing tired of your weakness. We cannot afford her memory returning," the crackling croaked. Orla stiffened at the command.

"But Master, she knows nothing…"

"Do you question me?" hissed the static.

"No Master, but her memories are gone…," the hooded figure said.

"Do it right this time, stop contracting out what you should be doing yourself," the voice crackled. "Or, I'll send my *Ain'grifer* for her and you next."

The static sound faded, and the bent figure righted itself. It stood from the stool it had been sitting on while taking a small scarf from the table in front of it. Before the figure draped the scarf over the orb, Owen and Orla saw the small blue sphere the figure had been speaking into.

Chamberlain stepped around the table and headed towards the door on the far wall. He stopped and turned back towards the fireplace. Owen and Orla had already kneeled within the hearth, hiding as best they could within its confines.

"You heard?" Chamberlain asked. Both Owen and Orla stiffened, thinking themselves discovered.

"Yes," came the answer from outside the fireplace, just to the left. Another dark robed figured stepped into view, and approached Chamberlain by the door. It stopped next to him; the second was slightly shorter, and thinner in the shoulders than the first.

"Will you be going to Narsus then?" the second asked. Orla and Owen made eye contact again, they knew that voice. Nem.

"Not just yet," Chamberlain answered, pausing a moment, stealing a look back to the covered orb on the table.

"Do it tonight, be quick about it…for her. She need not suffer. I'll deal with the sword witch and boy. Those two will feel my pain for losing her. We'll make it look as if the Sidhe killed them both, and then ended her own life," he said and then opened the door. Nem left first, followed by Chamberlain who closed the door behind him.

Owen and Orla both exhaled at the same time. They waited a moment longer before stepping from the fire pit. Owen was sweating profusely. Orla looked as cool and comfortable as always, if not slightly ruffled by what she'd overheard.

Owen turned to her, "We need to get out of here now, they could be back any minute."

"I know," Orla said, and quickly rushed to the door. She leaned her ear to it, and confident there was no one on the other side, shifted to leopard form. She sniffed the bottom of the door to make sure.

She looked back to Owen, and even in her leopard form, Owen could see the hurt in her eyes.

"Orla," he began, but the leopard shook her head.

Orla shifted back and eased the door open, and stepped out into the hallway of the servants' quarters. The hall was empty and quiet;

everyone was asleep at this time with the exception of the night watch. They were supposed to be awake at least. The room they had been in was a small den and study provided to the servants for their time off and recreation.

Orla leaned back into the room. "Now we know who sent me to you," she said, but it was clear in her tone, this was not a topic for conversation right now.

The two friends quickly exited the quarters and took the stairs down to the family's quarters and then down into the courtyard. As they stepped into the moonlight of the yard a lithe figure stepped from the shadows. Aiya wore her sea green cloak over her armor. She carried a small pack on her back, with a satchel over one shoulder. Her quiver and bow over the other.

"You're late, I was beginning to worry," she whispered, stepping in alongside the two as they approached the gardener's gate.

"We must be away, I am uneasy about this night," she said as they stepped out into the alleyway.

68

Boone was waiting for the threesome as they stepped out into the alley. Even he seemed on edge to Owen. Owen stole a glance towards Orla, he was worried how she was taking what they'd just found out in the catacombs beneath the house. She had been quiet since they overheard Chamberlain and Nem talking, but then again, sneaking out of the house in the middle of the night wasn't the most opportune time for conversation.

As they stepped into the alley the great dog again stepped from the shadows, padding softly over to Owen. He greeted his *Maou'r* by bumping his head into his stomach as normal but then paused. The dog stopped and looked into the boy's eyes.

You opened the door. It was a statement not a question. Owen couldn't hide it from the dog, he had no idea how he knew, but the *Duine Madra* knew; there was no questioning it or trying to deny it.

"Later," Owen said. "We need to get out of here quickly; you need to take us the fastest way." The dog nodded, turned, and headed down the alley towards the forest, leading west.

Aiya stepped in line, taking the rear guard, Owen and Orla staying close together, side by side, followed Boone. Owen continually looked over at his friend, concern creasing his face in the dim glow of the moonlight. Orla, however, was lost in thought; she focused on the dog in front of her and let herself follow the animal on autopilot while her mind raced through the night's events. She tried desperately to remember what had happened before being sent to Owen's world, anything that could explain how Nem and Chamberlain could do this to her. *Why were they robed? They didn't know we were there. Why would they hide their faces like that?*

The company traveled silently through the wood with only the occasional broken branch from Owen. It felt good to be hiking again, the familiar stretching and working of the muscles in his legs made him feel alive, as if during the last week he'd been lying in bed, never moving. He was surprised at how light the night truly was under the voyeur moon, and at how easily he moved within the wood.

They traveled quickly through the trees, not looking back, not even Orla. She had left a piece of herself behind in Quailan, a piece of her youth that in part saddened her, but in another part empowered her. She was the young Princess no more. Now she was a piece of something greater. She could sense that, the way she could sense the morning light upon her face in the early hours before being fully awake. She didn't know what that something greater was, or what part she would play, but in leaving Quailan with this small band of refugees and warriors, she was taking her first step in a very different direction than she had ever believed her life would take.

The storm clouds moved in quickly, less than an hour after their departure from Quailan and threatened the small band early in their journey. They could feel the sudden change in air pressure, and the sudden gusts of wind forcing its way through the humid skies in the valley of the Quailan Sylvans.

Boone led them into the mountains and ledges they had passed after crossing Fall's Bridge. They could hear the river and falls to their left, even though they never came in sight of them. The great dog led them into the cliffs and rock that ran parallel to the massive river that emptied into the falls.

It was in these cliffs when the rains finally came.

Boone found a series of rock over hangs that provided shelter from the rain and wind. The travelers hid beneath the lee and waited for the storm to pass. While waiting, they laid out their bed rolls and blankets and ate some of the hardtack they had brought with them. The company felt they were still too close to Quailan to risk a fire for cooking, or for drying off and chasing away the chill. The mood had become dark, brooding, and quiet with the foul weather, and everyone except Boone huddled under bedding and waited for the storm to pass.

Someone is coming, Boone said, his rumbling voice echoing in their minds. *Quite close. I just picked up the faintest sound, but whoever it is, is very good at going undetected. I should have picked up his scent by now, but he is being very careful to mask it from me. Be on your guard.*

Owen knocked an arrow into his bow, and freed himself of most of the blanket, making it easy enough to throw off if needed. Orla had already changed into her hybrid form, and even though Owen couldn't see Aiya from his vantage point, he knew she would be ready too.

"Is there room enough for another wet and weary traveler," a familiar voice called from above the rock ledge. It was the sound of a brisk winter wind on a bright and clear day.

"Winter!" Owen and Orla exclaimed at once, throwing off their bedding and racing towards the front of the overhang.

Boone too was up, but he was a bit more cautious, placing himself between the young ones and the traveler now appearing in the entrance of their dry retreat. The tall man stepped into the cramped space, hunching slightly from the low ceiling, and drew back his hood. The whitened red hair tumbled out from beneath the cowl, giving frame to the pale blue eyes. A slight smile creased the weather worn face as he looked down upon his three traveling companions.

"None of you look the worse for wear," he said, taking a seat along a rock wall and shaking the water from his shoulders. Boone, convinced of the true identity of the traveler retreated deeper within the shelter as Orla and Owen took seats to either side of the *Aingeal.*

"Now tell me, what have all of you been up to, and why are you making haste from Quailan?"

69

It seems you have all been as busy as I," Winter said after digesting all the news that Orla and Owen had delivered to him since his arrival. Aiya and Boone sat quietly; the former had actually not even been introduced formerly to the Hunter, only mentioned within the two young people's tale and indicated with a nod from Owen and Orla. Owen realized his rudeness on finishing his recapping of events. He was so excited at Winter's return, and in wanting to get the archer up to speed as quickly as possible, he had forgotten his manners.

"I'm sorry," he said quickly, standing and stepping beside Aiya, "Winter this Aiya, Aiya, Winter," Owen said awkwardly. Orla too blushed at her lapse in manners. She was visibly relieved to have Winter back amongst their company. His shear presence was a reassurance.

The *Aingeal* stood and bowed deeply, amazingly fluid and graceful for such a large man, to the Sidhe sitting across from him. She had seated herself within earshot of the two younger people telling their tale of the last week, but had not wanted to impose herself upon the friends. She sat quietly, hood up, in the shadows of the shelter. After Winter had stood and bowed, Aiya also stood, pulling back her hood and returned the gesture.

"It is an honor to meet one of the *Aingeal*," Aiya said, after standing from her bow. "The Sidhe are raised on the stories of your people."

Winter smiled slightly and inclined his head towards the Sword Maiden. It had been a long time since he'd been in the company of one of their race, and he'd forgotten how fair a people they were, and how elegant.

Owen and Orla had done well, enlisting one of their Sword Maidens to their cause.

"It is good that you were on your way, danger was closing in on Quailan from the outside, let alone within," the Hunter said, as he sat back down and pulled a piece of dried meat from a pouch at his belt. He un-slung his pack and quiver and laid them out alongside him. He removed his two-handed sword as well, placing it beside his other possessions. Owen noticed strapped to his pack what looked like another sword, wrapped in deerskin.

"Did you get your errands done?" Owen asked, filling the quiet.

"For the most part," the First Man replied. "The first was completed with the aid of the head of our clan. For the second, I finished what I set out to do, and that was to find that which was drawing my attention west. However, on finding the disturbance—for the time being—I was unable to affect any further course upon it."

None of the party said anything. Owen looked about their faces. Boone's eyes were closed and he was seemingly asleep, which Owen knew he wasn't. Aiya's face was its normal calm, stoic facade. Only in Orla did Owen seem to find the same blank stare Winter's explanation induced in him.

"I traveled as far as the Thorne Mountains and found that one of the Great Deymon's had been awakened, drawn forth, and unleashed upon Parathas," he said, his voice cold and distant like a January wind in the middle of a cold clear night. Boone lifted his head at the sound of the revelation. Even Aiya shifted slightly, stiffening at the news.

"But how?' she whispered.

"The Witch Queen brought it forth," Winter said simply, sadly.

"Lilith," Aiya said quietly, as if to say it any louder would bring the Queen of Darkness into their shelter with them.

"But, I thought….," Aiya began, but then cast her eyes to the ground.

"She was just stories like the First Men? Or possibly she was long since past like many of us?"

"Yes," Aiya said, embarrassed.

"No, she is very much real, and very much as dark as the stories. She must have felt the *Maou'r* and summoned the beast to find him and bring him to her."

70

The rain let up slightly in the early morning, long after three of the small band had called it a night. As Owen drifted off to sleep beneath his blanket, back to back with Orla in her hybrid form, his last sight was of the King of the Dogs and the Lord of the Hunt keeping watch by the mouth of their small, rock shelter.

Boone sat to one side of the opening, just inside and out of the rain and wind. His ears up and forward, scanning for any noise. The *Aingeal* of Winter and Hunting had managed to get to striking distance of the overhang before Boone had heard him. The fact that Winter was the hunter of myth made little difference to the dog, he had failed his watch in not spotting him sooner. He would not do so again. His eyes scanned the dark, looking for any movement within the shadows.

Winter sat leaning against the rock shelter. His hood pulled down to his brow, only his bearded chin and mouth visible from the shadows within. His great sword leaned against the wall behind him, while his quiver and bow lay next to him. Across his lap was the bundle Owen had noticed strapped to the side of his pack that now lay to the opposite side of him from his bow. His long legs were stretched out before him, and as Owen slipped into sleep he thought the once-god seemed weary.

The quieting of the wind brought Owen out of his slumber. He opened his eyes to find Boone in the same place he had been when Owen had fallen asleep. Winter too was where he left him; his head was tilted backwards however, resting the crown of his head along the wall behind him.

Owen sat up, realizing he was the last to awaken that morning. Orla and Aiya were closer to the back of the overhang, eating a meager breakfast, already dressed and ready to go.

"No rush, Owen," Winter said, without changing his position or looking at him. "The rain is beginning to lessen, and we will wait for it to stop further before we leave. The Vrok travels not by day, and we still have a bit of a lead. We will all do better to begin this journey dry, rather than not."

His voice filled the whole cave and Owen realized he had not been talking just to him, but to everyone within the shelter. Owen still didn't know anything about this Greater Deymon. The Vrok, Winter had just called it. It was unsettling to have yet another predator on their trail Owen knew nothing about. He would later regret learning more about it.

The rain didn't last much longer and the small band was again on their way. It was still early morning, but Chamberlain should have begun searching for Orla already. With Winter leading the small group, however, he had little concern of being discovered. *Although*, Owen thought, *the household never did anything else the way I thought they should.*

Winter took his usual place at point while Aiya took the rear guard. The elf had been her usual quiet self, but very interested in watching the archer through the morning while prepping for their journey. Boone took his place by Owen when the trail allowed it or behind him when it didn't. Owen and Orla again walked together unless they were traversing single file.

The band hadn't traveled far when Winter stopped to inspect the trail ahead of them. He said he found some unusual tracks in the cliffs on his way to their overhang last night, ones that had intersected the party's while he had been trailing them. He thought the sign he was seeing now was connected to what he saw the previous night.

Owen couldn't see anything on the trail other than leaves, moss, and dirt, but he took the Hunter's word for it. When asked what he thought the tracks belonged to, the Hunter kept silent and his opinion to himself as he moved the party in the direction they'd been heading.

The Hunter's mood had shifted again since the night before. His demeanor was similar to that before he left them on the edge of Quailan, he seemed distracted and elsewhere with his thoughts, a notable difference from his genuine excitement at seeing Orla and Owen the previous evening.

Understandable I guess, Owen thought as he hiked the rugged terrain behind the Hunter, *considering there's some new monster following us and Orla's own household was trying to kill her.* He had wanted to question Orla about the new threat, but they hadn't the time before leaving, and were never left alone long enough where he felt comfortable asking her. Orla's demeanor had changed for the better with Winter's return, as had his own, and he didn't want to chance bringing up Chamberlain and ruining that.

Winter stopped ahead of them on the trail and held up his hand, motioning them to stop. Boone pushed his way between Owen and Orla, taking a stance in front of them. Owen didn't hear it, but he was sure Aiya had unsheathed her sword as well. Orla stayed in Sylvan form for the moment, but Owen could feel the slight electrical static that charged the air right before she changed shape. Owen's hand flexed along his bow, free hand ready to reach for an arrow if need be.

He could now hear soft footsteps on the trail ahead of them. The sounds were quiet, careful steps taken by something large it sounded like. Owen braced himself for battle again. It seemed around every corner there was some new danger, some new threat waiting for them.

"All's I wanna do is t'talk t'the boy," he heard the gruff voice say from the trail ahead of them. From the growl that emitted from Boone's throat he recognized the voice as well.

Brule.

"About what?" Winter asked. Owen noticed the large man had not unsheathed his own sword, nor had he un-slung his bow. He seemed fairly calm. Owen was concerned he was under estimating the bounty hunter who'd followed them to his realm and back and had already cheated death at least once.

"It's between him and me, we got some things to discuss," Brule answered. He was closer now from the sounds of it. Not much further ahead of Winter on the trail. Boone growled deep and menacingly. "Looks like he's still got his puppy-dog too."

"Owen, come here a moment?" Winter asked, not turning away from Brule. He held his hand out behind him to guide Owen alongside him on the trail.

Owen hesitated and then went to Winter's side. He felt Boone close behind him; he knew the great dog wouldn't be far from him. Owen saw the bounty hunter then. His clothes were torn and tattered, the same ones he'd worn the day he'd fallen from the bridge. He wore no weapons, and held an unsheathed dagger in the palm of his hand, balancing the blade at the pommel and cross guard.

Brule looked healed, but not entirely fit. From what Orla had told him of trolls, they had very fast metabolisms and healing abilities, but the injuries Brule had suffered before falling from the bridge had been severe. Owen could only imagine the damage he had sustained from the fall. It was no small miracle that the troll had survived at all. *He probably hadn't been able to do anything but recuperate the whole time I was in Quailan*, Owen thought.

"On d'bridge, you risked yer own neck t'save mine from fallin'," he said, watching Owen carefully, "Why?"

Owen eyed the bounty hunter wearily, he figured this must be some sort of trick or trap; the troll had stopped at nothing, and kept pursuing Orla through everything.

"You helped us, fought for us against your cousins," Owen said. "Besides, you said you had nothing to do with my parents, only that the people who took them were the ones who hired you. I hoped you could help me find them." Owen looked the giant creature in the eyes. They were mostly brown irises with a dark, brick red rim instead of white.

"When I was hired," Brule began, and Owen immediately noticed a shift in the troll's speech. It was clearer, more articulate. He no longer used any slang, lost his accent, and sounded well educated. "It was by a robed figure, small, Sylvan height and build, but I never saw anything below the cloak and cowl. The job was simple. Bring back the realmjumper," Brule said, nodding his head in the direction of Orla. "It was a bounty I'd pulled many times," Brule explained.

"I don't always take back up, but I took my three cousins along because the Corps had given them leave and they could use the extra money. In hindsight, not the best idea I've ever had. Once we entered your world we picked up the leopard's trail and followed it to your house. My cousins don't do stealth, and before I knew it, they were inside your place. There was all sorts of yelling and screaming. But before my cousins or I could even get control of the situation, my employer was there, dark robe and all. He charmed both your parents, turning them to stone, and then ordered the rest of us to search the house. And as quick as he'd shown up, he was gone again. That was when you came in, I guess. I had left in search of my employer. I didn't like the way the caper was going down, and I thought it strange that he had come to your realm. That was when I found you up by the circle.

"After you two made your escape, he appeared again. He told me to continue the job in our realm, took my cousins and your parents, and left. That was the last I've seen of him," Brule said. He stood somewhat straighter once he'd finished, as if a weight had been lifted from his shoulders. He still felt weak, and the guilt over his involvement in this event bothered him still, but he felt he was finally on the right course for once.

"Why are you telling me this? Now?" Owen asked, still unsure of the large man's intentions.

"You did something on that bridge no one has ever done. You could have died trying to save me, for that, I owe you my life." Brule kneeled in front of Owen, causing the boy to stiffen slightly. The Trollbjorn held out the dagger he held in his hand. "I lost my sword on the bridge, but I hope you'll accept this blade in its place. I swear my sword and life to help you find your family, and safely return you to your world."

Owen looked at the monstrous person in front of him, and then up at Winter. The big man nodded his head and smiled slightly at the boy next him. Quite a bit had occurred in his short absence. The boy truly was the *Maou'r.*

Owen took the knife.

Brule looked at Owen, who nodded his own approval. Brule stood, and Owen offered him his dagger back, hilt first. "You'll need this until we can find a new sword for you." Brule tucked the weapon back into his belt.

"My horse is at the top of this ridge, he has some supplies on him already, but we can lighten everyone's loads if you like?"

Winter agreed as the two men headed up the rest of the ravine. Owen fell back in line with Orla. No one in the party spoke. Owen for one wasn't sure what to make of what just happened, and he wasn't sure if anyone else could either. The companions traveled to the top of the ridge where they found the biggest horse Owen had ever seen. It was a giant red horse, with a lighter, blondish mane and tail. Hanging from its saddle were two bags along with Brule's crossbow. The horse looked to Boone and then to Winter and finally to Owen, eyeing them all. Brule stroked the beast's neck gently in greeting. The party all pulled some of their supplies and stores from their packs and filled the horse's bags with them.

"What's his name?" Orla asked Brule as he pulled himself awkwardly up into the saddle.

"Dunno, he still hasn't told me," Brule answered. Owen thought he looked even more drained as he slouched heavily in the saddle. Orla turned to Owen and raised her eyebrows at him. Owen just shrugged and smiled back.

The party left as soon as they had lightened their loads. Brule took rear guard behind Aiya, following the Sidhe on his mount while Winter began leading them down the other side of the ridge and into the valleys beyond.

71

I *don't like it*, Boone's voice echoed in Owen's head. He was wondering how long the dog would keep quiet about Brule joining the party. Not long at all, actually. Owen smiled at his dog's suspicious and protective nature. It was reassuring.

"I know," Owen said, "and it will be good for us to stay on guard for a while."

The great dog grumbled and sighed behind him. Owen didn't need to hear his voice in his head to understand the meaning of his exasperation.

"If it wasn't for his help on the bridge, those trolls would have had us," Orla added. Her comment was greeted with the same grumbling.

She looked to Owen and the two friends exchanged smiles. She turned her attention to the valley before them. Orla was surprised at how good and happy she felt about being on the trail once more, even considering the circumstances. It would be good to finally be out of the foothills that they were still traveling through. The rocks and ledges felt confining to her, too many places for enemies to hide, even near Quailan.

They traveled quietly for most of the morning, stopping for a short break to eat the midday meal by a small creek. The creek bed was rock strewn, all moss covered. The deep, dark green moss and luscious ferns that grew along the river bed made the small clearing seem more magical than any of the wonders Owen had yet seen. This quiet place quickly became his favorite of everywhere he'd been thus far. The gentle trickle of the creek made a tranquil backdrop to the beautifully calming place.

Orla, Owen, and Boone sat along the creek sharing one large rock. Brule stood off by himself with his horse whom he had watered in the small creek. Aiya and Winter sat next to one another against an enormous black willow tree. It was the most Owen had seen Aiya speak to anyone besides her sister since he'd met the Sidhe. Owen actually even saw Winter smile a time or two as well as Aiya. He realized then that the two probably had more in common with each other than any of the other companions.

"So, what's a Vrok?" Owen asked. Boone sat up suddenly and looked at Owen as if the boy had suddenly begun howling at the noonday sun. Owen noticed that Orla stiffened slightly at mention of the beast as well.

"What?" he asked, looking around to make sure something hadn't sprouted from his head the way his two friends were looking at him.

Few speak that name so casually.

"Why's that?" Owen asked.

"The Greater Deymons are the Army of the Fallen. When the Fallen fell from Grace they brought forth the souls of their *Aingeal* brethren they had slain in the First War as Greater Deymon. Through torture and torment they turned them into the creatures they are now. They are the most evil and wicked things to ever walk Gaia. It brought great pleasure to the Fallen to turn the Creator's children into such evil creations," Orla said in a whisper, as if the wind would hear her words and carry them back to the Deymon or the Fallen themselves.

"So Lilith the Witch Queen is one of the Fallen then?"

"No, not exactly," Orla said. "Winter would know better, but she didn't participate in the War, I don't think."

Owen nodded and looked away for a while. This world was so amazing he thought. So much of it was like a fairy tale, so much of it an adventure. And yet, sometimes so much like a nightmare as well. It was easy for him to get caught up in the thrill of running from monsters or from meeting strange creatures and forget how real everything was, so much so that it usually overwhelmed any fears of his at the time. He would have loved to have met Orla and come here under different circumstances. Inevitably the guilt for having fun here while his parents were captive always resurfaced. He felt miserable that they were statues because of him, in someone else's possession, and a part of some scheme to hurt Orla and her world.

He wouldn't allow it anymore.

He knew where they were, they were in Narsus, the same city with Orla's father. They would head there, Vrok or no.

"Owen, what's wrong?" Orla asked. "Your expression has grown so dark," she added. Startled back from his own thoughts, Owen turned to his friend.

"I just wish I could have come here under different circumstances," Owen said looking about the small glen they were resting in. It truly was magical. So many different shades of vibrant green erupted from the place. The slight trickling of the creek through the moss covered rocks, the warm sunlight streaming through the hemlock and willow bows to the ferns below. Owen understood why Orla loved it so much here. A pang in his heart reminded him how much his father would have loved this same place. He turned back to Orla to meet her eyes.

"But everything you've seen since you've been here is the foulest; you've only seen the evil and hatred," Orla said with tears in her eyes.

"No, not everything," Owen said, smiling at her sadly, causing the small *Fey* to blush and briefly look away. "I wish I could have come here for a different reason."

A grumbling sigh from the large dog next to them broke the moment and turned their attention to the dog covering his face with his enormous forepaws.

"But I can't wait any longer," Owen said while standing. He walked briskly to where Winter sat with Aiya. The two were deep in conversation when Owen interrupted them.

"Winter," Owen said drawing the tall man's attention to him. Aiya stopped speaking as Owen spoke. She had been talking about her sister Silan and one of her visions.

"Yes Owen?" the archer answered. He sat beside a large boulder, from around which the willow sprouted, its top portion covered in thick moss while its sides were sparsely covered in olive green lichen. His hood slightly raised to the crown of his head, with his face plainly visible from its confines.

"We need to head to Narsus," Owen said. He didn't make it a request or question. He was going; he hoped the others would come with him.

"I don't think that's a good idea. The Vrok isn't far behind us, if we bring it into the city the casualties would be incredible," Winter said. He knew this wasn't what the boy wanted to hear, or even if we would understand the peril they were in with a Greater Deymon hunting them.

"My parents are in Narsus. We overheard them at Orla's house talking about them being there. They are planning on doing something, to them. I have to go; I can't leave them any longer. I've waited too long already." Owen was becoming emotional; he could feel his throat tightening and threatening to cut off his words.

Winter thought for a moment. If the boy's parents were indeed here, then someone could unleash an enormous amount of power using them for their own purposes, but the Vrok behind them was an immediate threat to the *Maou'r*. At that moment the fluttering of wings caught Winter's attention. It was the familiar sound of raven's wings, a sound he hadn't heard in a very long time.

The wing beats came to Owen as well, and the two men saw similar visions from the two birds, but neither knew what the other saw.

Winter heard the words spoken to him by his All Father on the night he was charged with protecting Owen and Orla "and the hunter may need to become the hunted," the Pilgrim's voice echoed his mind. "It is time old friend," the familiar, hoarse voice of the All Father permeated his mind.

Owen saw at last the creature that followed them in its entire unholy splendor. It was terrifying and wretched. He also saw a man confront the beast. Fighting with bow at first and then with sword, and the splintering of the great weapon, its shards falling upon the snow at the man's feet. He saw the vision and a sense of resolve settled on him, this was a task laid down long before the *Maou'r* had stepped back into Parathas and one that the Hunter would carry out. This sense of ease that the ravens laid on him receded quickly, however, and Owen soon began to regret his decision to push on towards Narsus.

"We shall go to Narsus then," the cool voice of winter emanated from the tall man's mouth as he looked to the boy in front of him.

"But," Owen started, already regretting his decision and the vision the birds brought to him.

"Some things are beyond our control, Owen, beyond our reach. They were woven into the fabric of time as the Creator laid forth this world for us," the Hunter said, standing and adjusting his gear.

"It is time to move," he said to the rest of the party as they quickly gathered their belongings and began to leave the small glen.

Owen watched him go, Orla and Boone by his side, and wondered what fate he had just condemned his friend to, or if he had ever really been given a choice in the matter.

72

Winter led the party out of the territory of the Sylvans as they walked into the evening hours. The *Aingeal* wanted to lead the Vrok out of range of the Sylvan villages and townships that lay between them and Narsus; he didn't want to leave the temptation there for the Greater Deymon as they moved closer to Owen's parents.

Owen had been adamant in his desire to head to the capital city, and he knew that Orla, Boone, and Aiya would go with him. To his surprise, Brule simply nodded when told their destination. Winter was the only one who was hesitant of the *Maou'r* heading towards the capital, but acquiesced in the end with one stipulation. That they head Northwest, drawing the beast from the Kingdom and then heading back to Narsus from the north where the city was more easily defendable.

After the short break to discuss their new course of travel, the companions broke camp once more and headed in their new direction. This bearing took them back along the hills, ledges, and cliffs they had traversed earlier. It did not bring them directly into the mountains but simply along the foothills.

Owen was pleased. The renewed strain in his muscles made him feel more like he was accomplishing more than all of the training he had done in Quailan. And somewhere deep within his chest, there was a core of determination to find and rescue his parents that was now being fed by the arduous journey and climbs.

No more running, he thought. *Now we're leading you*, he mused, *and once we have my parents then we'll deal with you, the way we've dealt with everyone else who's come for us.*

But still nagging in the recesses of his mind were the visions he had seen of the Vrok. They were not comforting, and he was determined to not let them come to pass. The foresight was fore-knowledge and with it he could change the outcome.

Orla watched Owen intensely as they left the glen and moved towards the borderlands along her Kingdom. A peace had settled on him in that glen that she had not seen in a very long time, not since their first leg of the journey that took them from the City of Cer'log de Mortem. And then, before her eyes, she watched as that calm was replaced with a dark brooding. Now a grim resolve enshrouded him. He had picked his course, one which she agreed with, and now with that plan in motion, he seemed less dark.

She just hoped that what they found waiting in Quailan would not be what they would find in Narsus, and that their reception there would be more welcoming. The trail Winter had taken dropped to single file and Owen stepped back for Orla to pass him on the trail. She smiled at him as she stepped in front and he returned the look. She too wished he could come here under different circumstances.

As the party divided itself into single file once more, the trail became too tight for Brule's horse to accompany them. They divided their belongings back amongst themselves, Brule taking the lion's share of the communal provisions. He patted his horse softly on the neck, speaking quietly to it, and then took his position in line. The horse slowly moved back down the hills into the forest beyond.

"He's a smart horse that one, he'll catch back up with us," Brule said, almost to reassure himself. Owen doubted as much, but kept his thoughts to himself.

Aiya slid to the rear guard position; keeping Brule in front of her while Winter remained in the lead followed by Orla and then Owen. Boone kept pace at Owen's heal, between him and Brule. Owen was sure that the bounty hunter could still feel the mistrust amongst the party and hoped the trollbjorn wouldn't take it to heart. He had yet to prove himself to the group, and Owen was afraid until then, the mistrust would remain.

As their climb leveled off and they worked their way through a spruce and fir grove Owen began to notice inverted trees. Mature trees had been ripped from the earth, stripped of all their bark and branches and then replaced inverted back into the earth, roots exposed. They looked like some odd foreign species of island tree to Owen. Or yellow power poles with large osprey nests atop them. They were sparse at first, but then began to occur more frequently as they continued their trek.

Owen looked to Winter and Orla in front of them to see how they were reacting to the trees. Winter seemed to pay them no mind, but Orla began to look anxiously about her, and seemed more agitated at their presence. She finally shifted into her hybrid form before Owen asked her about them.

"Um, what's up with the trees?" Owen asked, trying to sound casual and not as alarmed as he was becoming.

"Giants," she replied over her shoulder.

"Brilliant," he responded under his breath.

Winter heard his question as well and stopped at the tree next to him and waited for the companions to gather around him.

"Giants," he agreed, nodding to Orla. "They use them to mark their territories and to attract the attention of lady giants," Winter said smiling.

"Giants?" Owen asked looking about him.

"Nothing to worry about, really," Brule added. "Friendly sort, for the most part. Like gold, they do."

Winter nodded his agreement of the trollbjorn's assessment. "Especially the hill variety."

"What do they, um, eat?" Owen asked, still not convinced.

"They're herbivores for the most part," Brule offered.

"Yes, only a few of the different species eat meat. Frost giants are the only ones who are solely carnivorous, but that's simply because there isn't much vegetation where they live," Winter continued.

"Plains Giants are the ones you need to watch out for, though, ornery bunch they are," Brule continued again from where Winter left off, "evolved in the open where there's no cover, so they compensate for it by being overly aggressive. They're also some of the biggest of the giant kin, but they're extremely rare now-a-days."

Wonderful, Owen thought.

"They believe in mutual avoidance for the most part, hence the trees. Just letting us, and everyone else, know they're around and that they don't want to be bothered. It worked well for them until some hunters began using the trees as sign of giant presence and began hunting them out of those areas. Plains giants aren't the only species close to extinction now," Winter said coolly.

Owen stepped over to the bare tree next to Winter and ran his hand down the length of it. Teeth marks were present in the soft spruce wood.

"They eat the bark, the sap and pitch also holds a certain attraction for them," Winter said over his shoulder.

Owen smiled at this new understanding of giants. How easily explainable their existence seemed. *Just another piece of the puzzle*, he thought as the companions began their march once more.

They hiked into the evening hours until Winter decided to find shelter for the night; dark storm clouds threatened them from a distance and the Hunter wanted them to have dry bedding for the night. He found it on the lee of a ledge face that had a small overhang. The floor of the shelter was dry spruce and fir needles that had blown into the shelter and never been blown out.

The party laid out their bed rolls and Winter chanced a small cooking fire for them. Orla and Owen took the spots closest to the wall while Brule, Aiya, and Winter stayed close to the mouth of the small shelter. They, along with Boone, opted to have two watches during the night with two guards each. As always, Orla and Owen were left out of the equation.

During the evening, after dinner, Winter again pulled the wrapped parcel from his pack and laid it across his lap. As the night went on, and others turned in for their rest or turned to conversations amongst themselves, Winter sat beside Owen.

"This blade was forged by the *Aingeal* during the War of the Fallen, or the First War as it has become known, long before the Great Schism. It has long been passed down among our kind. I thought it lost, but it has recently been recovered by my liege. Its name in your tongue means GreenFyr, and I am afraid its time for its blade to be rekindled." Owen could see, however, even from beneath the deer hide that the blade was actually quite intact, and was unclear of the First Man's meaning.

The older man watched the fire, its light, turning his white beard to the orange and blonde of his youth before Owen. The boy glimpsed Winter in his prime, except for around his eyes, which were still creased by crow's feet in the firelight, eyes that had seen much, and forgotten little.

"Who are the Fallen?" Owen asked, already assuming the answer.

"My kin. Those who fell from Grace. Those who chose darkness over light," Winter said, not looking from the fire; as if in its flames he could scry the answers he sought.

"And the Schism, they didn't want the worlds split, did they," Owen asked.

"No."

"And the re-unification you and Orla have mentioned, it's them trying to have the worlds put back together," Owen asked, everything beginning to come together for him.

"Not entirely the Fallen. Although they long for it, many individuals from many races wish for our worlds to be one, once more," Winter answered. "But the Fallen are behind them in some form or other, even just as inspiration, they scheme and plot and manipulate." Turning his attention from the fire, he looked at Owen and smiled.

"The Fallen are at their strongest when they work from the shadows, gaining strength from their minions who carry out their schemes and plots, paying tribute to them by doing misdeeds. And I fear, Owen, one of the reasons Lilith and the others will purusue you so, is because of the powers the *Maou'r* possesses in those terms. One of the main reasons for the Schism was to separate Man from those that manipulated Man's faith in them. Faith can be a powerful shield, Owen, but an even deadlier sword."

The First Man's attention was again cast back to the fire as if in it he could foresee their futures.

"You were right in turning our course towards your parents, it is the right way, don't tarry from reaching them in Narsus. We all need to make haste, I fear some great evil is at work and plans on using your parents to help make it so.

"I still cannot sense them in this world. I believe whoever holds them won't release them from their stone prisons until the very last moment for that very reason."

"How will we find them then?" Owen asked, concern shadowing the optimism he had conjured for the rescuing of his parents.

Winter smiled at the boy again, "We will find a way, we always find a way. Now rest," Winter said, placing his hand on Owen's shoulder to help him stand. He placed himself at his post at the opening of the shelter, across from him stood Aiya, his partner for the first watch. He laid the still wrapped sword by his pack.

Owen stood and walked back to his sleeping roll where Orla had already arranged herself. Boone lay on the other side of Owen's bed roll watching his young *Maou'r* as he climbed into the bedding. The large dog laid his head next to Owen's as he drifted off to sleep.

73

Owen was jarred awake by a tremendous clap of thunder. The ledge-face shook from the vibrations above it. He looked to the entrance of their meager shelter and driving sheets of rain teemed down in front of Brule and Boone as they stood watch by the mouth of the opening. A bolt of lightning lit up the small cave and almost immediately another ear shattering thunder clap boomed through the mountains, causing dust and small pebbles to rain down on Owen and Orla.

Orla too was awake, waking only moments before Owen had. Her keen senses had picked up the glare of lightning and the sudden shift in air pressure before the storm had started. She looked at Owen as he rubbed the sleep from his eyes and surveyed their lodgings. Orla took in her companions as well.

Aiya lay asleep not far from Owen and Orla, her rhythmic breathing the only indication that she was still asleep in the storm, but Orla doubted her truly sleeping. Winter sat crossed legged before the small cook fire, staring into its embers as if reading the future, while Brule and Boone guarded their entrance.

Owen looked over at the Sylvan sitting next to him. "Been raining long?"

"Dunno. Don't think so, I woke up just before you did," Orla said, smiling back at the human.

"Are we the only ones who ever sleep?" Owen asked, looking back to the others.

"Yep. Aiya likes everyone to think she does, but I know better," Orla said loud enough for the Sidhe to hear. The elf rolled over, opened one eye at the two friends, and then rolled back over and went back to her rhythmic breathing.

"See?" Orla laughed.

Winter looked up from the fire and smiled gently at the two young people laughing in the corner. It was good for them to laugh, they needed that; it may be the only thing to get them through all this. *To get us all through this*, he thought.

"Get some sleep you two, it's going to be a long day tomorrow," Winter said, his voice like dry ice in the damp cave. Owen nodded to the older man, and laid his head back down. Orla did the same, and the two lay facing each other, watching the other fall back to sleep.

Winter was right. It was a long day.

They broke camp at first light just as the heaviest of the rain was dying off. It continued to drizzle and spit for the remainder of the morning with only a sudden cloudburst of a downpour just before the noonday meal. They stopped quickly, only taking enough time to pull provisions from their packs before moving onwards again.

It wasn't much past noon when Orla knew they were no longer in her Kingdom. She could just sense it. She didn't need the cloud cover to break, or see the mountain ranges along her side to know, it was a feeling deep within her soul that she was no longer home, and it brought a slight malaise to her as she left Sylvanni once more.

It was just past their crossing of the Sylvan Kingdom that Winter slowed his pace and began watching the trail more closely, not long after that he stopped all together. Boone passed Owen and trotted up alongside the *Aingeal* and the two convened briefly. The other members of the party worked their way up the line to the *Aingeal* and *Duine Madra*. Owen searched the ground for what the Hunter had found, and thought he saw a slight scuff mark on some moss covering a flat stone.

"Goblins," Winter said, answering all their questions at once. "I thought I saw signs of a war party a little ways back, but wanted to make certain. I was surprised to see them this close to the border," he added. "Boone said he picked up traces of their scent as well, but wanted to be certain because this is so out of character for them."

"Goblins? Impossible!" Orla said flabbergasted. "Not in our Kingdom."

"'Fraid so, Orla," Winter apologized.

"These were made just before first light as far as I can tell, they're not too far," he added.

"Are they after us?" Brule asked, leaning over Owen and Orla to look more closely at the sign on the trail. Owen wasn't sure if the troll could see anything more than he could make out, but Brule certainly acted as if he could.

"I don't think so," Winter said, looking around the forest floor for any other sign or indication of their intentions.

"Traveling light by the looks of it," the bounty hunter added, after straightening himself and finishing his inspection of the trail.

"I agree," Winter said, looking ahead of the party into the forest beyond as if willing it to reveal its occupants. "They were after something, but not us. They're heading the same direction we are, I'm certain they don't even know we're back here. Goblins don't usually keep rear scouts or guards."

"What do we do then?" Aiya asked, getting to the point.

"Well," Winter said, mulling his thoughts over, scratching his beard while doing so, "I would suggest we try and get a little closer to them and see what they're up to. I'd rather know what they're doing here than not."

The rest of the companions all nodded or stated their agreement to this. The idea of having a band of goblins this close and not knowing their intentions was unnerving to all of them.

The company set out once more. This time Brule and Winter took the front while Aiya and Boone kept rear guard. Boone stayed close to

Owen, not letting the *Maou'r* more than a stride ahead of him. Orla and Owen stayed close together. She had shifted to her hybrid form while Owen had drawn his bow like Winter. He wished now that he'd taken the time to make more arrows. *After this*, he thought as they worked their way through the woods.

Winter followed the almost invisible trail with ease. Owen couldn't even see most of what the Hunter followed, just trusting the archer's instincts. Winter slowed them, and then brought them to a stop by holding up his closed right fist. He had found something in the woods ahead. Owen peered around a small yellow birch as the Hunter began to approach the shape in the forest. Owen could make out, just barely, a dark shape, black in the forest, hunched over something on the ground. Winter approached slowly. Once close enough to discern what was on the ground he threw up his hands. A murder of crows flushed before him, cawing and screaming their anger and protest as they took to the trees around them. Winter called the rest of the small band to him to inspect his findings.

As Owen approached he discovered what the crows were gathered around. There was a corpse laying face down in the forest duff. The person was dressed in leather and metal. A corset of rings covered his torso while he wore iron shod boots. Thick leather breeches with matching gloves riveted with iron bands for bracers. The dead man's helmet lay tossed in the mud to his side. An axe blow to the back of the skull was the obvious cause of death. No other personal belongings remained on the dead man.

Owen then realized the scale of the person in the mud before him. Shorter than himself, with a burly, stocky build, the man couldn't be any taller than five feet, not much taller than a Sylvan, but much, much stouter. Owen looked up at Winter.

"Dwarf," the *Aingeal* said, answering Owen's unasked question. He bent closer to the corpse, "fresh, this morning."

"Goblin hatchet from the looks of the wound," Brule added, squatting down next to the corpse.

"Aye," was all Winter replied. He looked puzzled. "Not uncommon for skirmishes between goblins and dwarves, unusual to find them above ground, though." He looked around the ground, reading its tale. "He was the dwarfs' rear scout, the war party moved in quickly after this."

Owen looked at the dead man on the ground and felt queasiness deep in his stomach. This scene reminded him much of his first encounter here in Orla's world. Owen watched the forest around him with unease. He had seen death, and even killed since coming to this world, but he still couldn't emotionally detach himself from it. There was a distance and separation that Brule and Winter seemed to be able to apply that Owen was having difficulty with. He was just thankful the body wasn't old enough to have begun to decompose yet.

"We should bury him," he heard himself say.

"No time," Brule said. Winter looked at the troll and then to the human.

"The party is still close, I'm sure," Winter said.

Owen looked around him, "There are plenty of stones here."

Winter nodded, "We have time for a small cairn then. Brule take watch, stay close though. Boone secure a perimeter for us?" the *Aingeal* asked, as he laid down his bow and began lifting stones and bringing them back to the fallen dwarf. Aiya, Orla, and Owen joined him and shortly a small stone mound stood where the dwarf had once lay. Brule shifted impatiently, but held his tongue.

The party collected their gear, and each in their own way, in turn, paid their respects to the dwarf as they continued on the trail of his killers. They met up with Boone shortly.

Odd noise from ahead. Combat, but not a battle, more like a fist fight, really, the dog reported to Winter as the others approached.

"Aye, I hear it as well," the Hunter replied.

"Me too," Orla purred in her feline form. Owen looked to Aiya and Brule, both of whom seemed as if they could hear it as well. Boone tipped his head to either side to get better reception.

I guess I'm the only one who can't hear it, Owen thought as he notched an arrow into the string of his bow.

Winter looked down at the young human, bow in hand. He was troubled as to whether he should scout ahead and leave the others behind, but then part of him was reluctant to leave them with the goblins so close at hand. He was bothered at the size of the party they had been following, not a mere scouting band, but a full regiment of goblins had come above ground for this raid.

"I would rather scout ahead by myself, but I'm wary of splitting the party up with this many goblins in the wood," Winter said, drawing the others close to him. "I want everyone armed and alert, Owen and Orla with me, Brule and Aiya I want you on our wings, Boone keep track of our rear guard, I don't want any surprises.

"If any one sees or hears anything unusual, signal the others, I want everyone within visual contact," he said, drawing his own arrow from his quiver. Aiya did the same; Brule pulled his dagger from his belt. Owen thought the once well armed bounty hunter might have been a bit at a disadvantage, but then he felt Boone's nose nudge his hand and realized his *Duine Madra* went into every battle unarmed.

I'll be close, but stay close to the Aingeal.

Owen nodded his understanding and scratched the great dog's head between his ears, drawing the animal's eyes closed for the duration of the affection. "I'll be fine," Owen replied, which was answered by a sigh from the dog as he trotted off a distance to patrol the rear procession of the company.

Winter took point with Owen and Orla to either side of him. Owen could see his other companions fanned out in the woods about him. At two other occasions the party halted as Aiya and then Brule each found the other members of the dwarven rear guard, both slain from behind.

Winter lead the party to a sudden ledge and drop. At the bottom of the twenty foot cliff was the remains of the dwarf encampment. Tents, cook fires, and supplies were strewn about the ground. Bodies, of mostly unarmed and unarmored dwarves, littered the grounds as well. A few goblins had met their fate, but it was apparent, even to Owen, that the dwarves had been attacked unawares in the early morning hours.

One dwarf remained, however, as sport for the battalion of goblins. Some fifty or more goblins filled the space now, surrounding the last remaining unarmed dwarf. They had long polls with nooses on the ends of which they had tightened round the dwarf's neck, keeping him at polls length while goblins, one at a time, came up and fought him, bare fisted. He was battered, bruised, and bloody. His thick black beard was soaked with blood and his knuckles were raw and bloody. Several goblins lay crumpled in front of him, failed attempts at battling him unarmed.

Owen watched the ungainly creatures that reminded him of a combination of apes and dwarves. The creatures were bow-legged with short, truncated legs, but long, over sized arms and hands. They had huge yellow eyes with brick red pupils that seemed to absorb the sunlight. The goblins had pale yellow-green skin, long pointed ears, and triangular shaped jaws. Small needle like teeth filled their mouths that ran in several rows along their gums, and long pointed noses with small slits for nostrils. They were, for the most part, hairless with a few sporting top knots and tuffs of dark hair on the tops of their heads. They wore remnants of armor and dwarven or elven clothing, unkempt and dirty. Most wore scabbards with bows and quivers on their backs and carried scimitars in their hands; a few had shields and axes. The goblin axes reminded Owen of pictures of tomahawk hatchets. The blades of the weapons were wedge shaped with a small spike opposite the blade. The carved shafts of the axes were almost two feet in length. From what Owen could see, many of the goblins had adorned their weapons and shields with hair, feathers, bones, or other trophies from previous kills.

The goblins were so distracted that they didn't see the newcomers watching them from the cliff edge. They yelled, mocked, and screamed in their native language at their captive, who stood stone faced, and waited for his next opponent.

Owen looked up at Winter and saw reflected in the man's eyes his own feelings. They would not leave this man to face this fate alone. Owen knew he needed to free his parents, but how could he face them if he left this man here to torture and death. He couldn't, he wouldn't. Owen knew his parents would want him to do what he could for this sole dwarf.

Winter signaled to the rest of the party. Brule and Aiya worked their way down the cliff face to either flank of the goblins. Aiya stayed at bow range, but loosened her sword in its scabbard. Brule worked his way amongst the tents and boulders to close ranks with the goblins. He would melee with the wretched creatures as the others opened with arrows. Boone too worked his way down the ledge in front of Owen. He knew the dog had purposely positioned himself to fend off any goblins that tried to close on the archers. Orla worked her way down the ledge as well to help Boone where she could.

As a new goblin stepped into the make shift circle around the dwarf and the audience reached its crescendo of cheers and jeers, Winter let loose his first arrow. Owen and Aiya followed with theirs and before the goblins even realized they were under attack the three archers had already dropped several foes a piece. As confusion took hold in the tattered tent grounds, Brule stepped out from his hiding place and began working his way through the goblins.

He broke the necks of two before planting his dagger in a third. He retrieved two of the goblins curved scimitars from the ground and waded into their mass once more, swinging both blades with equal and efficient prowess.

A huge goblin in the center of the throng hefted a huge shield and began charging towards the archers on the foremost ridge. A growl and howl erupted and carried over the mass of confusion and hysteria below while Owen felt his heart surge, his courage strengthen, and he knew Boone saw the foe charging them.

Both Winter and Owen rained arrows down on the shield but none penetrated. The goblin, now with a small band of warriors surrounding him, pushed his way towards the *Maou'r* and *Aingeal*.

Brule worked his way through his own mass of goblins and began attacking the goblins to the rear of this sudden surge and retaliation, but he was out of reach of the tribal leader.

Owen turned his attention from the leader to those with him and began dropping his unshielded guard, which only seemed to anger the chieftain more as he bellowed his hatred. Winter too began to rain down arrows onto the chieftain's vanguard, dwindling their numbers greatly. Aiya fired her arrows into the goblins restraining the dwarf, freeing him of the catch poles.

Owen reached back and realized he had fired all but his last two arrows. He felt the familiar fletching of the one arrow Winter had given him for retrieving fletching resources, and was tempted to use it, but refrained. His finger tips touched his silver birch arrow, but he hesitated in retrieving it as well. He slung his bow over his shoulder, saving his last two arrows, and waited for the remaining goblins to reach him. He noticed a small cedar stump lying atop the ledge, and grabbed it, making himself a would-be club should he need it.

He noticed Aiya now engaged hand to hand with two goblins. She sliced through them easily and, moving into the clearing, found additional targets scampering amongst the dilapidated camp site. Brule too had worked his way through the throng of goblins and had now reached the bottom of the small ledge beneath the chieftain's remaining guard, most of who had pulled up short before the *Duine Madra.* No goblin was willing to engage the great, growling dog below the ledge.

The guards slowly began to back away from the dog when a bellow from their leader forced them unwillingly into combat with the King of the Dogs. Boone leapt from his purchase, tackling two goblins at once. Several others rushed to their comrade's aid, but Orla quickly leapt to the dog's assistance. Owen began to rush to his friend's side but a hand from Winter stayed him just before an anguished cry silenced the remaining fighting. Boone and Orla separated from the goblins before them, both of their fur was blood splattered.

Owen saw the source of the scream; the last remaining dwarf had retrieved two short swords from the wreckage of his camp and approached the goblins. In the thick harsh language of the goblins he spoke to the chieftain, pointing at him with his twin blades, challenging the much larger goblin.

The chieftain's guards lowered their weapons and stepped away from Boone and Orla. The dwarf closed on the large goblin who had lowered his shield while drawing an enormous axe. Owen could see that the handle of the axe was adorned with the beards of the dwarves the goblin had slain over the years. A thick mane of hair plumed from the shaft of the weapon.

Brule and Aiya took defensive positions along the rim of the camp, Aiya again held her bow, waiting for a target. Brule planted his scimitars in the earth before him and folded his muscled arms across his chest. A thick gash in his left bicep dripped onto the ground while the troll took no notice.

Owen watched while Boone and Orla climbed back up the ledge to beside Winter and the *Maou'r*. Boone's nose had been sliced and a deep red gash ran across his muzzle. Orla came up and stood next to Owen, she made the climb in two graceful leaps. She seemed unharmed, the blood that had splattered her white fur was goblin, not Sylvan.

"What do ya make of that?" she asked, a bit out of breath.

"Retribution," Winter said quietly, his voice hovering in the air like an early morning frost, lingering over bogs and wetlands.

The goblins still standing surrounded the dwarf and their leader, banging scimitars to shields, grunting and chanting. Owen wondered what they must be saying. The dwarf stood motionless, the way he had stood waiting for his next opponent. Owen wondered how long he'd fought them, one at a time; how many times he'd lost and been beaten to submission and how many times he'd won. He was amazed at the dwarf's stamina and endurance; how he could still be standing after such an ordeal was beyond the boy.

The chieftain banged his axe to his shield and charged the dwarf who suddenly sprang to life. He crouched low bringing both blades up at once, both making contact with the axe shaft, the first blade sliced the plume of dwarf beards, freeing it from its lanyard. The second blade parried the axe blow, but then reconnected as the goblin passed the dwarf as he easily sidestepped his larger opponent, bringing the blade sharply across the chief's back. The goblin cried in anger and pain while his followers screamed and chanted encouragement.

The dwarf turned and faced his attacker, still emotionless. Standing straight and waiting for the goblin to attack again. The plume of dwarf beards lay at his feet. This time the chief began to circle the dwarf who remained still. He allowed the goblin to get behind him and just as the goblin raised his axe above his head to bring it down upon him, the dwarf turned, swords raised and crossed. They caught the axe with their crossed guards, and with a quick turn of his wrists, the smaller dwarf wrenched the axe from its owner's hands.

The chief now stood weaponless. He flung his shield to the ground, and two goblins began to inch their way closer to the dwarf, only to be stopped by arrows fired into the ground at their feet by Winter. They recognized the warning for what it was and backed off.

The dwarf dropped his swords, both landing point down into the soft ground, wavering slightly as they stood blade first. The goblin barked, what Owen took to be a laugh, at the dwarf as he charged the smaller man again. This time the dwarf didn't sidestep or pivot, he landed an enormous upper cut to the goblin's chin, halting the creature in his tracks. He followed with a blow to the stomach, expelling the air from the chief's lungs, and then viciously kicked the goblin's left knee, hyper extending it backward with a nauseating crack of tendons, cartilage, and tissue. The goblin screamed in pain and for the first time, fear. The dwarf, still stoic, stepped behind the goblin quickly before the other could counter, taking the huge head in his hands. With one sudden twist and wrench he cracked the larger creature's neck, allowing the deceased chief to topple over to the ground.

A few goblins rushed the dwarf then, but they were all slain with quick arrows from Winter and Aiya. The few survivors scampered from the camp and disappeared into the woods.

The dwarf turned to Owen, Winter, and the others on the ledge and waited as the small band made its way down to him. Owen could now see that his beard was normally black, but saturated with blood and sweat, it took on almost an auburn sheen. His hair, plastered to his face, was long, straight, and thick. He had heavy brows, thick with hair as well. Under the large sockets were eyes the color of coal. His skin was rough and callused looking. He wore a chain shirt of fine silver rings that rippled and shown in the sun and moved silently as the man beneath them flexed and twisted. Like his fallen brothers, he wore iron shod boots, thick leather pants, and belted over his chain mail was a heavy, iron studded leather belt.

As Winter and Owen approached the dwarf eyed them equally. He finally settled his gaze on Winter and spoke in the common tongue.

"I am Balor, Captain of the Royal Guard of the Dwarf Kingdom, Dhunjharrow."

74

Balor sat crossed legged across from Owen around a small campfire Aiya had made to cook the dwarf a meal. The dwarf eyed Owen suspiciously. Winter sat next to Owen on one side with Orla to the other. Brule, Boone, and Aiya had extinguished the dwarven fires after searching for any survivors, and secured a perimeter around the trampled camp. Balor had just finished his meal, which the others had let him eat in peace, letting the weary man try and recoup some of his strength after his long ordeal.

"*Duenca* for the meal," the stout man said in a very deep, gravelly voice. To Owen it sounded as if it too came from the bowels of the earth.

Owen looked at the small man taking in as much of his unique qualities as possible. Shorter than Owen by almost a full head, the man was more than twice his girth, and Owen was sure, his strength. The dwarf seemed amazingly powerful and rugged for such a small man. His skin was thick, calloused, and dark like the soil he lived under. His eyes were the color of coal. His hair, coarse and black, was left loose except for two tight, thin, braids originating from his temples. The length of the free hair was kept cropped about his chin while the braids hung to his midsection. His beard and mustache below his sharply hooked nose was long and wiry, tucked neatly into the girdle about his waist. Again he had two tight braids that began just before his ears from his sideburns. His ears were small, round, and thick like the rest of the man. Balor's hands were wide and flat with short thick fingers. His finger nails looked to Owen to be as thick as nickels.

The small man noticed Owen studying him as well and nodded to the boy.

"I am in your debt," Balor said looking from Owen back to Winter. "Once I met their need for entertainment, they would have killed me soon enough."

"You're welcome," Winter said, his voice cool. "We were traveling this way and cut the war band's trail. We followed it and came across your rear scouts."

Balor nodded his understanding. He had figured they too must have fallen to the goblins, but hadn't been sure.

"We buried the first," Owen said, "but by the time we found the other two we were already close enough to hear the sounds of the goblins in your camp." He looked to the fire, becoming self conscious of speaking out.

The dwarf watched him again, and inclined his head in thanks, "*Duenca*," he said again. "I will collect the rest of my fellows and lay them to rest here, where they made their last stand, and met their fate like dwarves."

"We'll help you," Owen said, his voice firm and strong, leaving no doubt.

"But," Orla started. Owen turned to her and saw the look in Winter's face as well. He too was concerned about the Vrok. They had lost much time and distance investigating the goblins.

"It's still light,' Owen said, "and as long as we have light, we have hope." Winter smiled slightly beneath his beard and nodded his head to the wishes of the *Maou'r*. They would help the dwarf then, and maybe, still be ahead of the Vrok by nightfall.

Balor looked back at Owen and took the measure of him once more with his gaze. There was much more to this boy than he suspected. "Normally, I would refuse your help, but at this time, I am in no shape to do that," he said standing stiffly. "You and your friends make for an unusual band of travelers," he added.

"We have business in Narsus," Winter answered, quickly enough to avoid either Orla or Owen offering too much information to Balor.

The dwarf simply nodded.

Winter whistled gently, a sound one could misinterpret as a bird call, but the three companions guarding their borders emerged from the woods about them. Winter informed them of their plans and they decided that Boone would keep patrolling the perimeter while Brule and Aiya assisted in tending to the dead.

Balor was quiet, reserved, and distant. Only once did he say anything and that was when Brule had found a dwarven halberd amongst the dead and ruined. He held it up, examined it, and looked to the dwarf. There was no hint of a question on the half-troll's face, but the two warriors understood each other perfectly well.

It was a finely crafted weapon. Almost seven feet tall, solidly built of iron with twin axe blades on opposite sides of the shaft that ended in a long thin spear head almost a foot long. The blades were folded in iron and silver while the whole weapon was adorned in dwarven runes.

Never did the bounty hunter say a word. Balor looked at him and the weapon and finally nodded his solemn head. They both knew it was too splendid a weapon to leave on a funeral cairn.

"Dwendn would approve. He would rather see it cleave more goblin skulls than rot in a grave and, I think, in those hands it has a fair chance of doing so." He returned to the grim task of dragging his fallen friends to their final resting place while the others gathered stones and rocks for their cairns.

When the graves were done each of the party came silently to them, made their own thoughts, turned, and went back to the edge of the camp.

It was time to leave; the pending night was like a weight, heavy upon them.

Orla, Owen, and Balor were the last around the stone cairns, eleven in all counting the two scouts Brule had brought back to camp. Baelyn, the first scout to have fallen, was the twelfth. He was left where he was already laid to rest. Orla bent to the ground, touched the earth with thumb and forefinger. She brought them back to her heart and forehead before closing her eyes. Her lips moved, but Owen heard no sound. She opened her eyes and looked to him. A slight smile creased her lips as she turned from the graves. She gently touched his arm as she left to join the others.

Owen looked at the man across from him. Balor had dressed in the rest of his armor and battlements. He now wore a richly crafted breast plate over a shirt of fine mail, the links of which looking more like cloth than metal. On his arms he wore thick iron bracers that matched the greaves he strapped around his iron shod boots. He had belted his twin short swords to his leather girdle and stuffed a small hand axe into the top of his left boot.

Balor had buried all his men with their weapons and belongings with the exception of the halberd he'd passed on to Brule, sending each into the afterlife with everything they had carried into battle in life. All that was left in the camp were the ruined tents and provisions scattered across the ground.

"*Oft wug non Temblengurg, Duenca,*" he said in the rough, earthy language of the dwarves. Owen turned and began to leave. "Wait, young one," Balor said from across the cairns that separated the two men.

"*Duenca* for helping me send them on their way and for rescuing me from the same fate." Owen turned back and looked at the dwarf across from him.

"You're welcome, but it wasn't just me," he offered.

"Your friends killed many, but it is apparent that they follow you," he said, and Owen could tell he was still being studied. *He's trying to figure out who or what I am to them,* he thought to himself.

"Winter leads us, I follow him," Owen said. "What will you do now?" he asked, trying to change the subject. After a slight pause, Balor answered.

"As the green of summer follows, I'm sure," Balor said looking from Owen to Winter and back to the boy again. "Now? I go home. I am too few to carry out our mission and I must deliver the news of my mens' fate to their families and my liege."

"I'm sure we can travel with you to your home, if you want," Owen offered, not wanting to offend the dwarf, but wanting to offer their protection from any other bands that might be in the woods.

Balor nodded. Owen turned and left the man to say his final farewells in privacy and found Winter amongst the others. He approached the rest of the party who were all silent. Orla and Aiya stood together. Brule stood slightly apart from the others. Boone scratched an itch behind his ear, taking great huge swats at it with his enormous paw. Winter stood slightly in front of the others.

"We need to be away, Owen," the *Aingeal* said as Owen stepped next to him.

"I know," he looked up at the sky and the sun was already on its decent for the night. "I told Balor we'd take him to his home; I didn't think it safe for someone to be in the woods alone," Owen said, hoping Winter wouldn't disagree to his offer.

The tall man looked surprised for a moment. "What did he say?" he asked

"He thanked me, I think, and said yes."

"He did?" the archer scratched his beard for a moment. "That's unusual, most dwarves I've known would have declined, rudely at that, and had stormed off for such an offer," Winter said, looking up from Owen and to the approaching Balor.

As the stout man stepped beside Owen he looked up at Winter, "Your young friend has offered your companionship to my Kingdom, in return I offer you lodging and shelter from the approaching night. You do want shelter from the night, am I correct?" the dwarf said, already sensing their apprehension from the coming dark.

"Shelter will be appreciated, thank you," Winter replied.

Balor nodded and led their way from the camp. He took them into the uplands and the rocky outcrops that marked the beginning of the mountains hidden from view by the dense canopy of hemlocks. The temperature had changed as well, Owen noticed, becoming cooler with the coming night and elevation of the hills.

The dwarf kept them at a brisk pace. Winter had slid down and walked along with Owen and Orla. Boone stayed behind Balor and in front of Owen. He was sure the dog had done it in case the dwarf was planning on leading them into a trap. Aiya took rear guard, but stayed close, as Brule walked behind Winter. The journey wasn't difficult and Balor seemed to know the area well, leading the small band over the easiest terrain.

"Balor? If you don't mind my asking, I've been trying to ascertain why the goblins would have been above ground in such force. Had the Dwarven People discovered why?" Winter asked, as Balor stopped to give the others a rest. He seemed quite comfortable with his pace and Owen wondered if the small man could continue like this all day and into the night.

"Hmpf," Balor said, "the goblins have been going above ground in such force for a while now. We've been trying to discover the *why* ourselves." His demeanor wasn't pleasant and Owen could only imagine that he was still grieving after the loss of his men and friends.

"But I hadn't heard of such movements by them," Winter added.

"I'm not surprised by that," Balor quipped, his irritation almost palpable. "No one else in the Realm has concerned themselves with the Dwarf Goblin Wars in centuries."

"I was under the impression, apart from small border skirmishes, the war was over," Winter replied.

"Hardly," Balor retorted, his voice like grinding stones. The stout man stood from the boulder he'd leaned against and begun hiking again, silently calling an end to their break for the time being. The others quickly followed suit, and moved quickly to catch up to the taciturn man.

It was just nearing dusk when Balor led them into a slot canyon hidden by over grown hemlocks and yew growing along the cliff sides. Once in the slot, it opened slightly allowing them to walk two abreast. The dwarf turned to them then.

"No one other than a dwarf has entered this canyon and lived in over four hundred years. I am bringing you here now in appreciation and repayment for sparing my death to the goblins." The small man turned and walked deeper into the cavern which even in the darkening sky was veined in deep red and black marble. Owen had never seen rock more beautiful.

Balor came to a stop at the dead end of the canyon. He approached what to Owen looked like a blank wall and touched the flat surface with his thick hand. He shouted once, a bark in his own language that Owen couldn't discern. At the sound from his voice the door slid back into the face of the cliff revealing a long darkness within.

75

"Identify yer'self," a gravelly voice said from the dark as the companions stepped through the door and into the Dwarven Kingdom. The darkness felt alive, a suffocating, rough spun, living blanket, Owen thought as he froze, blind eyes searching the shadows for the owner of the voice. He felt Orla step closer to him, he knew her own senses were more acute and alert in their dark surroundings than his. Judging by the way she placed herself next to him, he figured she had just placed herself between him and the voice.

A gruff voice immediately in front of Owen answered the disembodied one. Owen recognized it as Balor's and even heard the dwarf's name spoken in the thick guttural tongue of the dwarves, which sounded to Owen like someone speaking German with a mouth full of stones.

"*Kapitan*," a voice answered in the dark and the darkness receded some, a pins and needle feeling spread over Owen as if the blood was returning to a limb which had fallen asleep, as if his whole body had been denied light instead of simply being in the dark. It was still dark; everything was a monotone gray to Owen, but still a marked improvement for him. He assumed it must be much better for the rest of his companions, who he now noticed had surrounded him in the small entrance to the Dwarven Kingdom.

Balor turned and faced Owen, looking to him, and then up to Winter behind him. "This is barely the border of our Kingdom," his gravelly voice explained, echoing off the stone walls as small, stout men slowly emerged from the walls in camouflaged clothing to envelop them. "We still have a long trek before us, but we will dine on roasted venison in the Halls of *Dweldwenfjord* this evening," Balor said, and then turned to a dwarf beside him. The man bowed deeply to Balor before the weary man embraced him, hugging him strongly. The two parted, and again in the language of the dwarves, Balor spoke quickly before the man nodded and stepped aside allowing Balor, the companions, and an escort of two more dwarven soldiers down a long and dark passage.

Balor took the lead with one of the two other dwarves; the second followed the party as they made their way down into the bowels of the Dwarven Kingdom. Winter followed closely to Balor while Orla and Owen walked behind him. Boone and Aiya followed them and Brule brought up the rear, closely watched and followed by the last dwarf who kept a firm grip on his battleaxe.

The corridors were large and spacious, easily allowing them to walk two abreast, but then there were times when the corridors shrunk in size. Squeezing them down to single file and lowering the ceilings until both Winter and Brule were hunched over and Aiya had to be careful of bumping her head as well.

At the ends of these bottlenecks they came to check points patrolled by more dwarven guards. *It's like a War Zone*, Owen thought, *and much better than the security at Orla's house*. The check points had an iron door built into the solid rock walls. The doors had small eye and arrow slits, and the few that the party passed through were usually adorned with goblin helms, armor, and once, a goblin skull.

Once through the doors they were greeted by more grim faced dwarves. All of whom looked tired and on edge, all of whom looked angry and red eyed from lack of sleep. Their beards were thick with food crumbs and their faces and hands were dark from soot put up by the small cooking fires in the tight corridors.

At these checkpoints, however, once Balor stepped through the door, the morale of the soldiers seemed to rise. His name whispered and repeated down the ranks of all the soldiers present until they all returned to clasp forearms with the Captain of the Guard as he made his way through their defenses or to simply watch him pass. Occasionally, Balor stepped to the side and spoke with the officer in charge before moving the party on.

During these periods amongst the lines of dwarves in the checkpoints, Owen noticed Winter closely following Balor and watching, and Owen assumed, listening to the conversations being carried out in the guttural language of the underground people. Winter never let on that he understood the language, but Owen had little doubt that the *Aingeal* was fluent in the harsh tongue.

Owen was also aware of the animosity and harsh looks and tones directed toward Aiya and Orla in these tunnels. They were usually carried out after Balor had already passed, and never in his presence, and even though the exact meaning and translation was lost to Owen, their tone and intent was clear in the expression and inflection of the speakers. Aiya and Orla took to speaking in the more musical and lilting language of the Sidhe and Sylvan folk, both being fluent in the other's language, during these periods as if fending off the harsh dwarven words.

In contrast, the dwarven men seemed to avoid looking at Boone and Brule altogether. The troll and the dog could simply not exist as far as the soldiers were concerned. Owen seemed to feel little noticed during these periods, as if he was just a shadow passing through. Occasionally, a dwarf would meet his gaze, but they took little interest in the boy.

Owen watched the men as he walked through their ranks. He'd felt weary and tired, even war torn at times, but these men seemed liked lost souls to Owen. *What have they seen?* he thought as he passed them by, *what have they had to do, become?* He wondered how long the goblins and dwarves had been fighting before his small band of friends found Balor a captive of his lifelong enemies.

Once through the check point he moved closer to Winter as the passageway opened again and Balor took a bit more of a lead before the others.

"Winter? How long have they been like this?" Owen asked, Orla stepping closer to him and Winter to hear the answer herself.

"Longer than most can remember," he answered soberly, his voice the cool of the season's first frost. "And many of us can remember for a very long while."

He looked over his shoulder at the *Maou'r* and smiled sadly. "In many ways the goblins and dwarves have forgotten what it's like to not be fighting, to not be terrified, to not hate."

Owen nodded his understanding; there were many people in his world that lived the same way.

He slowed his pace some and Winter parted from him and Orla. He looked at his friend who had remained in her Sylvan form since entering the tunnels. She had also become more sullen the further into the caves they traveled.

"You okay?" he asked.

"Hmm? Oh, yeah. I just don't like being underground. I feel too confined," she said, trying to smile strongly for Owen. She could see the look of worry he often had creep into his eyes. *When did I start to distinguish between his looks?* she thought.

"What have they been saying back there?" he asked, indicating the checkpoints over his shoulder.

"Not sure," she answered with a shrug. "Aiya said there's always been mistrust between the people below and the people above, especially those of the *Fey* line. Dwarves, even though magical creatures, wield no magic, so they distrust those that do. Historically more the Sidhe than Sylvan, but I think they've stop distinguishing between any *Fey.*"

"That's what you guys have been talking about?"

"Yes, sorry. She didn't want them to understand what she was saying," Orla apologized.

"S'alright," Owen said, feeling a little better about being left out of the loop.

Boone nuzzled his leg as they walked along the corridor as if sensing his loneliness and Owen lowered his hand, resting it on the massive head of his dog as they moved down the hallway. He scratched the thick, coarse fur of the *Duine Madra* and felt secure here in the dimly lit halls of the dwarves.

The party continued their long decent for several more hours, passing through three more checkpoints, each further apart than the last, until the corridor they traveled began to become large, more spacious, and much more ornate.

Owen was overcome with a strange feeling of comfort and safety. Walking amongst his friends, all of whom had sworn him their protection, and now in the deep confines of the Dwarven Kingdom, he felt secure. The corridors had been entirely warm and dry on their decent, but now that they had opened the air seemed crisper and Owen swore he could feel a slight breeze carrying fresh air. They were unlike any caves he had seen before.

The walls here were deeply carved of dwarven heroes and epics. More than once Owen thought some of the figures resembled their guide and host, Balor, as he walked them deeper into the Kingdom. Most of the scenes depicted battles with goblin armies, but as they moved along the walls the sculptures and reliefs began to look older, smoothed by age, and the stories they told moved away from the goblin war, although at intervals, the clashes of the two races re-emerged as a theme.

Some of the sculptures showed craftsman at work building great halls, others of tired dwarven miners uncovering wondrous jewels and ore, or working fine weapons and armor. Owen had become enraptured by the reliefs and almost walked into Winter's back as the tall man came to a stop before him.

"We part company here for a short while," he heard Balor say from the other side of Winter. Owen and the other members of the party spread out in the hall to better see and hear their host. Balor was standing in the middle of a crossroads within the large corridor. Directly behind him was a large hall that seemed to be alive with activity and noise, great earthen and flavorful smells of pottery and roasting meats and vegetables came from the hall as well as the clamor of noise and commerce.

The corridor to Balor's right was smaller and less noisy; the one to his left was quieter still. He looked at Owen as he stepped around the side of Winter, Orla following close behind him. The other's slowly coming about as well.

"Garrell will lead you to your quarters for your stay here, there you may refresh yourselves. I won't be long. I must meet with my liege and debrief him on the matters concerning my garrison and the goblins we encountered. I will come for you afterwards," Balor instructed.

"May we request a meeting with your King?" Winter asked.

Balor chewed on this for a minute, "Certainly," he replied. "It has been far too long since an *Aingeal* has ventured this deep into *Dweldonfjord*."

Winter nodded his thanks and agreement.

"When I return we will feast together. Until then," Balor said, turned, and headed down the left corridor alone. The dwarf he had been speaking with, Garrell, nodded and led them down the right corridor. The dwarf whom had followed them down the long tunnels stayed at the cross roads, arms akimbo, watching the way they had just come.

Garrell walked quickly, with loud commanding steps, his iron shod shoes slapping the flagstones and resonating down the corridor ahead of them. It didn't take them long, three rights and one left, passing what seemed to be residences along the way before they came to a small cluster of rooms, all of which were connected and seemed to be an unoccupied family apartment of sorts. Garrell showed them in, giving Winter and Brule rooms of their own, Orla and Aiya a room to share, and Boone and Owen their own room. The room was actually for Owen, he acknowledged Boone not at all. The rest of the apartment had a small library and study, with a small attached reading room with a short couch and comfortable looking chair and ottoman, a small dining room, and a fully stocked and functional kitchen.

Each bedroom consisted of a bed, chair, writing table, water basin and pitcher. The furniture was extremely well made and very sensible. There was very little style or complexity to each item, and all were dwarf size.

Brule washed in the basin, laid his bedroll upon the stone floor, and was quickly asleep; Winter sat in his bed using it more as a chair and seemed to meditate while Aiya and Orla washed themselves, and then their clothes as well, closing their door to the group of men in the other parts of the apartment.

Owen found himself alone with Boone. The large dog settled himself at the foot of the bed, blinked once at Owen, and was quickly asleep, his rhythmic breathing a comfort to the boy. Owen washed in the basin and then poured himself a mug of the fresh water left in the pitcher. The cool drink tasted wonderful. Owen drank it in one long continuous gulp; he had not realized how thirsty he'd been.

He sat on his bed and unpacked his fletching tools and supplies and began making more arrows from the spare shafts he'd picked up along their hike to the Dwarven Kingdom. He had found many potential shafts along their hike to the slot canyon and entrance to the Kingdom Below. Owen had become quite adept at the art and in a short time had produced quite a few high quality hunting arrows in addition to a few extra target arrows. He placed them in his quiver, along with the two he had spared from their fight with the goblins, and several he had salvaged from their battle, and continued to ponder on the thoughts that had occupied him while fletching his new missiles.

They were now on their way to the city where Owen believed his parents were being held. It was the same city where Orla's father was, to which she had tried to travel before being abducted and sent to his world; where her abductors then tried to have her killed, and when that failed, retrieved, supposedly. *Why would they want her dead? And when that didn't work, back alive?* Owen thought. *She must have learned what they were up to and tried to warn her father. But what?*

And in the meantime, they were being pursued by one of the Greater Deymons and now the guests of the Dwarven Kingdom. Owen wondered if they'd ever reach Narsus. And what would he do when they got there? *We should go to Orla's father. He might be able to help us, and when Winter speaks with him, maybe he'll believe us.*

Owen looked over the edge of the bed and down at Boone. Weariness finally caught up with him, and the sight of his great slumbering dog seemed to call to him. He slid from the bed, pulling the wool blanket from it, and curled up against his friend, using his shoulders and ribs as a huge pillow. The dog seemed to groan approvingly as Owen drifted off to sleep.

Balor turned and walked briskly down the corridor. It had been weeks since he'd been back to the Kingdom and almost as long since he'd last walked these halls. The goblins were on the move, but he still didn't know why. He had no answers to the questions he'd had when he last spoke to his liege and now he'd brought strangers into the depths of the Kingdom. His King would not be pleased. *But when was the last time an Aingeal walked these parts of the Realm,* he mused, *and in such company? This may be connected to the sudden increased activity of the goblins.*

Balor passed a few guards in the hall that stopped and waited at attention as he passed, he gave a quick salute while doing so. Normally, he would have stopped and chatted with his men of the Royal Guard, but he was consumed by his thoughts and his need to speak with his King. He continued walking until he came to the large ornate stone doors, shaped to look like two huge dragons locked in combat. His presence at the doors announced his arrival at the royal chambers.

Two large white bearded dwarves guarded the entrance. They looked at Balor while the one to his left spoke, "The King is expecting you." The dwarf on the right pulled a thick, braided cord and the large door ring in his hand while his partner took hold of the ring on the left side. As they pulled the large doors open they split along the dragons, separating the two fighting beasts.

Balor stepped through without waiting for the doors to be fully opened. The hall of the King was a large room, with eight pillars to either side of the main aisle, each sculpted as a large giant holding up the ceiling. Large braziers burning with coals lit and warmed the room, while a large fire roared in the enormous carved mouth of yet another dragon behind the throne of the King of the Dwarves. His throne was sculpted of platinum, pounded completely smooth and flat without a hint of a hammer blow to be seen.

The seat was occupied.

The King was an old man, even by dwarf standards. His beard was white, with long streaks of silver running through it. His ears were pierced with large gold hoops, while the crown which sat upon his head was a thick band of platinum, bejeweled in the center with a single ruby the size of Balor's fist. He wore a richly woven linen tunic and leather breeches. His boots were shod in gold, not iron, and each of his short, meaty fingers was adorned with gold and platinum rings. Each of which bore a different, enormous, perfect gem: sapphire, ruby, diamond, emerald, opal, pearl, topaz, garnet, dragon's tear, and *Duenguifenn's* Soul.

Balor walked to the foot of the throne and kneeled, lowering his head and gaze. His King looked as he had when Balor left him the last time he had been in this room, displeased.

"Sit up Balor, Kaptain of the Royal Guard, Prince of *Dweldonfjord*, and heir to the Kingdom of the Dwarves," the King's hoarse voice commanded.

Balor stood back up, and clasped his wrist behind his back. "My King, uncle, I bring unsettling news of the world above."

"And of visitors to the Kingdom Below," the King added not very pleased.

"And I bring guests, yes," Balor admitted, "however; I bring them, for if not for them, you and the Kingdom would be heirless." Balor had learned how to speak to his uncle. For one, he was allotted more lenience because of his relation, but also because he was direct with the King, which no one else dared to be.

The King did not answer. He waited for Balor to explain. He did not like the sound of what his nephew had just told him. He had on many occasions admonished his nephew for taking too many risks and asked him, but never commanded, to step down from his post as the Kaptain of the King's Guard. It was the honor and duty of the oldest son of the King's brother to serve as Kaptain. A duty that Balor had fulfilled since his own brother died, along with his father and cousin, the King's son, in the battle of *Feldongourge*. On that day Balor became both Kaptain of the Guard and heir to the Kingdom. He also, almost single handedly, handed the dwarves their victory in that battle and won himself a place in Dwarven Lore and History. Balor became the tragic and beloved son of the Kingdom Below when he slew the goblin general, breaking the spine and will of the remaining goblin army that occupied their historic cities.

"My garrison was ambushed and over thrown. Only I spared. I was to be sport until they grew tired of me. The *Aingeal* and his band came upon the goblins and slew them, saving me," Balor's voice was flat. He neither liked admitting defeat nor speaking of losing one of his men, let alone an entire garrison.

"The goblins over threw an entire garrison of the King's Guard?" the King demanded incredulously.

"Aye," Balor confirmed. "Never have I seen a goblin war party above in such force and number. I fear the goblins are up to something, but what, I am unsure."

The King sat silently, stone like, for a long while before answering. Balor was used to these long silences, but he was weary after his long ordeal and wished his uncle to say something. He was beginning to sway when his uncle finally spoke.

"I was told the party is of mixed race, the First Man, two or three *Fey*, and a troll. Is that so?"

"Yes my liege," Balor answered, regaining his balance and becoming more alert. Not sure if the smaller boy was a *Fey* or not, but unable to place him to any one race. "The *Aingeal* has requested an audience with you."

"Has he now?" the King mused. "After all these years they finally come to speak with the Dwarves.

"I will see them, refresh yourself nephew, son of my heart, and then bring them to me. I will know what they want, and of what they know of these new developments of the goblins."

Balor bowed and left his uncle. He was glad to be leaving. He wanted, needed, to refresh himself and eat something as well as rest some, but the rest would have to wait. Balor also truly wanted to speak with and learn more about these visitors. They acted unlike any above-grounders he had ever met before, and took great risks to free him from the goblins.

The knock to the door woke Owen from his sleep. Boone was still lying beneath him, acting as pillow, but Owen could tell the great dog was awake and waiting, alert to see who appeared from the other side of the door.

"Owen?" Orla's voice inquired from the other side. "May I come in?" she asked.

"Yeah, of course," Owen said, leaping to his feet and throwing the blanket back upon his bed. He quickly combed his hand through his hair and ignored the snort and grumble from Boone as he too stood, stretching and arching his long back as he did so.

Orla walked into his room.

She was wearing new clothes; they looked like something Aiya might have worn. Orla wore a cloak of poppy blue, a white, silk tunic, tied at the waist with her own silver belt, and leggings the color of balsam firs. Her feet were still bare and Owen was pleased to see she still wore her toe ring.

Her hair was pulled back and worn up on her head, pinned with her silver leopard pin; two thin locks fell to either side of her face. Owen was speechless as she entered. His eyes were drawn to the smooth curve of her bare neck as it stretched from her delicate jaw line to her shoulder.

"Napping?" she asked, smiling at the dumbfounded expression on his face.

"N, no," Owen stammered, "I mean, yeah, a little." Boone walked over and greeted Orla, raising his great head to look into her face; she smiled broadly and scratched him between his ears, while his tailed wagged in appreciation.

"Balor's here, he says the King will see us now," Orla said.

"Oh, okay," Owen answered awkwardly. He hesitated, looking back at his bow and quiver. "I don't need anything, do I?" he asked, feeling awkward leaving his bow behind.

"No," Orla smiled, "I don't think you'll need that here, besides, Balor said after our meeting we're coming back this way for dinner with him."

"Alright," Owen said, following Orla out of the room and closing the door behind. Balor was standing in the entryway to the apartment. Everyone else was already there. Owen was pleased to see that Orla was the only one to have put on new clothes; everyone else was still wearing their traveling clothes, including Balor, albeit, he did look cleaner and groomed. His long dark beard was washed, combed, and tucked back into his wide belt.

"If you would follow me," the dwarf said as he exited the apartment. The party fell into their usual marching order with Brule bringing up the rear. No other dwarves accompanied Balor this time through the tunnels. As a matter of fact, the only other dwarves they saw on their way to the King were the two ancient looking ones stationed outside his chambers. They followed the party into the room closing the great doors behind them.

The small band followed Balor down between the rows of stone giants. Owen was amazed by the dragon fireplace, its mouth agape with flames. He saw huge, beautifully woven tapestries that hung on the walls between the stone columns. And finally, sitting upon a shining throne, was the King of the Dwarves. He wore bright silver mail that matched the thick band of a crown around his head. His long beard hung over the ends of his bent knees. Across his lap was a large, double bladed axe encrusted with jewels.

Balor approached his King and then stood to the right of him, the rest of the party stopped before the old dwarf and kneeled or bowed as was the custom of their races. Brule and Winter both took to one knee while Orla and Aiya each inclined their head, but never lowering it lower than the King's. Owen decided to mirror Winter and took a knee while Boone stepped beside him and squared his shoulders. The *Duine Madra* bowed to no one.

"King Gavril, Liege of the Ground Beneath, and Thane Lord of the Dwarven Free Folk," Balor announced.

Owen noticed they weren't alone in the chamber and that an even older dwarf than the King along with two Royal Guards stood behind and to the left of the ruler of this underground world. Beside Balor, Garrell and two more dwarves approached, wearing the uniform of the Royal Guard. The King nodded his head and Winter stood up, followed by the rest of the companions.

"It is an honor and a privilege to be before the Dwarven King and in the halls of the Under Folk once more," Winter said, as warmly as Owen had ever heard him speak. His voice sounded like frost retreating from the morning sun on a spring day.

"It has been a long while since we last were host to one of the First Men; to what do we owe the pleasure of your company?" the King asked, with a somewhat bitter tone. Owen was sure the sound of sarcasm was intended. "It has been long said that the *Aingeal* were often absent when needed, and ever present when they desired a favor. Which is it this time?"

Owen was surprised at the way the King addressed Winter, but the *Aingeal* didn't seem affronted by the, if not impolite, less than civil chastising.

"The First Men have long walked this world and tried to help and counsel its people, but we oft find ourselves the bearers of ill-favored news. It is the ilk of our *wyrds* that we must bear, but we have ever held the safety and well being of Illeden's peoples first in our intentions.

"We are here simply as guests of your Captain. We met him upon the road, aided where we could, and he offered us lodging and board in return. We were road weary and accepted."

"So the *Aingeal* has no other purpose for being here?" the King asked doubtfully. "Well, a time for firsts, then," he added to a chuckle from his wizened advisor.

"Well, when we were welcomed into the Under Realm I asked for a meeting with his liege, so I could discuss current events, so to speak," Winter said, his voice becoming cooler, like an early winter breeze.

"Ah, as I expected and no less," the King scoffed.

Winter ignored the King's tone and continued with his thought. "We are on our way to Narsus to meet with one of its senators to discuss some disconcerting news. It seems there may be a plot against him and his kin, linked to the efforts of Re-Unification, by some in his household. However, there is to be a session of the Allied Nations to discuss this topic of Re-Unification, and it occurred to me that it has been too long since an ambassador of your nation had participated in such a discussion. I was hoping I could convince you to send a representative," Winter offered in his best impersonation of a politician. He had complete disdain for this type of thing and preferred to be on the trail of game rather than intoning polite politics, but this too was sometimes the calling of the First Men.

Owen could see a slight flare of anger in the eyes of the King. "Participate in a discussion on what happens in the Above World? What do we care of happenings Above Ground? When have they held a session to discuss the Goblin War or the Below? When have they sent aid to the besieged Dwarven Kingdom? I'll tell you, NEVER!" King Gavril roared.

"This may be a good time to broach that subject, your Highness. Make all the nations of Parathas aware of the plight of your people," Winter suggested.

"Dwarves need no assistance from up-worlders. We can deal with our "plight" on our own, thank you very much!"

"I meant no disrespect to your people, but involving yourself within the Above World again may help bring an end to this conflict. At the very least, open the Kingdom Below to the Kingdom Above and work towards better relations with your neighbors," Winter offered.

"We are dwarves, we need no one else," the King said simply. Winter could see there was no changing the royal mind.

"I see that, your Highness, and I thank you for your time. However, in connection to this plot against the Sylvan senator and with the attack upon your Captain and his men," Winter began, if he could manipulate the right amount of pride, guilt, and fear, he might be able to make this work. "If we hadn't helped your Captain than he wouldn't have been able to bring word of the goblin's activity and we wouldn't have been deterred from our course. However, now, we have made ourselves enemies of the goblins, who we may come across again before reaching Narsus. If you were to send a garrison of your troops along..." but the King interrupted Winter before he could finish.

"How dare you try and blackmail the King of the Dwarves? I should lock you and your companions away in the depths of *Buerradwelve* for your insult. Your aid will be rewarded by food, lodging, and safe passage through our Kingdom as promised, and nothing further. No dwarf shall step foot in Narsus as long as I am King!" the King roared. Winter simply inclined his head and said nothing further. No one in the party said anything.

Owen looked to the other dwarves within the chamber. All of whom were stoned faced except for Balor who seemed to be seething.

"I have nothing further to discuss with these people," the King declared. Balor stepped from his post and beckoned for Garrell. The dwarf approached.

"Show the guests back to their suite, I will be there shortly to bring them to dinner," the captain said, roughly dismissing the party.

Owen and the others turned and left the chambers, the two sentry dwarves closed the enormous dragon doors behind them as they walked back to their rooms in silence.

76

They were hardened dwarven military. They had spent their entire adult lives in the service of the Kingdom as soldiers, and yet they huddled together in fear. The fear in the tunnel, just inside the exterior door, was tangible. The smell of sweat and bile clung to the backs of their throats as well as their nostrils. The soldiers had long since forgotten their weapons and posts and cowered in the dark corners trying to make themselves small and insignificant.

The beast outside screamed its frustration once more.

A soldier retched in the dark, another wept unabashedly, the lanterns had long since been snuffed out, so the soldiers wouldn't have to see the fear in one another's eyes.

The beast raked its great talons along the outside of the door, long naked fingernails across a slate blackboard, gouging the stone with deep ruts.

The Vrok was angry and frustrated. It finally had cornered its quarry, but now was denied their flesh because of these troublesome dwarven doors. The entry way was much too small for it to enter, even if it could breach the dwarven crafted entrance.

Dwarves wielded no magic, and were extremely suspicious of those who did, but their craftsmanship was no less magical. They were inherently magical beings and it showed in the fine works they wrought.

The beast screamed once more. It could sense the fear and trepidation on the other side of the door, it could smell the stink of their flesh, taste their dread. It was still no consolation for being denied its prize. It would have to wait for its prey to leave the hole they had found in which to hide.

The Vrok leapt up onto the sheer wall above the entrance and scaled the surface as easily as a squirrel climbs a tree. It was soon lost in the shadows, enveloped in its own darkness within the night.

Its scream broke the silence once more, and was answered by a clap of thunder off to the south, followed shortly by a flash of lightning that illuminated the skyline revealing its perch upon the crest of the mountain.

77

C'mon in," Owen called from his bed. He had been fletching arrows while talking with Orla, who sat on the floor with her back against Boone, who was sleeping soundly lying along the cool stone wall. His tongue lolled from the side of his mouth and his eyes were closed, but Owen knew the dog was now awake and alert to who would be at his door.

The door slowly opened and Brule stepped and stooped through the small door. Orla quickly rose to her feet while the dog she'd been using as a pillow pulled his legs beneath him, liked coiled springs, and slowly raised his enormous head to watch the bounty hunter as he stepped into the room.

Owen, who had been working on some arrows, kept his newest one in hand, while resting his right hand upon the bow that lay on the bed next to him. Brule had been with the company for only a short time, and even though he'd fought alongside the companions, there was still unease amongst these four. It had been tough for Owen and Orla to look past the fact it wasn't that long ago that Brule had been hunting them down and working for those who sent Orla to Owen's world and kidnapped his parents.

Brule was well aware of all of this. It was honestly the first time he could ever recall feeling guilty for anything. A miserable emotion he now acknowledged. However, he did rationalize that this was the first time in his long career as a bounty hunter that he had ever taken a job where the mark wasn't a down and out louse who deserved to be hunted and brought to justice. To actually come across a mark who was decent and honorable was a shock to the calloused mercenary. *Who knew?* he thought to himself.

"Brought you this," Brule said as he walked into the center of the room, openly leaving his back exposed to Orla and Boone as he faced Owen on the bed. He didn't like the feeling, but he knew he needed to begin to build the trust between himself and the one the others called *Maou'r*.

"You've been lucky this far. Personally, I'm not one for gambling, and think you should take some precautions," Brule said, as he handed Owen a fine hauberk. The shirt of rings was superbly crafted and barely made a sound as Brule laid it on the bed. The finish had been dulled so as not to shine or glimmer, but Owen was still surprised at the beauty of the fine workmanship. Mouth agape, he looked up at Brule.

"Ach, don't look at me like that," Brule quickly said. "Consider it part of an apology for my part in all this, besides, you could use it," he quickly added.

Owen picked up the chain shirt and held it up to himself, it was lighter than a wool sweater, and much more resilient than anything he was wearing now. Owen was suddenly struck with how truly strange this all was. *I'm living in a dream, a story!* Some fantasy novel his mom might have written, but this was no novel. His mom and dad were prisoners by someone, for some unknown scheme. And he was here, in a room with a dog who could talk, a girl who could turn into a leopard, and a troll who was once hunting her, and who now was giving him armor for his protection.

"Thanks," was all Owen could say, laying the hauberk back on his bed.

"Don't mention it," Brule said with a curt nod. The large trollbjorn began to turn around to leave when Owen stopped him with a question.

"What's that?" Owen asked, indicating the bandolier over Brule's shoulder. The bounty hunter almost seemed pleased to be asked.

"Oh, these?" he said, sliding the bandolier off his shoulder and handing it to Owen. Brule could feel the interest from behind him as well.

"This was quite a find I tell ya. A nice set of dwarven throwers! A whole bandolier of them!" Owen took the bandolier of hammers, but just as quickly dropped them to the ground. What Brule had swung around with no effort almost pulled Owen over. The boy heard a quiet snicker from his dog behind Brule.

"Whoops, watch yerself, Lad, they're heavier than they look. But they're balanced for throwing, ye see, and pack a wallop if you can put enough English on them. If ya know what I mean?" the troll posed with a grin, pleased by his find in the market. The big man took one out of its sling and handed it to Owen. Owen held the small mallet and couldn't imagine throwing it farther than a meter and with no accuracy, but he didn't doubt that behind a heave from Brule these hammers would be deadly weapons. He handed the hammer back to the bounty hunter who quickly and nimbly slung it back into the bandolier.

"Not a bad bit of shopping if I say so myself, all of this for those two goblin scimitars I picked up and a bit of gold, not a bad deal at all. For folks who are always fighting these goblins there's quite a bit of demand for their stuff," he added, slinging the hammers over his shoulder once more.

"Well, I gotta get cleaned up fer dinner before that little host of ours shows up," Brule said, turning to leave.

"Brule?" Owen asked, stopping the bounty hunter once more.

"Hmm?" Brule hummed.

"Thanks," Owen said, nodding to the mail on the bed next to him.

"I said don't mention it," Brule said with a grin, turning and ducking his head below the doorjamb as he left the room.

Orla and Boone quickly came over to inspect the gift from Brule.

Don't know if I trust him any more, but he's right, you should have been wearing something this whole time. You have been lucky, Boone said.

"This is a truly nice shirt of mail," Orla commented. "Careful with it while it's here and you're not wearing it," Orla said as Aiya appeared in the doorway.

"Balor has returned, he's bringing us to our evening meal," she said before ducking back out of the doorway.

Owen had to admit, he had better manners than he was currently exhibiting, but he hadn't realized how hungry he was, not to mention how good the food tasted. *No doubt about it, dwarves can cook!* Owen thought as he took another bite of the venison on his plate. His plate was covered in an amazing and rich assortment of foods. Venison cooked within a light and flakey pastry stuffed with mushrooms and small onions, venison stew, boar ribs, roasted boar stuffed with mushrooms, baby potatoes, carrots, and seasoned with rosemary and garlic, sautéed mushrooms, and roasted sweet potatoes. Grease dribbled down his chin and fingers, but as he looked around the table the rest of his companions seemed just as famished. The dwarves didn't serve many vegetables with their fare, but Owen didn't care much, his dad was a meat and potatoes kind of guy, too.

Balor had greeted them in their guest suite and led them to a small private dining room where they could eat their evening meal and later relax in front of the large fireplace before returning to their quarters for the night. He had been the only dwarf to meet them and lead them to the dining room, and apart from the wait staff who served them, he was the only one to join them as well.

For most of the meal he was in a surly mood, even for Balor, and had done little more than eat and drink during their supper. Ignoring, for the most part, the few attempts to engage him in conversation by Winter.

Balor put down the last of his ribs and took his large mug of amber ale and drank it in one long draught. He placed the mug down again and wiped the froth from his beard with the back of his hand. The other members of the party were also finishing their meals and he surveyed each of them as they did so.

When Brule finally finished, the last of the party to do so, Balor turned his attention to Winter, sitting at the opposite end of the table from him, and Owen sitting next to him.

"So, tell me now, truthfully, why do you head to Narsus?" the dwarf asked, his demeanor somewhat milder after having his fill. Everyone at the table stopped what they were doing. Brule held a frothing mug of ale in midair just before his mouth. Aiya stopped while taking a sip of her mulled wine. Owen and Orla each paused and looked at each other over the spoonfuls of creamy, rich, raspberry chocolate mousse. Winter just smiled.

"Ah, yes, I thought there was more to you than met the eye," the *Aingeal* said. "I already told your King why we're heading to Narsus. He was quite clear on the dwarf's stance on that. Why would the Captain of the Royal Guard inquire further?"

Balor scowled the length of the table at Winter as if considering his answer. "I am Balor, son of Duendan, nephew to the King, and heir to the Kingdom," he said after a small pause. "My cousin, the King's true son and rightful heir, was killed during the Goblin War. I am his only remaining heir." Brule put his mug of ale down untouched. Aiya smiled, amused at the information, and Orla and Owen exchanged open-mouthed stares at one another. None of them would have ever guessed from his behavior during their journey to the Kingdom that they were in the company of the future dwarven King. "Being the King's heir, it is my duty to pursue the Dwarven Kingdom's best interests, even if at times, that is contrary to the King's verdict.

"Now, please answer my question," Balor said.

Winter nodded and simply looked to Owen. "It is your tale, if you choose to tell it." Owen looked down the table at Balor who now watched him even more carefully than before. He cleared his throat and put his spoon down. He felt Boone lay his head in his lap, sliding Owen's chair back from the table in doing so, to make room for it. Owen looked around the table at his companions, all of whom nodded or smiled their support in turn.

"My parents are there, prisoners, the last time I saw them they had been turned to stone." The words came more easily to Owen than he thought they might. It was as if he had exhaled and they simply slipped out with his breath. "It's why I'm here, and why everyone else is heading there, as well."

"So this conspiracy and plot," Balor asked, "was that a cover for your real reason?"

"No, that is a very real threat," Winter responded. "The boy's parents were taken during the attempted *re*-abduction of the Sylvan. We think she saw something she shouldn't have; she has no memory of how she came to be where she was found. Since her rescue, there have been attempts on both their lives. The boy's parents, from what we can tell, were in the wrong place at the wrong time. Those behind the plot have taken advantage of their misfortune and may attempt to use them to further their own agenda."

Balor mulled this over; he refilled his mug from a pitcher on the table, again draining it in one long swallow. He placed the mug down and wiped his beard in thought.

"Then why did you turn onto the trail of the goblins and take the time to free me?" Balor asked, he already knew the answer, but wanted, needed, to hear it in with his own ears.

"Because we couldn't leave you to that fate to save them from theirs," Owen said quietly. "No one deserves that."

Winter looked at the *Maou'r* and smiled, and Owen thought he sensed a bit of sadness in the look. Balor looked around the gathered party and took in each person's expression. *They all revere him*, he thought. *They would follow him to the Abyss, but why?*

"So, on the morrow then?" the dwarf asked breaking the silence.

"We continue on to Narsus, that part was true. We need to inform the senator of the abduction, murder, failed assassinations, and of the conspiracy within his household. We also, hopefully with his help, will find the boy's parents."

"So, when you asked for the dwarves to join you, it wasn't to aid in this fight?" Balor asked.

"No, I meant what I said; I think it long overdue for the Kingdom of the Dwarves to be heard Above Ground in the summit to be held. That is all, Balor, no ulterior motives." Winter poured himself a cup of tea from a steaming pot on the table. He stirred it with a spoonful of honey before taking a hesitant sip of the seeping beverage.

Balor nodded. He looked once more at Owen as if he was mining, delving into his soul, and appraising the worth of it. He abruptly pushed his chair back and stood from the table.

"If you'll excuse me, I have many things to consider this evening. I will send for you on the morrow for your morning meal, and for the ceremony our King wishes to have in your honor before you depart. I must ask you stay in your apartment for the evening, for this I apologize; I would have liked to allow you access to our halls and wonders, but during this time of war it is not safe to be about on your own. I will ask one of the servants to lead you back to your lodging when you are finished here." With that the stout man bowed and hastily left the room.

Winter looked at Owen, still smiling, and said, "You did well, Owen. Spoke very well." The Hunter grasped and squeezed the boy's forearm in approval and then returned his attention to his tea. He stared into its steaming contents for long periods before gingerly taking sips of the brewed leaves.

"You do think we can trust him though, right?" Owen asked, a little nervous about revealing so much to a stranger. After what had happened in Quailan he was still nervous about trusting anyone.

"Oh, I think we can trust Balor. His uncle or some of the other members of the court I would say certainly not, but Balor is honorable." Smiling again, Winter continued, "I think we can trust him to do the right thing, I'm sure he will keep what was said in this room to himself."

Owen wasn't so convinced, but returned to finishing his dessert, which took some effort to actually finish. When he was done he felt as though he would burst from eating so much. Winter and Aiya were again engaged in conversation which Brule seemed to be part of. Boone had returned to his place by the door and Orla was just finishing her dessert as well. The young Sylvan was beginning to look very sleepy.

"I think it's time we asked our escort to lead us back to our room," Winter said, noticing how tired his two young charges looked. "We have a long day ahead of us tomorrow."

Brule stood and went to the door of the kitchen and asked someone to lead them back to their rooms. The rest of the companions stood, Owen stretched as the servant appeared from the kitchen doors. He was a small dwarf, not much taller than Orla, with a thick red beard braided into two long braids originating from his square chin.

The dwarf didn't speak as he led them back to their rooms. Once back in their apartment the party retired to their rooms to rest before continuing their trek on the morrow.

78

Owen woke to a knock on his door. He hadn't slept that heavily since coming to this world. He wiped the sleep from his eyes as he rolled from bed. He grabbed his pants from the floor and looked over at Boone sitting patiently by the door.

"One sec," Owen said, pulling his pants on. "Who is it?" he asked Boone.

Winter. His *Duine Madra* answered. *Hurry up, sleepy, some of us are hungry and don't have thumbs to open doors.*

"Come on in," Owen said, grabbing his tunic from the floor as Winter walked in.

"Time to break our fast," the large man said inclining his head to fit through the doorway as he entered. "Dress for traveling and all that entails, we will be leaving right after this ceremony Balor mentioned, which should immediately follow our morning meal."

Winter noticed the set of rings lying on the chair beside Owen's bed. He walked over and inspected them. "A very nice set of Sidhe chain," the Hunter commented, "where did you get them?"

"Sidhe? They're elvin? I thought they were made here? Brule bought them for me," Owen answered, surprised by the set's origin.

"Definitely of elfish craftsmanship and certainly not dwarven. Brule you say? Did he say where he bought them?"

"At the market," Owen answered. "I think he ducked in there when we were coming back from meeting with the King." Owen took the hauberk from Winter and inspected it once more. It was still an amazing piece of workmanship, he thought.

"Ah, he had mentioned something about buying some supplies. Well, he must have found them in the marketplace and assumed they were dwarven then," Winter hypothesized.

"So, if it wasn't made here, then how'd the dwarves get them?" Owen asked.

Winter looked at his young charge with a sad smile, *he's still so young and innocent even after all he's seen and been through*, the tall man thought looking at Owen.

"Would you fancy a guess? I have my own assumptions, but I would like to hear your's first," he said.

Owen thought for a moment and Winter could see the sudden revelation appear on his face, a brief hesitation and passing revulsion, "The owner died and someone looted the armor and his belongings," the boy answered.

Winter nodded. "I would guess, not that it would help any, that they passed from elf to goblin, before being claimed by the dwarves. Long has there been animosity between those two races, but it usually falls short of bloodshed." Winter turned and was about to leave when he stopped, "Be quick now, the sooner we're on our way the better, and be sure to wear those rings beneath your jacket."

"Winter?" Owen asked.

The tall man turned and waited for the boy to ask his question.

"Do you think Brule knew and just didn't want to tell me?"

Winter considered this possibility, "To be honest, Owen, yes, I think he might have."

Owen nodded as Winter left. Boone came over and sat beside his *Maou'r* as he finished dressing and packing his things before they left their room to meet the others for breakfast.

When they had finished breaking their fast they were led past their apartments and to the main set of tunnels from which they first entered. They had eaten their meal in the same room they had the previous night, but they had eaten alone. Only the red bearded dwarf was there and served them. Balor was absent and no other representative of the Dwarven Free Folk was present.

It, again, had been a rich fare with sausages, ham, bacon, stewed mushrooms, and fried potatoes, thick dark breads fried in the fat of the meats, butter, crème, pastries, and honey as well as an assortment of berries, dates, and plums. Dark, strong coffee and tea were also plentiful. They ate their fill and several of the party, Owen included, packed extra provisions in their packs with the leftover food.

Their escort paused at the junction to the large room that housed the market. There were two dwarven guards dressed formally in ceremonial armor and clothes. Functional and practical for combat, but still cleaned, polished, and more ornate than any of the armor Owen had seen the soldiers wearing previously. Neither guard looked particularly happy about being assigned to this detail, but Owen was beginning to realize that the unpleasant look was quite common amongst the dwarves.

The two guards led them down the center hall that opened into the larger chamber where the company had not been taken when they first arrived. It had been the chamber filled with pleasant smells and the noise of commerce Owen remembered, but as they walked down the hall to the room the chamber was quiet and just the lingering scent of those same smells was present.

At the doorway to the main chamber the guards were greeted by four more, all heavily armed and armored. They too seemed to be unhappy with their detail. Behind them two large ornate doors, depicting two enormous giants bracing the very same doors, could be seen pushed open revealing an enormous gathered crowd. The two guards led them past the four and into the room. The room was the largest structure Owen had ever seen. It was bigger than any football or baseball stadium he'd seen on television. The room had two rows of pillars that ran the length of it, each one depicting a different dragon. Some breathing flames, some in flight, and others coiled around the pillar as if sleeping. The gathered crowd was split to either side of a long aisle down which the guards led them. As they walked,

Owen heard a loud boom, and turning, could see that the guards had closed the doors behind them.

The gathered dwarves were curious of the strangers in their Kingdom and jockeyed for position along the aisle as the company passed them. Owen's attention was focused on the far end of the room, however, where he could see a small throne was erected in which the King was seated, surrounded by a small band of guards and advisors. Behind the King a thin waterfall spilled from the sheer cliff. But Owen could hear no running water in the room. As he approached the dais he could see that behind the stone chair the ground gave way to a straight drop where the water fell and emptied, disappearing behind the throne.

The hall was bright as noonday, but Owen couldn't see how they lit the underground chamber, just another marvel of dwarven architecture as he stepped up before the King. The aisle had been large enough for all of the party to walk abreast and as they halted before the King they stayed fanned out. Owen stood next to Winter in the center with Orla on his left. The companions kneeled or bowed as they had the previous night.

Owen noticed as they walked down the aisle that many dwarven soldiers had stood along their path to prevent the crowd from stepping out and approaching them. He noticed now, that there were a large number of guards at the front of the room around the King, as well. The thing that struck Owen as odd, however, was there was no sign of Balor anywhere among the gathered dwarves.

Owen felt small in this room full of so many people. He was one of the taller people in the chamber, but the sheer size of the structure coupled with the might and authority of those gathered was humbling. He was only fifteen, and in the whole time he'd been in this world, this was the first time he really felt his age. The world seemed about ready to collapse in on him when the King spoke. His voice, hard and gravelly, boomed through the chamber without any aid or amplification, another ode to the skill of the dwarven crafters who mastered the acoustics of the chamber.

"We are gathered here this morning to thank and acknowledge the bravery of these Up-Worlders before us. Because of their courage and brave deeds they…" but before the King could finish his prepared statement two loud booms echoed from the back of the room as the doors were flung open. Standing between the doors and walking towards the company was a tall dwarf, easily recognizable at that distance to Owen as Balor only because of the twin short swords worn on his belt.

A horrified gasp escaped from the crowd.

Owen saw many dwarves turn their horrified faces away from him, averting their eyes from his visage, as he walked towards them. He strode down the aisle and the soldiers, who had at first drawn their weapons at the interruption of the ceremony, quickly sheathed or relaxed their grips on them. It wasn't until Balor was halfway to the throne that Owen noticed the dwarf was clean shaven.

The dwarf's appearance was very different without his beard. His hooked nose was much more noticeable over his bare upper lip than it had been over his thick mustache. His lips were thick, with a wide mouth, and a square, strong jaw, with a cleft in the center. His cheekbones were prominent and his black eyes, deep set, under thick brows still heavy with dark eyebrows. His hair was worn loose and hung to either side of his face freely.

He wore banded armor of hardened, boiled leather, wrapped in steel bands about his ribs and chest, in place of the exquisitely crafted rings and plate mail he had worn the previous day. He had steel shoulder guards partly hidden beneath a dark scarlet cloak that fell from his shoulders and to the ground behind him. His iron shod boots thumped the stone floors as he approached, and the buckles on his sword belt clinked in the silent room.

Balor approached and passed the party, without any acknowledgement, and only stopped once he was before his King. As he passed Owen, the boy could see that the freshly shaved dwarf already had a shadow along his jaw line of the beard he'd just shaved.

The gasps of surprise, shock, and disgust were quelled when the Captain of the Royal Guard began to speak.

"I am Balor the Beardless, *Duaegar* to the Dwarven People!" the statement was greeted by another outburst of cries and shouts of anger and disbelief from the throng of gathered dwarves. The shock sounding behind Owen was the audible expression of the King's face.

"Balor, how could you?" the King began quietly, behind the thick, ringed hand he'd raised to his face, but was quickly cut off by Balor.

"I resign my commission as Kapitan of the Guard and renounce my claim to the throne!" Again shock and dismay echoed through the chamber from the gathered crowd as Balor spoke.

"What does *Duaegar* mean?" Owen whispered to Winter beneath the clamor of the dwarves.

"Outlaw, renegade, banished. There is no exact translation to the common tongue," Winter quickly said, not wanting to miss anything transpiring before him.

"Nephew, how could you?" Owen heard the King mutter.

"My life was saved from torment and death at the hands of goblins by the people behind me, and for that, I owe them my life. The debt is mine, and mine alone, and I am HONOR bound to uphold that debt. It shames me to think that my own King would brush aside honor, and instead, embrace bigotry of the World Above!"

The chamber had grown deathly quiet. The initial shock and surprise on the King's face was slowly being replaced by anger.

"I have shaved my beard, and will remain beardless, until I and our Kingdom have regained our honor," Balor said. He squared his shoulders and looked at his King, meeting his gaze.

"Balor, what have you done?" the King asked again, "Do you know what you say?" he shouted, his voice echoing throughout the chamber.

"I do, and I have made my decision," the dwarf said.

"Then go and never return, forever onward, you will be *Duaegar* to the Dwarven People!" the King bellowed. He stood abruptly, and along with his guard and advisors, left the dais and exited through a door next to the throne in the wall the waterfall fell from.

Balor turned to his companions, looking to Winter and then Owen, "I pledge my life and swords to your cause. May I regain my honor in doing so, or die trying," he kneeled before them. Owen looked up at Winter, at a loss for words.

"Stand brave dwarf and join our small band. Your honor is not in question, but may you find what you're seeking in our company, none the less," Winter quickly said noticing the troop of guards approaching them. "However, I feel we need to make haste and leave your Kingdom before we have further worn out our welcome."

Before Winter could finish his statement the small party was surrounded by a garrison of heavily armed soldiers all of whom with weapons at the ready.

79

Kaptain we should move quickly," Garrell said, as he moved through the ranks of his men.

"I agree," said Balor who turned to the rest of the party. "I may now be *Duaegar*, but I still have many who are loyal to me, but I don't want to endanger them for assisting us. We need to move, quickly," the stout man turned and headed to the opposite side of the falls that the King exited by. Along that side of the wall was a passage as well. The door opened after Balor pushed on a small rune carved into the wall.

"This will take us Up World. I hope you have all of your belongings, we won't be coming back here anytime soon," he said before turning and entering the tunnel. Half of the garrison went with the party while the other half stayed in the chamber below to prevent anyone from following. Garrell and four other soldiers, along with Balor, led the group while Winter led the small party, again falling back into their marching order, before being followed by the remains of the half-garrison of dwarves.

"This passage isn't too long, but it will put us on the far side of the mountain. However, it is in part of the country where the goblin activity has been most intense, so I wanted the escort to make sure the opening was clear before we exited."

Winter nodded his understanding. Owen was still trying to sort out what had just happened.

He turned to Orla who looked a bit concerned as well. "I guess we're not finishing the ceremony then," he said with a smile. Orla smirked back before shifting to her hybrid form. It had been almost a full day since she'd shifted and she had been missing it. She hadn't wanted to shift in front of any dwarves, but now that they were moving quickly, and into goblin country, she wanted to be ready if anything happened. She also took pleasure in the looks on the faces of the soldiers with her, and on how they avoided getting too close, now that she'd changed.

In no time they'd reached the exit to the Above World. The party quietly opened the dwarven door and dispatched a small party of dwarves to scout the area. Owen and the rest of his companions emerged when the party returned and gave the all clear. Balor made quick goodbyes to many of the soldiers with them, the longest of which was with Garrell, who gave his former captain a hug before returning to the tunnel and sealing the door behind him.

Owen breathed in the mountain air deeply. He had thought it would seem cleaner or fresher after emerging from the tunnels, but the dwarves had done a remarkable job of venting their underground world. The ground and trees were wet and the sky overcast. A storm had just passed, and the birds were quiet still in the gray morning.

Winter seemed distracted at first as Owen looked at him, but as if sensing Owen's gaze the *Aingeal* changed his expression.

"We want to move quickly, we have lost ground to the Vrok, and need to make it up this day," he took the lead, not waiting for anyone to fall in behind him. Owen and Orla both jogged to catch up with him before settling into their normal marching pace. Balor settled into the marching order behind Aiya and before Brule, walking briskly to keep up with the long legged Winter as he moved the companions quickly through the countryside.

80

"GreenFyr," Winter said, as he looked at the sword he'd pulled from its scabbard and laid in his lap. "*Graenn'eldur* in the tongue of the First Men," he continued as he looked at the blade as if it spoke to him. Owen sat next to him, entranced by the blade as well. He had been curious about it ever since the Hunter had spoken its name to him the first time only a few days ago.

There were runes etched into the length of the blade that when illuminated looked like silver flames dancing along its edge. The hilt was wrapped in forest green leather and set into the pommel was a large emerald. The cross guard was simple and straight, but the green metal rippled like flames in the light. The blade was slightly longer than the long swords Aiya had trained him with, but the hilt was long enough for it to be swung one or two handed.

Winter slid the blade home into its scabbard of dyed green leather and silver fastenings once more. It wasn't time yet, he reassured himself, as he wrapped the weapon once more into the deerskin he carried it within. Owen watched reverently as he did so. *The boy desires to wield it*, he thought as he tied the bundle tight about the weapon. *Does it call to him, I wonder? Not yet Owen, in time, but not yet.*

The lunch they had eaten seemed meager and little compared to the fare they had dined on in the Dwarven Kingdom. Owen had taken some of the extra food from his breakfast with him, but hadn't wanted to eat it just yet. He was saving it for later in their trip when he was feeling hungrier.

Winter had pushed them hard through the morning. His demeanor was very similar to the way he had acted before leaving Orla and Owen on the edge of the Sylvan territory. He could feel the Vrok behind them, close behind them, and he was desperately trying to open some distance between them. No one in the party complained about the pace, they all knew Winter wouldn't push this hard if he didn't feel it necessary.

Along their trek they crossed two sets of goblin war party tracks, but didn't waste any moments following them this time. Owen could see the look in Balor's eyes and knew that the dwarf wanted to scout after the goblins to know what they were up to, but he had pledged his allegiance to Owen and wouldn't break that oath. The thought that there were bands of goblins loose in these woods concerned all the company, but Owen was confident Winter could lead them around any trouble.

After packing away the sword, *GreenFyr,* Winter called the group together once more and continued their Northeastern journey. He still intended to lead them first away from the Sylvan Kingdom, to draw the Vrok as far from the Sylvan villages as possible, before turning and heading back down into Narsus. The route from the north into the capital was a difficult route through the mountains, but it would lead the Vrok towards the city from its most defendable position.

Owen had watched Balor during lunch, and was surprised when the dwarf had sat himself next to Brule, and the two had spoken some during their meal. Owen thought it good that Brule had someone to speak with during their journey. He had thought the bounty hunter might join Orla, Boone, and himself after he had bought Owen his elvin armor, but the trollbjorn had resumed his quiet demeanor amongst the company once they had taken to the road again. Owen wondered what the two men might have discussed during lunch: weapons, battles, or even past adventures?

Winter pushed them hard again into the evening, stopping just before nightfall in a small hemlock grove. The weather had turned cold, and what had begun as a slight mist in the late afternoon, had turned to flurries by the time they stopped for the night. The hemlocks would act as a canopy to keep the snow off them during the night if it should turn to heavier snow.

Even with the chill air, they opted to not light a fire that night. They planned on eating their dried provisions and hardtack, but Balor produced two large wheels of smoked cheese, a loaf of the dwarven dark, hard, crust bread for each, and four large, dried sausages to divide amongst them. He also had carried several wine skins and handed them out as well. He had strong ale for Brule and himself and sweet wine for Winter and Aiya. For Orla and Owen he handed them a large skin to share, which he said was a favorite amongst dwarven youth their age. It seemed to be a sparkling cider of some kind, but Owen could not place the source of the flavor. For Boone he had carried a dried, hollow gourd filled with crisp cool water from the deep wells of the Dwarven Kingdom. His provisions brought much cheer into an otherwise gloomy evening. All of the party was aware of the proximity of the Vrok to them, and the cool wet weather had certainly dampened their spirits some, but this fine fare was a welcome surprise and diversion.

Owen noticed that Winter intently watched the mountain behind them as if he could see the Deymon following their trail. The *Aingeal* told the party that he would take the first watch, that they might have to wake early before dawn, and be on their way to stay ahead of the Vrok. He would wake Brule and Balor after a few hours to take over his watch and then he and Aiya would finish the night. Owen thought Boone seemed a bit offended by being left out of the watches, but the large dog settled down with Owen and Orla on the far side of the camp, and quickly went to sleep without saying a word. Aiya was a bit reluctant to let Winter take the first watch as well, but she acquiesced, and finally turned in herself.

Sleep came to Owen quickly in the night. He had not realized how tired he was until he'd climbed into his bed roll. The hard hike that day had taken its toll on him and he could feel the tired muscles in his quadriceps and calf muscles as he drifted off into sleep.

The ravens came to him at some point that night, but he wasn't sure how long he had been asleep before they arrived. They showed him the sword GreenFyr, unsheathed, and ablaze in glowing green fire. He also saw a man moving quickly through the forest. He moved with great haste and a determined gait. He made no sound and was like a ghost in the wood.

The ravens then showed Owen the Vrok.

It was moving through a short slot canyon just into the foothills of the mountain, it moved quickly, sniffing the air as if a giant bloodhound on a scent. It was monstrous and horrifying. It screamed in the night, shaking the canyon and silencing the nocturnal forest animals.

Owen woke.

He lay still for a moment, remembering where he was, not wanting to move in case the Vrok was there within the camp. As if home in his room, frozen to his bed, afraid of what might be beneath it. The sky above him was a deep gray and full of large thick snowflakes. The snow was kept from his face by the hemlock branches just above him, but he could already see the thick snow blanketing the surrounding ground.

He slowly turned his head to the side; the one Orla had gone to sleep on, moving slowly in case there was some unseen monster lurking in camp. Lying in between him and Orla, was the sword GreenFyr, removed from the deerskin and laying in its green leather and silver buckled sheath. Owen raised his head to see that Brule and Balor were on watch, speaking in hushed tones on the far side of the camp. Aiya was presumably asleep, and Winter's bedroll was empty. His pack was laid next to it, but his bow and sword were gone.

In the distance Owen heard wing beats and he remembered.

He slowly began to get up. He kept an eye on the troll and dwarf being sure not to draw their attention. He slowly pulled his feet beneath him, took hold of the scabbarded sword next to him in one hand and his bow and quiver in the other, and was about to slip into the hemlock grove when Orla grabbed his wrist. He looked down at her quickly, realizing her eyes were open, but she hadn't moved her head at all. *How long was she watching me?* he wondered.

"Where are you going? And with that?" she whispered, looking quickly down at the sword.

"Winter's gone," Owen said quickly, looking back over his shoulder towards Brule and Balor.

"Gone where?" she asked squirming out from under her own blanket, but not relinquishing her grip on his wrist.

"Dunno, but I have a hunch," he said, trying to twist it free, but the Sylvan was far stronger.

"If you think you're going alone," Orla said as she quickly and quietly stood, "then you really don't know me that well."

"Okay, but quietly," Owen said as he and Orla quickly moved under the cover of the hemlocks. Under the bows there wasn't much snow, but enough had fallen to quiet their escape from the camp. As they were just reaching the edge of the grove a large and familiar shape blocked their path.

Where do you think you're going? Boone's voice boomed in their minds.

"After Winter," Owen said, not stopping, but walking past Boone who sidestepped in front of the boy. "Move or come along, Boone, this isn't open for discussion," Owen said angrily.

The Aingeal have always chosen their own path, they go their own way.

"Well, this time he's getting some help. Now move!" Owen demanded, starting on his way again. The great dog reluctantly let him pass.

I can track him better, even in the snow, the King of Dog's voice boomed in their mind as he bounded past, quickly picking up Winter's trail. Even though the sky was heavy with snow, and laden with deep gray storm clouds, it was a bright night. The snow captured what light there was from behind the clouds and illuminated the forest below. Even for Owen it was relatively easy to make out the landscape around him.

Owen and Orla quickly followed Boone into the thick countryside. Orla shifted to her hybrid form, and when she did, she too picked up Winter's slight trail. Occasionally, in the snow, they caught a glimpse of his tracks but it was quickly being covered by the newly fallen snow. She too was glad Boone had decided to come; his nose was much more sensitive than hers.

They had been hiking for the better part of an hour when Boone came to an abrupt stop. The dog froze in place, the hairs along his shoulders and back raising. His ears pricked up and faced forward, his large plume of a tail arched up and over his back. Owen could see the muscles ripple and tighten along his shoulders even beneath the dense fir.

"What is it Boone?" Owen whispered, just as Orla caught the scent, and gasped audibly.

The air is feted, the massive animal said.

"The Deymon is close," Orla whispered next to Owen. He noticed she was shivering in the night and knew it wasn't due to the cold.

"Winter is close then," Owen began just as the Vrok screamed, shattering the silence, and driving Owen and Orla to the ground, buckling their knees with fright. Boone stayed still, rigid, and on guard. He could hear the faint sounds of bowstrings, and knew Winter had engaged the beast. But he wasn't sure what to do, he was the *Duine Madra* of the *Maou'r*, sworn to protect and serve him, but what happened when those two purposes were in conflict with one another?

The great dog leaned his head back and howled. He howled for Owen. He howled for Winter, and he howled to let the evil beast know Winter wasn't alone in the woods this night.

Owen stood.

It took every ounce of strength he had, even with Boone's howl chasing the evil from his heart. He was filled with terror, never had he been this afraid, never had he been this frozen by the world around him, but still he struggled to his feet. Owen stood and walked to Boone. The dog never changed his position; he just looked into the shadows of the forest. His eyes were blind to the battle being waged in its shadows, but the world was alight to his other senses, and he heard and smelled the battle through the trees.

Orla shakily began to get to her feet, the effort was enormous, and she was amazed that Owen had done it with what seemed like little effort. The Vrok screamed again, freezing her in place, somewhere between a crouch and kneeling.

"Winter is out there fighting it, isn't he?" Owen asked Boone, through teeth he struggled to keep from chattering. Cold sweat ran down the back of his neck. His stomach tightened and cramped, contracting from the fear that tingled through his synapses.

Yes, was all Boone could bring himself to say. His inner struggle to serve and protect the Man next to him was tearing at the very fabric of his conscience.

"Then I must go to him. Protect Orla at all costs," was all Owen said before he bolted into the direction of the screams and the direction in which Boone was looking. He thought for a moment he heard Orla shout his name, but it was drowned out by the voice in his mind.

Be safe, I will be behind you once she is safe. The battle is already engaged and the Aingeal seems to be holding his own.

It didn't take long to find the battle. Owen ran to the edge of a short ledge, barely stopping in time before careening over the side of it. He had run right to where Winter had attacked the beast. Owen stood upon the archer's tracks and beside him was the Hunter's bow. He had ambushed the beast as it entered into this small slot canyon.

And then he saw the Deymon below.

The canyon wasn't more than twenty feet high and barely half that in width. The beast took up most of that space, standing erect it almost reached the top of the canyon with its head on the long snake-like neck. It thrashed and swished around Winter, trying to gain an advantage, it crashed into the sides of the canyon, sending rocks and shrapnel flying. Owen could see down the length of the rock walls huge scars where the beast had climbed and clung to its surface.

Owen could also see arrows stuck into the beast, but none seemed to have hindered or hurt it any. Owen drew his bow from his back just as the Deymon sensed his presence. It screamed and tried to find him along the rock ledge, but his attention was continuously brought back to Winter as he fought the beast with his great sword. Sparks flew as the blade kissed the Vrok's carapace, and hissed as he parried the beast's talons. The blade seemed to not even scratch the unholy creature below.

The beast dodged a great blow from Winter and saw Owen along the rocks; it leapt, trying to break free from the combat. Winter followed the beast's course with his eyes and saw Owen amongst the ledges as well.

"To me, you villain! To me!" Winter shouted, leaping and barring the beast's path from Owen. He brought down his great blade, cleaving through the snow and wind. The blade seemed to glow blue as it struck the Vrok. The air was pierced with the sound of breaking ice as the weapon shattered.

Winter's sword splintered, sending shards in all directions. Falling like so many icicles in the newly fallen snow. The Vrok screamed, but again seemed unhurt. It slowly turned its attention back to Winter, the shadows gathered around it and him like great falcon wings mantling its prey.

"Owen run!" Winter said through clenched teeth, still gripping the hilt of his ruined sword. The air went cold, and Owen felt as if his fingers would turn black from frostbite. Frost froze along the edges of his hair and his eyebrows, and he felt the hair inside his nose freeze as well. The wind howled and blew down on the great, evil beast, and hoarfrost formed along its horns. It screamed its contempt at the *Aingeal* of winter and gnashed its jaws at him.

Like a coiled snake it thrust its long neck out, biting into the rock ledge where Winter once stood; he leapt back down into the canyon, off the small perch he had been on between Owen and the monster, leaving the beast open to approach the *Maou'r*.

But the Deymon sensed victory, and could taste the death of yet another *Aingeal* at its jaws, and turned to face the Hunter. Winter looked briefly up at Owen, who held aloft GreenFyr still sheathed in its scabbard.

"Winter!" Owen shouted, and launched the sword from the rock ledge. The weapon was thrown well, Winter took one step to his side, grabbing it by its hilt, and quickly removing the scabbard with his free hand. But the time it took to catch and draw the blade, was all the time the Vrok needed.

With one fearsome, taloned hand it grabbed the First Man about his torso; two eagle-like fingers digging their talons into and past his collar bones while two more buried into his sides, just under his ribs. The Hunter gasped slightly, his face veiling the pain.

Owen screamed the name of his friend again. Watching as the Vrok pulled the First Man close to its visage, its fetid breath spilling over the man's face. Owen's attempt at help had opened the Hunter to this fate. The young boy, his bow forgotten where he had dropped it, quickly began scampering down the ledge as he heard a great howling from behind him.

Boone was coming!

His howl again nurtured Owen's heart with strength and courage, driving Owen faster down the ledge. He looked to Winter to see that the howl had done the same for him; his face was hardened, stronger. He drew the sword GreenFyr up, running it home into the beast's carapace; a great, green, glow emitted from the blade from inside the beast.

The Vrok screamed again as if in answer to Boone's howl. It was another scream of contempt and anger, not one of pain and dying, as Owen had expected. It brought Winter closer still to his gaping maw, and constricted its grip, driving all four of his talons deep into the *Aingeal's* chest and under his ribs. The Hunter's expression changed and quickly turned blank as stillness enveloped his body.

The Vrok shrieked in victory and turned its attention to the boy behind it, not relinquishing its grip on the now lifeless archer.

Another howl answered the beast from Boone, but he was still not to the canyon. Owen faced the Deymon, alone and weaponless.

GreenFyr still glowed from its place within the Deymon, the emerald hilt calling to Owen. He forced himself not to see Winter still in the beast's grip, and was ready to move when the Deymon finally attacked. Owen launched himself from the ledge, dropping a good two meters from its edge, hitting the snow and ground in a tucked roll, quickly getting to his feet as the beast wheeled about, narrowly missing Owen with its enormous serpent's tail as it did so.

"Owen!" he heard Orla call from the ledge.

We are here. The familiar voice of his dog rang in his ears. Owen thought he sensed a tone of remorse in the sound. He was sure the two friends could see Winter's fate all too well, but then he heard the sound of bowstrings. *The others have come as well. They discovered us gone and quickly followed.*

"No!" Owen shouted. "It only wants me!" One friend had already died for him this night; he couldn't bear to lose another. It wanted him, and he was not willing to lose anyone else this night. "Get outta here!" the boy screamed to his friends.

Owen heard a great war cry from behind the beast, and watched as Brule leapt from atop the ledge, and onto the Deymon's back, bringing down the dwarven halberd with a massive stroke. Brule attacked the Deymon, only to have his weapon explode on contact with the Vrok's armored carapace. The beast bucked, heaving the bounty hunter from it, and with lightning speed, lashed out with its tail, slapping the troll into the stone wall. He slid down amid a small avalanche of rock and shale and lay still, slumped amidst the ruin.

Owen heard the hiss and screams of a large cat and knew that Orla had shifted into her full leopard form. She too leapt from the ledge; landing along the creature's back, digging her claws into the beast, before leaping off, over its head, and landing beside Owen.

She too had lost a friend this night. She too would not stand to lose another.

Aiya fired more arrows into the neck of the Deymon, but it paid them no mind. Its prize was before it, and it had no other desire than to claim it for its mistress. Owen heard the rumble of more rocks and a cry from Balor as he charged the beast from behind; he met the same fate as Brule and was slammed by the lashing tail. The tail caught the dwarf just beneath his arm, knocking the breath from him, but he managed to drive his twin short swords into its flesh before being launched into the canyon walls.

Owen caught a glimpse of Boone along the ledge just before the massive dog leapt and landed at his side. Owen stood before the Vrok, flanked to either side by Orla, in her snow leopard splendor, and by Boone, King of Dogs, last of the *Duine Madra*.

We meet our fate, whatever it be this night, together, my friends, the dog's voice echoed in their minds, muffling the scream of the beast before them.

The Vrok lunged once more, but Owen leapt beneath the beast, avoiding its jaws, which drove deep into the snow and earth where he once stood. Boone bit deeply into the neck of the beast while Orla unloaded with a flurry of slashes and scratches of her claws. The Vrok reeled back, unfazed by the attacks, Boone still shaking and biting. The Deymon shook its long sinewy neck, casting the dog from it. Boone hit the wall, but landed on his feet, charging back into the fray once more. Owen found himself standing beneath the beast. Its attention momentarily on Boone, and he realized the sword, GreenFyr, was just above his head, driven deeply into the Deymon's carapace.

Owen reached up, taking the sword hilt in his hand. The leather was warm to his touch, as if welcoming his hand, while the emerald seemed to shine at his touch. With a mighty pull he took the blade from the beast, sliding it easily from its unholy sheath.

The Vrok screamed again, but this time, it seemed to Owen, in surprise and frustration. The Deymon drew back to its full height, and then just as quickly, lunged back down at him. Its jaws wide, death and decay issuing forth from them. But Owen sidestepped the attack, as easily as Aiya had taught him to, and just as quickly, brought GreenFyr down with a devastating blow.

The sword took the beast by its neck, just behind the skull and horns, cleaving its head from it with the mighty stroke. The head fell to the ground while the neck flailed about, for the briefest of seconds, until a sudden wind pulled inward towards the Vrok's body.

Owen watched as the headless Deymon reeled back, Winter still in its grasp, and the once dark body of the Vrok turned bright white. The body seemed to expand and then collaspe in upon itself.

The lifeless void that had once been the Vrok's vessel was destroyed, and life now rushed in to fill it. With hurricane winds, the empty cavity pulled life into it, until it was full, and then with the same force, the void exploded back—driving everyone in and around the canyon to the ground.

The Vrok was no more, taking Winter's body with him.

Owen landed in a heap, twenty feet from where he'd been standing. He moved quickly to stand again, but once he saw the beast was gone, he slumped back down, letting darkness claim him.

81

Lilith stood at her window licking her fingertips as if they were covered in blood. *So my minion has failed to bring me my prize, but oh, what a sweet failure it has been. Yes, this failure could still be worth my effort and time after all.*

She walked away from her window where the fierce winds and storms of Winter blew against her mountains. They were still quite impassable, and would remain so, for a long while to come. But now she had something else to occupy her with in the meantime.

She took a long Alpaca robe from her wardrobe and wrapped it about her bare shoulders. Her preferred silk shrifts were not warm enough, even for her, against this chill winter air. The fire in her hearth roared to life from her gaze while a little flame did a dance along its edge, masquerading as a Greater Deymon in miniature form.

She walked to the door of her chambers and opened it. Looking once more back to her window, and the inhospitable weather without, she smiled to herself. Yes, her trip to the dungeons would be well worth it, she would certainly find enjoyment in this failure.

82

The boy wept.

Before Owen was fully conscience he was already weeping. Even his subconscious knew what had happened, what was waiting for him on his awakening, and the consequence of it.

Winter was gone.

A howl drowned out the sound of his crying, a mournful, baying sound. Boone's call, which usually filled Owen's heart with love, strength, and courage, now only intensified his feelings of loss and sorrow. He saw the dog's silhouette on the rock outcrop that marked where Owen had first come across Winter and the Vrok in the valley. It was the place the First Man came to end the pursuit of the beast.

It was where he intended to make his last stand.

Boone lifted his massive head back and howled his sorrow into the night. One of the pack had left on his final journey.

A moan and sniffle, from next to Owen, brought his gaze around quickly. Orla was just coming to as well, and with it, her own realization of what had transpired. Owen, stiff and sore from the fight, crawled to her. As tears spilled from the brim of her eyes, she looked into his own tear stained face, and buried her face in his chest and sobbed.

Winter was gone.

Just audible above Orla's crying, Owen could hear the faint sound of singing. Beautiful singing; the sound, as if all of nature could be contained in one harmonious, beautiful voice, singing a sorrowful song. Owen couldn't understand the language Aiya sang in, but he understood the emotion behind the quiet tune. She sat upon a stone near where Winter fell, and sang a song of passage from this world into the next. It was a traditional Sidhe song of mourning, and one Aiya had already sung for her sister only a few days previously.

As Owen held Orla, and tried to comfort her through his own pain, he noticed Brule sitting on a rock only a few feet from where Owen had been lying. The large man sat watching over the boy and Sylvan. He had climbed from the rubble and checked on both of them, once he was convinced they were fine, he sat and waited, guarding them, to make sure nothing else came in the night.

Owen heard a faint tapping and clicking coming from down the canyon. He could make out the solid, stout shape of Balor hunched over something in about the place the Vrok met its end. The dwarf seemed busy at work.

When Orla had finally quieted some, Owen slowly stood and helped her to her feet. Boone had since stopped his howling and come down to them. The three friends walked down the canyon to the dwarf. Brule stood and followed.

Balor had been building a small monument to Winter where he fell and where the Vrok was vanquished. Owen knelt beside the rocks as the dwarf used a small mallet and chisel to etch the stone. He had carved a dwarven word into the top most rock of a small cairn he built from the canyon's rocks. Owen laid his hand on the man's shoulder, who nodded to the boy, and then continued his work.

"What does it say?" Owen asked, his voice sounding like a stranger's to him.

"*GwenderObenUbahn*," the somber, small man said.

"What does it mean?" Owen croaked, his voice catching in his throat.

"Our name for him. He who makes the Above like Below. Winter," Balor answered, his voice heavy with grief.

Owen stood as Aiya worked her way down the rock ledge. She

handed Owen his bow and laid Winter's by the rock pile. The snow had continued to fall, and when Balor had finished his work, there was already several inches upon the stone.

The companions retreated to a small alcove within the canyon, which was to the lee of the wind, and sheltered them from the snow. They set no watches; few of them could sleep anyway. Orla finally drifted off just before dawn while the others sat and stared blankly out into the night.

83

You are Alpha now.

Boone's familiar voice echoed through Owen's mind. Morning had dawned, but the light was still a dull gray, the storm clouds and snow keeping the glowing orb from lighting an otherwise very dark day. The companions had huddled together out of the wind and snow as best they could until morning. Orla was the only one to have slept any, and even that was restless at best. She woke as the night began to fade into a monotone gray morning.

This was my favorite time, Owen thought, *early morning during a snow storm*, thinking now, how nothing could ever make him happy again. "What do you mean?" he asked Boone, realizing the dog had meant him.

With the passing of the Aingeal, you are now Alpha of the pack, you decide where we go.

Owen couldn't believe what Boone was saying. He looked to the rest of the party to see what they were thinking. Brule nodded his agreement. Balor looked pensive, and Orla still seemed lost in thought.

"He is right Owen. It is time for the *Maou'r* to lead, Winter would have wanted it thus," Aiya said simply, and Owen thought, sadly.

"This is nuts, I don't even know what a *Maou'r* is! I wish everyone would stop calling me it!" He threw his hands in the air and began pacing amongst the boulders that had been their shelter for the night.

He stopped abruptly and looked back at his friends. "I'm just a kid, a kid that back in my world, got pushed around and bullied all the time. I'm no leader. Look at all of you! You can transform into animals, are magic, or warriors. I have no magic, I have no powers," Owen said, sitting down on a boulder, and burying his face in his hands. *How can they expect me to lead?*

"Hogswallow!" Balor said, standing from his seat, and walking towards Owen. The boy lifted his head and looked up at the stout man. "No warrior? You slew the dark beast yerself, Man!

"No magic either, eh? Look about you boy, and tell me what you see?" the dwarf demanded, standing in front of Owen. Owen was quiet for a moment, thinking the question rhetorical, but when the dwarf simply crossed his arms over his chest, he looked back at the rest of his companions.

"Us, I see all of us," Owen stammered, not knowing what Balor wanted him to say.

"Exactly!" the dwarf exclaimed. "And what are all of us?"

"I, I don't know Balor...tell me...I don't know," Owen said, too overwhelmed to comply with all of Balor's questions.

"Fine, I'll tell you, then. There's a Sidhe Sword Maiden, possibly the most skilled warriors in all of Parathus, and she's sworn to protect you, fight for you! There's the *Duine Madra*, King of the Dogs, last of his kind, and he's sworn to serve you. There's a trollbjorn bounty hunter, by definition someone who swears allegiance to the highest payer, but I believe he's sworn his sword to you, for not a sickel. There's a Sylvan Princess, who not only calls you friend, but stands side by side with you in the face of evil incarnate. And," he paused only briefly here, "there's a dwarf, who would rather be *Duaegar* to his Kingdom, and travel with you, than take up the crown.

"And then there's Winter. Let me tell you something boy, the *Aingeal* are an odd lot, but I've never heard of one of them to lay down his life for *anyone* before. And he did. For you." Owen looked away, the thought of Winter dying for him wasn't something he needed to hear right now. Hot tears streamed from his eyes, and down his cold cheeks, why was Balor doing this?

"And if that's not magic, then I don't know what is. You might not be the strongest among us, or throw enchantments, or wield a blade as mightily, but there's magic in you, boy. When I left my Kingdom, I wasn't sure I was doing the right thing, but I can tell you now, if there's not magic in that heart of yours, than I'm no dwarf!"

Owen looked back to Balor and couldn't believe what the dwarf had said. No one had ever spoken to him, of him, that way before. No one had ever even seen him like that before, *how could they see me that way?*

He looked back to the rest of the party, all of whom in turn met his gaze, and all in turn nodded their agreement. He looked to Orla last, who through watery eyes, met his stare and held it. She too felt that way, she would follow him to the end of the world, would die for him. She too believed in him the way no one had ever done before. Orla smiled at the dumbfounded look on his face, stood, and walked over to him. She sat down beside him and rested her head on his shoulder.

"That is who the *Maou'r* is, that is why we will follow you," she whispered.

Owen stood and walked out into the storm. He walked down the slot canyon until he came to Winter's cairn. The rock Balor had carved for the fallen archer, the one in which his name was carved, and on which his long bow hung. Owen stopped and looked down at the stone.

"Is this what you intended all along?" Owen asked. "You knew, didn't you? Why did you do it? I can't lead them, I don't know how, I can't do this alone," Owen said, feeling his throat tightening against the emotions that weld up in him.

You are not alone.

Owen turned to see his friends gathered behind him.

"You are not alone," Orla repeated, "the *Maou'r* will never stand alone."

84

Owen took one last look down into the canyon at the monument to the *Aingeal,* where Winter fell. The snow was still falling, but it had lessened in intensity. The wind, too, had died down as the companions had readied themselves to begin their journey again. Owen noticed as Orla pushed her hand into the snow to touch the earth, her heart, and forehead, then giving thanks to Gaia. He looked up into the gray sky, as the snow gently touched and melted on his face, and wondered what she had to be thankful for?

"And where are we heading, Lad?" Balor asked Owen, stepping up beside the boy, and surveying the canyon again, as if for the first time.

"Back to camp," Owen said flatly. "We need to collect the rest of Winter's things and our own bedrolls."

"And from there?" Balor asked, looking Owen in his eyes.

"We keep heading to Narsus, along the path Winter had chosen," Owen said.

"Alright then," Balor said. He looked to Aiya who had joined their conversation.

"I'll take point then," she said, as if it was the most logical choice. She looked at the dwarf, having to look down at him to meet his gaze. Owen could see he wasn't pleased, but also saw it made the most sense. His coal black eyes, shadowed beneath his heavy brows, met the Sidhe's and they didn't speak for a spell.

"Fine," Balor finally conceded, rubbing the sandpaper stubble remains of his beard. "Makes most sense to have you in the lead; little can get past an elf's eyes and ears." Balor looked to Owen to see if the boy had anything to add, which he didn't. He didn't want the mantle of leader, and besides, he had never been a part of deciding their marching order, and he wasn't about to start now.

"Then the dog, his nose is keenest, Owen and the Sylvan, myself and the troll bringing up the rear," Balor concluded with a nod of agreement from Aiya who seemed pleased with the order. She un-slung her bow, knocked an arrow, and waited by the forest edge.

Owen looked down once more into the canyon. Orla stepped up on the ledge with him, and squeezed his hand gently in hers. She shifted to her hybrid form, and as she did so let go, conscience of her lingering touch. Owen smiled at her and turned back to his companions, all of whom had gathered around him, ready to continue their journey.

They fell into their marching order without discussion and Owen continued to expect to see the tall man leading the group whenever he'd look up from the trail.

85

Snow fell heavily on the gray clad figure standing amongst the grove of ancient wooden statues. Each one of infinite detail and long since petrified to the elements. The Gray Pilgrim stood before the statue of the Hunter as it looked down on his friend and liege, bow drawn and at the ready. Snow lay on his friend's wooden shoulders while the old man seemed only to see how lifeless he was.

"It's true then," the familiar and burning voice came from behind him. He didn't need to see her to know who it was, didn't need to see the anger and hurt in her eyes. "He has fallen then?"

The wanderer simply nodded and continued looking at the avatar of his old friend.

"You knew he wouldn't return from this errand you sent him on, you knew," her voice crackled and hissed accusingly behind him. He bowed his head to the elements, seeking refuge within the dark confines of his cloak's hood.

He heard the soft footsteps as another of his *Aingeals* entered the sacred grove. *Is this all, just two?* he thought as the familiar voice came from beside him.

"It was a Vrok that slew him?" the comforting voice asked.

"Yes," the Pilgrim answered, his voice heavy. His throat felt like a corn husk being shucked, letting his voice free to the world.

"A Vrok?" the burning voice said again, "Who let it loose?"

"Haven't you scried for it?" the Pilgrim asked, finally turning to his subjects.

A stout woman with mouse brown hair puttered about her statue across from the Hunter's. She brushed snow and dirt from the base of her likeness as the Pilgrim then looked to the other woman standing before him. She was tall and thin, her hair the color of fire and flame, orange, red, and warm, even in the falling snow. Her eyes were a vibrant green and burning in the night. Her skin was fair and her cheeks bright and flushed in the cool air. She was much angrier than the last time he had seen her.

"No," her voice simmered. "I came as soon as the ravens called to me." As if in response the two birds quorked and chortled their greeting while perched on two other statues.

"Ah," the Pilgrim said, turning his face to the snow above him. Large full flakes fell from the sky quickly blanketing the ground and tree bows about them. He stuck his tongue out and collected the falling snow for a time. It had been many, many years since he'd done such a thing, and he was surprised at himself for doing it now of all times.

"Who called it forth?" the burning voice asked.

"Lilith." The Pilgrim was surprised at how weary his voice sounded. So many years, so many friends, lost.

The wanderer looked back at the woman before him and then down the long line of statues. A tall, dark haired girl with a long sword belted around her thin hips leaned against a similar wooden statue, while a smaller, slight, ginger haired man smirked from beneath an alder tree at the end of the grove. *So, not just two, then. And more, who refused to come, for now.*

"He knew the importance of the appointed task," he said, his voice softening, becoming that of the grandfather, the nurturing father he could be. "He chose his path; I did not choose it for him." A clap of thunder distracted him for a moment.

"Thunder snow?" questioned the matronly woman across from the Pilgrim.

"That's what it seems," he answered.

"What of you? Have you seen the boy from your flames?" the Pilgrim asked the angry, young woman.

"Yes, I see what it sees, when they permit me," the *Aingeal* responded, growing less angry, and more sorrowful, "they have been lighting fires less and less.

"So is he gone then?" the flaming haired woman asked then, her voice cooling to tepid warmth.

The Pilgrim looked back into the falling snow. He scented the air and let his mind open to his ravens. He saw the Thorne Mountains before him, and a young boy wielding a sword bathed in green fire. The flakes fell about them; building on his cloaked shoulders. His birds shook their feathers, shaking the white flakes from them. The snow steamed and hissed before touching the red haired woman. The Pilgrim looked down at the snow covered ground and exhaled slowly, watching his warm breath steam in the cool air. He smiled at the girl in front of him.

He held out his large calloused hand, wrapped in and old scarf, letting the snow slowly accumulate upon it. Once there was a fair amount, he upended his hand and let the snow fall to the ground.

"It appears Winter is still among us."

86

They cut the first set of tracks shortly into their trek back to their original camp. A goblin war band was in their general location, and seemed to be working in a search pattern through the area. The snow through the night should have covered their tracks to the fight with the Vrok, but the goblins were very intent on searching this area.

Aiya had done a fine job leading them around the goblins for the time being, but the creatures seemed determined. Owen didn't like the fact they were so close. He was, however, glad the snow was coming down so heavily and quickly covering their tracks behind them.

The company traveled in silence through the morning. It didn't take them any time to reach the campsite, which seemed to be undisturbed and unmolested by the goblins. Surprising, considering the number of tracks they saw on their way through the woods. They quickly broke camp, shaking the snow from their bedding and supplies. No one touched Winter's things until they had all finished with their own. At first they just stood around it, looking down at the meager possessions of the *Aingeal*, but then Owen bent over and rolled the simple, rough spun wool blanket and cinched it to his own bag, took the small leather pack, with its wine skin and few provisions, and tucked it in with his own. Everything else the Hunter carried on his person.

Owen stood and looked at his companions, all of them foresworn and morose. He knew how they felt; he too was still having trouble coming to terms with Winter's passing. He looked to Orla and she again touched her forehead, and heart before pushing her hand through the snow to touch the earth beneath. It was the second time he'd seen her do it this morning, the last time was in front of Winter's stone, before they left to come here. He had seen her do it many times, but these last two had touched him more than the others. There seemed to be more meaning in it now than before.

"I think we should keep going, the way Winter intended," Owen heard himself saying. He looked to Balor and Aiya, both of whom nodded their agreement.

"We head Northeast, and then come down into Narsus through the mountains."

A horn interrupted their thoughts, breaking the silence of the woods and snow. It was loud and had seemed close.

The dwarf cursed, looking about him anxiously. "Goblin horn, the devils are practically upon us," he growled.

"Most likely, who ever blew that horn, has crossed our trail. We need to move, now!" Aiya said, knocking an arrow as she did so. The companions quickly left camp in the order they'd arrived. Orla shifted into her hybrid form while she stepped into line with the others.

Another horn, further off, answered the first. Owen thought the noise was reminiscent of a conk shell being blown; he assumed it was some type of animal horn they were using. A third, just off in front of them responded to the second trumpet. Aiya stopped them in their tracks and quickly turned them east, and began consciously heading through the thick hemlock understory. The young evergreens, thriving in the shadows beneath the canopy, provided excellent cover for the companions, and also made it near impossible to track through their grove.

Owen could faintly make out shouting deeper in the forest. Aiya moved quickly and decisively, she wasted little time considering her next move. A fourth horn erupted from behind them, right on top of their trail.

Whatever happens, stay close. Boone's voice rumbled through Owen's mind.

Owen checked on Orla to make sure she was close by; he also chanced a quick glance behind them. Balor wasn't too far back, but Brule wasn't in sight. Owen hoped the bounty hunter was fine, but figured he probably had slowed his pace some to keep the rear protected from the coming goblins.

Aiya slowed and then stopped along a small granite wall to the north where a massive sugar maple grew. Its bark roughly plated and fissured.

The companions all moved in close to one another. Owen saw Brule stop just within eyesight of the group and keep watch for any incoming pursuers. Owen tried breathing through his nose and out his mouth, trying to catch his breath. He wasn't sure if he was feeling winded because of their pace or because the goblins were on their trail.

"They're all about us," Aiya said, arrow still knocked, looking at the forest around her, as if waiting for a goblin to step through into the clearing.

"Aye, they're hot on our trail," Balor added. The dwarf didn't seem out of breath or nervous at all. *He's in his element*, Owen thought looking at the veteran of so many goblin wars and battles.

"What do we do then?" Owen asked, anxious to get moving again. He didn't like standing still.

Aiya seemed pensive. It was the first time since meeting the Sidhe that she seemed unsure, Owen thought. *We really must be surrounded*, he thought, *if she's this worried.*

"There's an entrance into the Below World not too far off," Balor suggested. To Owen, it seemed as if the dwarf was reluctant to mention it. "It may not be any safer, though. With this many goblins above ground the Below may be just as hostile. And..." Balor paused as if considering his words, "that part of the Below was lost to the dwarves many years ago, it's goblin occupied now."

"What good will that do us, then?" Orla growled in her hybrid form. Owen could tell she wasn't too keen on returning to the tunnels of the dwarves again. She preferred the open and fresh air.

"It might not do us any," Balor admitted, "but right now, the Above isn't fairing very well, either." The dwarf looked to Aiya and then to

Owen. He would leave the decision to them. He had another reason for not wanting to return to the Below Ground. He was *Duaegar* now, if he was caught, and they with him, they would be treated as criminals and traitors by his own people, and that was something he did not want to bear.

"How far?" Owen asked, thinking anything was better than standing here and waiting to be found.

Balor inclined his head and looked at the wall they stood beside. He took in the grain of the rock, the folds, and heaves of the different types of minerals within its side. He then looked at the sky, and through the thick snow clouds, found the paleness behind them that indicated the sun.

"Half-mile, bit more maybe, in the direction we want to be going," he said after some consideration.

Aiya looked at the dwarf and Owen, she too didn't want to enter the Below Ground again, but she also knew the danger they were in here. She looked in the direction they needed to head as if willing it to reveal any hidden dangers, but when it didn't, she looked back to her companions.

"I think we should head that way," was all the Sidhe offered.

"Me too. If the way opens, we can stay above ground," Owen said.

And if danger persists, we head below, Boone rumbled through all their minds. Orla didn't look happy, but Owen knew she was resigned to do whatever the party deemed best. They moved back into their marching order and moved from the shelter of the wall.

87

Sssshhh," Aiya said, as she scooted back to where Owen, Orla, and the others had ducked down into the thick fir and spruce. It hadn't taken them long to reach the entrance to the tunnels, but they had already avoided two different sets of goblins along the way. The snow was continuing to fall heavily and covering their tracks, but they weren't sure for how long.

"Is there any other way in?" she asked after checking that she hadn't been followed back. She looked over her shoulder once more and then back to Balor.

"Probably," the taciturn dwarf answered.

"Probably?" Owen asked, less reassured than he'd been when the dwarf first recommended this course.

"Hrrmmfff," Balor sighed, "Yes, probably. These mountains and hills are full of caverns, tunnels, mines, and halls. Most are now abandoned, condemned, or occupied by the enemy!" Balor seemed agitated by the direction of the conversation.

"But this is the only one I know of, other than the one we left through," he added, glowering and scowling off into the distance of the opening. "What's wrong with this one?"

"Guarded," Aiya answered. "I saw four guards. Not impossible to get by, but there may be more." She, too, was tense.

"Or they might sound an alarm if not dispatched quickly enough," Balor added.

"I'll go," Brule interjected. It was the first thing the bounty hunter had said, or contributed, since they'd left Winter's canyon.

"Is there no other way?" Orla asked, not bothering to hide her trepidation at entering Below again. She looked to Balor, Aiya, and Owen all in turn.

"I'm afraid not," Balor said, not opening the subject to debate again.

"I agree," Aiya added, more compassionately. "There are far too many goblins searching these forests."

"Aye, but searching for what, or should I say who?" Brule said. "How and why are the goblins about? Why do the goblins care?"

The company grew silent once more. Owen had assumed from the start that the goblins in the wood were out looking for them, but Brule was right, why? A better question would be who told them they were in the woods in the first place.

"Fair point," Balor acknowledged. "Goblins themselves wouldn't care a bit, they'd as soon come across any other race as you or the *Fey*, anything other than a goblin is fair game to them. But if they were working for someone else, well, that would make more sense."

"Can't we discuss this some other time and place?" Orla suggested.

"Yes, we can, if we can get into the underground then we might buy ourselves some time from these search parties. We can always come back to the surface a little ways from here to break up our tracks," Aiya said.

What tracks? Boone asked. *The snow has been covering our trail. They're tracking us some other way.*

"He's right," Balor said. "Bah, we need to get some place safe, so we can sort through all this."

"I'll take care of the guards then," Brule offered again.

"It would be safer from a distance," Aiya offered hefting her bow a bit.

"Aye, but they might sound the alarm if each shot wasn't just right," Balor conceded. "The bounty hunter's right, up close and personal is the way to go on this one. I'll go with him."

Brule nodded his agreement as well as a reluctant Aiya. The dwarf and trollbjorn left the small group, quickly splitting up, and approaching the guards from opposite sides. The companions' vantage point did not offer a view of the door to the Below Ground, so they sat quietly waiting for any sound that might clue them in as to what was happening. Aiya and Boone stood guard on either side of Owen and Orla, both straining their exceptional senses for any sign of danger and approaching goblins.

It seemed like hours passed as the snow slowly accumulated on their shoulders. Owen looked up into the sky and wondered if Winter had anything to do with the storm. It had begun just before he had fallen to the Deymon. Owen shook his head, he had seen a lot of strange and unbelievable things since coming to Orla's world, but he knew what he saw. Winter had died that night, not even one night ago; but there was no way he could have survived what he'd seen. No matter what he wanted to believe.

A soft groan and a muffled shout came from the direction of the goblin guards. Owen, Orla, and the others went on guard, waiting for an alarm signaling their discovery, but one never came. It didn't take long for Balor to come back the way he'd left to let them know the coast was clear. He led them back to the entrance.

Brule was disposing of the goblins when they got there. He had piled the corpses on the far side of the entrance beneath some hobblebush growing in the understory amongst the spruce. Owen watched the bounty hunter take a short sword, dirk, and hand axe from the corpses. He slid the sword and dirk into his belt and the axe into his belt at the small of his back. He broke some of the spruce bows off the trees and laid them atop the goblins. He turned and saw Owen watching him and quickly came back over to the group. He stopped next to Owen.

"I know it looks disputable, but don't let good equipment or gear go to waste. You never know when you'll need it." The trollbjorn slapped Owen on the shoulder. "C'mon, let's get out of the snow."

Owen adjusted GreenFyr in its scabbard on his belt. Aiya had taken a position to the left of the entrance, Orla by her side, Brule, Boone, and Owen on the right side. Balor approached the door. He studied the seam around the edge and then the locking mechanism.

"Animals!" he growled. "No respect for craftsmanship," he muttered.

"Can you open it?" Aiya asked, nervous about being exposed along the rock wall.

"Can I open it?" Balor scoffed. "There isn't a dwarven made door that I can't open," he said, lifting the latch and shoving the door open. The door had not been locked. He drew his twin swords and walked into the dark opening, its shadows enveloping him as he did so.

Aiya, Owen, and the rest of the companions followed him. The tunnel was dark, dimly lit by torches in sconces sparsely spaced along the rock walls. The craftsmanship was again remarkable and unmistakably dwarven, but the care and cleanliness of the tunnels were undoubtedly goblin. Trash and waste were strewn all along the halls. Garbage, junk, bones, and carcasses lay randomly about. The stench made Owen retch; catching vomit in the back of his throat, he couldn't imagine anything living this way. Brule closed and sealed the large stone door behind them. He took one of the hammers from his bandolier and hammered a spear point, from a broken shaft he'd found in the tunnel, wedging it between the stone hinges, pinning the door closed and preventing anyone from following them.

Or us escaping, Orla thought as she felt the walls close in about her. *It's just a room, just a hallway in my house,* she tried to convince herself.

"I think it best you lead while we're in here," Aiya said, "I'll step to the back with Brule."

"Agreed," the dwarf said, and Owen could have sworn he sensed a pleased tone to Balor's voice. He knew the dwarf liked leading the group, being more in control.

"Where will this tunnel take us?" Owen asked.

"This one heads north, but it will have many junctions and offshoots that we can take to bring us back down into the Sylvan Kingdom. If I recall correctly, there is one that will head right into the capital city."

The companions followed Balor into the Below. The slope began to descend as they moved deeper into the rockface. As they moved away from the entrance the debris and trash lessened and eventually vanished. Goblin graffiti was scrolled along the rockface over the original dwarven sculptures and writings. Every time they passed such vandalism Balor would rant and rave about the barbarian animals that his people were waging war against. They weren't in the tunnel for very long before they could hear a low rumble following down the corridor behind them.

"They've breached the door," Brule said flatly. Owen noticed he slackened his formation from the others, keeping a little more space between himself and them.

A horn sounded from behind them. The trumpet followed them down the corridor and passed them like a wave down into the depths of the mountain. Another horn sounded from the deep.

Balor stopped their procession. He waited for anymore horns to sound, but no others answered. He turned and looked back at the others, all of their faces grim from the sudden realization that they were trapped between the two groups of goblins.

"Quickly now," the stout man said, turning and plunging deeper into the depths of the tunnel—not the direction Owen might have chosen, but then again, back the other way wasn't a great option, either. Balor moved at a fair trot, as quietly as he could, and surprisingly, the solid man could move across the rock floor with amazingly little noise. The rest of the group, except Brule, was also silent. The chain shirt Owen wore made no noise and his soft black boots kissed the floor tenderly and silently.

They ran downhill along the tunnel, the horns sounding at regular intervals, the one behind them somewhat distant, but the one in front growing louder with each call. Balor continually turned his head from side to side, searching the rock walls for something. He had put away his twin swords, but he instinctively clenched and unclenched his fists as he ran. Owen noticed that both Boone and Orla would lift their noses to scents in the tunnels, trying to catch the scent of their pursuers. Owen just tried to maintain the pace at which they traveled without tripping over anything in the dark corridors. As they moved further into the depths of the Below, the torches became more scarce and eventually vanished altogether. The unparalleled craftsman of the dwarves allowed for some light in the tunnel from light shafts and other means of reflecting light down into the depths, but it had long since grown quite dark. Orla had cast a small charm for Owen, with a look of surprise from Aiya, to help light his way. She had picked up a small pebble along the floor and spoke a quiet word above it. At the word the pebble began to glow, dimly at first, but then a little more strongly. The pale green light reminded Owen of a glow stick from back home, and even though the pebble didn't throw much light, the bit it did was a marked improvement. He felt embarrassed by the tool; however, because he was otherwise sure no one else in the party would have needed the aid.

He held the stone between thumb, index and middle fingers as he jogged behind Boone, he could barely hear Orla behind him, the soft padding of her paws on the rock and her steady breathing. The soft green glow gave the tunnels and eerie, sick feeling.

Balor came to a sudden stop in front, causing Boone to almost run him over, and Owen to almost crash into the both of them. The others slowed down without any problems. Balor turned to a small outcrop, almost imperceptible to the eye unless looking right at it; Owen knew he would have walked by it without even a second glance.

"In here, quickly," Balor ordered, leading the way into the small space. The alcove led steeply downward. The space was cramped; Owen needed to incline his head to avoid braining himself.

"Cripes, could you have found a smaller hole for us to crawl into?" Brule grumbled from behind. Owen could only imagine the difficulty he was having moving through the tunnel.

"You could stay behind," Balor grumbled in return. "It has been a very long while since I've been here, but I thought I remembered this route on my last journey."

"Where does it lead?" Owen asked.

"Dunno, didn't explore it last time, just remembered passing it," Balor confessed.

"Great," Owen mumbled.

"Wonderful," Orla added under her own breath.

The tunnel was much steeper than the first one they entered; it switched back and forth at sharp corners driving the group deep below ground. The walls were much rougher in their workmanship. This was not a tunnel for show, this was an expressway not intended for everyone. The air in this part of the passages was stale and thick, with a sour taste to it.

It was the first time since entering the network of corridors that the horns were not easily discernable. For now, they seemed to have put some distance between themselves and the goblins.

The companions were just turning another sharp bend of the switch back when suddenly the way was blocked by a rockslide. Small, soccer ball sized rocks had fallen from the ceiling and wall across the small tunnel, blocking the way.

"Geezum Crow," Owen mumbled.

"Bloody Hell!" Balor growled as he quickly approached the slide to investigate it. He climbed up onto the rocks, tried shifting some of them, and then inspected the side walls and ceiling around the collapse.

"What do we do now?" Aiya asked from down the line. The tunnel was too small for them to shift their marching order, or to help Balor with the inspection.

"What's going on up there?" Brule grumbled from down the line.

"Cave in," Orla responded, sounding more despondent than she wanted.

"Ssshh, I'm thinking," the dwarf grumbled back. "Do you feel that?"

"Feel what?" Owen asked.

"That breeze," Balor answered, frantically trying to find the source of the air current.

Owen held his breath trying to feel the air filtering into the passage. He could only hear Brule, cramped, and grumpy at the end of the line muttering to himself. Boone too, lifted his nose to try and find the breeze. Owen could only imagine how this collapse was affecting Orla, she hated to be down here in the first place, and now her fears were made real with the collapse.

"It's here!" Balor exclaimed, a little louder than Owen would have liked. "There's air being pulled into the tunnel here!" The dwarf climbed up the small pile of rocks that blocked their way, and very carefully, shifted some of the rocks around the source of the breeze. He was careful not to disturb the pile while doing so, making sure the remains of the ceiling and wall were still well supported by the other downed rocks. The dwarf was able to move enough of the rocks to make a sufficient space for the party to crawl through.

"What about Boone?" Owen asked stepping up beside the dog.

I'll fit, I'll just go last to make sure I don't dislodge any for anyone else, his voice echoed in their minds. Owen didn't like the idea, it wouldn't be easy for the big dog to drag himself through the rubble, but he honestly saw no other way.

"I'll go first and investigate the other side," Balor offered, climbing back up the pile of debris.

He quickly disappeared down the hole he'd made, not shifting a single rock. He was only gone a short while, during which the companions remained absolutely quiet and still, listening for any sound of the dwarf or the goblins behind them. The dwarf quickly returned, poking his head out the hole.

"Opens into a fairly large cavern, seems deserted, I didn't investigate thoroughly, however," he said, brushing dust off his brow. "The slide seems sturdy enough. Follow me through and I'll secure the far side." He quickly disappeared back through the tunnel.

Owen turned and looked back down the length of his companions. He wasn't thrilled about going next. Boone had laid down before him so he could step over him to climb the slide up to the hole.

"I'll go next, Owen," Aiya said, slipping by Orla as the small Sylvan squeezed into the wall to try and make room. "It would be better for Balor to have someone on the other side to help secure the cavern," she said, before lightly climbing up the rocks and slipping in and vanishing into the hole as well.

"Sure," Owen said, feeling worse that someone else had gone before him. *Make up your mind,* he thought as he stepped over Boone, *am I your leader or not.* "Be careful," he said to the big dog as he climbed up the rocks to the hole, which seemed much larger up close than it did back in the tunnel. It seemed large enough for the troll and Boone, but it wouldn't be a comfortable fit for either of them.

Owen entered the hole with his left hand extended before him, holding the glow-stone Orla had charmed for him. It was difficult to crawl through the space using only one arm, but he didn't want to be without the light in such a confined space. He did realize at one point that the ceiling above him was higher than he realized. It had given way to the rocks, dropping them into the corridor, but he didn't want to shine his light above his head and see all the millions of tons of stone above him. The fact that some of them had already fallen onto this passage made him feel less like inspecting the hole he now crawled through. It was easier for him to put faith in Balor's inspection, after all he, more than Owen, knew what he was looking for.

Now that he was in the hole, he could feel the breeze. It blew steadily into his face, much fresher and cleaner air than what had been in the tunnel. Owen couldn't see or hear Aiya in front of him. He felt like he was barely making any progress. His breathing was increasing into rapid short breaths and he thought he could hear his heartbeat echoing off the rocks around him. Sweat began to drip down his forehead and into his eyes.

"Owen?" Orla's quiet, tense voice came from behind him.

"Yeah?" he replied hoarsely.

"I'm not sure I can do this," she said, her voice, even in her hybrid form, cracking and sounding scared. More scared than Owen had ever heard her sound before.

Somehow she had gotten to right behind him, if he looked back he could see her as close to him as she could get without crawling up onto his back. Her eyes were wide and dilated in the faint green light, glowing like a cat's in a car's headlights by the light of his stone. Her leopard ears were laid flat against her skull.

"You can do this, Orla. You can, and you will," Owen said, trying to overcome his own fears and sound strong for his friend. He wished he could reach back and take her hand, leading her out, but there really wasn't enough room for that. They probably could fit side by side if they tried, especially if she shifted back to her *Fey* form, because Balor had made the passage big enough to accommodate Brule and Boone, but neither one of them wanted to feel any tighter or more crowded right now. He took a deep breath and tried to control his own breathing and heart rate.

"Look at me," he said to her. She looked at him with her large, green, cat eyes and he could see the naked fear there, completely bare. "I'll help you get through this. I'll watch out for you," he said more assuredly.

He could see her swallow and try to muster her courage. She never broke eye contact with him, as if doing that would be the end of her. Orla took a deep breath in through her nose and let it out through her mouth.

"I'll try," she finally said, and even though it was hard to tell in this shape, Owen thought she tried to smile for him.

"Hold my leg if you want, squeeze if you need to or want me to stop," he said. "I'm going to get us out of here, okay?" She nodded her answer even though the last thing she wanted was for him to turn away. In his eyes she could find her courage, she could find a place where the walls didn't seem so close or the rock above her so oppressively heavy.

Owen turned and began crawling again. He could feel her wrap one of her hybrid hands around his ankle. She held it firmly and tightly, and Owen was certain if she got scared enough she could snap the bones in it without much effort. He began to speak to her softly as they went. Quietly, gently, encouraging her to keep moving and telling her that everything else would be alright and that soon, very soon, they'd see the sky again.

"Almost there, Orla, I can see the end of the tunnel now, almost there," he said as they closed in on the end of the passage, which hadn't been more than twenty feet, but felt to them as if they'd crawled a mile.

When he reached the opening he quickly pulled himself free, turned, and helped Orla out as well. She let him guide her to the opening where she leapt with cat-like grace from the hole at the top of the slide to the floor beneath. She perched on the floor, knees bent, with one hand steadying her against the stone ground. She shook her body, as if physically and literally shaking off the encroaching vibe of the walls.

Orla looked back to Owen and again smiled her awkward hybrid smile at him. Her eyes were less large now and she seemed better. She nodded her head to him in thanks and he returned the smile and nod. He was sure he was going to have a bruise around his ankle in the morning.

He took in the cavern from his perch upon the rockslide, holding his glow-stone up slightly to illuminate their surroundings. He saw Balor to one side of the slide beneath him and Aiya walking over to check on Orla. The room was enormous, with what looked like another rock slide in the far corner. Owen couldn't see the ceiling above them, nor could he make out one of the far walls, to the East he thought, but around him were what appeared to be the remains of a battlefield. Large and small skeletons lay strewn across what looked to have been a great dwarven hall at one time. Large sculpted columns graced its center and middle, broken, rotten furniture was scattered about the floor between corpses.

Owen slowly worked his way down the slide as he heard Boone and Brule working their way through the hole. The rocks were looser on this side and he slid and ran the length of the slope. The sound of the tumbling stones reverberated and echoed off the chamber, sounding like rolling thunder across the Great Plains. Owen winced at the noise he'd made, hoping it would be contained in the great hall.

"Don't worry, Lad, the great halls of old were always hewn to have acoustics like that, to throw the Thane's voice so everyone in attendance could hear him," Balor offered, but Owen could see the small man looking about his surroundings, wondering the same as Owen. Had anyone else have heard the disturbance?

Brule hoisted himself from the hole, dusted himself off and worked his way down the slope. Much to Owen's embarrassment, he didn't dislodge a single rock on his way down. The grace in which the enormous trollbjorn carried himself was always deceiving.

Boone emerged from the hole, but he, like Orla, chose to leap down. He wasn't as graceful as Orla, but he landed well, thudding against the floor once, and trotted over to Owen to check on his *Maou'r*.

"What is this place?" Owen asked.

"It was once the great hall of *D'mjohl Dunne*, but it has long since fallen from the minds and tongues of dwarves. It was the place of the final battle between the dwarves and the Under-Elves. In this hall was where it ended, no one who fought that day ever lived to tell how, however," Balor explained, again looking about the hall with an eerie respect and apprehension.

"Are you sure? How can you be certain?" Aiya asked.

Balor seemed annoyed at being questioned. He was not quick to respond, he walked amongst the ruins close to the hole they'd climbed through. "Location, first of all," he grumbled, "but also the skeletons, many thick boned dwarves, and an equal number of light boned corpses; your dark cousins," he said, lifting the forearm bones of one of the delicate skeletons he mentioned.

"Also, this hall matches the descriptions of *D'mjohl Dunne*," Balor looked around the hall. "We should look about the place; see if we can find any other ways out of here."

"Where should we look first?" Owen asked.

"There seems to be a greater concentration of bodies northeast of here," Aiya said, her keen Sidhe eyes allowing her a better perspective of the surrounding area.

"No one has been in this hall since the battle?" Brule asked, looking about the destruction. "And how long has that been?" The bounty hunter was taking in the scene about him as well.

"I'm sure goblins have been all through here," Aiya suggested bending closer to the stone floor. She dragged her finger along a broken bench to judge the amount of dust. "Considering how long it's been, it's remarkably clean."

"It's been more than ten generations of dwarves since the battle. For the Kingdom to reclaim this hall, especially now, from the ill begotten scum that reside in these burrows," Balor began, but then held his tongue, remembering he was no longer a part of the Dwarven Free Folk.

Owen watched as the stout man stopped himself, but still considered what this discovery would mean to his people. He had sworn his life and honor to helping Owen find his family and rescue them, but now, he was faced with one of the greatest halls of his people.

He knew the internal struggle within Balor must be immense. As Owen watched the dwarf, Balor turned to him and smiled. Something the dwarf, any dwarf, did seldom.

"It has been here for these many centuries, it will still be here for that many more. My place is here, with you," Balor said, as if sensing Owen's thoughts. Owen smiled in spite of himself.

The companions dispersed and began working their way through the ruined hall. Aiya and Balor took point, Owen and Orla following, with Boone and Brule bringing up the rear. They weaved in and out of the old broken furniture and sculptures. Huge blast marks scarred the granite and marble, scorching pillars and tables. Swords, axes, and pole-arms of dwarven soldiers littered the floor along with the thin rapiers and daggers of the Under-Elves.

"What happened to the Under-Elves?" Owen asked, amazed at the destruction and show of power in the vast room. He stopped at a crater at the bottom of which lay a score of broken dwarf skeletons. The ground around the edge of the crater was reflective, turned to glass from whatever had been detonated or exploded on the site.

"They retreated deeper, further than even we dare to go," Balor said hesitantly. "But that's just what folk say, no one really knows."

Brule stopped and inspected a dwarven axe, only to place it back from where he'd taken it. He continued on, looking over certain pieces, and moving on. The companions passed another place where the ceiling had collapsed, leaving a large pile of rock and rubble across the floor, broken limbs jutting out from under the debris. The skeleton of a large reptile or serpent's tail exteneded from beneath the massive rockslide; judging by the size of the tail, Owen estimated the animal had easily been the size of one of the largest dinosaurs. Banners and tapestries, rotted beyond cipher, lay strewn across the room, more evidence of the destruction that occurred in this place.

"It's a tomb," Aiya whispered, and slowly began to sing her song. The one she'd sung for her sister and Winter. She held her bow before her, arrow at the ready, while her voice traveled through the vast room, like soft spring rain on the leaves of a parched forest.

"There," Balor said, nodding his head in the direction of another pile of rubble. The dwarf began heading in its direction; the others followed. As they approached, Owen realized the pile of debris was not rock, from another cave in, but corpses. Skeletons long since dried and devoid of flesh and tendon piled in a heap of death. Atop the pile sat a lone figure, crossed legged, with a large war hammer across his lap. He wore an enormous helm that covered the upper portion of his face, but left exposed his nose and mouth. In life he wore a red beard, the remains of which still clung to his dried, mummified chin and mouth. The helmet still shone in the filtered light of the hall, gold and platinum glinted through the otherwise dim darkness. Eye slits peered across the field of destruction and the death on which he sat. A long dark cloak fell from his shoulders and plated armor, gauntleted arms and hands rested upon the shaft of the mighty hammer. The man was much taller than any dwarf and built much more solidly than any *Fey.*

"*D'onner G'ott,*" Balor whispered at the sight of the corpse. The mass grave of bodies was as large as any of the rockslides. The pile of bodies were all Under-Elf, hundreds of them. The ground beneath and around them was again blasted and devastated, the floor cracked and scarred.

"Who was he?" Orla asked, stepping closer to Owen. So much death; it seemed senseless to her. The Below had troubled her before this for its close confines, but now, more than ever, it seemed like a large grave to her.

"*Aingeal,*" was all Aiya said. The word carried enough meaning; she needed to say nothing else.

"He fought beside the dwarves of *D'mjohl,*" Balor said, more to himself than the party. "We had *not* fought alone."

"He didn't just fight with them," Brule said, approaching the pile, "he died with them." Balor looked to the big man and nodded an acknowledgement between the two warriors of the significance of the sacrifice. Balor kneeled before the pile of corpses, laying his swords on the ground before him.

Brule looked up at the pile, he tried to calculate the sturdiness of its construction, whether he could climb it or not. He wanted to investigate, to appraise that weapon, and armor. The trollbjorn looked at his companions, his friends, and wondered what they would think of him if he did so. He knew Balor wouldn't appreciate the affront to the First Man who'd died with his kin. The dwarf had granted him a weapon at their first encounter, now armed; he didn't think the honorable man would appreciate him robbing this grave. The wealth of the weapon was not worth the cost of their friendship. He turned his back to the corpse.

"But it looks like he won," Owen said, staring at the man atop the lurid heap. "Why did he stay here to die?"

Balor looked back up at the man. "Maybe he was grievously wounded and wouldn't have lived anyway."

"Or maybe after this day, he no longer wanted to live," Aiya suggested, taking in the full horribleness of the death and destruction about them.

"Aye, or maybe that," Balor said, suddenly sounding tired and weary.

"We need to keep moving," Brule suggested. He'd been looking around the room for any sign of an exit from this tomb, but hadn't seen one. There was a possibility, but it too had been blocked by a rockslide.

"I'll go scout about for an exit, why don't the rest of you rest some," Balor suggested. He stood and sheathed his swords.

"I'll go with you," Brule said.

"Do you think it wise to separate?" Aiya asked.

"With the acoustics of the hall, I'm certain we would hear anyone who enters the hall, it should be fine," Balor said. He looked to Orla and Owen and then back to Aiya as if suggesting the rest could do them good. Aiya nodded.

"Why don't we move more to the center of the hall, and away from here," Aiya suggested to Owen and Orla who silently agreed. The three of them and Boone walked away to find a more suitable place to rest.

"Where do you want to start?" Brule asked.

Owen, Aiya, Orla, and Boone all made camp a little ways from the First Man and started a small cooking fire. They heated some of their provisions and rested while Brule and Balor completed a search of the hall, trying to find an exit out of the vast room. Once during that time the companions heard the faint trumpeting of a horn back in the direction of the rockslide they'd climbed through to reach *D'mjohl Dunne*. Shortly after the horn blast the dwarf and bounty hunter returned. They had been gone for close to an hour.

"We found another passage we can squeeze through to exit the hall. We must hurry however; I fear the goblins have discovered our last route," Balor said quickly, taking a piece of dried meat and dark bread from the food the others had left for him and Brule.

"We heard the signal as well," Aiya and the others were already prepared to depart. Brule and Balor grabbed their share of the meal, and the companions quickly headed to the passage the friends had discovered as a second horn blast resounded throughout the chamber. The hall amplified the horn, casting it off of the walls, echoing in the deep. They could now hear screams and growls as the goblins picked up their trail. Great beastly howls erupted from the hounds the goblins had used to find the scent of the party. Swords and axes banged against shields as the goblins poured into the hall from the small hole through which the party had entered.

The companions rushed to the new exit as they heard their pursuers chasing them through the hall. Chancing a quick look over his shoulder as he ran, Owen saw that it was indeed a large war band behind them. Two of the goblins in front had huge hounds on thick iron chains and collars dragging them after the party. The dogs looked like huge mastiffs with thick bristling hairs down their spines and short, docked tails. Their shoulder muscles rippled as they pulled their handlers on.

Owen could hear the rumbling and growling emitting from Boone, and he could feel that the dog wanted to stop and fight, facing these traitors to his race, but the King of Dogs continued on with the others, not willing to lead his *Maou'r* into such a fight.

They reached the other entrance and Aiya and Balor immediately turned and shouted for Orla and Owen to push their way through first. Aiya un-slung her bow and knocked an arrow. Balor unsheathed his short swords, waiting for the first clash. Boone spun and howled in the chamber, drowning out all other sounds and filling the hearts of his allies with courage and his enemies with fear. The *Duine Madra* wanted blood, and their pursuers now knew it.

Brule let out a war cry and spun to face the onslaught of goblins holding a dwarven thrower in each hand. "Who will be the first to allow me to practice with my new hammers!" he shouted back at the goblins.

Orla leapt up the slope of rocks, not pausing an instant. She shifted to full leopard form for better traction up the slope as she entered the opening. This passage was larger, not as broken as the last. Parts of the bracings of the ceiling were still intact as Owen followed her through, hearing the first volley of arrows fired by Aiya at the oncoming goblins. The passage was dark, almost pitch black. Owen fumbled for his glow-stone as he tried to keep from falling as he moved into the exit.

"Orla!" he shouted. "Orla I can't see, wait up!" he shouted after her. He suddenly heard a loud crashing and what sounded like bottled thunder as he felt the rocks he crawled across begin to slide out from under him.

He heard Orla cry out in front of him, "Ooooooowweennnnn!" as the rocks drowned out her voice and the passage caved in around them.

88

Dust and pebbles exploded from behind the four companions who faced the oncoming goblins. The roar of the rocks sliding and shifting drowned out the noise of the villains as well as the companions' own cries of horror.

Aiya continued to fire arrows into the advancing goblins, dropping an enemy with each shaft. Boone's howl shifted from defiance and courage to one of fear and doubt. The great dog leapt onto the rockslide behind him, and with his massive forelegs began pulling and digging the heavy stones away from the now closed opening.

"Help him!" Aiya shouted, as she fired more arrows. She knew she didn't have many shafts left, but a Sidhe Sword Maiden was more than just an archer. *Let them come!* she thought, letting fly more arrows and felling more goblins.

Balor turned and sheathed his swords while scampering up the slope. He had to dodge several beach ball size boulders from Boone as he did so.

"Boone! Easy Boone!" he shouted, as he got up alongside the dog. The massive animal was frantic, his mouth agape and frothing, his paws bloody from digging and moving the large stones. He whimpered and howled as he desperately tried to excavate the rockslide. "Boone! You have to slow down, boy! You'll cause another slide!" Balor pleaded with him while he tried to inspect the damage to the entrance.

It was now blocked, but *by the Abyss how deep does the collapse go?* Balor thought as he too started shifting stones out of the way.

"Rrrrrrraaaaarrrrrr!" Brule bellowed as he sent two hammers sailing across the expanse between the party and the goblins. The hammers each met their marks, crushing the skulls of the two large hounds the goblins had been using to track them.

Brule had heard Aiya's cry to start moving rocks, but the oncoming goblins were still too many, even with her picking off the leading troops. He could lessen their numbers before they reached him and his allies; besides, too many bodies on that slope would not help things. Balor and Boone were more than capable of reopening that hole. Brule was sure they would find Owen and Orla safe on the far side.

Aiya slung her bow over her shoulder. She was nearly out of arrows, only a few left. If she didn't draw her sword now, and replace the bow, the goblins would be on them before she had time. She pulled the long curved blade from the scabbard on her belt. The shimmering silver blade, the epitome of elvin craftsmanship, glimmered in the dim hall light. She took a two handed hold on the hilt and prepared for the first goblin to reach her.

Brule slid the goblin short sword from his belt and pulled another hammer from his bandolier. As the first goblin reached him, he brought the small mallet down just off the shoulder of the creature that engaged him, driving the wretched creature to the ground with the sound of shattering bones. Three more goblins dropped as they reached the half-troll.

Brule looked up at the goblins around him. Most of their number had now reached him and Aiya. The Sword Maiden had laid to rest several of her own goblins. Her sword dripping crimson. The goblins' long noses twitched, their long pointed ears wiggled, they shifted their weight from one foot to the other. And then, they all charged at once.

Aiya took the first goblin through the stomach, slicing him nearly in half. She decapitated the next, and cleaved another's head in two. She had just disarmed a fourth while dodging a wild slash from another when she chanced a glance to the troll next to her. Brule was fairing as well as she, but she could barely make out the giant man from behind the wave of goblins surrounding him.

"Aiya! Brule! We have a path, I'm going through!" Balor shouted from the slope. Boone had already stuck his nose in and had gotten both scents, but he couldn't tell anything more. They were close by, but that was all.

"I'll call back to you if the way is clear," Balor said to the dog as he pulled himself into the cleared passage.

Boone turned back to see the fray unfolding below him. He very much wanted to vent his frustrations on some goblin necks, but he also wanted to be right there to move through the opening once Balor secured the passage.

Aiya sliced two more goblins and began working her way towards Brule. She needed to reach him to buy the company some time and much needed space.

Brule brought his sword around in a blinding arc, driving back the surge of goblins and downing two of them that didn't get out of the way in time. With his hammer, he smashed the face of one goblin trying to rush in behind his sword.

Aiya slew two more goblins before leaping up onto the slope to stand beside Boone. The goblins had fallen back. A horn sounded below them and was answered immediately by one close to their original entrance into the hall and by two more further up the tunnel.

Bbbbbbaaaaaaaaarrrrrrrooooooooo.

Brule worked his way up the slope as he cleaved through a lingering goblin. The war party that had fallen on them was in shambles, with the remaining numbers falling away from the two warriors. The remnants of the first band merged into the other now charging across the hall. It didn't take long for the newly formed war party to start banging their shields and chanting again. Two more horns sounded in the distance, but both seemed to be growing closer.

Bbbaaaaaaaaaaarrrrrrrrrrooooooooooooooooooo.

Owen shook his head, not so much to shake the dust free, but to clear his thoughts. Touching the back of his head, he felt a mighty lump already forming, checking his hand, he was glad it came away without any blood. He still couldn't see anything, the darkness seemed to lighten to a pale gray, but so much dust now floated in the air it was like a thick fog.

"Orla!" his voice echoed down what seemed like a long corridor.

A rattling chortle of a laugh met his voice, bouncing back up the corridor to him.

"Gots somthin' o' yers, I wager," a nasally voice mocked him.

Owen stood, barely; his legs were wobbly, and his head felt cloudy and dizzy while the lump on the back of it throbbed. The dust was clearing some, and he could better make out his surroundings. The slide had slid further into the corridor, essentially removing their floor while they were crawling through the passage. Looking behind him, it did seem like more of the ceiling gave way in the process, blocking his friends from him and trapping them on the far side from the war band. Not that things were much better over here, though.

Owen drew GreenFyr from its sheath, the blade glowed pale green in the dust filled hallway. His legs were shaky, but he took a tentative step in the direction of the laugh. *What had happened to Orla?* he thought.

"Wassa matta, goblin gots yer tongue?" the mocking voice drifted through the floating sediment once more.

"Orla?" Owen asked cautiously. He didn't want to give away his position, but he needed to know she was okay.

"Oiy, she's fine, tasty, she is," again the mocking, grating laughter.

"If you harm her…" Owen started, anger replacing the fear. It spread through him, clearing his head, and steadying his legs.

"Wha'? Wha' ya gunna do den?" the voice gnashed back, no longer mocking, but sinister, evil, and full of malice.

"I'll make you pay, I'll make you regret the day you were born," Owen answered, with his clearing mind, the visibility in the passage was clearing as well. He could make out two shapes about ten meters distant against the far wall, one much larger than the other. The smaller one seemed to be holding something, Orla perhaps. The dust was still heavy enough to make it difficult for Owen to make out his adversaries.

"Oiy, boy, I already regret dat," the creature mocked again. "You gotta do betta den dat!" Howling laughter from the small one and what seemed like chuckling from the larger.

"What do you want?" Owen asked. He wasn't sure if the two villains could see him yet.

"Well, now dat's mo' like it. Tricky question, ain't it, wha' I wan', eh? Wha ya got?" the voice sneered. Owen was truly beginning to hate it. It grated on his nerves like nothing he'd ever heard before, as if grinding metal could speak.

"I want to know she's okay, first," Owen said, trying to buy himself more time. He moved closer to the wall to his left. More shadows remained against that wall, he carefully stepped, inching his way closer.

"She's fine boy, but ya keep tryin' t'be sneaky, an's come any closa, she won't be as pretty as ya 'members hers." That got a larger chuckle from the big one. It was taller than Brule, but not as muscular looking. It had an exceptionally large head for its body, more slender shoulders, but longer arms. It slouched, letting the long arms hang even further, and it looked like it held a weapon in its left hand. Through the dust, which was clearing still, it looked like the ogre Owen had met on the road beyond the City. In the clearing gloom it looked as if the creature held a large wooden club. The smaller one now definitely looked like he was holding Orla. He held her in front of him, with one hand around her throat and the other holding a wicked looking knife to her face.

The anger that had flowed through Owen was ebbing to fear again. What could he do to help her? He was powerless, and these two creatures seemed so much more than a match for him.

"I want to hear it from her," he said, trying to keep his voice firm, in control.

"Go ahead den m'sweets, tell yer hero yer fine den," the creature mocked again. The dust had all but cleared now and Owen could finally see clearly. Rocks were strewn across the hallway, and it seemed that these two creatures were squatters living down here for some time. Heaps of garbage and loot lay about, two ragtag piles of bedding lay in one corner, and the familiar script of graffiti was written over everything.

Owen could also see that the one holding Orla was another goblin, a larger one than the ones they'd already faced, but still with the familiar traits of his kind. He had a long pointed nose, over thin lips, housing a mouth of sharp pointed teeth. His ears were long and pointed, angling off to the sides of his head, weighed down by their weight and size.

He was a dark, sickly green color, the color of pond slime in mid August. The goblin had long, straggly, black hair that grew sparsely from his head and hung limply down his back in a loose braid. He held Orla close before him, and wasn't much taller than she, but wider. However, the knife he held close to Orla's cheek kept bringing Owen's attention back to it. Orla was barely conscious and seemed dazed, possibly from the rockslide. She had reverted back to her Sylvan, *Fey*, form.

Owen gave the goblin's friend a quick glance, and the creature seemed as dumb as it was large. It had a large sloped forehead ending in a wide protruding brow, over dim, deeply set eyes. It had a flat nose, with a broad mouth, and large, widely spaced yellow teeth. The creature was large and powerful looking, but had little muscle tone. To Owen it seemed like an out of shape monster, with flabby arms and potbelly that hung from beneath the potato sack it wore for a shirt, and over its loosely belted wool trousers. It was bare footed with enormous feet and large hairy toes with long, dirty toenails. It seemed to lean on the club, and was easily distracted by the swarms of flies that flew about it and its master.

"Oiy! Yer jus' a boy!" the goblin exclaimed, laughing harder as he did so. "Ah, but dat is a nice lil pig-sticker ya got 'dere," he added, seeing GreenFyr in Owen's hand.

Owen felt his cheeks flush and turn red, but he could worry about his hurt pride later. He needed to figure out a way to get Orla away from these two thugs. He didn't like how dazed she looked hanging in the goblin's arms.

"Alright boy, enuff chit chat. I wan' dat sword of yers, and anyt'ing else yous gots," his shrill voice commanded.

"Release the girl first," Owen countered.

"Oiy! Ya tink I'm a fool den? I could just kill 'er now den," the goblin spat. "Ach, enuff of dis, Deedle take his stuff!" he shouted at his large companion, who suddenly seemed animated for the first time since the dust cleared.

The large ogre lumbered towards Owen, raising his massive club as he did so.

"Orla!" Owen cried. He needed her to wake up, right away.

"Oiy! She can't save ya, boy, she's my tasty lil treat fer later, she is!"

The ogre slammed the club into the ground where Owen had stood a scant moment before, he easily sidestepped the beast, but with surprising speed it turned quickly around to face him again, negating the small window Owen had been given. He wouldn't under estimate the dim creature again.

"Deedle, stop toyin' wit da boy!" the goblin scolded, which the giant beast seemed to take to heart. It roared its agitation at Owen as it swung the club like a baseball bat at Owen's head. Owen ducked and rolled, only to have to leap out of the way again, as the club smashed the rock floor where he had just tumbled.

"Orla!" he shouted again only to the delight of the goblin who erupted in yet more shrilling laughter.

Owen rolled and stood, just as the ogre was bringing down his club once more. Owen brought GreenFyr up to meet the wooden weapon this time, and in a flash of bright green flames, the blade sliced right through the club, cleaving it in two. The charred stump of the weapon fell to the ground as the dim creature lifted the small remaining handle up to inspect it. It let out a despondent moan that turned to anger directed at Owen.

"Oiy! Deedle, I wanna dat sticker, now git it fer me!" the goblin yelled. But this time, Orla had woken up enough, to take in the scene. She stayed limp in the villain's arms, not to clue him in on her recovery. She saw Owen duck under a wild punch at his head from the ogre and sidestep another swipe at his face.

"Oiy, Pretty, ya think I don't know yous awake, do ya?" the goblin whispered in Orla's ear, which made her skin crawl and her stomach retch. She tasted bile in the back of her throat as she felt the creature's warm breath on her neck. His filthy hand tightened around her neck, making her breathing difficult. "Tell yer boyfriend t'stop fightin', or else I'm gunna ring yer pretty lil neck."

Orla could see the knife tip being waived in front of her nose; the blade wasn't more than six inches in length. She turned her head slightly and saw the filthy green arm of the goblin holding the blade, and bit it. As she did, she shifted into her full leopard form, the sudden growth forced his hand from around her neck, and the sudden bite from her leopard form, broke the bones in his hand, causing him to drop the knife. His shrill scream filled the passageway, only drowned out by the sudden growling of the snow leopard now standing before him.

Owen heard the sudden scream and growling, and had a good idea of what had transpired, but had his own hands full at the moment. The ogre took another swing at him, causing him to duck once more, but this time as Owen ducked beneath the swing, the giant creature brought his large foot up, kicking Owen like a soccer ball across the room.

Owen landed in a heap, still holding GreenFyr, but the wind had been forced from him. He stood, gasping for breath as the ogre charged him. The dim-witted beast lunged for Owen, reaching out with his giant shovel of a hand, just as Owen brought GreenFyr up to meet it. The blade sliced down the webbing between the monster's middle and ring fingers, cleaving Deedle's two smaller fingers, and a sizable portion of his hand, clean off. The giant screamed, not a monstrous growl, but a scream, like a child whose toy has just been broken. It grabbed the bleeding hand with its other, and ran from Owen towards its master, who was already quickly back peddling down the passageway from the very agitated snow leopard.

The cat stopped and watched them run away, as Owen stepped up beside her. She shifted back to *Fey* form, and leaned her head on his shoulder.

"Thank you," she said.

"For what?" Owen asked, honestly surprised. "You got yourself outta that."

"I wouldn't have been able to if you hadn't been fighting an enraged ogre all by yourself," she laughed. Owen smiled, despite himself. If only the kids at school could see him now. That felt so long ago, and literally a world away. He wasn't sure if he really knew that boy anymore.

Owen and Orla walked over to the wall closest to them and slowly slid down it until they were resting on it as much as each other.

"I hope the others are alright," Orla said, as a muffled howl could be heard coming from the other side of the rockslide.

"Me too," Owen said.

89

"Praise be to Durin!" Balor cheered as he poked his head through a small hole in the rockslide and saw Owen and Orla resting along the passage wall. He pushed one more rock to his left and promptly came tumbling out of the hole and down the rock slope.

Owen and Orla dashed to his side as he careened into the stone floor. Both stifled laughs as he righted himself, adjusting his swords, pushing his hair from his face, and straightening his armor.

"It's good to see you both, we feared the worst!" He clasped Owen about his forearm and put a tender arm around Orla, squeezing her tightly into his side.

"But I have to get back and tell the others they can come through, the goblins are pressing the fight." Just as Balor was turning to head up the slope, Boone came pushing his way through the hole, leaping from the top of the rock pile and onto the floor. He bounded once from the floor and then straight into Owen, tackling him to the ground. He wagged his tail furiously while dropping his massive chest onto Owen's, pinning him to the floor.

I was so worried! I'm VERY pleased you're well. You too! his voice boomed as he looked over to Orla standing beside them, who had given up on stifling her laughter and was currently smiling and laughing freely. Owen smiled too; he hadn't seen her laugh like that in what felt like a very long time. It was worth not being able to breathe while under Boone's mass.

"G'off," Owen exhaled. Boone jumped off him and ran around him while he got up, bumping his shoulders into his legs while he did so.

"We need to move this little reunion," Brule said, coming down the rockslide behind Aiya. Both had come through while Boone was greeting Owen. Neither the elf nor the troll looked injured.

"The goblins have brought reinforcements, it won't be long before they push forward again," Aiya said, stepping down off the rocks. She looked at both Owen and Orla and then to the garbage and belongings, "What happened over here?"

"The rocks began to slide; I ended up falling and hitting my head. I blacked out. When I woke up, a goblin had me, and Owen was fighting an ogre," Orla said as if she was talking about the weather. Smiling, she looked at Owen who returned the smile.

"What?" Balor asked grabbing the hilts of his swords. Boone stopped his romping and put his nose to the air, breathing deeply.

There were two of them. Been down here a long while, I should have picked up there scents.

"What happened to them?" Brule asked, looking around for any bodies.

"They took off when things stopped going their way," Owen said with a shrug.

"It seems our young charges are coming into their own," Brule quipped. "We still need to move." Getting sidetracked, he began to poke around in the belongings of the squatters.

"Were they injured?" Aiya asked drawing her sword again. Orla noticed now the blood along the Sword Maiden's bracers and armor. She looked to Brule and he too wore the gore of battle.

Her smile no longer graced her face, things were no longer fun, and she suddenly remembered Winter and an ache caught her deeply in her chest.

"Not bad," Owen said suddenly aware of Orla's change in mood. "The goblin had a bite to his hand and arm, the big one was missing part of his hand. Both left without weapons. We didn't follow them; we figured we'd wait for you four."

"Good thinking," Balor said.

"Any chance we could rig that opening so it collapses on them as they come through?" Brule asked Balor looking back up the slide.

"I can give it a shot," Balor said scurrying back up the rocks. He began to fiddle with the rocks, and supports along the ceiling.

"Careful," Orla said to the dwarf as a few stray rocks slid down beneath him. Boone busied himself with picking up the scent of the goblin and ogre; it was easy enough to find their blood trail. He meandered over to where they kept their garbage to smell what they'd been feeding upon while living down here.

Brule and Aiya rested themselves. Both were winded from their battle with the first wave of goblins. Brule examined his weapons and armor. It was the bounty hunter's way of relaxing.

Owen busied himself by investigating the hovel where the two occupants had been dwelling. Filth covered almost every square inch of the small passageway. Most of which Owen didn't even want to go near, let alone touch, but he did find something of interest over by where the duo slept. Alongside the goblin's sleeping mat was a small hole chiseled out of the rock wall. No more than a foot high by a foot wide. Owen peered into the shallow depression and saw that it was stuffed with a small wooden chest. He pulled the chest out.

The wood was old, but sturdy. Not very big, it fit snugly into the hole. Close to a foot long and not quite as wide, the box was only half that tall. It had two iron hinges along its back and one latch on the front. The latch and lock on the front had been broken, presumably by the goblin in an attempt to open it, when the box came into his possession. There was fine writing along the top of it, in a language Owen couldn't read, but that looked similiar to some of the other forms of elvish he'd seen in Quailan.

He slowly opened the box. It opened without any resistance. In it were a number of coins, mostly copper and silver, but a few gold mixed in as well. A few polished stones, and one ruby about the size of Owen's thumb. There was a small pair of round, wire framed eye glasses. Two rings, one gold with a large diamond in it and the other silver with an emerald in it. There was a leather pouch that looked to be filled with little stone animal figurines. An exquisitely crafted and delicate necklace made of platinum, with an intricate medallion enclosing a small off center jewel that seemed to capture and radiate with the dim light of the hall. There was a velvet pouch with different types and shaped dice. The box also contained numerous different types of teeth and a few claws from assorted different species and races. The collection was actually quite extensive. There was also what appeared to Owen to be a shrunken head. For such a small box, it contained a wealth of oddities that the goblin considered treasure.

"Whatcha got?" Orla asked from behind Owen, causing him to jump.

"Oh, sorry," she said, smirking slightly.

"No problem, didn't hear you," he said. At least when she was in Sylvan form he had a chance to hear her bells, but as a leopard or hybrid she moved silently when she wanted.

"Anything good?" Orla asked, peering over Owen's shoulder. Owen shrugged; many of the items were nice, or interesting, but nothing of real use, he thought. He slowly plucked through the lot again showing her each piece, as he moved the leather pouch out of the way he heard a slight squeak from behind him. Turning around he saw Orla, eyes wide, with her hand covering her mouth.

"What? You like the figurines? Take 'em," Owen said, handing her the pouch. She shook her head vigorously, and looking with disbelief looked back into the box and pointed to the necklace.

"Oh, yeah, I thought that was nice too. Here," Owen said, reaching in and pulling it out. As the medallion spun in the dim light it seemed to collect all the light from the room and redirect it through itself. It was the prettiest prism Owen had ever seen. It possessed no color of its own, but collected the light around it and presented it back to the world through its lens. He genuinely wanted Orla to have it. *Maybe*, he thought, *she could wear it and think of me.*

"I can't," she said, straightening up and taking a step back.

"Why not?" Owen asked, pushing the necklace towards her.

"Don't you know what it....it's much too nice," she said, holding her hands up in protest.

"Orla, it's very nice, but not too nice. Take it. I want you to," he said, draping the chain over her head. She closed her hand over the medallion and looked back at Owen. She smiled then, a heartfelt, happy smile.

"Thank you," she said. Owen smiled too; it wasn't like he'd bought it or anything. He'd found it in some dirty 'ol goblin's piggy bank and given it to her. *Well, at least she likes it*, he thought. He looked back at the chest and then back to Orla.

"What should I do…?" Owen started to ask, but then realized Orla had already wandered away. She sat at the foot of the rocks by herself, back in her Sylvan form, and looked at the necklace she cupped in her hands. She saw Owen watching her and smiled at him again, before sneaking the medallion beneath her tunic.

Owen returned the smile and turned back to the box. "Hmmm, what might be useful?" he asked aloud to himself. He took the coins, ruby, and the rings. He was about to slide the box back where he found it, when on second thought he took the leather and felt pouches. He left the rest in the box and slid them back into their place in the wall. He walked back over to Orla, who Boone had come back to sit alongside. She slowly scratched the top of his head while he watched Owen walk back to them. Owen sat down next to Orla and they waited for Balor to finish his work on the rockslide.

90

B *bbbbbaaaaaaaaaaarrrrrrrrrrooooooooooooooooooooo.*
The horn blasted from the other side of the rockslide as Balor came trudging down the slope.

"We're all set," the dwarf said smacking the dust off his hands and knees.

"Let's move then," Brule said. The rest of the company stood and prepared to go as well.

They fell into their marching order without discussion. This passage was big enough for them to walk two abreast so Boone and Balor took the lead and Brule and Aiya guarded their rear. Owen and Orla walked along next to each other.

Owen followed the blood trail of the goblin and ogre as they started their trek. The trail was easy to follow and headed in their same direction. This passage seemed level to Owen, neither delving further into the deep nor ascending towards the surface. This passage again was well decorated with carvings depicting dwarven heroes and epic adventures. It was also covered in the now familiar goblin graffiti as well.

Not too long into their journey they heard a soft rumbling and shaking from behind them. Balor clapped his hands and laughed at the underground thunder.

"HA!" the dwarfed shouted. "That'll teach 'em for trying to follow a son of the earth in his own Kingdom!"

"Let's just hope it delays them for some time," Aiya offered from the back.

"Are we even heading in the right direction anymore?" Owen asked, completely turned around and lost now in the Below.

"At the moment, no," Balor admitted. "We needed to make adjustments to our travels in avoiding the goblins. I should be able to get us back on course shortly," he said to Owen, and more quietly, "I hope," to himself.

They kept a good pace, close to a trot, to try and out distance the goblins behind them, but always wary of the blood trail in front of them. An injured goblin and ogre, who felt cornered, were dangerous indeed. They hadn't gone very far before an earth shaking explosion erupted from behind them. The blast sent a shock wave of wind and heat past them in the corridor, almost knocking Owen over as the force overcame them.

"What was that?" Orla exclaimed. The party stopped and all looked at one another.

"I have no idea," Balor admitted.

"Some sort of spell," Aiya offered. "It felt arcane in nature," she added.

"Goblins have never possessed such magics," Balor quipped, "fools all of them, they'd sooner blow themselves up then get an enchantment right."

"Then let's hope that's what they did," Brule grumbled.

"Yeah, but let's not wait around to find out," Owen added, bringing the group back to the matter at hand.

They again turned to head back down the corridor. The companions hadn't gone for very long when the trail split, one way to the left and one to the right. Balor chose quickly, sending the group down the right passage. They all headed down the tunnel, the corridor did not have any torches. Owen reached into his pocket and found his glow-stone. He pulled it out and kept it in front of him while they moved quickly down the corridor. This one seemed to be moving downward, but also didn't seem to keep a straight line; it zigzagged continuously. Owen suddenly realized the blood trail had stopped.

"Hey, what happened to the goblin's trail?" he asked.

"They took the left fork," Balor answered.

I'm still getting strong goblin scent in this passage, though, Boone said.

"Aye, goblins are all through these tunnels, infested with the scum," Balor spat.

The scent is strong and fresh.

"Like I said, infested."

"Maybe we should slow down, or…" Aiya began when they came around another bend and happened upon a lounging band of goblins. Balor and Boone stopped immediately, surprised at how quickly they came upon the villains. The goblins too were surprised, most didn't even notice the intrusion until one screamed an alarm.

Aiya felled that goblin with an arrow, but the alarm had already been sounded. Balor drew his swords and began yelling insults in goblin, while Boone raised his hackles and let loose a warning growl that made many of the goblins take pause. One, however, in the back of the band, let blast a warning on the bone horn he wore about his neck. The blast was surprisingly loud and blew past the company and down the way they had come. It was answered three times. Two came from behind the already alerted band of goblins. The third came from behind the company, still a fair way behind them.

Bbbbaaaaaaaarrrrrrrrrrooooooooooooo.

The horns cried in the Deep. Their blasts carried and echoed long past their initial sounding. The goblins rolled from straw mats, threw down loaves of rotten bread, and the carcasses of small animals, and grabbed their weapons. They didn't wait for a plan, they simply charged straight at the companions.

"Quickly now! The way we came!" Aiya shouted. She and Owen began laying down cover fire with their bows, dropping goblins as quickly as they tried to engage the small party. Brule fired a dwarven thrower from his bandolier, caving in the face of one goblin that got dangerously close to Owen before meeting his fate.

"Move!" Brule bellowed. Balor was reluctant to leave the fight with the creatures; Boone never left Owen's side. "Balor, there are more coming, move!" the troll shouted again, finally getting the dwarf to change direction and begin leading them back the way they had come. Brule stayed behind with Aiya to give her some protection while she kept the band at bay with her bow, using the last of her arrows. The other four bolted down the corridor, heading back towards the fork.

Bbbbaaaaaaaaarrrrrrrooooooooooooooo.

The horns cried once more, all closer still, the goblins were coming. Owen and his friends ran down the passage. They heard a blast from behind them and the screams of goblins afterwards, but kept moving. Owen hoped Brule and Aiya were fine. They reached the fork, and turned down the left side. Owen immediately saw the blood trail again.

Bbbbaaaaaarrrrrrooooooooooooooo.

Closer still the horns wailed, but none came from the left fork.

"Quickly now!" Balor shouted. "Down this shaft!"

"But Brule and Aiya!" Orla shouted through her hybrid lips.

"We're here!" Aiya shouted from down the hall behind them. She and Brule were in a full run; she fleet footed, and Brule a lumbering mass of muscle and brawn. The party once more complete, headed down the left corridor. They ran without caution, careening around corners. Balor looked desperately for some sign of which direction they were heading or for signs of new tunnels or directions to take. Any kind of clues he had learned to search for in the Deep to determine his way as they ran as fast as they could. They clanged and banged with their equipment and armor rattling against them.

Bbbbbbaaaaaaaaarrrrrrrooooooooooooooooooooooo.

The horns wailed again, closer still. They no longer seemed to be that far apart, they sounded as if they had merged and were coming from the same direction as the first trumpet.

Bbbbbbbbaaaaaaaaarrrrrrrooooooooooooooooooooooo.

The companions pushed harder still. Owen felt his thighs burn, his chest felt as if it was on fire. He was breathing from his mouth, taking deep, gasping breaths. He wasn't sure how much longer he could run at this pace. The *Maou'r* noticed Balor looking along the right wall; he wasn't watching the passage anymore. The dwarf was looking for some sign along the wall.

He never saw the body lying on the floor. The dwarf tripped over the corpse and went flying down the corridor, slamming into the rock floor, hard, three times before skidding to a stop. A soft, pained, grunt escaped the small man's mouth before he started pushing himself up from the floor. His companions had all come to a stop at the corpse he tripped over.

"What was that?" the dwarf asked, shifting his jaw from side to side.

"Dead body," Owen answered, looking down at the corpse.

"Bloody well lucky he's already dead," the dwarf grumbled as he stumbled back to his friends, "or else I'd kill 'em."

The body was old, but no more than a month or so, Aiya and Brule surmised as Balor walked back to them. He had been Sylvan judging from his size and build. His clothing, what was left of it, was unmistakably that of the house guard of Orla's home.

"I can't believe it. What would one of our guards be doing down here?" Orla whispered from behind her furred hand.

"Dunno," Owen answered, but finally feeling like many of the dots were being connected for them.

"No time to worry now," Brule said looking back down the corridor the way they had come.

Bbbbbbbaaaaaaaaaarrrrrrrroooooooooooooo.

The trumpets sounded as if they were right on top of them. Goblin shouts and screams could be heard once the din of the horns passed.

"They are on us!" Brule yelled, readying for war.

Owen looked down the hall and saw Balor running passed them, the dwarf seemed no worse for wear. He drew his twin blades as he passed, bellowing his own battle cry. "Let them come!" he shouted, taking position next to his troll comrade.

Boone had stepped between the oncoming goblins and Owen and Orla. The companions could now hear the onslaught charging them. The sounds of scimitars bashing shields, screams, growls, and the clamor of armor and boots on stone rushed before the war bands like ripples across a pond.

"Run!" Brule shouted. "Leave us!"

"No!" Owen screamed back. He would not abandon his friends.

"We can hold them off, the corridor is narrow enough where they can only approach us a few at a time," Balor tried to explain. "Take any routes upwards and to the east," he said, jaw set.

"It's the only way," Brule added, looking over his shoulder briefly at the boy who desperately tried to save his life on the bridge. "Let us repay our debts," he said.

"No!" Owen shouted again. He looked to Aiya for support, but he could see the Sidhe felt the same.

"You three run, reach the surface, get to Narsus, we will hold them off," she said, standing and unsheathing her sword.

"'Fraid not," Brule said. "They need your help beyond here." He looked to the dwarf next to him who simply nodded his agreement and firm resolve. Without another word between them, Brule brought one of his hammers up into the ceiling, knocking a support beam loose from between him and his other companions. The mallet laid a devastating blow to the wooden support, dropping the small portion of ceiling between them in a rush of rock, dust, and dirt.

"Brule! Balor!" Owen yelled after the passage had become eerily silent.

"We're fine!" came the muffled reply. He could not tell which one of them had shouted it. Owen turned to the stunned looks on the faces of Orla and Aiya. They could not believe it either.

"We can't leave them!" Owen shouted, and he thought he could hear the muffled sound of combat from beyond the rockslide. "We can't!"

"We must," Aiya said sadly. She felt her place was on the other side of this wall with the dwarf and troll, not here. She was a Sidhe Sword Maiden; she was prepared to lay down her life for the *Maou'r*, and did not appreciate being denied that honor.

"What?" Owen and Orla asked at once. Boone had come up to the slide and was listening to the fighting coming from beyond it. He tipped his head from side to side listening to the cries of battle.

"Do not let their sacrifice be in vain," was all Aiya said. She stood and sheathed her sword. "We need to move, now." The Sidhe did not leave this open to argument. They were now solely her charges; she would see them to their destination.

Boone turned as well. He looked at Owen expectantly. He needn't speak to his master to communicate what he thought. Owen could see it in his deep brown eyes.

"Let's go," Owen said starting down the corridor once more. Boone took the lead while Aiya again took rear guard.

91

Do you think they're safe?" Orla asked, leaning against the smooth rock wall. They had found the exit to the world Above, but had waited to recuperate some before leaving the Below. The exterior door was quite cold to the touch, and Aiya believed the weather was still frigid. She lit a small fire in the anterior room at the entrance to the Dwarven Kingdom.

The goblins had wrought their destruction and desecrated the stout people's homes and tunnels. The once fine furnishing, tapestries, and craftsmanship lay in ruin, defiled and violated. Aiya used the old wood, rotten food, and moldy rugs and weavings to feed her fire.

Owen had gone off with Boone to try and find some extra layers of clothing to fend off the cold for when they made way for Narsus. They inspected the immediate adjacent rooms, but did not venture far from Orla and Aiya. Both companions kept an always vigilant ear for footsteps through the dark halls. They had not seen nor heard any sign of the goblin or ogre since the blood trail had run dry after separating from Brule and Balor.

Aiya looked at Orla. She knew what the young girl wanted to hear, but she did not believe them safe. No. On the contrary, she believed even two as valiant, brave, and skilled as Brule and Balor could not win against a horde of goblins in the Deep. Sheer numbers would have eventually won out, overwhelming the two warriors after exhaustion set in, and their bodies weakened.

"I think they are safe, I think Gaia cradles them in the palm of her hand," Aiya answered. Orla looked at the Sword Maiden. It wasn't the answer she wanted to hear, but she appreciated the other woman's honesty. *Yes, if the two warriors fell, they would indeed find grace in the loving embrace of Gaia,* Orla thought and truly believed.

She leaned back and tried to make herself comfortable. She closed her eyes and tried to think of quieter, happier times.

"No one in your community knows you are a practitioner of the arts, do they?" Aiya asked. "Not even your father?" Aiya already suspected the answer.

"No, just Chamberlain, he too practices. When I was younger he recognized my potential for it and began teaching me in secret. Sylvan society gave up magic a long time ago and it has since become taboo to practice." Orla found herself speaking freely to Aiya. It felt wonderful to have someone, another adult besides Chamberlain, with whom she could trust. She paused, reflecting on that last thought. She could no longer trust Chamberlain, she probably never could have. "Especially for a senator's daughter," she added almost as an afterthought.

"And who taught Chamberlain?" Aiya asked. She hadn't trusted the steward when she and her sister had been guests at the house. Especially after his reaction to Silan's offer of assistance to restore Orla's memory, and then the attack by the *Ain'griefer*; she had her doubts about the man.

"I, I don't know," Orla stammered. She had never asked, never thought to, it had just never even occurred to her. The surprise was evident upon her face. "I just never considered it," she said apologetically.

"I think it, and a few other questions, will be good for us to ask when we find your father in Narsus," Aiya said while stoking the fire.

They were warriors Owen. They met their fate the way they'd wished for all their lives.

"What?" Owen said. "Are you mad? Do you have rabies?" he asked indignant.

I'm fairly certain, no. But they fought against unspeakable odds, for a cause they believed in, there are many worse ways to die.

"There's no good way to die, no matter how you go, you go. You're still dead!"

There's a lot to be said on how one passes into the next world. To do so honorably, bravely, or for a righteous cause, is far better than many other ways.

"Yeah, well, watch the news some time in my world and you'll see what I've seen. Thousands of people all over the world kill each other, or themselves, everyday for all sorts of causes, in the name of everything imaginable. And for what? Because they're right and someone else is wrong? Money? Peace? Land? I don't buy it," Owen said. "There's no right or wrong great enough in the world to force it down some else's throat! As long as they're not hurting or oppressing you or someone else, then let them alone." He found a small wardrobe in what looked to be a guard, or sentry apartment. There was the wardrobe, small desk and chair, and a few small bunks. He opened the wardrobe.

Those men didn't fight the goblins because of a difference in philosophy. They fought them because if they didn't, those villains would have murdered you and everyone else or worse. With the exception of Balor, I don't think any of us would have confronted those creatures, and Balor is unfortunately the result of a long conflict, that most of the participants have long since forgotten the reasons for why they're fighting.

Owen looked from behind the wardrobe door at Boone who was now sitting watching him. He looked up at the *Maou'r* with his deep brown eyes. There was an immense intelligence in those eyes, one that transcended animal or dog. He saw and understood things that most people never considered; most people just took as dogma and went about their business.

"You're an amazing person," Owen said. "Smarter than most folks I know," to this Boone wagged his tail. He opened his mouth slightly, in what to Owen looked like a smile.

"I know they died honorably," he said, looking back in the wardrobe, moving pieces of clothing back and forth along the rack.

"It's just hard to accept, ya know? I mean, so did Winter, and now them, and they all died for one reason. One STUPID reason!" Owen shouted, slamming the wardrobe door which split down the middle and fell from its hinges. The boy turned and looked at his dog that had closed his mouth and stopped wagging his tail, but that looked back at him with deep undying devotion, and deep unfettered compassion.

"Me," Owen said weakly. A tear ran down his face, one single tear. He had cried so much the last few days, most times late at night when he thought everyone else asleep. "For me. And I wish they hadn't," he was beyond crying anymore.

Boone stood and walked over to his *Maou'r*. He lifted his great head, leaning it against Owen's chest. Owen placed one hand upon the top of Boone's head and the other beneath his chin. He stroked the great dog's thick, coarse fur.

And if you asked them if they would do it again, they all would say yes, without question, I'm sure. And for one reason only, because they know you would do the same for them, without a second thought.

Owen bent over and placed his face to Boone's, pressing his lips and nose between the large dog's eyes. Owen closed his eyes and breathed deeply, taking in the rich scent and aroma of his dog, a scent he had grown to love, one which had grown to soothe him. He stood back up and sighed deeply.

Owen reached in between the broken doors of the wardrobe and pulled out a thick, gray, wool cloak, scarf, and wool gloves.

"This should help some," he said stuffing the articles into his bag, "let's go find the girls."

92

When Owen stepped back into the antechamber he noticed Aiya had started a fire, preparing them a warm meal before they headed out into the cold surface world. The dim light of the fire lit the small room, and even amongst the ruined furnishings, it provided a warm, cozy atmosphere in the depths of the darkness of the Below.

Orla sat crossed legged before the fire. She looked tired, but smiled wearily as he walked into the room. Aiya even looked happier to see him return.

"We thought you'd left us," Orla teased.

"You know I wouldn't," Owen said, sitting down beside her. Boone walked over to the large dwarven door and lay in front of it. His body yearned to be out in the cold, he'd been underground too long. He desired to see the stars, smell the firs, and tread on earth, not stone, once more. His thick, dense fur insulated him from the coldest temperatures, and the door's cold felt good against his long body.

"You may," she teased. Owen couldn't tell if she was teasing or serious. She was tired, exhausted really, and near sleep. The only thing keeping her awake was the savory smells from the cook pot over the fire. Aiya was making something special from their rations it seemed.

"Never," Owen swore in a mocking tone. He laid his bow, quiver, pack, and GreenFyr beside him. He thought of unrolling his bed mat, but they wouldn't be there much longer. He would not sleep tonight. He had decided he would not lay his head in the Below ever again.

"MmmmHmmm," Orla hummed. "Is it ready yet?" she asked Aiya.

"It should be," the Sidhe said. She reached over the fire and took the pot using her cloak as a pot holder. She spooned out the contents into their own small wooden bowls. The aroma wafted up to Owen's nose and the smell immediately made his stomach gurgle and his mouth water.

"*G'lemghesh*," Aiya said as Owen smelled the broth. He saw a few different types of chopped mushrooms, some of the dried venison from the dwarves, a mix of spices, fragrances, and smells he couldn't place.

"Eat, it has soothing and healing properties," Aiya said, handing out some of the hard, dark bread of Balor's people. Orla spooned the Sidhe soup into her mouth while Owen dunked the stale bread into it, letting it soak up the broth. The soup was very good, with enough spice to warm them through. By the time Owen finished his, Orla had already fallen asleep. She had lain back, using her small pack as a pillow. She hadn't even finished her own dinner. Owen tipped his bowl back, drinking the rest of it.

"Rest, Owen, we can afford a little time. We will need to move quickly and for long periods." Aiya too had finished her bowl. Owen leaned back and rested his head on his pack as well. The warm soup, which still seemed to be warming him outward from his belly, and the warmth from the campfire, were enough to lull him to sleep. He drifted off quickly and without a fight, barely realizing he was falling asleep.

Aiya woke them both a few hours later. Boone too was awake and sitting by the door, anxious to be out of the underground. Owen felt much more refreshed than he would have imagined. The *G'lemghesh* was so much more filling and invigorating than he expected it to be. He felt as if he'd slept for a week and eaten a full course meal earlier that morning.

Both Owen and Orla stood and stretched. Owen strapped on his gear and weapons while Orla helped Aiya douse the fire and try and minimize their sign of passing. Aiya had already prepared her own gear. She had cleaned off her armor, and Orla presumed, her sword.

Owen buckled on his sword belt and turned to Boone and the sealed door to the outside world. "How do we open it?"

"I should be able to," Orla said. She walked over and investigated the door. "From the outside I probably couldn't, but I would think from the inside...," she said while looking around the door frame. There were many inscriptions and runes around the door, but even though Orla couldn't read them, she knew the dwarves were very superstitious of spells and casters, so those wouldn't have been charms. She figured there must be some simple locking mechanism that to a dwarf would be apparent, but anyone else looking would be nearly invisible. Instead of looking any further, she simply spoke a word of command for open while placing her hand upon the cool stone. The familiar blue glow emitted from her hand.

The door, stirred, shuddered, and then, slowly, opened.

Cold air blasted them as soon as the door moved. Snow and gale force winds assaulted them through the now open portal. The storm had not let up at all. Boone stepped out into the Above, into snow drifts that he had to leap through to get past. The snow depth was already up to his belly, and in the drifts, well over his head. Owen pulled the hood of the dwarven cloak up over his head, and tightened the scarf about his neck, pulling it up over his mouth and nose. Orla shifted into her leopard form, which like Boone, was made for this type of weather. Aiya, otherwise indifferent to the climate and temperature, actually added a layer of clothes over her armor, a thick wool sweater.

"Head for the forest edge, if we can get into the tree line, it will shelter us some from the wind," Aiya said, guiding the companions down the small hillside of the mountain into the forest below. They reached the tree line, which consisted mostly of stunted spruce and balsam fir at this elevation, but were still big enough to act as a wind block from the gusting storm.

They traveled through the day, stopping once for a midday meal and slight rest. The snow depth amongst the trees was less, but they still ended up having to wade their way through the snow. Their progress was exhausting and they ate slowly and recuperated at the noon time break.

The temperatures were biting cold, but when traveling their body temperatures kept them warmer, while sitting and eating Owen began to catch a chill, feeling his toes and fingers growing cold and painful. He finished his meal of dried venison, stale bread, and sharp cheese, and began to walk in place trying to keep warm.

Aiya quickly finished her own meal, cutting it short, to get the group moving again. Orla and Boone seemed the least affected by the temperatures. Boone, actually, seemed like a puppy; leaping, and running in circles around them, burying his face beneath the snow, only to lift it up again covered in the flakes and frost. The companions intersected a set of moose tracks along their journey during the afternoon, and Boone had to control his desire to follow the tracks and chase down the cervid. The companions kept moving, Owen wishing he had snowshoes. His thighs burned from high stepping through the snow.

"Are we even going in the right direction?" Owen finally asked out of frustration and exhaustion. Thankfully his question had the desired response; they stopped their trek for a short conference.

"I believe so," Aiya answered. She looked up into the thick gray sky, through the blankets of falling snowflakes.

"How? We can't even see the sun to get a direction," Owen said, he'd been turned around ever since they'd emerged from the Below.

"I believe we came out on the eastern side of the *Durrim's Vein*, which runs north out of the Sylvan Kingdom. If I'm correct, and we follow the line north, we should come to *Ful'aing C'Rag*, a range that collides with *Durrim's* and runs southeast back into Narsus. I believe this is the route Winter originally intended for us to take," she explained. She knew the pace was too much for them, but she needed to push them, the weather was beyond anything she had seen in decades and she didn't know if the goblins would follow them out of the Below.

Owen nodded. Aiya's logic was sound and he trusted her judgment. The cold was beginning to seep into his bones, and the reprieve had been enough for him to catch his breath, but now he wanted to start moving to ward off the cold again.

They turned their attention back to their journey. The landscape had changed since they first emerged from the mountains. They had worked their way into the bottomlands of the foothills. The trees had changed from the short stunted spruce and fir common along the higher elevations of the mountains to a mixed hardwood forest. Many birches and maples grew along this east facing slope. They occasionally hiked through hemlock stands that made it easier to wade through the snow, their thick bows holding large loads of snow above their heads as they passed.

They came across several sets of tracks in the snow. Large paw prints, Owen would have categorized as dog.

Dire Wolves. I picked up their scent further back.

"Really!" Owen said excited, he'd never seen wolf tracks before.

Yes. They seem to have picked up the scent of that moose we passed a ways back. They will pay us no mind; they have no interest in Fey or Man.

The companions pushed on through the day. It was getting close to dusk when they stopped and made camp. They had seen no sign of other creatures in the forest that might be searching for them, nor had they seen any sign of pursuit, so they decided to chance a fire. They found a small outcropping that would provide some shelter from the snow amongst a hemlock stand. Careful to build their fire out from under any snow laden bows they made a small conflagration to sit and warm by. Boone lay down beside Owen and Orla shifted into her hybrid form and sat by him on the other. The fire felt good, and after their short meal, they all helped collect as much wood to keep it stoked through the night. They decided to watch in two shifts. Owen and Boone on one and Orla and Aiya on the other, it was the first time that Owen and Orla actually felt they were contributing to the watches.

Their camp was in the shadow of the *C'Rag*. It was a deep gray and whitewashed monolith behind the curtain of snow, but it was still comforting to know it was there, and that they were drawing closer to their destination.

"Do we need to cross it?" Owen asked when they first came upon it.

"No," Aiya had answered. "Not here, there is a pass closer to Narsus that we will use," she had continued. "We will begin heading southeast from here in the morning, following the mountains to the pass, and then once we cross, we'll pick up the road into the capital."

"How much further?" Owen asked again, trying not to sound too tired.

"Another day and a half I would wager based on the conditions," she answered.

They all slept, when they weren't on watch, soundly. Nothing disturbed them through the evening, and the fire kept the cold at bay for most of the night. In the morning they ate a light breakfast, extinguished the fire, and were quickly on their way.

Again their journey and route was a hard one. At the rate they were going, Aiya estimated they would reach the pass by nightfall, camp there, and then cross it in the morning. By their midday meal, they were already weary, and by nightfall they were all exhausted. Aiya and Orla took the first watch and Aiya let Orla rest when she fell asleep on watch. The Sidhe had expected her to, and when she did, did not bother waking her. She had even let Boone and Owen sleep longer than their arranged watch time, but eventually needed some rest herself, and had to wake the great dog and boy to take their shift.

She had curled close to the campfire and fallen quickly asleep. Her rest was uneasy and often troubled by visions of Narsus. She saw dark shapes in the shadows of a tall tower, and felt the foulness of the *Ain'griefer* about her. When she woke the next morning she felt as if she hadn't slept at all.

93

Aiya woke in the morning to the smell of cooking meat. Boone had scented a deer close to the camp, and Owen had taken the animal with a single arrow shot. It was a well placed hit, so the animal hadn't run far before succumbing to the wound. Boone easily trailed it and dragged it back to camp, where Owen then butchered it the way his father had shown him.

Owen had first felt guilty about taking the spike buck because he knew they would not be able to use the entire animal, but Boone had assured him the carcass would not go to waste. The dog was certain that with this unusual snow many of the animals would be in need of an easy meal.

Orla, in her snow leopard form, had awoken first and was delighted to see the venison roasting over their small fire. She shifted to her hybrid form and licked her lips.

"May Gaia bless you, Owen McInish," she said sitting down next to him and Boone. "You're a Prince," she added, nudging him with her furry elbow.

"It was Boone's idea," Owen said, "I only shot it because I thought if I didn't he would have gone off chasing it," Owen laughed. Boone sighed deeply and turned his back to the two friends. He was beyond such temptations, he knew, even if the urge and idea had occurred to him.

"You didn't stray far, did you?" Aiya asked as she rolled her bedding and joined the others at the fire.

"No. He was just outside camp, and Boone dragged him back," Owen said.

"Good, and thank you, it smells wonderful," she said.

After finishing their meal they broke camp quickly. The journey to the pass was not a long one. The pass had been used for centuries, and there was a worn trail up into the mountains, but the companions chose not to use it until they absolutely had no choice. The small band stayed in sight of the trail along the forest edge, but kept to the cover of the tree line, out of sight from the pass as they moved closer to Narsus.

The weather had not ceased its attack on the travelers. The wind blew down from the mountains driving snow into their faces and blinding them. The visibility was no more than a few meters forcing the four companions to make sure not to lose each other in the forest.

They kept to the forest until they reached the bottom of the pass road that crept down from the mountains. The snow was fresh, without any tracks, as the travelers stepped from the tree line and began their trek up the mountain road.

94

Boone had taken the lead again, working his way up the trail that cut between two of the peaks of the *Ful'aing C'Rag* and came out on the other side of the mountain range. Boone kept his nose into the wind, but no strange or out of place scents was driven to him on it. They crested the top of the pass, and began working their way down into the valley on the other side.

The pass was a well worn road, Owen thought, as they moved up and over the mountain range. The elevation was very high at this point over the range where the pass cut up and over a shallow saddle between two peaks. The snow was much deeper along the road, which ran along two high walls covered in thick, blue, glacial ice. Once they crested the pass, the downward trek moved quickly and easily.

The hike into Narsus was not a long one; Owen hoped they would reach it by nightfall. The main road into the capital ran right along the base of the mountain on the opposite side of the pass. The companions quickly turned onto it, no longer fearing bands of goblins. The main road on any other day would have been busy with traffic, but the fierce weather was keeping most travelers at bay.

By the time they reached the bottom of the pass on the far side of the mountain it was near time for their midday meal. They had not bothered to light a fire, but had found some shelter from the driving wind and snow from a large boulder that had rolled from the mountains to the tree line many years before. The rock blocked the worst of the wind and precipitation, allowing them to warm some under their wool cloaks and extra blankets they pulled from their packs.

The temperatures had warmed a bit once they had finally reached the valley. Owen could not believe the change in weather and climate in just a few days. Part of him knew why winter had come so quickly and savagely, but another part of his brain, the part that still belonged to his world, refused to fully accept it.

When the companions had finished their meal, they started their trek towards Narsus. The friends didn't speak during this last leg of their journey. All of them were consumed by their own thoughts as to what was waiting for them in the city.

The storm gray sky was just beginning to darken further with the coming of evening when the road became a bit larger, and beneath the snow, cobbled. They soon came before a large gate and stone wall. The wall wrapped around the lower city of the capital and attached to the mountains to either side of Narsus. The wall stood close to twelve feet high from what Owen could tell. He saw Sylvan guards walking along the top of it; most were bundled tightly in cloaks to block out the snow and driving wind.

The gate itself was a large wooden door, reinforced with iron bars. It stood open, allowing traffic to pass freely through it. On a clear day, Owen imagined the gate would have been quite busy. Three guards stood huddled about a small cauldron filled with burning coal in the middle of the road, but paid the few citizens little mind as they trudged past them into the city.

Just outside the city walls were several vendors hawking their wares. A small cart, with a small cooking fire and stove on the back of it, was selling spicy smelling dishes, while another sold furs, and yet another sold wild grown plants and herbs. The atmosphere to Owen seemed more like a farmers market, even in this frigid storm. These were the poorer folk, and not allowed or unable to afford to be a part of the true market within the city.

Owen pulled his hood lower down his brow as they entered the city. Boone stayed close and few people paid the large dog any attention.

They had decided back along the road that it would be better for the *Duine Madra* to accompany the party into the city. Very few people would even remember the stories of the race, and fewer still would make the connection between the great dog and Owen. They all felt it safer to have Boone traveling with them in the large city.

As they passed beneath the arches of the city, Owen and Orla both couldn't help but exhale slightly, breathing a little easier now that they had come this far in their journey, and that maybe their adventure was drawing a little closer to an end.

95

Owen immediately saw a difference between the homes and architecture of Narsus to Quailan. Each home in Quailan seemed fashioned to that family's animal selves, more of an extension of those forms. There were burrow homes, tree homes, stone homes, and log homes. In Narsus, however, most homes were of the same stone design; the stone itself looked as if it had been quarried from the surrounding mountains.

In this lower section of the city, the homes were small and tightly lined along well marked roads. The main street through the gate led directly into the mercantile district of the city. Most of the buildings lining the roads were small stores and shops, or restaurants and cafés. All seemed to have awnings that could be opened in the spring to provide shade and shelter for tables and chairs or sidewalk shopping. However, with the current climate the shops were well sealed with smoke pumping from their tiny stone chimneys, quickly being carried away by the driving weather.

Some of the buildings had large windows in them, but were fogged or hidden behind drifts of snow, so Owen had a difficult time seeing in them. He seemed to be the only one who was distracted with sightseeing. Aiya and Boone were alert and ready for any potential dangers while Orla was preoccupied on remembering how to find her father now that she had reached the city.

There were many more people out on the streets within the city than outside the walls; the weather had not seemed to affect the daily business happenings around them in the slightest. On the contrary, it seemed to be the main topic of conversation and small talk.

"I haven't seen snow like this," one would say while another, "I hear it's a result of that global cooling they've been talking about," or another, "the weather is becoming more violent, I've never seen weather like this, I swear it's a sign of..." and so on. Most conversations, though, were in some form of *Fey* or other, and Owen was left to speculate on what they were saying.

There was also a much greater diversity of people here in Narsus than in Quailan. With the exception of Aiya, Silan, and himself everyone else he had seen in the smaller town had been Sylvan. Here in Narsus, however, there were all types of races. He saw little people with butterfly wings that couldn't be more than a foot long and others closer to a meter long that had wasp or dragon fly looking wings. There were others he thought must have been gnomes, with long bulbous noses and long beards below them. He saw tall elves that looked like Aiya, and may have been Sidhe, but also smaller elves, still taller than Orla, but of finer, fairer skin with brightly colored hair and longer, larger, pointed ears.

Owen even saw a woman that looked like she possessed the body and legs of a deer, but the upper torso of an elven maiden. She wore a bow and quiver across her back and a long thin dagger in a bandolier across her chest. Her hair was long and chestnut colored, braided loosely, and draped over her right shoulder. She saw the four companions as they walked through the city and smiled at Owen as he passed her.

As the friends turned onto another road the fresh smell of baked goods reached their noses and Owen's stomach grumbled loudly enough so that Orla could hear. She laughed at the noise, resting her hand on her own stomach to quell any outbursts from it.

"Judging by the sound of it, maybe we should stop and get Owen something to eat," she teased as they approached the bakery. It was the only building on the street that had regular traffic in and out of it, ringing a small bell on the door, and releasing its aroma onto the road every time the door opened.

The whole street, even with the blustery wind, was filled with the mouth watering smells of cinnamon buns, cookies, cakes, and breads. The four companions stopped in front of the establishment's window and looked in. It looked warm and inviting. There was a fire in a stone hearth with several tables in front of it. A glass counter full of pastries sat in front of a large kitchen.

Owen looked at Aiya and Orla, both of whom looked as hungry as he felt.

I'll wait here. Go in, warm up, and get something to eat, Boone said lying down in front of the large window. *It's too warm in there for me, anyway.*

"Okay, we won't be long," Owen said as he and the other two friends stepped inside the bakery. Again they were buffeted with the sumptuous smells of the baked goods. The room was crowded with several people in line ahead of them. Owen, taller than most Sylvans, was able to see over their heads and into the cabinet. There was a large pastry that had a shortbread crust, covered in raspberries, which were covered in white chocolate. Owen knew immediately what he wanted. He also saw that they had hot chocolate as well.

"Um," Owen whispered, "I took some money from the tunnels before we left, should we pay with that?"

"No. I'll pay for it," Aiya said. "Do you know what you want?" Owen was able to point out the pastry he wanted, over the heads of the Sylvans, because Aiya was also much taller than the smaller *Fey*, so she could see the counter as well.

"I'll get us a table by the fire," Owen said. Orla and Aiya stayed to order and bring back the drinks and baked goods. Owen walked over to the tables surrounding the fire. Several of the tables were taken by small groups of Sylvan's. There was a mother with three children at one, all eating enormous frosted cupcakes, while she drank a steaming hot beverage. Another table was occupied by two Sylvan men, who looked like merchants or businessmen, discussing a business venture over tea. One other table was occupied with three Sylvans and two smaller looking *Fey* people, all of whom were laughing and chortling.

As Owen was walking by the last occupied table, taken by a tall Sidhe, the man spoke to Owen. Surprised, Owen stopped and peered at the man from beneath his hood.

"You and your friends look to be weary travelers," the man said to Owen. He wore a long elegant cloak over an ornate tunic and breeches. His clothes were of the finest materials and details. They had intricate runes stitched into the seams and Owen could tell they were of the highest quality. He wore a large brimmed hat made of woven birch bark. It looked to Owen like it was more of a sun hat, rather than for winter, but he imagined the wide brim did keep the snow and wind from its wearer's face.

He looked older than Aiya, but like most Sidhe, his age was difficult to determine. His sharp features were accentuated by the shadows cast from beneath his hat.

"Traveling from afar?" he asked Owen as the boy tried to think of a way out of the conversation. Owen tried to keep his own head tipped, so the shadows of his hood hid his more un-*Fey* like features from the Sidhe.

"No, um, not too far," Owen answered, starting to step away from the table.

"Ah, good, frightful weather to be coming from too distant a place," the man answered. Just as he did so, a large black and red, tiger-striped spider stepped out from behind the back of his hat, walking along the brim. Owen unconsciously took a step back from the man, catching a gasp just before it escaped his mouth. It was the same type of spider Owen had seen in Orla's basement.

The spider stepped to the very edge of the hat, and while holding on with its four hind legs, it reached and wriggled its fore legs at Owen. Owen gulped.

"So what brings you to the capital city of the land of Sylvans?" the stranger asked curiously. He had such a strange, and yet polite way about him. Owen wanted nothing more than to get away, but found his feet rooted in place.

"Nothing in particular, really," Owen answered, unable to take his eyes off the spider. The man took a single gold piece from somewhere within his robes and placed it on the table with a slight spin. The coin twirled in place for a moment before wobbling to a stop. Owen watched the coin and then looked back at the stranger who smiled, not so unsimilarly to a cat who has just eaten a mouse.

"Ah, and your business?" the Sidhe asked, standing from his chair beside Owen. The stranger was taller than Aiya, but not nearly as tall as Brule.

Owen didn't answer, he watched as the spider moved from the front of the brim, where it had been reaching at Owen, to back behind the crown of the hat. The stranger straightened his clothing, pulling his cloak more tightly about him.

"Ah, well, keep your secrets then," he said with a smile, but with no mirth behind it, "good to have made your acquaintance," he added without any warmth at all. Somewhere in the back of Owen's mind he felt that this chance meeting, with this stranger, hadn't been chance at all.

The Sidhe left as Aiya and Orla began to walk over to the fire where Owen suddenly found himself alone. Owen sat at an empty table next to the fire while Orla and Aiya sat down with him.

"Who was that?" Aiya asked. "He looked like he was Sidhe by his build, but his face was hidden beneath his hat."

"I dunno," Owen said, trying to remember the stranger, "he never gave me his name." And after a moment's thought he added, "but he did ask a lot of questions."

Aiya looked back after the man who had been talking to Owen. "I wish I could have gotten a better look at him," she mused.

"Did you see the spider on his hat?" Owen asked. Both Orla and Aiya looked at him strangely. "It was one of those big ones like in Quailan," he said, looking at Orla, "like in your house."

Orla's expression turned cold.

"I only know of one spider in Quailan," she said through a mouth full of pumpkin spice cake. She swallowed the dessert before finishing her sentence.

"Chamberlain."

96

Chamberlain?" Owen exclaimed. He nearly choked on his Dragon Claw Danish. All those times he sat in the bath and Chamberlain was scampering over him into the tunnels under the city.

"Yes. So he's here too," Orla said, not realizing that Owen had seen him all those times and never knew it was him.

"But who was he with?" Aiya asked while sipping her tea, she too had taken a pumpkin spice cake.

"Well, they know we're here then. I'm sure Chamberlain would have recognized me, not to mention you two," Owen said. He sipped his hot chocolate from a great big, blue mug.

"We should get moving then," Aiya said, suddenly realizing Owen was right and they could be in danger, even here. "Where can we find your father?"

Orla thought for a moment, he should be done with his session by now, but would he be back to the Senators' Chambers already, or out at other meetings, or even dinner? He could be anywhere within the city.

"We should start at the Senators' Chambers," she said, slipping the last of her cake into her mouth, and chasing it with her hot chocolate.

Owen stood, took a last swig of his own drink, and slid the Dragon's Claw into his pocket. The three companions quickly left the café. They found Boone waiting below the window where they had left him. A skiff of snow lay along his body and head.

456

"Did you see a Sidhe, wearing a large hat, leave?" Owen asked immediately.

I don't get a snack? the great animal asked while standing up.

"Oh, sorry, almost forgot," Owen said, pulling the pastry out of his pocket and handing it over to the dog. Boone gently took it from his hand, and quickly swallowed it, not losing a single crumb.

Saw him. He went down the road, left after the first block, he said after he finished licking his lips.

The four companions headed out of the lower city and into High Narsus. There was another gate that they passed through, but again the guards paid them little mind as they walked through the archway. It was immediately apparent that they had just entered a much more affluent part of the city. The houses were still the same stone, but they were larger, and much more richly crafted with small front and side yards. Many of these buildings were now houses, apartments, and offices. It was also apparent they had just left the mercantile quarter of the city. There were many more constables in this portion of the city, which Owen wasn't sure if it reassured him, or made him more nervous.

It was beginning to grow dark, and as they walked down the road, street lamps began to come on. Owen stopped to investigate these because he had yet to see anyone use electricity. He looked up at the closest one and noticed it was very similar to the glow-stone he carried in his pocket that Orla had made him. In each glass lamp was an orb about the size of a bowling ball of pure light. The light from the lamps seemed to catch each flake of snow and glisten in the sky around them.

The companions hurried down the street towards the government buildings and politician's housing. It had been several years since Orla had been to the capital and she was having trouble remembering exactly the right way.

Orla finally came across a street that she remembered and the companions quickly took it. Now dark, the temperature was quickly dropping, the thought of having a warm bed to sleep in that night was making them colder still when they came to a third gate. On the far side of the gate was the capital building along with the politicians, diplomats, and embassies. There was also a very tall tower standing just behind the capital building. Its pinnacle stood higher than the tallest peak of the *C'Rag* that surrounded the small valley in which the city was nestled.

"What's that?" Owen asked, looking up at the structure.

"It's the Tower of the Stars," Orla said, forgetting Owen had never been here before, or seen any of its wonders. "It was supposedly built here long before the Sylvanni ever settled here, by the *Aingeal*, before the Great Schism. They say it was built that tall by them, so they could sit in it and feel as if they were once again back amongst the stars," Orla said wistfully.

"So what's it used for now?" Owen asked.

"Nothing, the Sylvan have never used it. It's just a monument, really," she said.

As they approached the gate two guards stepped forward to block their entry. Owen slouched more, trying to be closer to Sylvan height and made sure his face was well shadowed within the cloak. Both Aiya and Orla stepped forward to meet the guards.

"Official personnel only," the first said as they stood in the entryway.

"We are indeed here on official business," Aiya answered.

"Identification?" the second guard asked.

"I am Orla of Quailan," Orla said quietly, but both guards turned their attention to her. "My father would want to be informed of my presence," she added. The guards looked at her in her road weary and travel stained clothes and doubted her for the briefest moment.

"Take me and my friends to my father," she said less quietly and more stately. The two guards quickly spun and walked the companions back to the gate where they met with two more guards. After a brief explanation, the first two guards escorted Owen and the others to the Senators' Chambers.

97

The guards led the companions into the government compound. The two leading them seemed pleased with being able to get away from their posts for a time. One of the other guards at the check point acted as a runner and went ahead to try and find the senator. The remaining guard, who stayed at the gate, occasionally cast glances back at Orla and Aiya, paying little mind to the large dog and their hooded companion. Owen at first chalked it up to the fact that Orla was looking little like a Princess at the moment and Aiya, even travel worn, was always a breathtaking combination of beauty and fierceness. The stories of the Sword Maidens were legendary; their numbers few, but their skill and prowess made them seem legion.

Owen too, looked to Orla often, but he did so for other reasons. He could see the tension resting between her shoulder blades and in the crease between her thin arched brows. He wanted nothing more than to relieve her of that, say something that would ease the tightness, make her laugh. He hoped that her father would have some answers for the young Princess as to why she was trying to get to him in the first place, and why someone would have been so desperate to prevent her from reaching him.

The guards led them into the actual capital building which was splendid and ornate. Gold leafing was laid over fine carvings and sculptures. The work was much more delicate, and overall on a much smaller scale, than what Owen had witnessed of dwarven craftsmanship, but by no means any less beautiful.

The company continued down a flight of stairs and then into a large chamber, reminiscent to Owen of his own government's Senate chambers. At the bottom of the stairs, leading down into the chambers, and past the large rows of seats at the foot of a large bench, stood a small group of people. There were a few Sylvans wearing fine robes matched by an equal number of Sidhe. One of which, was the stranger who had been wearing the woven birch bark hat Owen had spoken to at the bakery.

The guard who had run ahead of them came back up the stairs and met with the companions' escort briefly; speaking in hushed tones, and then walked past the four friends on his way out of the room.

"Orla!" a tall distinguished looking Sylvan exclaimed from the floor of the Chambers. He moved up the stairs while Orla pushed her way past the escorts to meet her father. They embraced, her father holding her tightly, lifting her off the ground as he did so. "Where have you been? What happened to you?" he asked, holding his daughter out from him, so he could see her fully.

Owen could see that additional guards had stopped just behind Orla and her father.

The senator was taller than Orla, closer to Owen's own height, with long silver hair, the sides of which were pulled back into a single braid while the top and back were left loose down his back. He too, like all *Fey*, had high arching brows the color of his hair, sharp features, with dark nut brown skin, in sharp contrast to his hair. His eyes were a bright green, like his daughter's, and after looking her over, they quickly jumped to her companions. In the briefest of glances, fully observing and analyzing them. There was a keen intelligence in the man's eyes, and Owen could also see a deeper honor and nobility in them—a look that again reminded him of Orla.

"Senator," the tall Sidhe, who Owen had spoken with, began, "the girl's companions." The tone was not quite a request, and yet, not quite a command either. It walked the thin line of two people still trying to determine each other's place in the hierarchy.

Owen looked quickly to Aiya and saw recognition in her expression as she looked at the Sidhe. It was not a happy expression. He looked back to Orla and her father and saw the elder Sylvan eyeing him closely.

"Orla, your companions? Who are they, and how do you know them?" was all her father asked.

"Senator, a more…." the Sidhe behind him began again, but Orla's father simply held up his hand for silence, with which the stranger obliged him.

Orla looked at him questioningly, and he simply smiled and nodded in the direction of her friends. She smiled back, and cleared her throat.

"Aiya, and her sister Silan, came to our home in Quailan to meet with you as ambassadors of their people, but you had already left to come to Narsus. They were invited to wait as guests until you returned. Her sister was murdered in our home by *Ain'griefer*. And Owen," she began, but a soft deep voice rumbled through her mind.

Do not mention where he is from, and treat me as if I am simply a dog, pay me no mind, Boone told her.

"And Owen," she began again, "found me, saved me from a pack of Death Dogs, and brought me back to Quailan after I had first been abducted," her voice faltered some because she saw her father's features slowly growing angrier. He slowly turned away from Orla and back to the *Fey* standing behind him, one in particular, had slowly stepped from behind the others. Chamberlain.

The old steward's face did not change or show any sign of emotion, he simply looked at his old master and acknowledged his anger with a slight bow.

Owen hadn't seen the Sylvan amongst the others when he had first entered the chambers before becoming distracted by Orla's father. Now that the senator's glare was no longer upon him, Chamberlain looked at Owen. His eyes burned as he looked at the boy. Owen felt somewhat protected from the steward's eyes beneath the hood of his cloak, but still they brought great unease. The man's eyes were penetrating and they never left Owen for the remainder of his time in the chambers.

"Orla, you are to come with me while I have the guards bring your friends to lodgings of their own. But," her father said, turning to Owen and Aiya, "I should inform you that guards will be posted outside your room, and that you are not allowed to leave without expressed permission from me or another member of the council," he said flatly, without any pleasure or politeness. Owen could not read this man. He was a flat slate, devoid of any hint of his motives or agenda.

"Senator," Aiya countered, "I am a sworn Sword Maiden of the Sidhe and will not be treated like a common criminal, my companion and I have protected your daughter whilst bringing her safely to you, and this is our repayment?" Aiya did not hide the anger or contempt from her voice.

"The fact that you are who you are is the only thing keeping you from a prison cell!" her father answered angrily, his face contorting into a vestage of rage. "There are questions I need answers to—from all those involved—and until then, you will remain in your rooms until we either free you, or bring you before the council for your trial!" The senator spun on his heel, grabbing Orla beneath her arm as he did so, and pulling her down the remaining stairs with him. Owen and Aiya began to take a step in their direction, but the two guards before them drew their swords, barring their path while the guards behind Orla and the senator parted, allowing the two to pass, and then quickly took positions behind the first two guards. The doors to the chambers opened as if on cue and poured forth Sylvan reinforcements.

"Don't!" Orla shouted over her shoulder as her father walked her from the room, "I'll take care of this!" she shouted once more, as she was dragged through the door and out of sight, followed by Chamberlain and the other Sylvans and Sidhe politicians that had also been in the room.

Owen looked at Aiya questioningly; he wasn't sure what to do. He was sure that Boone and Aiya could easily deal with most of these guards, but creating a blood bath on the senate floor would not do anything to further their cause or prove their innocence.

"Not now. Orla will see this remedied," Aiya said through clenched teeth. It was apparent that the warrior did not appreciate the treatment she was receiving from the Sylvans. "We will go with them, for now," she said as the guards led them back out of the chambers the way they had entered.

98

Owen paced pensively through the small apartment. It consisted of three rooms, a kitchen, bedroom, and what could have been described as a study, in addition to a small bathing room and toilet. The bedroom had one small Sylvan sized bed and a wardrobe, the study had two small—albeit comfortable—chairs, writing table, and a stool. The kitchen had a small cooking stove and chopping table with two stools. The apartment was practical and functional, but by no means was it comfortable for the three companions.

The guards had originally attempted to place Boone in the kennels, but when it became apparent that Aiya and Owen were willing to draw swords if they tried to separate the dog from them, they acquiesced.

But then they realized how small the apartment was.

There were no windows with the exception of a small skylight over the kitchen table. Owen could tell that Aiya's claustrophobia had been bothering her since she entered the small building. She had sat, legs curled beneath her, on one of the small chairs in the reading room. Boone had laid himself in the bedroom next to the small bed, while Owen paced through all three rooms.

"How long are we supposed to stay here?" he asked, pausing in the reading room before Aiya. She looked up to him and he could see the tension around her eyes.

"How long we will, may be less than what they intended," she said. Owen nodded his agreement.

In all the ways he had envisioned the reunion between Orla and her father, this was not one of the scenarios. He couldn't help be worried for Orla, the thought of her with Chamberlain and that strange Sidhe was unnerving to say the least. He had not been reassured by her father's reaction either, he hoped that once he heard Orla's side, he would change his mind, but Owen wasn't so sure.

Owen began pacing again while Boone slept and Aiya stared off into space envisioning open meadows and old forests.

99

W hat are you doing?" Orla asked her father, as he led her into a
small private chamber off the senate floor. Her father closed the
door to the room in Chamberlain's face as the steward tried to follow
the senator. The senator turned and hugged his daughter once more,
some of the fire and anger leaving his face as he did so. She could feel
the tension leave his back and shoulders as she hugged him back.

"They're my friends, he's the one you should've locked up," Orla
said as they separated from their embrace, nodding in the direction of
the door and her former teacher behind it.

Her father held her at arm's length and looked at his daughter; he
stared deeply into her eyes, looking for any sign of things other than the
girl he knew. She stared back at him with a mixture of anger and
bewilderment. There was nothing there that he didn't recognize,
nothing that wasn't her, nothing unexplainable. There was the same
determined, strong, independent, and intelligent girl he knew. She was
so much like her mother, he mused.

He stepped further into the room, bringing her with him. Senator
Negu sat her down on the sofa, while he stayed standing. He began
slowly pacing about the room. He stroked his chin lightly with his hand
while he strode about.

Orla looked at the closed door, she could tell that Chamberlain and
the others were still out there, and if she knew Chamberlain, he had also

already cast an *Ethereal Ear* incantation. One of the first charms he taught her. He also taught her the counter to it.

She looked back at her father still engrossed in his own thoughts, and then back to the door; drawing a simple design with her finger on the sofa cushion next to her as she whispered the word of command, "*BodHar*." There was a slight trembling to the air, like a sound without noise, and then the room was sealed from any sounds escaping its confines.

"Did you say something?" Orla's father asked, turning to her. Orla smiled and shook her head. She looked at her father and could only imagine what Chamberlain must have told him.

"I want you to tell me everything," he said, kneeling down in front of his daughter. He placed his hands on hers and looked her in the eyes. It had been so long it seemed since she'd spoken to him, looked at him, or held his hand. She missed him, there was no doubt, but his association with the Sidhe, and the fact Chamberlain was here, worried her. She did not want to betray her friends to the likes of Chamberlain and the others in the dark robes. Was her father one of the dark robed conspirators? Could she trust him with the truth?

Orla looked into his eyes and knew the answer. He was the man who'd raised her, cared for her, been there for her when her mother died, who never stopped loving her. He was the man she'd known her all life. He was her father.

She told him everything.

100

When Orla had finished telling her tale, she took a deep breath and felt a huge weight lift from her shoulders. She looked at her father, and watched as his expression changed from concern, to anger, to troubled doubt. She had even told him about her lessons from Chamberlain and all she had learned from the steward. She had paused in her story then. When a brief horrified look crossed his face, but he had quickly composed himself, and with a gentle squeeze of her hand, encouraged her to continue her story. He believed her. She could see it in his eyes, but there was also much doubt there too, but deep inside, somehow, she knew it wasn't directed at her.

He slowly stood from where he had knelt for the entirety of his daughter's story and began pacing again, gently stroking his chin. A deep furrowed crease had appeared between his eyebrows. Orla watched him for a short time and then turned her attention to the door. She had lost all sense of time in telling her story and with her charm in place she could not tell what was happening on the other side of the door.

"How deep does it go?" the senator asked no one in particular. He turned to his daughter and the magnitude fully hit him. "They would attack my family? Go after my daughters? Maya!" he said, suddenly realizing his youngest daughter was still vulnerable.

"She's fine," Orla reassured him. "I sent her to stay with friends before I left to come here," she continued. "She doesn't know anything, just that the household was attacked, and unsafe, and that you would come for her as soon as possible."

Orla's father looked at his daughter and saw her quite differently than the last time he'd looked at her back home in Quailan. She had become a Princess since last he saw her, no longer a young girl, she was now, suddenly, so much older. He was still trying to process everything she had told him, there was so much to think about, and not to mention, that there was a human here. A human!

"Is he trustworthy?" the senator asked of Owen. Orla knew who he meant.

"Completely," she said, looking away from her father's gaze for the first time, a slight blush, and heat coming to her cheeks.

"But, how do you know, the stories…" he began but trailed off.

Orla didn't answer; she had reacted the same way when she had first met Owen. It was just how every story and tale was told about them. They were the tales told to children in her world. The stories of hopeful, brave *Fey* heroes, and their courageous deeds, opposed by the villainous and despicable humans. They were the monsters in their stories, told at night to keep young children in their beds, and well behaved during the day. He was a fairytale come to life.

101

How deep does this go?" the senator asked again. He stopped and looked at his daughter, knowing she wouldn't have the answer, but at that moment she was the only constant, the only truth he could rely on, nothing else seemed trustworthy or real anymore.

"I don't know what you mean," Orla said looking at her father, she had never seen him so troubled or disillusioned before, "what goes?"

"The conspiracy," he said in a whisper suddenly aware of their vulnerability here in the chamber, wondering who could hear them.

"It's okay," Orla said as if reading his mind, "we can talk safely," she said smiling, "I took care of that."

He nodded, even though the thought of his own daughter wielding magicks frightened him more than he'd admit, it was a necessity right now.

"It's got to be the Reunification," he said, suddenly angry. "That's why I had to leave two months back. Why I've been here, and why we've been quagmired in hearings and meetings for that whole time!" He slammed his fist into his open hand, and then sat down on the sofa next to his daughter, taking her hand in his.

"There are very strong forces at work, pushing for Reunification. Our worlds are connected to each other. Ours is dying; the damage the humans have done in their world is overwhelming and threatening our own. That is fueling support to reunify the two worlds, in an attempt to save ours by saving them both. And if peaceful cohabitation with the humans still isn't possible after all this time, then they propose open warfare!" Orla couldn't believe what she was hearing. The whole concept seemed so preposterous, so absurd, but here she was sitting with her father discussing it.

"But what do I have to do with that?" she asked. Somewhere in the back of her mind she felt an itch. An itch she couldn't scratch, but one she knew was there, and if she could just itch it, she would have her answer.

"I don't know about that, but maybe they were trying to get to me, through you," he said.

"Why?" she asked, suddenly drawn away from that itch.

"Because I'm the loudest opposition to their proposal," the senator said, a bit embarrassed.

"But what about Owen's parents, why would they be in Narsus?" she asked. Her father looked at her, but he didn't have any answer for her. He knew little of humans, mostly just stories really, and much of what Orla had told him had been news to him. The Sylvans had little interest in magic or much of the world in which surrounded it. He did, however, feel that it was somehow linked to the Reunification.

"I don't know. I don't know what use they would be in winning approval for their agenda," he started, but then stopped, "unless they're not using them to seek approval. Anyone who would go through the efforts they have in attacking you, wouldn't care about policy or Realm approval, they would move ahead with their own agenda. No matter the cost or obstacle."

"But how?" Orla asked, "What could they do with them?" she asked, but then remembered Winter telling Owen that just his presence in this Realm increased many being's power. *What could someone do with two humans?* she thought.

"I don't know, honestly," her father confessed, "you know more about the arcane than I do," he said with a bit more anger than he intended. He looked at his daughter and could see the hurt it caused her, and the sadness in hiding it from him had caused. She wasn't to blame; she was a victim in this.

"I'm sorry, sweetheart," he said, squeezing her hand. "This is all so overwhelming, so unbelievable."

Orla smiled, but then suddenly, a thought occurred to her. "Where are Owen and Aiya?" she asked, concern filling her voice.

"They are being held," he began, but then paused; he stood suddenly looking back at his daughter, his face a mask of concern.

"They are not safe," he said, striding towards the door of the chamber.

102

Black raven feathers fluttered through the night carrying news of things yet to come. The twin birds flew about the Star Tower, circling its entire length as they descended to the ground. Black birds in a black sky, dark omens for a dark night. The soft quorking filled Owen's ears, but the chortles and clucking were words and stories to him. Owen saw two statues poised at the top of the tower before a shining, pulsing sphere. Its pinkish, lavender hews in sharp contrast to the dark stone gray figures standing before it. A huge spider hung from the ceiling above the orb and Owen's parents, spinning an intricate web. The ravens landed at the steps of the tower, facing east as the morning dawned, the sun breaking blood red upon the winter landscape. Rustling feathers and wing beats sounded deep within Owen's consciousness in the dark of night.

Owen woke with a cramp in his neck and shoulders. The Sylvan bed in Quailan hadn't been this short, he thought, or had he grown? Either way, the bed was as evil as the Vrok, he considered as he untwisted himself and climbed from it. Boone snored loudly at the foot of the bed, taking up nearly half the floor space.

Owen walked from the room careful not to disturb the dog. In the sitting room he realized Aiya was no longer in the chair she had occupied for most of the day and night. He found her in the kitchen, sitting crossed legged upon the table, head inclined, looking out through the skylight into the night. She looked at Owen as he approached her. Aiya looked more tired than Owen had ever seen her; she looked wearier than the night that Winter had passed.

"The night is foul, Owen. The Kingdom is infested," she said, her voice harsh, her eyes bloodshot and red.

"They will be coming for us shortly," Aiya whispered, and looked back to the skylight.

"Who?" Owen asked. *The guards?* he thought.

"The *Ain'griefer*," she hissed through clenched teeth.

"How do you know?" Owen asked, leaning closer, he had been concerned all along that someone had been watching and listening to them since being put in here.

"They sent them for us once before, now they have us trapped, why wouldn't they send them again?" Aiya kept her eyes on the window above their heads.

"Then let's get out of here," Owen said while turning towards the door.

"It's sealed," Aiya said causally, "I tried it while you were resting." She looked down at him apologetically, "So is the window," she said, turning her attention back to the portal.

"Then what do we do?" Owen asked, beginning to feel trapped and claustrophobic himself.

"We wait, Owen. We wait. It won't be long now," she said.

Wait for what? Boone asked.

"For our guests to arrive," Aiya answered, and as if on cue, the three companions heard soft footsteps above them on the roof.

Aiya silently leapt from the table and unsheathed her sword. Owen took his own blade out, much more carefully, while trying to remain quiet. Boone tipped his head from side to side listening to the footsteps above them. The three friends slowly spread out in the tiny room, encircling the small table in the middle.

Owen looked up through the window and at the gray clouds beyond; then, suddenly, the clouds were blocked out, blackened by a shape over the window. Just as he was realizing what the shape was, he turned away from the sound of breaking glass.

103

As the window shattered and glass fell, Owen wielded GreenFyr, the ancient sword lit the small room in pale emerald light. A single figure leapt through the broken window, landing on the kitchen table silently. Both Aiya and Owen had brought back their weapons to attack, but held at the last moment. In the glow of the sword, the creature's feline characteristics were obvious.

"Orla!" they both said at the same time.

"Let's go! I'm here to rescue you," she said, jumping off the table.

"Little short for a stormtrooper, aren't you?" Owen asked, with a snort, not being able to help himself.

"What?" Orla asked. "What's a stormtrooper?"

"Nothing, never mind, just a joke," he said embarrassed. "I am *such* a geek," he said quietly to himself, but tried quickly to recover. "What's up? What's going on?"

"Not entirely sure, but I think you're safer outta here," she said, smiling at Owen's awkwardness.

"I agree," Aiya added, leaping onto the table. Her affect seemed much different, just the fresh air alone had improved her state. She leapt up and out of the window just as gracefully as Orla had entered.

Owen looked over at Boone and then at the window. Owen knew he couldn't make it, but he wasn't sure about the dog.

"Boone, jump, and I'll catch you," Aiya said, leaning back into the opening.

Boone jumped up onto the table, sending glass onto the floor. Owen realized how loud the crashing window had been and now the scattering of the shards.

"Sssshhhh," he hissed.

"It's okay, I've taken care of that," Orla said. She had cast a containment spell around the kitchen before she'd entered, to silence any noise of breaking glass.

"Let me get up there first, so I can help her," Orla said, springing to the window ledge from the floor. Owen felt inferior; everyone else was so much more adept at everything it seemed. Both Orla and Aiya leaned over the edge of the window as the great dog, belying his size, leapt with ease and grace up to the window ledge. He was able to grasp the edge of the window with his huge front paws as Orla and Aiya both grabbed clumps of fur and skin around the scruff of his neck. They kept him from falling back down into the room, while he kicked with his back legs until he gained purchase and traction on the wall, just under the window. With the help of his two friends he made it through with little effort.

Owen ran back to his room and grabbed his pack, throwing his dwarven cloak and gloves into it along with the rest of his belongings he'd taken off in the room. Placing his quiver across his back along with his bow, he ran back from the room and back into the kitchen.

Owen climbed up onto the table and looked up at the window. It was higher than he could jump. Orla leaned over the edge again. She was still in her hybrid form, but it looked like she was trying to smile.

"Did you think we forgot you?" she asked teasingly.

"No, it's..." Owen started, "I can't make the jump," he finished, embarrassed by his limitations.

"I know, it's okay. That's why I'm here," she said, not teasing anymore. "Just jump as high as you can, I'll grab your arm when you do," she said, making it sound easy.

"Okay, but I'm not sure I can jump even that high, and what if I'm too heavy?"

"It's okay, Aiya's got me," she said, trying to make her feline face smile again. "I'm not that strong!"

Owen smiled. Orla had a way of making him feel better about himself, not doubt himself, or feel awkward about things that he couldn't do. He stepped to the edge of the table and taking a one step run, he leapt as high as he could, stretching out his arm as he did.

Orla caught him about the wrist and forearm. She tightened her feline hands around his arm, her claws digging in slightly, holding on. He looked up into her bright green cat eyes as she looked down into his sky blue ones. Again, he thought, she attempted a smile.

"Going up," she said lightly as he was pulled up and through the window.

"Now what?" he said on top of the small building attached to the Council and Senate's Chambers. It was a small one story structure, unimpressive and nondescript compared to the much grander political building.

"My father is waiting for us," Orla said. "I told him everything, I hope that was okay," she said, looking to Owen. She had shifted into her Sylvan form, and he could see she hadn't even taken the time to wash or change out of her traveling clothes. She must have spent the better part of the evening trying to convince her father to release them.

"Where's he?" Owen asked.

"He's making arrangements to get us out of the city and to a safe place," she said.

"Why didn't he come?" Aiya asked, surveying the alleys and roads around them.

"We were supposed to come together, but I didn't want to wait for him to make all the arrangements," she said, knowing that both Owen and Aiya wouldn't trust her father anytime soon after their first meeting.

"I just had a bad feeling about leaving you in their any longer," she said, looking out over the dark city, street lights burned in the blowing snow, while dim lights filtered through the drifts from homes and houses.

"*Ain'griefers*," Aiya said the word, and just the mention of the creatures seemed to make the night colder somehow.

"Yeah," Orla said, knowing that was the feeling she'd had in her stomach all night.

"They're here in the city," Aiya said again, her voice being torn from her mouth by the blasting wind. Owen could see the look in her eyes, the memory of her sister's death at the hands of the deymon assassins.

"Let's go," Orla said, not wanting to stand in the cold and dark any longer with the deymons about.

"Not that way," Owen said, stopping the Sylvan after only a step.

"What do you mean?" she said, looking back him, "My father's this way."

"I'm not going that way. There," Owen said, turning back and pointing to the Star Tower. The four companions stood in its shadow, having to crane their necks to see the pinnacle. "That's the way I'm going. My parents are in there."

"How? The ravens? Are you sure?" Orla asked. She looked up at the tower as if imagining the birds flying around it. Orla was beginning to trust Owen's sight and the news the ravens brought to him. Aiya also turned and looked at him. The time was coming for her to honor her pledge to the *Maou'r*.

"Did they come to you?" she asked, watching him closely.

"Yeah, while I was sleeping," he said, self conscious of his visions. He still didn't understand anything about them, but they were coming much more frequently, and becoming easier to interpret.

"But my father," Orla said, but she already knew he would have to wait. Owen would head to the tower and she would go with him.

"He will wait," Aiya said. "The *Ain'griefer* are here. They're here for a reason."

"It's tonight, whatever they're going to do with my parents, they're doing tonight," Owen said. He walked to the edge of the roof; the tower was not very far from the capital building. Turning, he looked back at his companions watching him. He wanted to tell them he would go alone. They had already helped him enough, risked more than enough, but he knew he couldn't save his parents without them. He also knew, deep down, that none of them would ever leave him. There was still a piece of him that needed to try, however.

"Orla, you shouldn't come though, your father..." Owen began as the Sylvan stepped beside him.

"Don't," was all she said before hopping off the roof of the building to the small street below.

Aiya stepped alongside Owen, smiling slightly, "That went well," she said before jumping off the roof after Orla. Boone leapt off the side next, landing heavily, but gracefully.

Owen peered over the edge of the roof, there was a small shed a few meters down the length of the roof that he walked over to, hopped onto, and then once more onto the road below. The others met him as he landed. The road was empty, the snow falling steadily, making the night quiet.

"How long did I sleep for?" Owen asked, looking up at the sky trying to get a bearing on the time.

"Barely an hour," Aiya said, "The night is young, just after mid," she added.

Aiya led them through the streets of Narsus to the Star Tower of the First Men, or the Tower of the Once Men she knew some called it. She knew the history of the building better than most of the Sylvans living in the city around it. It was erected by the *Aingeal* not long after their battle with their brethren, the Battle of the Fallen they called it, long before the Great Schism, when many of their kind fell from grace. The tower was built in memory of the Fallen, but had long been left in disrepair since the decline of the First Men and the waning of their power and numbers. For centuries it had just been another part of the landscape to the Sylvans, just another peak amidst the mountains.

The snow had accumulated since they had been sequestered to the apartment; at least a foot of the powder lay in the streets and walks. No other tracks dotted the cityscape as they made their way to the tower. Owen and Orla walked along side each other while Aiya walked ahead; keeping a close eye on the buildings they passed. Boone stayed behind, trying to stay in the shadows of the buildings. It didn't take long to come to the tower; it was just a matter of circling the round capital building until they came to the far side of the structure. As they approached, Aiya motioned them into the shadows of one of the many alcove entrances to the Council Chambers. As they leaned into the darkness of the entry way they could see several figures outside the main entrance.

The tower had a large staircase leading to the large wooden doors marking its entrance. They were ornately carved and seemed not to have suffered from time and aging. The figures at the entrance were engaged in an intercourse almost on the verge of arguing. One then, abruptly, turned and left down the stairs.

The Sidhe stranger, the one Owen had spoken to in the bakery, was leaving. He headed back to the capital building. He left standing in front of the tower doors what looked to be a small unit of Sylvan guards while another robed individual entered and closed the doors to the tower.

"Who is this guy?" Owen wondered aloud.

"Sumiel," Aiya said the name with the slightest hint of disgust. "Why and how he is involved with the council is beyond me. He has always been one of immense ambition and segregation within the Sidhe."

"Well, he's the guy I saw in the bakery with Chamberlain crawling around his hat," Owen said. Sumiel entered a small building, next to the senate building, through an entrance opposite the tower. "He was there with your dad in the senate chambers too."

"Chamberlain," Orla hissed.

"Yup, they must be in this together," Owen said, not really expecting a reply from any of his friends.

"My father thinks it has to do with the Reunification," Orla offered. Aiya looked back to her a bit surprised, but considered it.

"If I remember correctly, Sumiel was often outspoken for the *Fey's* right to reclaim both Realms, it would make sense then if he was here pushing that agenda," Aiya surmised. "He was never one of much power, though. I don't know how he's become so influential."

"But what does that have to do with my parents?" Owen asked, trying to get a better look at the guards in front of the tower.

"My father also wondered if this whole thing wasn't completely political, if the dark robes weren't actually plotting something else, trying to go ahead with it some other way on their own," Orla offered.

"Can they do that, is it even possible?" Owen asked.

"He didn't know. Sylvans don't know much about things like that," she answered.

"Oh, it's possible," Aiya said, suddenly looking worried. "They would need a source of unfathomable power to do it."

Standing up, Owen turned to Aiya and Orla. He looked at them, wondering if they were thinking what he was. He kept hearing Winter's voice over and over telling him how his presence could increase the power of certain beings in this world. *What could they do with two humans?* he thought as he looked at his companions. Owen could see that they were thinking along those same lines.

"We need to find your parents, Owen. I fear they, and all of us, could be in grave danger," Aiya said as she began to loosen her sword in her scabbard. "There are only four guards; they should not be much resistance."

"Wait, let me try first, they may just be capital guards, not a part of the Reunification," Orla suggested. The Sword Maiden relinquished. Aiya, Owen, and Boone waited while Orla approached the tower entrance. Owen slid several arrows from his quiver, ones he'd fletched back in the Dwarven Kingdom and handed them to Aiya. She slipped the shafts into her empty quiver.

Orla noticed right away all four guards came to attention as she approached. Two stayed close to the door, while two came down the stairs to greet her, none of whom took out their weapons. They assumed the small Sylvan girl approaching wasn't any one dangerous, thankfully none of them recognized her.

The guards, however, approached tentatively. Anyone out in this weather, and out at this time of night, was suspect. They were capital guards and Orla was, after all, a defenseless Sylvan girl, they presumed.

"*Creidii!*" she intoned, raising her hands, and moving them intricately through the storm swept air. There was no visible sign of the charm, no bright lights, or noise. The guards didn't know how to react at first, but then again, they couldn't—even if they'd wanted to, except for one.

The two guards closest to the door, both went rigid, standing in place as if frozen, while one of the guards that had been approaching Orla did also, but the fourth guard did not. At first he didn't know what to make of her hand waving and strange language, but then he noticed his partners' state. He charged Orla then, quickly reaching for his short sword in the process. He never reached her, however; two arrows pierced his chest and hauberk, dropping him a meter from her.

She exhaled in relief, and guilt replaced the air in her lungs. She had hoped she could prevent any needless deaths. She looked at the victims of her spell. The first was quite paralyzed, and so were the other two by the door. They shouldn't remember anything that happened while under the effects, but they would remember seeing the Sylvan girl approach. When they woke to find their dead friend, they'd know who to blame. Orla found herself hoping Owen was right about the tower. It was one thing to run away and battle goblins and the like, but they had just attacked and killed a capital guard. They could all be charged with murder and she with treason.

Owen and Aiya moved the frozen guard and corpse up onto the landing before the large tower stairs. From a distance anyone would still see three guards present, standing at attention, before the ancient building.

Orla didn't look at the guard; she didn't want to know what he looked like, know whether he was old or young, to wonder if he had a family.

"We had to, Orla," Owen said. "You saved three of them, we had no choice."

"I…I know," she said after a pause. "It's just…" she couldn't bring herself to say, *but what if you're wrong? What if your parents aren't in there? What if we just killed this man for no reason?* And what bothered her even more to think, *but he was a Sylvan.* "There's just been so much killing, and we still don't really know why," was what she said instead.

Owen touched her arm, hesitantly, and only for a moment, but it was a gentle, caring touch. He understood, she knew he did, he didn't want to do this either. "I know," was all he ended up saying.

"It's locked," Aiya informed them after inspecting the door. Orla stepped up to the twin oaken doors and placed her hands over the large wrought iron lock. The familiar blue glow emanated from her hands, spreading from her fingertips like blue wildfire, penetrating the door and lock. There was a quiet CLICK from within the locking mechanism.

Owen and Aiya slowly opened the door to the tower. The inside of the building sparkled and glittered. There was no visible light source, but the anteroom seemed to be illuminated. The room was as bright as a clear night under a full moon. The room was completely hewn from white marble with silver veins running through the stone. The workmanship made the dwarven halls and Kingdom look like the work of young children.

Owen wasn't the only one in awe; Aiya had never seen such beauty and gallantry. They could hear running water through the doors to the main portion of the ground floor. As they followed the sound, Owen couldn't believe the spectacle before him. It was raining inside the tower, but there were no clouds and the ceiling glistened like a clear winter sky, as if there was no building above them at all, only the stars and heavens.

Owen at first thought there was no ceiling or roof to the tower, but then realized that if that was the case, the sky would have been filled with storm clouds and falling snow. But the tower looked as if it had a clear winter sky filled with bright stars, but it was actually raining, and without rain clouds, and *inside*, he thought.

In the center of the tower's first floor was a small pool, around which a thin staircase circled up the tower, disappearing into the night sky. The rain fell all about them, but never touched them. It seemed to dissipate before actually falling on them, but the raindrops dotted and rippled the surface of the small pool. The floor, walls, and stairwell were made of the same marble as the entryway, and like the guests, remained perfectly dry.

"*Aingeal* tears," Aiya whispered.

Owen noticed as he and his friends approached the stairs, that the walls were sculpted to resemble a great battle. *Aingeal* battled each other while others plummeted from their aerial combat into a great abyss. To Owen the fallen figures resembled deymons or gargoyles. And the detail was so exceptional; the figures seemed so life like, that the walls actually seemed to move.

Angels fought and deymons fell.

Aiya stepped upon the stairs and the others followed her. As they climbed the stairwell they realized that the center of the tower was hollow, there was a round balcony around the outer edge of the tower at intervals for each floor. The stairs ringed the inner edge of the tower, stepping up through the floor of each balcony. Each floor's ceiling appeared as a perfectly clear night. The friends didn't stop to investigate the floors, they continued on towards the top of the spire.

"Owen, where did you see them?" Orla asked after they had already surpassed nineteen balconies.

"I think it was the top, it was a room, different from these," he said, indicating the balconies. Just then an emptiness enveloped them. The tower, even with the clear night sky and raining atmosphere, had been warm and comfortable. Now, however, their skin became gooseflesh and the hair on Owen's arms stood on end. The companions all looked at one another and knew that chill, they knew that void.

"'*Griefers* are here," Owen said. The others nodded as they pushed on up the stairs at a renewed pace.

After they passed three more balconies they began to hear chanting coming from above them. With each following balcony the chanting grew louder. After two more levels, and on entering the third, they were greeted by four stone statues at the top of the stairs that opened into a large room at the very pinnacle of the tower. The four marble statues were similar to the sculptures that had followed them along the walls of the tower. There were two very angelic looking with large eagle wings, casting down two gargoyle looking figures with bat-like wings, with short horns protruding from their foreheads.

The stairway passed between the figures with an angel and deymon on either side of it. The chanting was loudest now, and as the four companions moved from the lower levels to the top of the tower, the night sky gave way to a clear and protected view of the raging storm outside the tower. Billowing snow clouds gathered around the tower's spire while white blankets of snow buffeted the structure. The exterior walls and ceiling of the room were made from a finely polished crystal, stronger than stone, and as transparent as any window Owen had ever looked through.

Owen's attention was quickly drawn to the room while he took in several things happening at once. There was the pulsing sphere from his vision floating in the middle of the room, its pinkish, purplish glow coloring the people and clouds around it. On either side of the sphere were two statues, Owen's mother and father, and standing next to each of them were two dark robed figures. Moving between the figures, and around the orb, were three other black robed figures. His mom and dad were still the way he remembered them, except they were no longer holding the baseball bat or rifle.

Owen recognized the man standing next to his mother; he would never forget the Sylvan. Chamberlain was dressed in ornate robes and was painting runes and symbols onto his mother's statue as they stepped into the room. A Sidhe was performing the same ritual on the statue of Owen's father.

Owen stood dumbfounded, he couldn't believe he had actually found them and come this far. The *Fey* in the chamber had not noticed the late arrivals and continued in their incantation.

Finishing painting the runes on the figures, Chamberlain and his Sidhe counterpart turned towards one another and began chanting louder while each drawing a long thin dagger from their belts. An increased sense of urgency took Owen as he turned to Orla.

"What are they doing?" he whispered in her ear while she looked on. She was looking intently at the magicians across from them. She understood most of what they were saying, but some of the words and meanings were lost to her, these were spells and charms well above her station.

"They're trying to make them flesh again, but..." she paused, but not just flesh; there was something she was missing. Owen slid an arrow from his quiver, and knocking it, took aim at the Sidhe next to his father. "Don't disrupt the spell until they're flesh again," Orla instructed. Owen nodded his understanding. Aiya followed Owen's example and armed herself with her bow. She took aim at Chamberlain.

There was a soft red glimmer around the two statues, and their gray stone skin began to lighten and pinken until they were flesh again, but frozen and rigid in place. Just as the glow began to fade a shout rang out across the room from one of the other robed figures. One of the other attendents was shouting and pointing their way. Owen and Aiya loosed their arrows. Owen's found its place in the chest of the Sidhe just as he was bringing down his blade to Owen's father's now vulnerable neck.

Chamberlain, alarmed by the yelling, moved just enough to avoid a fatal blow from Aiya's arrow. The missile slid across his chest as he pivoted to look in their direction the way his servant had been pointing. The blade of the arrow sliced through the ceremonial robes and his flesh below. A long angry gash ran along the mage's chest. He screamed in pain and anger as he saw the intruders at the top of the stairwell, standing between the tower guardians.

The human statues were flesh and held firm. Maron, his Sidhe counterpart, was dead, so he would have to finish the sacrificial spell himself, but nothing was disrupted. He could take some time to finish these meddling fools.

"*Beo!*" he shouted.

Owen and Aiya both began to reach for another arrow when sudden movement to their sides prompted them to drop their bows and reach for their swords. Owen spun to see the marble angels and deymons come to life.

"I've got these two," Aiya said spinning and facing the two statues closest to her. She drew her sword in a wide arc in front of her, her Sidhe blade actually slicing the marble of the attackers.

Owen pulled GreenFyr from its sheath; flames erupted from the blade as he did so. Orla leapt at the stone angel, attacking the golem, but her claws didn't even scratch the marble. She leapt over the creature's head as it flailed its stone fists at her.

The gargoyle attacked Owen, swiping at him with long, stone talons. Owen dodged and evaded the first two attacks while bringing his blade up into the creature's torso, pushing the burning blade deep into stone. The blade sliced into the creature, melting the marble, and slicing the statue in two. As the two halves fell to the floor, the creature became lifeless stone once more, shattering as it landed.

Boone leapt at the angel attacking Orla, his teeth no use against the marble, but he was able to draw the attacks away from the Sylvan and to him. He had dodged two punches when five bursts of red light slashed through the air and into the great dog. Three took him in his ribs while two more shot into his neck. He grunted as the five missiles knocked him to the ground.

"I've got this one, take Chamberlain!" Owen shouted, turning his attention to the marble angel. The workmanship of the creature made the being seem so lifelike and real, and yet it was only stone, Owen thought. The statue displayed no feeling or emotion as the creature moved towards the fallen dog. Owen stepped between the two, holding the flaming sword before the angel.

Aiya's blade was not as devastating as Owen's, but no less deadly, when wielded correctly. The gargoyle slashed at her, but she evaded the attacks with ease, even though the marble creatures were surprisingly fast, they were not as quick footed as the Sidhe. She counter attacked, taking deep cuts and slices from the rock being. The marble angel charged her, lunging and swinging strong, stone fists at her. Aiya parried the attacks, slicing one arm off completely while taking a deep chunk from the second. The creatures were mindless drones, uncreative in their attacks, but also unceasing and untiring.

Orla turned to her one time teacher. He was standing next to Owen's mother, wearing a torn robe and bleeding freely from his chest. He was in the middle of an incantation, but the thought of battling her former master was intimidating. She cast a quick shield spell, throwing the center of the spell over Owen. Just as she had finished her spell, blue fire flashed from Chamberlain's fingertips, dancing along the outer edge of the shield around Owen. Chamberlain sneered in response, and turned his attention to Orla.

The chill of the deymons coming from below was growing stronger. Owen slashed at the angel as it lunged for him, cleaving its head from its rock shoulders. Again the statue fell lifeless to the ground.

Aiya ducked another attack from her angel, spinning around behind the golem as the creature passed her; she kicked it from behind, sending it crashing down the stairwell it defended. But then the other stone statue was quickly on her, driving its attacks, but a green glow stopped it in its tracks as GreenFyr erupted from its chest. Owen pulled the blade from the statue as Aiya sliced her blade through the rock neck of the gargoyle.

Turning, Owen and Aiya watched as Chamberlain lashed out with blasts of eldritch energy, sending Orla back into the marble wall as her defenses fell before the onslaught from her master. Owen heard the girl scream as she collapsed to the ground.

The air was cold from the foul creatures coming from below. Owen turned to Aiya for the briefest of seconds. Boone stood wearily, smoke rose from the wounds along his flank and neck, the dog moved stiffly and with great effort.

"Guard the floor from the *'Griefers*!" Owen shouted as he charged across the floor towards Chamberlain. He raised GreenFyr above his head, the blade ablaze.

"Fool," Chamberlain muttered, spittle playing across his lips in disgust. With a simple gesture of his left hand and a flash of light Owen froze in place, and with another gesture from Chamberlain's right, bright yellow energy flashed across the room, striking Owen in the chest. He cried out from the intensity of the pain as his consciousness began to fade. It felt as if his very life force was dwindling.

He could hear shouting across the room and growling from a distance, but then there was a blinding flash of blue light that rocked Chamberlain from his feet, breaking his hold on Owen. The mage was shot across the room and slammed into the marble wall, crumpling to the ground.

Owen fell to his knees trying to catch his breath. He looked across the room to Orla, who was in the same state as he; she too was just getting back to her feet, a faint blue glow fading from her hands.

Aiya and Boone were quickly to his side, helping him to his feet while Orla slowly made her way over to them. She moved awkwardly, as if every movement caused her excruciating pain.

"The *Ain'griefer* are close," Aiya said. She held Owen beneath his arm, helping him support his weight.

"My parents," he said feeling as though his tongue was swollen, making it hard to speak. The Sidhe nodded, then helped walk him over to them. Owen looked up at his mother, frozen in place. She still had powders and paints on her face and clothing from where Chamberlain had painted her. Her eyes were open, but it still seemed as if she wasn't there. Owen touched her gently; she was rigid as stone.

"It's okay," Orla said. "They're held the same way the guards are downstairs."

"Can you break the spell?" Owen asked, his voice cracking with emotion.

Orla nodded, "I can try," she said. Owen noticed that Boone and Aiya had turned to face the stairs. Two dark shapes had just stepped into the room bringing with them the cold void of the Abyss. Owen felt the fear that had chilled him back in the courtyard in Quailan return.

The dark figures drew their slim short swords and daggers while they slowly approached Owen, his parents, and his friends.

Leave them to us, the rumbling sounded through their minds. Aiya and the injured dog slowly stepped from Owen. Boone still didn't seem fully recovered from the blow he'd received from Chamberlain, but he faced the deymon assassins none the less.

Orla closed her eyes and touched Owen's mother's forehead where she had touched her back in Owen's home. She spoke quietly to herself and a faint green glow appeared where her fingers touched the woman's forehead. She repeated a few more words, and then Owen's mother blinked.

Orla stumbled slightly, but Owen quickly grabbed her about the waist, supporting her, and keeping her from falling.

"Owen?" Mrs. McInish asked suddenly, her limbs dropping from their frozen positions. "Owen! There are monsters in the house!" she said, not entirely believing what she was saying, but she knew what she had seen. And then she realized what her son was wearing and the elf looking girl he was holding. "What's going on?"

"No time to explain, mom," Owen said quickly, "follow me," he said over his shoulder as he helped Orla over to his father.

"No time to…? You wait one minute, Owen McInish! Now tell me right this…," but then his mother noticed where she was standing. In a glass room, atop a huge tower, with a frightening blizzard outside while the largest dog she had ever seen, and an elven woman, fought two dark figures that caused her stomach to clench in fear. The elf swung her sword, disarming the dark figure, and quickly bringing her blade back and slicing through the creature's neck. The figure evaporated into the air. The dog had tackled the other creature and was tearing into its neck when it too vanished into nothingness.

Mrs. McInish quickly followed after her son.

She stopped when she realized who they were standing before. Mrs. McInish raised her hand and touched her husband's hair gently, brushing it away from his forehead. "What happened?" she whispered.

"One sec," Owen said, "can you do this?" he asked Orla, who looked exhausted. She smiled at him then, and the look made his heart swell.

"I've got to, right?" she said. She again touched his father's head and repeated the words she had said to his mother. The same green glow appeared at her finger tips, but then her body was rocked by a convulsion, shaking her violently. Owen's father opened his eyes, just as Orla's closed, and the young *Fey* went limp in Owen's arms.

104

O wen!" Mr. McInish said, recognizing the oddly dressed young man as his son. He reached out and hugged his son, pulling him close. Suddenly noticing the small girl his son held in his arms between them. He could immediately see the difference in the boy's stature and musculature. He was no longer the boy he once knew.

"Owen, what's happening?" Mrs. McInish asked her son again, stepping closer to him and her husband. She looked slowly around the room, realization slowly seeping in.

"Owen, where are we?" she asked. She looked closely at Owen. It was him to be sure, but he was different, he seemed older than he looked, than she remembered. His cheeks were red and weathered; his skin healthy and darker than before. His eyes were bright and clear, but seemed to have a weight about them that they had never had before. And the clothes he wore looked as if from one of her stories. He smiled then, seeing her and his father analyzing him, momentarily distracted from the Sylvan in his arms.

"It's really me," he said, but then Mrs. McInish finally identified the greatest difference she was seeing. He was comfortable with himself, as if he'd finally found out who he was.

"You won't believe me, and we really don't have a lot of time," he said as the enormous dog and woman came and stood by Owen and the small girl.

"The *'Griefers* have been dealt with," Aiya said eyeing Owen's parents carefully, almost in wonder. "And Chamberlain's servants are tending to him," she added nodding her head in the Sylvan's direction.

"Okay," Owen said. He looked back to his parents, sighing, he began to explain what had happened over the last month, but then a sudden cold chill entered the tower again, silencing him and drawing the group closer together.

"*'Griefers,'*" Owen and Aiya both said at the same time. The chill was overpowering, stronger than any fear he'd felt from the deymon mercenaries before.

"There must be many for their aura to be this potent," Aiya said. Owen noticed his mother and father looking, mouths agape, at the Sidhe Sword Maiden before them. He knew what his mom was thinking; *she's everything I ever imagined an elf would be!*

"They're blocking our escape," Owen said looking towards the stairs. "Mom...," Owen began, but Aiya silenced him with her hand upon his forearm. She looked back down at Orla still lying in his arms.

"We will deal with them. You protect your family and Orla; see them safely out and home. We will clear the way before you. By my life or my sword, we will see you safely from this tower," the tall, elven woman said as she drew her sword once more. A grim satisfaction had settled upon her. Finally she would be living up to her vow.

We will pave your way with the blood of your enemies, Boone's voice echoed in their minds. Owen's parents looked around them for the source of the voice and then both settled on the intelligent looking animal before them. The immense dog nudged Owen with his massive head before leaping off after Aiya. *Watch yourself!* he said as he disappeared from view.

His parents stared at Owen in awe. The boy who was picked on at school, or who spent his afternoons reading in his bedroom, or walking alone through their back woods was no more. In his place stood a young man that enchanted beings and warrior maidens protected with their lives.

"Owen, tell us what happened," Mr. McInish said kneeling down to look in Owen's eyes. The small elf girl still lay crumpled in his son's arms.

Owen looked from his mother to his father, even standing here amongst all this wonder and magic; he doubted whether they could believe all that had happened. He looked back down at the girl in his lap, her breathing was regular and deep, she looked as if she were in a deep sleep. He looked back up at his parents. His mother had turned and was looking at the dark figures behind them, they had pulled the other elf into a sitting position from the heap he'd been lying in on the floor.

"I found these tracks in the snow…," Owen began, and quickly told them of the events that led to the trolls coming looking for Orla and how they had been turned to stone. "I came here with her to find a cure, I didn't know until later that they had taken you here too," Owen said. He looked up and saw two dark robed minions walking towards him and his family. He placed Orla on the ground. Standing quickly, he unslung his bow, knocked an arrow, and fired it in one fluid motion. His arrow shot towards the first figure, and just before it struck, the servant vanished. As the robe fell, a small blue, black, and white bird flew quickly from out of the cowl and shot down the stairs. Owen drew another arrow to fire at the second figure when that figure too transformed into a small arctic fox. Owen was about to take aim when his mother grabbed his arm.

"OWEN!" she shouted, "What do you think you're doing?" Mrs. McInish said, grabbing Owen's arm and pulling up his bow, spoiling his shot. The fox followed the bird down the stairs.

"Mom, you don't understand!" Owen shouted, fully aware that Chamberlain was on his feet.

"I do, you tried to shoot that, that, that thing," she stammered at a loss for what she'd just seen. "You can't, you don't just shoot at…," she stopped, remembering the things she'd just seen. "At stuff, you just don't shoot at anything alive!"

Chamberlain held his arms above his head; soft chanting began to fill the room while the orb in the middle of the room began pulsing in cadence to the rhythm of the words. The sphere began to expand.

"What's he doing?" Mr. McInish asked, looking back at Owen.

That's when Owen realized that the paints and powders on his parents were pulsing as well. The different colors and designs came to life, glowing brightly with each chant.

"I don't know," Owen said, looking back to Chamberlain. "Mom, you don't understand. These are evil people and they are trying to use us to do very bad things." The look in his mother's eyes was more than he could bear. She'd never looked at him that way before. He couldn't think about that now, though. He began to pull another arrow from his quiver when his father's hand made him pause.

"Wait," his father said. "Get your mom outta here, I'll talk to this guy." He squeezed his son's arm before letting go. Mr. McInish turned and began walking towards Chamberlain. "I'll catch up," he said over his shoulder.

"Mom, I can..." Owen began, but an abrupt flash of light cut him off.

"No, you heard your dad, let's go," she said, standing up. "Do you need help?" she asked looking back at Owen, suddenly realizing her son was frozen in place. His eyes wide with fear.

Owen couldn't believe this. What was he supposed to do?

Just as he was lifting Orla in his arms a sudden flash of light sent by Chamberlain struck him, freezing him in place. He couldn't move a muscle. There was no pain, but just a sudden numbness that encapsulated his whole body. All he could do was watch as his unsuspecting father closed on the dark robed magician while his mother turned back to look at him horrified. Owen couldn't help watching the runes glowing along his mother as she stared at him in disbelief. When he looked back at his father he couldn't believe what he was seeing. He couldn't believe what was happening. He had come so close. How could everything unravel now? How could everything come apart so fast?

"Listen, pal, I'm not sure what's really going on here, but..." Mr. McInish had begun to say to the small man in the dark robes, but something stopped him in mid-sentence; a tingling along his neck that made the hairs on his neck and arms stand on end, a static charge in the air that prickled along his skin. "Mister, I don't...," he began again just as the man before him suddenly threw open his robes. Four enormous spider arms stretched from its dark confines, just as the hood of the cloak fell away revealing a gigantic spider's head. Mr. Mcinish tried to back peddle away from the hideous monster, but the arms were too fast, quickly reaching out and easily lifting him off the ground.

"Oh God, Owen," his mother whispered, grabbing her son by his arm and trying to shake him free of his charm. When she couldn't free Owen of his hex, she turned to look for her husband.

Chamberlain had shifted into his hybrid form. The chanting was no longer coming from him, it seemed to be emanating from the room itself, while the sphere continued to grow and throb.

Chamberlain had the head of his spider self, along with four spider arms, two that grew up from above his shoulders and two from below his Sylvan arms. He still had humanoid legs, but thick black and red striped, coarse hair sprouted from beneath the dark robes. His fangs clacked together as if in agitation, while two of the spider arms held Owen's father off the ground. He'd struggled to free himself, but the thick hairs on the ends of the spider feet acted as if covered in adhesive and easily hefted the man aloft.

The elder McInish struggled to get free, but made no sound, he hadn't wanted to draw attention to his plight and chance his family not making a clean get away. He glanced over his shoulder at them, hoping to see them disappearing down the stairwell, but instead saw his wife and son till standing where he'd left them. "GO!" he shouted.

Owen screamed inside his head. His voice was gone, but his mind shouted for Chamberlain to drop his father. He looked at his mother and screamed at her to run and leave them, but the voice only echoed within his mind.

"Oh God, Owen," Mrs. McInish whispered. "What is that thing?" She let go of her son, and then grabbed him again, tugging on him, almost causing Owen to fall over. She let go again, opening and closing her hands. And then she saw the Sidhe magician's knife laying on the floor. She picked it up, her hands shaking terribly as she did so.

"I'll help your father," she said, not as confidently as she would have liked. "Once he's safe, we'll get you outta here," she added, turning back towards Chamberlain and Mr. McInish. The runes painted onto Owen's parents were glowing brightly now, like little neon signs all over them. Owen couldn't take his eyes off his parents. He tried to move, his brain shouted commands to his legs, his arms, but they wouldn't respond. It was as if his mind was closed in a room with his body locked outside.

Mrs. McInish looked back over her shoulder, "I love you, Owen," she said as she turned and rushed towards Chamberlain.

Owen knew his mother didn't understand. She had no idea what kind of monster Chamberlain really was. She had no idea what he was capable of.

He had to do something, they didn't stand a chance. He felt as if his eyes were going to explode. He couldn't move, he couldn't help, and finally, he couldn't even look away.

The sounds of combat echoed from below. A great howling that gave Owen courage reverberated up the stairwell, filling his heart with hope and strength. He thought with the strength of Boone's howl he might be able to break the spell. He felt himself teeter; he could swear he felt a tremor run through his body. *This is it!* he thought. *A little more!*

As Owen focused back on his parents, pausing in his attempts to free himself, he saw that the orb had grown in size and girth, it was filling the room, a great pulsating mass, radiating heat and light like a small sun. Chamberlain stood before the giant sphere, part Sylvan, part spider, holding Owen's father in his large hybrid spider arms. Mrs. McInish charged Chamberlain, leaping into his body, driving her shoulder into his torso, just as a loud humming began to emit from the sphere.

The blow caused Chamberlain to stumble, turning the mage and causing him to lose his balance. Mrs. McInish slashed at the spider-creature with her knife, causing the creature to step back. The spider creature's head shot quickly around, looking for Owen, before the bent elbow of one of Chamberlain's spider arms, closest to the orb, gently brushed against the whirling sphere.

That was all it took.

The orb gripped Chamberlain and began drawing him into it. The gravity and pull of the pulsing ball latched onto the mage. A scream erupted from his spider-like maw as the creature panicked. He reached out and grabbed Owen's mother, trying desperately to pull himself free. Owen's mother dropped the knife in her struggle to escape.

Owen screamed in response, but no sound came from his mouth. Only he could hear himself wailing inside his mind. His parents struggled, but Chamberlain did not relinquish his grasp. The mage fought to regain his footing and pull himself free, but he would not give up his prey to do so. The sphere drew him deeper into it.

Owen's mother kicked out, hitting Chamberlain square in the chest, pushing the spider creature deeper into the orb. Without solid footing, the creature was suddenly, completely, consumed by the sphere, drawing both of Owen's parents with it.

All three people vanished within the swirling mass with a slight *pop.*

"NOOOOOO!" Owen screamed, his voice rising above the humming of the orb.

With the absorption of Mr. and Mrs. McInish a backlash of energy erupted from the sphere, slamming into Owen and knocking him and Orla back into the wall. He dropped his friend as he slid down the crystal. He slowly pulled himself back up. The Sylvan stirred in a daze, looking up at Owen. Her eyes flicked open one second and closed the next and then open again. She saw him and looked into his eyes, tears filling hers.

"I remember," was all she said before unconsciousness claimed her once more.

Owen bolted over the top of her and towards where his parents had just been. The sphere had shrunk drastically; it was no larger than a basketball now, whirling in the center of the room. Glowing runes, floating in mid air, scattered around the room, the chararcters looked strikingly like the ones that had once been painted on Owen's parents. The air was calmer, still, even the storm outside the crystal spire had ceased.

Owen ran towards the orb, collapsing to the ground just before it. Hot tears gushed from his eyes.

"NO!" he screamed; anguish choking the word from his throat. This was impossible, how could he have come this far, freed them, and been so close to getting them away? How could he have come so close to have this happen?

The boy kneeled before the orb whose color had changed and was now a soft, pale orange, shimmering slightly. He leaned forward, stretching his hand to touch the spinning sphere.

Don't.

The voice said, carried to him on raven wings, disturbing the quiet of the pinnacle. Owen's hand stopped millimeters from touching the orb. His fingertips hovered just above the glowing object. The voice had sounded different than how the birds normally sounded to Owen.

The hairs on the back of Owen's neck stood on end. A deep chill slowly crawled down his spine, a vast wasteland of emptiness began to surround his heart, and Owen recognized the feeling creeping into the lower reaches of his abdomen.

"'*Griefers*," he whispered. He could feel their presence in the chamber with him.

"Weeping won't spare your life, boy," the cold, lifeless voice said from behind Owen. He knew what it was, but he didn't care anymore, he had no will to fight anymore. Why bother?

You must fight, the ravens delivered the disembodied voice again. It was feminine Owen noticed this time, and sounded remarkably like...his mother! Owen's head snapped up and looked at the sphere before him. It was impossible, and yet so many other things in this world seemed impossible.

"You're all alone now, boy," the *Ain'griefer* said from behind him, his voice like ice water being poured down his back.

Not alone, his father's voice said with the soft rustling of wing feathers.

Never alone, his mother said. *You must fight, Owen.*

You are the Maou'r, both his parents said. The word sounded strange being spoken by his parents. But he knew they were right, and somehow, hearing it from them made him believe it a little more.

"My minions below are dealing with your friends, leaving you to me," the deymon intoned again, sounding slightly closer.

Owen stood and turned to face the creature. At first glance he looked similar to the other 'Griefers Owen had already faced, but this one wore a tattered maroon cloak about his shoulders, the hem of which was torn and stained. He also wielded two Sidhe crafted swords. These blades gleamed silver in the dim light of the room, not the same flat black blades his deymon mercenaries wielded.

As Owen stood, he felt the familiar weight land upon his shoulders. This time, however, he knew it was not the ravens landing to whisper their secrets to him, but instead, he felt his parents resting their hands upon his shoulders, standing with him before the 'Griefer.

"Tell me deymon; is your master in the Abyss?" Owen asked, gripping the hilt of GreenFyr. He felt the familiar warmth of the sword begin to spread through his fingers, palm, and hand as he grasped it.

"Why?" the Ain'griefer hissed, slicing his swords through the air, slowly stepping around Owen and the orb.

"Because I've got a message to send back with you!" Owen shouted, freeing GreenFyr from its sheath, bathing the room in its pale green light. The light illuminated from the crystal spire, painting the storm clouds in its firey emerald glow.

The deymon hissed its response at the boy, sending chills and spasms of fear running through him. The fear was more intense than what he'd felt in the courtyard, this time it seemed more directed at him and not just an ambient presence. The deymon was trying to work him; he could sense it now, because along with the fear, he also felt something else, something stronger.

A strength emanated from his chest, spreading outward like a brush fire through dry kindling until it felt as if he couldn't contain it any longer. So he didn't, and the warmth erupted from him. Green flames spread up his arm from the sword and sheathed him in its embrace. He could feel its warmth, but he did not burn. The deymon took a step backward away from the flames.

"Your tricks won't save you, boy," it hissed again, but it didn't step any closer to Owen. "And once my servants deal with your friends we'll extinguish you, forever."

"You're the only one who'll get by them, and I'm sure you did it by sneaking in the shadows," Owen mocked, he felt more sure of himself than ever before. He could feel the weight still upon his shoulders, and almost felt invincible.

The deymon hissed in response to Owen's baiting and lunged toward the boy, slashing savagely with his Sidhe blades. But GreenFyr flashed up in Owen's hands, connecting and blocking the attacks. Sending its flames along to the Sidhe swords, engulfing and spreading along their lengths until the deymon was enveloped by their tongues.

The *Ain'Grifer* dropped to its knees in front of Owen, the flames rippling up his arms. Its dark features contorting into a grimace, its indigo, unfeeling eyes turning on Owen, finding the boy's.

"What's your message?" it hissed as the flames consumed it.

"Tell them they've awoken the *Maou'r*," Owen said sheathing his sword.

The creature screamed in agony, an unholy shrill that caused Owen to drop to his knees. The *Ain'griefer* crumpled into ash, its scream echoing through the tower long after the deymon had returned to the Abyss.

The chamber was eerily quiet. The distant sound of combat below occasionally worked its way into the room. Owen looked back to the orb, now the size of a tennis ball, spinning. He suddenly remembered Orla. He raced to the wall where he'd left the Sylvan. He sat next to her, feeling the ache that he had harbored in his chest since first seeing his parents as statues return.

He couldn't believe his parents were gone. Of all the strange things that had happened in this world, this seemed somehow the most impossible to believe. He had found them. He had freed them. How could it end like this? It wasn't possible. Another howl from Boone warmed his heart, not dulling his ache at all, but in some way giving him the courage to face it.

Owen looked down at Orla again, tracing her hair behind her ear. He scooped his arms beneath her knees and under her arms, and lifting her gently, he slowly began the long journey down the Tower of the Star.

105

Owen sat in the small study, wrapped in a wool blanket, before a large fire in the room's hearth. He stared blankly into the flames. He blinked occasionally, but otherwise his expression never changed. He'd sat this way, every day for the last three; never leaving the chair, never eating or drinking.

Boone lay curled at the foot of his chair. He would not leave him and would be there for him when he needed him. Unbeknownst to him, just his sheer presence was a comfort to his *Maou'r*, even though the boy couldn't bring himself to tell him.

Aiya was also in the small quarters with the boy and his dog. The accommodations were larger than when they had first arrived, and the fare that was delivered to them daily for their meals, was much more appetizing.

He also paid little attention to the slight Sylvan girl who came in the morning, sitting next to him by the fire daily, and leaving just before bed every evening. Orla came and sat with Owen each day. Aiya had told her what had happened in the Star Tower and how Owen had carried her down to find her and Boone waiting for him at the bottom of the structure. He had told them then what had happened to Chamberlain and his parents, but then had become silent. He carried her out of the tower where they were met by a small army of capital guards led there by Orla's father.

When his daughter hadn't rendezvoused at the appointed location, he had called his most trusted guards and dispatched them throughout the city looking for any signs of his daughter and her friends. When one came back and informed them of the state of the guards posted outside the tower, he sent word back to gather everyone to that location. They had just arrived outside its doors to see the Sword Maiden and dog battling a handful of *Ain'griefer*. The senator and his men stood dumbfounded staring at the dark creatures. Every one of them knew exactly what they were, but none had believed the bedtime stories they had been told were true. Even in this magical world, there were things so dark, people never thought them real. And even Orla's father, after hearing about them from his own daughter, still doubted on some level.

It hadn't taken long for the two warriors to finish the deymons, and it was only moments after that when Owen stepped through the large doors carrying the senator's daughter in his arms. The senator rushed up the stairs and took his daughter from the battered looking boy. His eyes were glassy and they seemed to focus on places and things somewhere else.

"Orla!" the senator called to his daughter, squeezing her slightly. Her eyes fluttered open and she muttered the same words she had said to Owen on the stairs.

"I remember," she said softly.

The guards had stepped up and surrounded the companions, drawing their weapons, but their looks seemed less sure. They had seen what the woman and dog had just done to the unholy.

"These people are to be treated as guests of the city, bring them to my personal guest suite, and meet all their needs," the senator said looking to Owen and then to Aiya. "Bring me a healer at once," he cried, as he rushed down the stairs and made his way back to his own quarters.

Even though the guards had been instructed to treat them as guests their attitudes were still those of guards escorting prisoners. When they had reached the senator's guest lodging there was an awkward silence while the captain of the guard considered asking for the warrior's weapons. Aiya knew what the man thought; it was written simply across his uncomplicated face. She also knew she would not be separated from her weapons while those in league with Chamberlain were still free in the city.

For the captain's part, he too noticed the set expression upon the women's face. Despite his simple looks, he was more in tune than most gave him credit for, and he made no mention of the companions surrendering their weapons. He hoped that it would not come to such a request.

The apartment this time was more spacious and had several large windows that overlooked the tower and the mountain ranges surrounding Narsus. Aiya sat and exhaled deeply after the guards had left them alone. She had been concerned they were to be sequestered again like animals in a cage; her heart had already begun to race and cold sweat to collect on the back of her neck.

This space was much more comfortable, with ornate and yet comfortable furnishings. The books and texts in the study were actual works Aiya found to her liking. There was a wide range of subjects and topics to choose from, and even though the Sword Maiden had always been more interested in physical pursuits than literary ones, there were a few that she used to pass the time. Books were Silan's passion, not Aiya's. The Sidhe smiled now when she thought of her sister. Not that the pain was any less, or the memories more distant, but the thoughts of her sister made her feel in the other women's presence once more. It hurt just the same, but with it came a warmth as well. She could not explain it, but somehow she knew the two feelings would always be with her in equal shares.

Orla noticed Owen turn his attention from the fire out the small portal window, which allowed a view of the pinnacle spire of the Star Tower. It was the first time she'd seen him move these past few days. She wasn't sure if he would hear her or not, but she took this moment to speak with him.

"Owen, I'm not sure you can hear me, or want to hear, but you need to know. They are preparing a tribunal for you. They are not sure what should be done with you. Aiya and I are no longer in trouble, but it seems the Sidhe, Sumiel, is trying to make a statement by forcing this hearing on you. After my memories came back, and from what the other guards outside the tower remembered when they came out from under their charms...did I mentioned that? Oh, I'm sorry; I've forgotten how much there is to tell you. Supposedly Chamberlain charmed the guards outside the tower and after he...," she paused, not sure as to what really happened to him. No one did except for Owen. "Well, after he disappeared, all the spells he'd cast were undone, including the memory charm he'd placed on me." She stopped again as Owen turned and looked at her.

"I don't care what they do to me," he said flatly, his eyes watery. He turned and looked back out the window.

"Owen, what happened up there?" Orla asked quietly. Owen didn't answer right away. He kept his attention out the window as if the longer he could hold off saying it the less true it would be. He finally turned and looked back at his friend sitting next to him.

"I failed. I failed them," Owen said, his voice raspy after not speaking for three days. "Chamberlain got up and started the spell again," Owen began, his voice distant, "but before I could do anything, he froze me," he stammered, looking away again, back towards the spire of the tower. "My mom and dad tried to stop him, but they got pulled into that sphere. They all just disappeared."

He turned back to Orla and he could see that she was crying too, thin rivulets of tears slid down her cheeks, dripping from her chin. "And then there was this explosion, it knocked me back to the wall, but then I was able to move again," he said, his voice choking in his throat once more. He looked back into the fire as if the flames would burn the images from his memories.

"You said you remembered," Owen said suddenly, remembering the delirious comment his friend had made. Orla smiled slightly and nodded.

"Everything," she said. Owen smiled too. He wanted to know what had happened to his friend, but he needed to finish his own story, he needed to tell his friend what he had seen.

"You passed out again, and I ran to the orb." Orla watched him. She already knew what he was going to say.

"But they were gone, all of them, just the ball was left, but it was so much smaller," he looked back to his friend again, and had never felt more helpless.

"Owen, I'm so sorry," Orla said as she leaned towards him, and very gently touched his arm. The touch was warmer than Owen would have thought and he was amazed at how good and comforting it felt. The sad, sunken feeling that had rooted itself in his gut began to unwind itself again, the overwhelming feeling of being alone.

Not alone, a voice sounding strikingly like his mother's whispered in the recesses of his mind.

Never alone, his father's deeper, soothing, voice echoed his mother's.

"Owen, the *Maou'r* will never walk alone," Orla said, echoing her own words the day after Winter had passed. She squeezed his arm gently from where she still held him.

And the aching in his gut eased more, a part of him believed their words. As if sensing his thoughts Boone inclined his great head and rested it along Owen's feet.

"You remembered?" Owen asked stepping from his own self wallowing for a minute.

"I did. I do, I mean," Orla corrected herself, smiling self consciously now that Owen's attention was upon her.

"Everything?" Owen asked, suddenly aware of what this could mean. Orla nodded her answer, she remembered everything.

"Was it Chamberlain then, who sent you to my world with the Death Dogs?" Owen asked impatiently not waiting for Orla to tell her own story.

She nodded again and cleared her throat.

"I don't know where to start exactly," she said quietly and then with a nervous giggle, "at the beginning, I suppose, might be a good place," she added.

"I overheard Chamberlain talking in his study one day, he talked about my father heading into Narsus and how their plans were moving along as scheduled. How my father didn't suspect anything. He spoke of his pupil and how she was coming along nicely as well. He never mentioned Reunification, but he mentioned their plan, and alluded to a plot, it seemed. I couldn't hear any voices talking back, but he continued the conversation. I was so intent on listening I hadn't realized his assistant, a boy named Vulpes, had come up behind me.

"I quickly made up an excuse about needing to be somewhere else and went back to my room. He must have told Chamberlain that I had been outside his door, he probably had been watching me longer than I'd realized at the time.

"It was then that I decided I needed to go and find my father here, I had just some things to take with me when Nem came into my room. She seemed surprised and asked what I was doing, where I was going, trying to stop me and talk me out of it. As I was arguing with her, Chamberlain and Vulpes came in. Chamberlain seemed annoyed, angry almost, Vulpes looked guilty and nervous. Before I knew what was happening, Nem had placed the collar around my neck. I remembered changing and seeing Chamberlain casting a spell. The moment I had changed I leapt out over the balcony of my room and out into the courtyard. I was running on instinct at that point. Chamberlain had cast a memory charm, so I remembered nothing of what had just happened. I just felt this overwhelming need to run. As I was leaping over the wall around our home I remembered a sudden, jarring pain, and then nothing but blackness. After that I remember waking in your world. I was there a day before seeing you. The hounds came sometime in the night before you rescued me."

Orla paused then and looked back at her friend. She had already told this story to her father, but retelling it again to Owen felt different. It still felt like she was telling someone else's tale and not her own, but it also felt by telling it, it was somehow more true, and more believable.

"You know the rest," she added, looking away shyly.

"Yeah, I do," Owen said realizing Aiya had stepped to the doorway to listen to Orla's tale. She smiled at Owen, truly thankful to see the boy responsive and back to this world. He smiled back, and Aiya saw a glint of his former self in his eyes.

"But now Sumiel wants to put you on trial for what happened," Orla said, realizing why she had started the story in the first place.

"My father says he's a big supporter of Reunification and thinks he had something to do with Chamberlain. I told my father we saw him outside the tower before we went in, but he's denied ever being there. Supposedly he has an alibi."

"Orla's right, he's a proponent of reunifying the worlds, but he was never this influential before," Aiya added. Owen remembered her thinking that the night they entered the tower.

"My father says he's been getting much more powerful political allies of late and has been throwing his weight around, like now. Sumiel says it's your fault for enchanting the guards, killing one in the process, and for Chamberlain's disappearance. He has even gone so far as to say you encharmed us and that you're responsible for my disappearance."

"What's he suggesting they do to me?" Owen asked flatly, he didn't seem nearly as worried or as emotional as Orla would have thought.

"I don't know," Orla admitted. "He's just been pushing for this open hearing to decide."

Just then a knock came from the door of the apartment. Owen and Orla stood and stepped into the hall as Aiya stepped to the door. She opened it hesitantly, and once she saw who it was, opened it fully. Boone had stepped into the hall as well, blocking Owen and Orla from those at the door.

The guest was the captain of the guard and several of his men who had escorted them to these lodgings three nights ago.

"The Council is convening a tribunal. We are here to escort you all," he said matter of fact. The guards stood stoically, all of them hoping the companions agreed to come along.

106

Owen stepped from his bedroom washed and wearing his least ripped and dirty set of clothes. He wore the leopard pendent Orla had given him, clasping his dwarven cloak about his shoulders, and wore GreenFyr on his hip with his bow and arrows slung across his back. He had dunked his whole head into the water basin in his room, and after drying his hair slightly, had run his fingers through it as a comb trying to manage it somehow.

"Good Sir," the captain said surprised, and slightly sterner than he would have wanted in the presence of the massive dog at the boy's side.

"Your weapons," he added less forcefully. He looked to Aiya and Orla as if they would understand, but was met with twin glaring stares.

"What about them?" Owen asked. To be fair he hadn't thought much about them when he had put them on. Over the past month they had simply become a part of him, but now that the captain was calling attention to his wearing them, he wasn't about to release them.

"This is a tribunal, Sir. To determine what the Realm shall do with you. You can't possibly…," the Sylvan started, but was quickly cut off by Aiya.

"What can't he do?" she hissed through clenched teeth, her own hand sliding to the hilt of her sword. Orla looked at the woman and knew she wouldn't let the guards disarm Owen. She realized that she too was running through a laundry list of appropriate spells to cast should it come to that, but quickly realized it couldn't go that far. It was just what their opposition wanted, another reason to cast Owen as the villain in this plot.

"He is a hero to the Realm, and should be treated as such. No one has asked for my blade, nor would they, until charged with a crime," Aiya spat.

The captain of the guard took a step backwards, his own men bringing hands to their weapons.

"But you have committed no crime, there are no charges brought against *you*," he countered.

"Are there charges set against him?" Aiya insisted.

"None yet, but..."

"Then he keeps his arms." Aiya made it a statement, she was not seeking permission.

"He is the companion of a Sword Maiden, I think you can trust in her judgment, if not in him," Orla suggested, meeting the guards stare as if to remind him who she was and his position within the capital.

"Yes, Princess," he said, inclining his head and looking to Aiya as he did so.

"May we escort you to the hearing room?" he asked in a much more respectful tone.

The four companions followed the captain down the corridor while the six guards followed behind them. The tension was palpable.

The corridor was fanciful and ornately decorated. The Sylvans had spent a small fortune on the work wrought upon the capital building, and in particular, the living quarters of those senators serving their government. Owen paid little attention to the halls they were led through. He paid little attention to the people around him as well. He was just intent on facing his accuser in the tribunal. Someone amongst them, this Sumiel possibly, was at fault for what happened to his family and he wanted to see him. He wanted to know what they had in store for him now that his parents were gone and their plans ruined.

Their escort finally stopped outside a pair of large doors gilded in gold. He turned and faced the companions. He looked quickly again at Owen and his weapons, but said nothing this time. He had his reservations about the boy being armed, but then again, the Princess and Sidhe were correct. He had not been formally charged, and if the Sidhe considered him a warrior, than it would be disrespectful and a dishonor to demand he turn them over.

He bowed his head slightly, stepped aside while opening the doors, allowing the companions to walk past him into the large hearing room. Owen did allow himself to absorb these surroundings.

It was a long narrow room lined on either side with dark wooden pews. At the end of the room was a large stadium seated bench. Along the walls were lanterns that lit the space. Each lamp held one of the glowing balls of light similar to the street lamps.

The pews were lined with many people all curious to see the Man that they had heard about in the capital. The majority of citizens that turned out were Sylvan and Sidhe—of high status and of affluent wealth, judging by their clothes, Owen thought. *Looks like I'm the main attraction in town*, he mused. There were also a small cluster of butterfly winged people hovering to one side. Each of their wings a different color and design from one of the others. They whispered and pointed at Owen as he walked down the aisle.

In the back of the room was a pile of old robes and clothes, at first glance appearing as just a pile of old cloaks and garments, but the pile of laundry took some shape and moved slightly as Owen entered the room. It was the only person in attendance that didn't seem to have worn their best clothes for the occasion. It looked as if a pile of laundry had just taken up residence for the day to avoid the cold and snow outside.

There were also a few other people with wings that soared around the large room. Their wings moving in a blur, Owen assuming they looked like dragonfly wings. They blurred by him, not too closely, but close enough where Owen could hear the buzz of their flying.

Along the front of the room, seated in the gallery of long benches, were many more Sidhe and Sylvan, but again Owen saw representatives of other nations there as well. He saw three small men, all with long white beards, wearing drooping, floppy hats, and none of them much taller than three feet. They immediately reminded Owen of the garden gnomes he'd seen on front lawns.

Along the back of the benches were again several types of flying *Fey* that hovered over the rest of the gathered senators. In the middle of the bench was a hunched black bear with finely brushed thick fur wearing thin, wire framed spectacles, a red plaid vest, and who eyed Owen warily as he approached. To Owen he looked like a very well dressed bear, but there was something to the creature's eyes that gave him a most insightful gleam. Seated to the creature's right was a finely dressed man with two ram horns protruding from his temples and wrapping behind and below his pointed ears. He wore a fine tunic with a silk vest over it. He had a thin mustache and goatee. To the left of the spectacle wearing bear sat a beautiful woman. Her hair was the color of ferns, her skin the color of snow, and her eyes sparkled like a mountain spring. She wore a thin white dress whose thin straps rested lightly upon her bare shoulders. As Owen watched her, he couldn't help but think that a slight breeze touched her, and no one else along the pulpit, stirring her hair and dress slightly.

Also in the stand was the Sidhe Owen had come to know as Sumiel and Orla's father. It seemed that Senator Negu held some place of prominence among the council.

Owen looked away. He seemed numbed to the stares at this point. Still in his heart there was the empty feeling and ache for his parents. Orla's father stood before the gathered Council of Nations. Owen noted several vacant seats among the gathered and wondered if those places belonged to the absent dwarves. Another pang shook his heart at the remembrance of the stout people and their errant heir, Balor.

The guard escorted Owen through a small gate, which he tried to close behind the boy, but quickly took a step back as Boone eyed him. The large dog shouldered his way through to stand next to his *Maou'r* while the guard indicated to Aiya and Orla that they were to sit behind Owen on the opposite side of the small gate.

The guard then exited behind, leaving the boy and his dog before the gathered politicians and assembled who came to see the Man that had stepped into their world.

Owen could feel Boone standing next to him. The dog stood leaning, slightly, against his thigh as a reassurance to his boy, and as a sign of solidarity before the council. Owen's hand found the top of the massive head of the animal next to him, and rested it upon the animal's brow. He raised his eyes and looked across the gathered council, taking in each member, holding each one's stare for a moment before moving on to the next.

Owen had nothing to be ashamed of, nothing to apologize for. He had come here to rescue his parents. He had not needed permission in doing that, and now in failing to save them, he owed the citizens of this world nothing. It had been they who had taken his parents from him, he hadn't forgotten that. He wouldn't forget that, and he certainly wouldn't shrink away from their gazes now because of it.

"Thank you for coming," Senator Negu said, inclining his head slightly. Owen just looked at the Sylvan and the rest of the council. He still didn't know what to make of Orla's father. He had seemed distant and guarded from the moment Owen had met him, but Orla had said that he was a part of their escape the night his parents died.

"Do you know why you are here?" the senator asked Owen. Owen shook his head slowly; honestly, he wasn't quite sure why he was there.

"Each of our nations has many regulations and laws regarding our citizens or residents traveling to your world, but none of our respected countries had ever had the foresight to develop any means of dealing with a human who might come through to our world," the senator explained. "Simply, Owen, we are trying to figure out what to do with you now that you are here."

The council members around Sumiel snickered and laughed at something the Sidhe muttered under his breath to the few gathered about him, drawing Owen and Senator Negu's attention back to them.

Orla's father seemed annoyed at the interruption, but turned his attention back to Owen. "Any suggestions on your part?" he asked the boy. *He looks so young*, the senator thought.

"Send me back home," Owen said through a dry, tight throat. He hadn't realized how nervous and tense he had become.

Another outburst from the council members around Sumiel turned the attention of the gathered to the group of politicians.

"Ambassador Sumiel, do you have something to add to these proceedings?" Negu asked with overt annoyance.

"As a matter of fact, Senator, I do," the Sidhe said, pleased he had manipulated Negu into giving him the opening. He stood, gaining a level of intimidation amongst the gathered. Sidhe were much taller than the other gathered *Fey* and Sumiel was a particularly tall Sidhe.

"How can we send this *spy* back to his world? We have no idea of his intentions. Our greatest security from *his* kind has been their ignorance in knowing of our existence, but if we send him back there, then we have no idea what he will tell them about us.

"Furthermore, what of all the destruction, discord, and death this human has sown since arriving in our world? Are we to let that go unpunished?" A gasp, followed by shouts of agreement, drifted from the assembled citizens behind Owen. Sumiel looked at Owen, but he didn't let his emotions play across his face. Owen tried desperately to remain as impassive as possible. Growing up and bullied his whole life, he'd learned it was better to not let your feelings to the surface. In most cases it just encouraged the bullies even more. And in standing before this tribunal, he began to think of Sumiel as just that. Standing with his supporters amongst the politicians and trying to force his own views and agendas on those weaker senators who might have differing opinions from him.

The once intimidating visage of the Sidhe began to replace itself with nothing more than a school yard bully to Owen. He became less concerned with what the *Fey* had to say during these proceedings.

"Exactly that, Ambassador," Negu interjected. "He came to this world to seek out his parents, who had been abducted by our own citizens."

"A likely story," Sumiel jabbed. "Where's the proof of that?"

"Even still, our laws do not say what to do when a Man comes to our Realm, but they are explicit in that we are not to engage them at any cost. Our laws are very clear on that!" Senator Negu argued. Many of the politicians within the council nodded in agreement. Sumiel could see that Negu had the majority of the members on his side, but he might still be able to win something here.

"I will grant you that, Senator. However, in that regard, then we have the question of how we deal with those who aided him whence he was in our Realm. You are right; our laws are quite explicit on how we interact once we are within their presence." A thin smile creased the otherwise placid face of the Sidhe ambassador while Negu's own temper flared.

"How dare you? This was discussed in our closed session and has been nullified. Any involvement with the human has been dealt with already and decreed as necessity by our citizens," Negu spat. He had never encountered such a dishonorable and despicable politician before. There was no limit to the man's underhandedness. But the damage was done; the fact that citizens of the Realm had been cleared during a closed session of the council, to keep the details from the citizenry, had just been made public. Negu knew that questions would now ensue as to why such details and facts, and who had been connected to the human, would have needed to be kept from the public.

"So we give the boy what he wants, we send him back," Sumiel added as if succumbing to the wishes of the senator, "but he must go alone," he added turning and looking directly at Boone. "His mangy companion would have to stay here, of course."

NEVER! A Duine Madra can not be separated from his Maou'r! Boone's voice roared through the minds of those gathered. It was followed by his deep growls and the gnashing of his teeth. His lips curled back to reveal his large white teeth, while the hackles along his back rose. His enormous paws tightened and gripped the ground while his thick nails cracked the stone floor beneath them.

Sumiel quickly brought his hands up to begin to perform a charm in response to the threatening posture of the large dog, but before he could finish, Owen's own hands moved in a blur. Without thought, that would have slowed his movements; the boy drew an arrow, unslung his bow, and brought the two together on their target before the Sidhe could even finish his spell. Those not watching Owen, thought the weapons just materialized. Those watching him saw the boy achieve it in blinding speed. Those that knew the *Aingeal* archer couldn't help but be reminded of the Hunter.

"Finish that spell, and I'll tack you to the wall behind you," Owen said coldly, not moving his eyes from the Sidhe. In Owen's peripheral vision he saw Sumiel's companions begin their own charms. "Anyone of you even thinks about casting your own, and I'll drop him where he stands," the boy added.

Boone's growls filled the auditorium which had grown silent otherwise.

No one can break the bond of the Maou'r and Duine Madra, NO ONE!

"He comes with me, or we fall together, here, now," Owen added. He felt the familiar tingle along his arms and spine just before Orla shifted into her other self. She would stand with them, and even without seeing her, he knew Aiya had loosened her own weapon in its sheath.

He and Boone would not stand alone before their foes.

Not alone, his mother's voice soothingly said to him on raven's wings, *never alone*, his father's voice echoed. While the familiar weight landed upon his shoulders.

They will sing of the deeds we perform this day, Boone's voice rumbled through Owen's mind for only him to here.

"No one will ever take my Duine Madra from me," Owen said through clenched teeth. He would die here and now before he ever let them lead Boone from his side. Fate had brought them together, and not even she could separate them now. The great dog, as if in response, leaned his massive head back letting spill a great howl. The walls and ceiling shook from its might and Owen could see that Sumiel was physically shaken from its intensity. The noise again filled Owen with courage and hope.

"And no one shall," a low, deep voice said quietly behind him. Owen did not turn to see who it was, he would not let Sumiel from his sight, but the voice was familiar. And it carried with it a sense of power and authority Owen had felt before in its presence. Wing beats accompanied their master's presence as Owen continued to eye the soft spot of Sumiel's throat just below his chin.

"No blood will be spilt in this chamber of law and order, and no past mistakes will be made again when it comes to the bond between the *Maou'r* and his *Madra*," the Pilgrim added, stepping through the small gate to stand beside the human boy and King of Dogs.

"You have no authority over this council, Wanderer," Sumiel spat at the All Father of the *Aingeals.*

"No, but their council has always meant much to its members," said the woman with the fern colored hair. Her voice was like the gentle, soothing, rambling of a brook over moss covered stones.

Sumiel turned to her sharply, but then slowly looked away, not willing to make conflict with the other *Fey.* He brought his anger back to the *Aingeal.*

"It was your own decree that broke the bond in the first place! You should still stand by your folly now, if you feel it thus!" Sumiel's composure was lost; he had not counted on the presence of one of the *First* during this hearing.

"Temper yourself Sidhe; do not taunt the gentle breeze, for it might turn to a gale before you. Mind you, you do not want to see the Lord of the *Aingeal* unmantled," the Pilgrim said with malice beneath the gentle tones. Owen had never heard such threat and dread laced into simple words before.

"Lower your bow, Owen, there is no longer any need of it now," the voice added in more soothing tones. Boone had stopped his own growling, and even though he still stood with his broad chest and head squared, Owen could tell that the great dog knew that the immediate threat was over.

Owen obliged the *Aingeal* and lowered his weapon. He watched the Sidhe ambassador as he did so, but Sumiel made no effort to finish his hex even though the threat of attack still lingered in his eyes and stare.

Owen noticed the ambassador's stare find the captain of the guard and anger flared as the small Sylvan did not meet the Sidhe's gaze.

"Possibly the greatest mistake made during the Schism was in the separation of these two races. Let us not ignore the wisdom of the Creator in bringing the two together in the first place, let us now correct a wrong done long years ago, by allowing the two to remain as one," the Pilgrim implored the Council.

Senator Negu looked at Owen and Boone and nodded his head along with the majority of other council members. Sumiel and his contingent did not add their support to the suggestion.

Senator Negu's gaze drifted from Owen to his daughter and his face lightened, but in it was also a deep sorrow. His heart broke for the sadness that shown on his daughter's face.

The look did not go unnoticed by Sumiel and he grasped at the chance to wreak even more grief and pain.

"Fine, send the flea ridden beast from this Realm. Good riddance, but let the council be firm in its decree that no *Fey* should accompany the human to his Realm, now, or in the future." Negu and Sumiel exchanged heated stares, but no one in the council argued the Sidhe ambassador's point.

"So be it," the Pilgrim added, "May no *Fey* accompany the boy to his Realm." Owen looked up at the tall man then; dressed in ragged traveling clothes that he recognized as the pile of laundry he had seen when he'd first entered the council chambers. From beneath the wide cowl, Owen swore that the old man winked his one remaining eye at him.

The large man rested the enormous paw of a hand then on Owen's shoulder. Owen was comforted at the touch and looked back to his friends seated behind him. Both wore similar expressions of happiness and pain, sadness and elation. Owen was free, no charges had been brought, but their companion was leaving them and never to be seen again.

"Then these proceedings are ended. On the morrow, Owen McInish, will return from whence his journey began, and return to his own Realm," Senator Negu proclaimed, striking a small gavel to announce the hearing's end.

Sumiel and his supporters left quickly through a side door into private chambers, while the other members of the council mingled, or worked their way closer to the human. The Pilgrim looked down at the boy while his friends and companions gathered about him. Orla's father even approached the small group.

"Thank you," Owen said to the *Aingeal* who waved his giant hand before him.

"Nonsense, I did nothing for my part."

"We can leave here and retire to my private chambers, so we may have some privacy," Negu interjected, guiding the companions out of the hearing room through another side door. The gathered craned and stretched their necks to get one last glimpse of the human before he left the room.

107

The mood was somber in the chambers of Senator Negu.

Owen sat by the large fireplace with Boone lying at his feet, sound asleep, and Orla by his side. The two friends spoke little, but when they did it was easy and light. Neither mentioned what lay before them the following day, but spoke of past adventures and happenings. Orla asked many questions about Owen's world, something she had never done before, and the few questions Owen asked about her Realm, she answered without hesitation.

Aiya, Orla's father, and the Pilgrim all stood to one side of the room and discussed the plans for the following day. The First Man would lead Owen and a small company of Narsus guards to the City where Owen had first entered their world. Aiya, Orla, and her father would accompany them as far as Quailan. Aiya left the chambers to make arrangements for their journey while the *Aingeal* and the senator joined Orla and Owen by the fire.

"I've been thinking," Owen said looking at the tall man with the long white beard standing next to the fireplace.

"Hmmm?" he mused stroking his beard.

"When I first arrived here, there were a lot of people who could sense my presence. It was why you sent Winter with us, to protect us; won't they sense me now? Won't they come after me again?" Owen asked. He had not spent much time with this *Aingeal*, but there was much about him that reminded him of Winter, and yet he knew this man was also very different from the archer.

The *Aingeal* considered the boy. He had known immediately when he first met him that he was the *Maou'r*, but even then a small piece of doubt had lingered with him. After parting from the boy, there was not a moment he had not thought about him, nor a moment his ravens not watched him, and yet he still felt that he did not truly know this Man. He had even spoken at great length with his friend, the Hunter, when he had retrieved the boy's sword from the *Aingeal*. Winter had not doubted the boy's lineage then, and even still, the Pilgrim found himself wondering if this small Man was the chosen one.

The wanderer stroked his beard as he continued to watch the boy who wasn't impatient for an answer; the boy himself seemed to be considering the *Aingeal*. Owen was amazed at the person before him. He was the spitting image of several characters he'd read about through countless fantasy and mythological stories. His white beard cascaded down his chest, while his bushy eyebrows cast his one good eye in shadow and hid the empty socket of the other. He wore a long gray cloak over an old set of rings from which a faded blue tunic shown through. His gray breeches were tucked into tall, brown riding boots that he folded just below his knees. He had left his tall spear by the door to their chambers. His long hair was pulled back, with the sides braided into a thin line down the back of his head.

"What name do you go by?" Owen asked. "Winter had many, but that one suited him best, I thought," he added.

"I still hadn't answered your first question," the Pilgrim mused, stepping away from the fire and taking a seat in a high back wooden chair next to Owen.

"It seems I have a new name with every age and in every land," he contemplated, looking into the fire. "A new name for every tale. You find one you like, and use that, I'm sure it will be fine by me.

"As for your first question, no. No one or thing should be able to sense your presence while you're still here."

Owen didn't reply at first. He considered what the *Aingeal* had told him. Orla stood and sat down next to Boone on the floor and began petting the giant dog as he slept. The realization that he and Owen would be leaving shortly, and never to return, and her forbidden to ever travel to his Realm, was beginning to sink in. She didn't like the feeling; there was an uneasy sensation in her gut, and a dull ache in her heart.

"Athaeyr," Owen said quietly, looking once more at the *Aingeal*.

"Pardon me?" the tall man asked, looking back to the boy.

"Athaeyr, it's what I'll call you," Owen explained.

"It's one I have not been called before, but it is a good name, none the less. Where does it come from?" the older man asked. Looking at the boy, realizing there were depths to this *Maou'r* he had not counted on.

"It's the name of a character from one of my mother's stories. You remind me of him," Owen explained, looking to the fire in an attempt to hide the tears welling in his eyes. He quietly cleared his throat trying to squelch the emotion that was building there with the thoughts of his mother.

"Then I am pleased you've honored me with it," Athaeyr said, placing his large hand on the boy's shoulder and squeezing gently. He stood then and headed to the door where his spear stood. He pulled his hood upon his head, and took up his spear.

"It is growing late, and this has been a long day. We have another long day ahead of us on the morrow, so I will take my leave of you. Sleep this night, your journey is not at an end, just yet," the *Aingeal* said as he stepped from their room.

"It is getting late," Negu said standing as well. He paused for a moment and took in the scene of his daughter lying beside the great dog at the boy's feet. His daughter was dwarfed by the animal's size. He waited another moment, awkwardly. As if waiting for Orla to stand as well. When she did not, he too walked to the door to the study. He paused again. The father in him wanted to call his daughter to bed, but she had been traveling alone with this boy for the past month or more, and this was to be their last night before setting out on their final journey together. He could not bring himself to separate the two friends on their last night in Narsus.

"Goodnight then, do get some sleep this evening. The road is long and you will need your strength for it," he said before retiring to his own bedroom for the night. He wearily walked the stairs to his set of rooms. The toll of the last few days had grown on the small man. He was not looking forward to the journey the following day.

Owen and Orla sat before the fire, but neither spoke. Neither could find the words, nor muster the courage to say how they felt. They had battled deymons together, never faltering, but now trepidation and fear gripped and held them from talking to the other. Just sitting alone was a comfort, however. It did not take long for the pair to fall asleep, Owen in his chair, and Orla asleep with Boone as her pillow.

108

Owen woke in the early morning. The household was still quiet and a gray dawn appeared behind the partially drawn curtains. He felt Boone still asleep at his feet, and when he looked down, he saw that Orla was awake; watching him.

"How long you been up?" he said, stretching and rubbing the sleep from his eyes.

"Not long," she answered, smiling.

"How long you been watching me sleep?" he asked again, looking down at his friend.

"Not long," she said, smiling wider.

He smiled too. The morning felt good. Owen could feel the impending gloom of goodbyes on the horizon, but he paid it no mind. He would cross that bridge when he came to it. For now, the awkwardness of the night before was gone, and things between him and his friend seemed back to normal.

"Wonder what's for breakfast," Orla mused standing up and stretching as well. Boone perked up at the mention of breakfast and snorted awake. He lifted his giant head, yawned widely, showing off his large white teeth. He stood, shaking himself as he did so.

The three friends walked down the hall to the kitchen of the senator's quarters. They could smell the fragrant scents of breakfast, and hear the bustle of the kitchen staff, as they approached.

Senator Negu's staff greeted Orla and Owen warmly, providing them with a morning feast of warm toast, creamy maple butter, marmalades and preserves, crisp bacon, fresh yogurt, maple syrup, cereal, and raspberry and blackberries the size of Owen's thumb.

The chef found a large lamb shank for Boone that he had been planning on serving for dinner, but with the senator leaving for Quailan, there was no point anymore. The dog was pleased and wagged his tail furiously, humming while he consumed his meal.

Owen and Orla ate ravenously, smiling at each other while they gorged themselves. They still hadn't gotten used to being able to eat as much as they wished, whenever they wished. In the recesses of their minds they still remembered the scant meals at the end of long days of hiking, or measly morning meals that didn't even fill their bellies.

They had almost finished by the time Athaeyr and the senator joined them in the kitchen. The staff was unaccustomed to having so many guests in their midst while preparing meals, and moved through the room uncomfortably and awkwardly, but the senator had felt that a formal sitting meal was unnecessary on a day when they would be getting an early start on their journey.

"I see you've both already eaten then?" the politician said as he entered the room, laying his hands upon his daughter's shoulders, and kissing her lightly on her cheek. He smiled warmly at Owen as he pulled up a seat across from them at the butcher's block where they had been eating.

The staff provided the senator with his own plate which he began to fill with the fare before him. The chef poured him tea and left a cup and spoon of honey for him.

"We want to be leaving shortly, are the two of you ready?" Negu asked, eyeing the two young people from over his tea cup.

The friends exchanged a look and then in unison answered the senator.

"Not yet," they said both stifling smiles.

"Then you better go get ready," the senator said as Athaeyr seated himself at the small table taking Owen's seat as he vacated it.

"Aiya has our escort ready along with all our provisions for the road.

I asked her to join us, but she said she had some last minute things to attend to," the *Aingeal* said as he helped himself to a mouthful of berries.

"She said she would meet us by the stables once we were ready," he added after swallowing. He smiled at Owen and Orla as they left down the hall they had entered from, on their way to pack their belongings for the trip. Owen had never even brought his things from the study where he had fallen asleep the previous night. He had very little packing to do. As Orla headed to her room, he walked through the study, looking at books on shelves with titles written along the spines in languages he couldn't read. He stopped and looked at a small painted picture of a young Sylvan and baby. The woman holding the baby looked very much like Orla except for her blue, not green, eyes and a slightly broader nose. Owen guessed it was her mother and Orla the baby. The thought made him think of his own parents and the pain that accompanied those memories made him quickly think of the journey before him.

Owen adjusted his quiver and bow along his back, and GreenFyr in its sheath. His traveling cloths were washed and pressed, and felt somewhat stiff against his skin. They had lost the soft well worn feeling of the road. Owen was sure once he had put a day's travel on them they would once again feel as comfortable as before. He used his leopard cloak clasp even though he had not chanced wearing it while traveling before. The road would be easier this time around and he wanted everyone to see him wear it as he left Narsus. A gift to the human by a Sylvan Princess, he hoped Sumiel would be somewhere watching as he left.

"What are you doing?" Orla asked from behind him.

"Um, nothing," Owen said, dropping his hand from the clasp and adjusting his sword belt once more.

Orla smiled, she'd seen him touching the leopard clasp she'd given him, and she was glad to see him doing it. She was self conscious of him seeing her touch the medallion she wore beneath her tunic whenever she was around him.

"Ready?" he asked, changing the subject, uncomfortable with Orla smiling at him like that.

"Yes," she said. Orla shouldered a small leather bag, and waited for Owen to heft his own pack.

"That's all you're bringing?" he asked swinging his pack into place. Orla blushed slightly.

"No, I had another pack, but one of the servants insisted on carrying it down to the stable." It was Owen's turn to smile at his friend.

"Life's tough being a princess, huh?" he teased.

"Quiet," she said shoving him slightly as they exited through the door Athaeyr had left through the previous night.

The day was gray; the storm clouds had finally stopped their assault, but lingered threateningly overhead. The wind blew bitterly from the north, whirling, and drifting the already fallen snow. At times it looked as if the storms had begun again, but it was only the wind moving the capital's powdery blanket.

The gray wanderer met Orla and Owen as they exited the building prepared for traveling. He and the senator led the two friends to a horse drawn sleigh that they had prepared. The sleigh was actually an enclosed room on skies pulled by two large, twin, draft horses. They were mottled gray in color with long black manes and tails. Aiya rode up next to Orla and Owen as they stepped up onto the sleigh. Her horse was a white mare with striking blue eyes. The horse almost blended in with the snow blowing about it. Owen had never seen anything more spectacular than Aiya in all her splendor upon that magnificent horse. She had polished her armor the night before and even in the dull gray day it sparkled and shone. The wind blew her dark hair about her while she and the horse were the embodiment of calm and control.

In addition to the sleigh, its driver, and Aiya, they were to be accompanied by a garrison of twenty Sylvan soldiers all of whom had been placed under Aiya's command until Quailan. An unusual circumstance, but considering the renown of the Sidhe Sword Maidens the senator had arranged for it to happen. Athaeyr, Boone, and the soldiers would travel on foot while accompanying the royals and Owen to Quailan. From Quailan the *Aingeal* would lead Owen and Boone back to the City while the senator and Princess would remain in the village. Aiya would be free to go her own way, presumably home, from there. The soldiers would also escort Owen on to the City. None of them were excited about the trek in these conditions and especially in the company of the human. Ever since Owen had appeared in Narsus the city had been running wild with rumors about the boy. No one, apart from those who actually knew Owen, had any idea what was true or not. Most of the residents after hearing what happened at the tribunal, quickly brought in their children, closed their shutters, and waited for word of the human's passing. The excitement had quickly turned to trepidation at the fear that all the nursery rhymes they had been told as children would come true.

The Sylvan children were just as excited as ever, however, because their parents kept them home from school. Grandparents told dark and frightening tales of humans that their grandparents had told them. Many children went to bed that evening scared to close their eyes or step from their beds for fear of the human lurking beneath it or in their closets.

Both Owen and Orla, seated in their sleigh, noticed the lack of fanfare as they left the capital city. Seated in their sleigh with them was the senator. He had a large wool blanket, hemmed in thick white fur, draped over his lap. Other blankets and pillows were stored in the coach as the horses slowly trudged through the deep drifts that covered the road.

"Not exactly the way the two of you came to Narsus," Negu said as he smiled at his daughter

"No," Orla answered smiling at her father. That journey, and the others Owen and she had undertaken, seemed so long ago now; ancient history. And yet, it was just a blink of an eye, really, in all the history of Parathas. But still, it seemed like she'd known Owen her whole life. She had trouble trying to see what it would be like without him.

Orla quickly pushed that thought from her mind, but not quickly enough. Her father had seen the melancholy expression appear across her face. He looked at his daughter thoughtfully, but then turned his attention to the window of the coach as they began to move.

They made good progress throughout the day. Owen and Orla again recounted their story to her father to pass the time. Each taking turns in telling the tale, or in adding an important detail the other missed along the way, and finishing each other's sentences. They laughed and shed tears along the retelling, and even though the events seemed so far off, they still brought the same feelings closely to the surface in their recalling.

Owen was thankful for the two windows on either side of the sleigh. He often lost himself in watching the countryside pass by. On their journey to Quailan and Narsus he often was lost in the trek itself, and rarely noticed or took the time to see the country for its rare beauty. He marveled at the world he traveled through and wondered if he could ever appreciate his own world again.

The travelers stopped once for their midday meal. The chef had sent them with plenty of provisions along with a thick venison stew with carrots, potatoes, leaks, and peas, with loaves of dark bread, sharp cheese, and butter. They ate their meal in a jovial mood, washed it down with wine, ale, and water, and were off again as soon as they had finished.

The company made good time considering the depth of the snow. Aiya had moved to the front of the party along with several of the soldiers who had shifted into their other selves. Owen caught glimpses of a great stag, black bear, and big horn sheep. He had also seen several members of the company during their noon meal coming and going as assorted birds, keeping a watch further down the trails before and behind them. The sleigh was pulled behind Aiya to help trample down the trail for those soldiers still traveling by two feet. Neither Boone nor the gray wanderer seemed bothered by the deep snow. On the contrary, Owen often saw Boone playing in the drifts alongside the sleigh throughout the day.

As they stopped for the night, Senator Negu offered Owen to stay in the sleigh with himself and Orla. There was quite a bit of room, and supposedly the seats they had been sitting on during the day each pulled out into beds, but Owen politely declined. He thought he sensed disappointment in Orla's expression but wasn't sure.

"Thank you, Senator, but I haven't seen Boone, but for lunch, and I think I'd like to spend the night with him, if it's all the same?" Owen explained. Again he thought he noticed the expression on Orla's face. If he didn't know any better, he would have guessed she would have preferred to curl up with the great dog herself than sleep in the coach for the night.

The soldiers had erected canvas tents for themselves and some of the soldiers had doubled up so Owen and Boone could have one of their own. Aiya had her own which was much more elegant and ornate than the military issue the Sylvans used.

Athaeyr simply sat beneath a large hemlock tree, whose bows were laden with snow, wrapped his cloak about him, and pulled down his cowl slightly. The watches through the night would be managed by the soldiers.

If it wasn't for Boone, Owen would have been cold through the night, but between his sleeping roll, wool blanket, and the dense fur of the dog, he was quite warm. Boone seemed content and pleased that Owen had decided to join him. He, too, had missed the boy during their travels through the day.

They woke to a knock on their tent door in the morning and immediately smelled the cookfire and smells of breakfast. Aiya told them that the morning meal was almost finished being prepared and that they would be leaving shortly. The two quickly woke and exited their tent to meet the others for their meal.

When they had finished eating they returned to their tent to break it down for the day, only to find that the soldiers had done it for them. Owen was unaccustomed to all the help while traveling, but was quite happy with it thus far.

He joined Orla and her father again in the sleigh for the day's journey. The next three days continued, uneventfully, following this routine.

109

Boone woke Owen on the fourth morning.
When Boone heard the stirrings in camp of morning, he leaned over and touched his cool, wet nose to Owen's cheek. The boy stirred and slowly opened his eyes to look at his friend staring down from above him.

Time to wake up, the roaring voice echoed through Owen's mind.

"Got it," Owen said while stretching. His dog stood and poked his nose through the tent flap, looking out into the camp beyond.

"G'morning," Owen said, pushing his hands through his hair trying to neaten it some from his nights sleep. Since coming to Orla's Realm it had become a mass of thick, uncombed hair. Back home he would have been embarrassed to ever let his hair get this way, but here, after everything that happened, he had forgotten about it, and now in its current state, liked it.

His dog sat and waited for him by the front of the tent. There was very little to pack being a dog, Owen however, had to roll his bedding back together and pack his blankets. He buckled GreenFyr back about his waist and again slung his bow and quiver to his back. When he was finished he looked back to Boone.

"Ready?" Owen asked with a slight smile.

Yes. The dog held his head tipped slightly to one side. His master had seemed more distant and reserved since their night in the Star Tower and losing his parents. Boone expected as much, but thought Owen would seem more anxious about his trip back home without them.

Athaeyr nodded to the boy from across the campfire as he and the dog emerged from their tent. The tall man was sitting by himself, again, below a tall hemlock.

After breakfast their tent was again already packed for them. Owen climbed back into the sleigh while Boone lingered at the door. He decided he would run along side the sleigh that day and not leave Owen's side; he had been missing traveling with his *Maou'r*.

It was another uneventful day of travel, which found both Owen and Orla drifting off to sleep throughout the morning's trek. The snow was still deep and powdery which made for easy travel of the sleigh while the rest of the party had fallen into their routine. The clouds were still thick and threatening, but no snow had fallen on their journey to hamper their travels.

At their midday meal, Owen and Boone sat with the senator and Orla. Athaeyr was not with them and Aiya had ridden ahead to scout the upcoming valley along with several of her soldiers. When they had finished eating the senator stepped away to speak with the captain of their company.

"Owen," Orla began, for the past four days she had been trying think of the words that would express how she would feel once Owen returned to his world, but she just couldn't find the right ones. She knew they were running out of time, and her father had not let her from his sight for more than a moment during the journey. "Owen, I…," she began again, but faltered.

"I know, me too," the boy said, placing his hand upon the young *Fey's*. "Not sure what I'm going to do if I can't see you every day," the boy said before blushing slightly.

"Well, we're only about a day away now," Orla's father said as he stepped up beside his daughter and her friend, causing Owen to snatch back his hand. "The snow had certainly slowed us down a bit," he added when the two looked back at him and smiled weakly. He had the feeling he had intruded upon a conversation he was not supposed to be a part of. The two friends went back to sipping from their cups while the awkward silence permeated. This growing realization that his daughter was quickly growing up was not sitting well with him.

The three climbed back into their coach while Boone took up his place by its side and Aiya came riding back into the encampment. Athaeyr too stepped from amongst the trees and the pair conferred with the captain. They quickly formed ranks and began moving again towards Quailan.

The road soon began to descend into a low-lying valley. The hills that surrounded it were not excessively large mountains, reminding Owen of the Green Mountains from his home. The white hills surrounded the small basin they entered. The dense fir and spruce cover they left was replaced with silver and red maples, willows, and alders. Their leaves long since dropped before the coming winter and now buried beneath a blanket of snow.

The company made its way through the valley in short time and again climbed back into the mountains and the thick stands of snow-laden conifers. Owen again drifted off to sleep. It wasn't a very relaxing sleep and he found himself continually awoken from branches being dragged along the coach or ruts and bumps in the road.

It hadn't taken them very long before stopping for the evening and their nightly meal. Owen and Orla were able to sneak off to the edge of the encampment for a short while.

They didn't say much; just being able to sit by themselves for a bit was pleasant enough. Orla noticed her father watching them from the cookfire. "We should get back," she said motioning towards her father.

"Orla, wait one sec?" Owen asked. "Ya know, I just," he began and now it was Orla's turn to smile knowingly. "You've been the best friend I've ever had these past weeks, ever really, and I'm going to miss you. A lot, but I'll never forget you," he said feeling less awkward than he imagined he would when he first thought of telling her how he felt. "I miss my parents a ton, but I'll never regret meeting you or coming here," Owen said as he stood up from where they'd been sitting. He, too, could see the senator from across the camp. He held out his hand to Orla, which she took with the saddest of smiles.

The young elf leaned on her tip toes and kissed Owen on his cheek then, just before turning to walk back to her father, guiding the boy behind her. They hadn't gotten far when he saw the Pilgrim step from the wood along the trail. "I'll be there in a sec," he said, nodding towards the *Aingeal*. Orla smiled her understanding and walked back to her father while Owen walked to where the First Man was standing by the forest edge.

"Ah, there is the *Maou'r* now," the old man said as Owen stepped next to him. "What can I do for you?" the *Aingeal* asked in his raspy voice that seemed to emanate from beneath his long white beard. He looked down from beneath his thick brows, which looked more like clouds than eyebrows to Owen. His one eye pale as a winter's sky, the other simply shadow where the orb used to be.

"I wanted…," Owen began and then faltered. He looked down at the ground, deep with snow, which reminded him of someone else special to him he'd lost. "I just wanted to ask you about my parents," he said again, saying the words quickly, not letting them slip from his tongue again.

"Ah," Athaeyr said again. "What would you like to know?"

"What they…fell into…," Owen began, but couldn't find the word for what he had seen that night.

"The nexus," the wanderer offered.

"Yes, what was it?" Owen asked, not a little frightened by what the answer might be.

"It was an anchor point, part of the fabric that holds our Realm to yours," the Pilgrim explained.

"So Chamberlain was hoping to break that point using the power unleashed by my parent's sacrifice?" Owen surmised. He had spent many an hour and sleepless night trying to put the Reunifiers scheme together.

"No, not exactly, no. I believe they were trying to establish a bridge from that point to your world," Athaeyr suggested. He too had spent many long hours trying to determine what exactly, or more accurately, how exactly the insurgents were trying to accomplish their goal.

"So then what happened to them?" Owen asked, still not able to grasp the notion of what he had seen.

"Your parents and the Sylvan were pulled into the nexus that exits between Earth and Parathas. Their very essences became a part of that space and fabric," Athaeyr explained.

"So they're gone then, that's it," Owen said, looking away from the *Aingeal* and into the north wind, letting the cold air blow the tears from his eyes as they began to swell.

"I don't follow," the wanderer countered.

"They're dead, that was the end?" Owen asked, still with his face to the wind. There was something familiar in its touch; he closed his eyes letting the last tears be pushed from their corners.

"The end? Absolutely not. It is not the end when we die, Parathas no, but only the very beginning, my young *Maou'r*. When we pass from this life we simply move from one state to another. Does the caterpillar die when it leaves its cocoon as a butterfly, does a tadpole die when it metamorphoses into a frog. Death is not our final state, only the next step in our journey, Owen." The *Aingeal* rested his giant hand upon the slight shoulder of the boy to his side, and remembered after so many years, how young and innocent humans truly were in their deepest selves. Just children lost in the giant wood of the universe, stumbling to find their way amongst so many dangers and sinkholes, so many wrong paths, and so many deceivers willing to misdirect them.

"So, they're okay then," Owen asked looking up at the man whom he'd envisioned in so many tales, described slightly different in each, by various names, but now so very real.

"Oh, my dear boy, they are as fine as they can be," he said with a sad expression upon his well-worn and weathered face. *He is so young, and yet we ask so much of him. He is our Maou'r, but we mustn't forget he is just a boy.* "They are as fine as they can be, without their son," he added with the slightest of sad smiles beneath his white beard.

Owen met the old man's eye and held it for the briefest of seconds. He wanted to know what he said was true and not something an adult might tell someone younger to ease the pain or hurt. He needed to know that his parents were truly okay, but then he looked away again, back into the north wind. Winter's cold embrace pushed the tears from his eyes and quickly from his cheeks as Owen stood silently next to the first of the *Aingeal* while night came. The sounds of the cookfires and dinner being served brought them slowly back to the others after they had finished talking, and Owen had said his goodbyes into the wind. His farewell was not the absolute goodbye he thought it might be, he knew now there would come a time when he would be with his parents again.

110

Light snow flurries greeted the small band of travelers the following morning. The effect was a slight refreshening of the snow that had fallen over the past week. Owen slept well the previous night, it was possibly the first decent night's sleep he'd had in a very long time. In his dream he was home again, his mom downstairs in the kitchen making breakfast, his father was out in the yard raking leaves. When he woke that morning the smell of his mom's cooking seemed to still be in his tent.

The sudden realization that he was not home gave him a pang in his heart, but he quickly remembered his conversation with Athaeyr the night before, which seemed to ease the pain slightly.

Boone was still asleep next to Owen, but as soon as the boy softly scratched behind the dog's ear, he rolled over on his back exposing his belly. Owen accommodated by scratching the dog's stomach as the animal's tongue lolled from the side of his smiling mouth.

"Good morning," Owen said, patting the dog's deep chest and standing up. He stretched, touching the top of the tent doing so, and then quickly prepared his possessions for the last leg of their trip to Quailan.

As Owen stepped from behind his tent flap he saw Orla and her father already seated about their small fire, they were just being served. Orla immediately saw Owen, smiling, she beckoned him to them.

There was already a place set for him next to her and his meal was quickly served as he sat down.

"You look well this morning," Negu said as Owen took his plate.

"Thanks," Owen said, "first time in a while, I think, I got a good night's sleep." Orla smiled at that. The three ate their morning meal, occasionally, the senator would make polite conversation regarding the weather, the landscape, and Orla and Owen would exchange bemused smiles at each other.

Towards the end of their meal they noticed Aiya and Athaeyr walking down the road they were to travel that morning. It was not uncommon for the Sidhe to scout ahead each morning before the progression, but on this morning she and the *Aingeal* seemed deep in conversation.

Owen and Orla climbed into the coach, but the senator closed the door behind them and exchanged a few words with the wanderer before climbing in as well. The group was quickly on there way. Owen watched as Boone trotted alongside the sleigh, bounding through the deep snow drifts. The dog seemed as happy as Owen had ever seen him while running through the white powder.

"An animal in his element," Negu had commented once along their trek while Boone ran alongside the sleigh. "There is nothing more beautiful." The remark had reminded Owen of Orla in leopard form moving along the mountains while traveling to Narsus. He had felt the same way then. He was not looking forward to saying goodbye to his new friend.

Close to their midday meal, shouts from the soldiers brought Owen and his two coach companions back from their own thoughts to their current surroundings. They were shouting in their native language and Owen couldn't understand anything they were saying. He saw Boone standing at attention next to the sleigh, his head held high, his chest squared, and his plume of a tail arching over his back.

The door opposite from where Boone stood guard suddenly opened, causing all the coach's occupants to jump with fright. Standing in the opening was the Pilgrim.

"It's alright now; I think you should come see this. There is another sleigh before us!" He said in his booming voice waving the three occupants out.

Boone quickly came around the sleigh and greeted Owen and Orla. As they weaved their way amongst the soldiers Owen could gleam glimpses of the other sleigh and what appeared to be several figures standing in the road before it. As they got closer, one of the figures suddenly disappeared, Owen thought, but he quickly realized the figure had simply changed into a snowshoe hare, and came bolting down the rest of the road toward the senator and his daughter.

"Maya!" Orla exclaimed as the hare leapt into her arms, shifting into the young girl Owen had met during his time in Quailan. Negu quickly embraced his two daughters as the remaining travelers hurried down the road to greet them.

"Oh, I feared I'd never see either of you again," the young Sylvan said burying her face in her older sister's shoulder. Orla burst into tears holding onto her sibling tightly. Just then the rest of Maya's companions arrived. Fawn and Luna were there, looking a bit awkward and intimidated by all the soldiers and Aiya still on horseback standing over everyone. They both also eyed Athaeyr warily, being sure not to get too close to the tall man.

Urma, Orla's robust housekeeper, grabbed Owen and squeezed him in an enormous bear hug. Owen was at first surprised to see her; he had heard many of the household servants had left once they heard of Chamberlain's fate. It appeared the steward had been filling many of the positions with persons loyal to him, and once he was discovered, they quickly departed. Urma had been one of the steadfast attendants from the beginning and taken over in the absence of the steward in refilling all the openings.

"Oh, my dear boy!" she bellowed while squeezing him. "I am again indebted to you for keeping my Princess safe!" Senator Negu, Orla, and the others all smiled and laughed at the raucous woman.

The housekeeper released the boy, but then took hold of her Princess. She lifted the Sylvan up in the air and twirled her in the lightly falling snow. It was the first time in a long while where Owen actually felt good and happy, but it was not to be long lasted.

"The day is waning, I hate to be the one to mention it, but none of us are to our destinations yet," the *Aingeal* said as the reunion was coming to an end. Aiya agreed and turned back to speak with her soldiers, Negu nodded as well.

"But Quailan is so close, aren't we all heading there?" Orla asked. Even Owen could tell they were close to her home village. He had noticed the change in terrain over the last few hours; they were again in the valley of giant Sentinel trees. He was amazed at the size of the behemoths that grew around him.

"Not all of us," the wanderer said sadly to Orla, looking to Owen.

"The senate was quite clear in their charge," Senator Negu continued. "We are to bring Owen as quickly as possible to the circle in which he passed into our world, and send him back through it."

"But, he can at least spend one night at Quailan, it's only fair to give the soldiers rest," Orla argued. Her father answered her with a simple, sad smile.

"No, sweetheart, we have our orders, Athaeyr and Owen along with the soldiers must continue on this evening." He placed his hand on his daughter's shoulder to comfort her, but she quickly turned away from her father.

The senator retracted his hand and turning to Owen said, "Owen, it was a pleasure to meet you, I wish we could have met under different circumstances, but I am eternally indebted to you for all you have done for my daughter." He glanced once more at Orla, who still had her back to him, and retired back to his sleigh. Maya and Urma went with the senator, Urma stuffing a large sack into Owen's hand before going, while Fawn and Luna returned to the sleigh in which they had come. One of Negu's household guards was waiting to return them back to the village.

Orla turned back to Owen once her father had left them.

"I thought we would have had another day at least," she began, but stopped when tears caused her vision to blur. She looked up into the storm clouds overhead, trying to keep from letting them spill from her eyes.

"Me too," Owen said. There was so much he wanted to say, so much he wished Orla to know. And for the first time in his life he realized there was really nothing from keeping him from telling this person, this girl, what he was feeling. He faced trolls, deymons, and goblins, why should telling Orla what he felt be so frightening?

"Orla…," he began, and yet there weren't words to express how he truly felt, how could he even give them value or scope? What words could really do them justice?

"I don't want you to go," she finally said looking back down from the sky at him. She had given up on willing herself not to cry and let the tears teem off her cheeks.

Owen smiled, "I don't want to," he said.

Orla bent over and ran her hand through Boone's thick fur. She hugged the King of Dogs then, wrapping her arms about his neck, her hands barely touching. She let go and placed a kiss on the small white patch of fur between his eyes. "You take care of him," she said quietly. The huge dog's brown eyes twinkled back at her as he nodded his head slightly. She stood back up and looked at Owen. She could not remember ever feeling this sad and lonely before.

She hugged Owen then, something he was completely unprepared for; she almost knocked the two of them to the ground. Orla buried her face into the fabric of his tunic while Owen rested his chin on the crown of her head.

"Orla, back home, I…," Owen began and faltered. "I don't know what I'll do if I can't see you every day." She squeezed him tightly then, and he knew she understood what he meant, he knew she felt the same.

"I'll never forget you, Owen McInish," she whispered as she let go and hurried back to her father's coach. Owen watched her go, the wind swirling the drifting snow about her as she left, thinking he hadn't said any of things he truly felt. She climbed into the sled and closed the door without looking back.

"Goodbyes and farewells are strange things," the Pilgrim said from beside Owen who hadn't realized the man had stepped next to him. "Sometimes they are simply the titles to new chapters."

Owen looked up at the tall man who also had an air of melancholy about him. "Or new beginnings," Owen added. Athaeyr smiled at the young boy and then looked away. He looked west, in the same direction and manner in which Winter's attention was usually pulled. In that brief moment the two *Aingeal* seemed so alike to Owen.

"I too am not traveling with you to the City, I am afraid. Important matters pull me elsewhere," he said looking back down at the boy. The disappointment was clear on the lad's face, he thought. "I have grave errands to run and little time to do them," he said and Owen remembered another *Aingeal* leaving him to tend to his errands. It seemed the First Men were always needed elsewhere, Owen thought.

"Thank you, Owen," the wanderer said, and Owen found it funny that the man was thanking him. "I'm afraid I haven't heard enough people in this world express those sentiments to you, but this Realm has an enormous debt owed you." Owen smiled at this, despite the abject misery he was feeling at the moment.

"Aiya will see you to your destination and I have absolute faith in her abilities," Athaeyr added while he again grasped Owen's shoulder, squeezing it tenderly for a moment before letting go. At that moment Aiya slid from her horse's back next to Owen. The Pilgrim smiled at her and then pulled his hood down snuggly before turning and heading westward, leaving the road and entering the thick wood. It wasn't long before Owen lost view of him.

Aiya looked back down at her charge. "It has always been thus with the *Aingeal*. They come when they are needed, and leave as soon as they are no longer." Owen looked up at her and smiled. He suddenly remembered the sack in his hand and opened it. It was filled with warm meat pasties, fruit pies, chocolate goblin eyes, and a thermos of what Owen could only hope was Grumbling Goblin hot chocolate.

"We all walk from here," Aiya said as one of the soldiers led her mount back to the senator's sleigh. "The snow will slow us some, but we will still need to move quickly," the Sword Maiden said, handing Owen a pair of snow shoes as the senator's sleigh passed them on its way to Quailan. Owen saw Orla in the window of the sleigh briefly as it rode by. She looked out the glass at him as it passed, holding her hand to the window. Aiya's mount had been tied to the back of the sleigh and trotted along behind it.

Suddenly Owen was left with only Aiya, Boone, and the Narsus soldiers. She gave a few quick commands and the garrison split in two. The Sylvan scouts morphed into their other selves and broke before and aft of the party while the second half walked before and behind Aiya. They ate their midday meal as they walked in silence.

111

Owen was surprised to find that as they moved further away from Quailan the snow depth lessened, the sky seemed less gray, and the chill wind didn't blow as fiercely. It hadn't taken long to circumvent Quailan. The main road itself splintered off taking Owen and Aiya along with their escort around the village. When they came to the mountains they followed them down to the river that bore its way through them. Once in the valley, Owen looked back towards the mountains trying to find the expanse that they had crossed along the bridge, but he was unable to see it from the lowlands.

The river was frozen in parts, but could be heard running heavily below the thin ice. In places Owen could see holes in the ice and the river beneath. The group followed the river as it lead them from the Sylvan Kingdom, it wasn't the direct route Orla had taken them on into her Kingdom, but due to the weather, Aiya felt it best to avoid the mountains. She said they would make up the time once they reached the plains, which they did.

The Sidhe pushed Owen and the soldiers from first light until dusk everyday. They ate their midday meal on foot, only stopping at the end of the night, and waking everyone while it was still dark to break their fast and be ready to move at first light. At night, Boone and Owen still had their own tent, but usually they fell asleep by the fireside with Aiya. She would wake them gently during the night, and send them into their tent while retiring to her own for a few hours each evening. She didn't sleep much now that the *Aingeal* was gone, and when she did, it was not a sound sleep. It caused her great pain to think of never seeing Owen again, but she felt he would be safer back in his own world, away from all those here who would do him harm.

She woke the boy and his dog again before first light; both stumbled from their tent still half asleep, finding their way to the cookfire for their morning meal. Owen rubbed sleep from his eyes and then ran his hand through his hair.

"We reach Cer'log De Mortem today," the captain of the soldiers said as he sat down across from Owen.

"We do," Aiya answered, sipping tea from a small travel cup she carried in her waist pouch.

"The men are uncomfortable entering the Dead City," he said quietly, as if embarrassed to admit it.

"We have our orders," she said between sips. "And we shall reach it by day," she added. "The dead sleep by day." The captain considered this before rising and returning to his men. Aiya watched him go with a disapproving look.

"They don't need to come into the City with me," Owen said once the captain was out of ear shot. "I know where I need to go." Aiya looked at Owen for a moment, considering his statement.

"You've seen it?" she asked simply. She knew the *Maou'r* had the sight and didn't question his ability to see glimpses of the future, but she was still unwilling to have Owen walk into the City alone.

"No, but I remember the way Orla and I left when we first arrived," Owen added, taking the last bite of his oatmeal.

As was their routine they traveled hard and fast across the plains. They reached the Silvermoor by lunch, crossed it and entered the woods that surrounded the City of the Dead. Owen wondered if he would meet any Gypsylvanians while crossing through this wood once more, but he figured even if they did, Aiya wouldn't take the time to stop and speak with them. As it was, they did not, and by mid afternoon they had reached the edge of the wood and could see the City before them.

The soldiers lined themselves along the forest edge and took in the scene. Parts of the City were in flames, the once white stone buildings black from soot and fire. Dark shapes flew about the buildings, some man shaped, others not. Cries and screams could be heard from the wood's edge.

Owen looked to Aiya who looked grim. He stepped over to her, "Aiya, none of you need to come with me," he said quietly.

She looked at him with a mixture of contempt and admiration. "I have sworn to protect you and escort you to the City," she began, but Owen interrupted her.

"And you have, here we are," he said quietly. "And you know as well as I do, if we bring these men into that City, most of them will not make it out again." She looked down the line of trees where the Sylvans had spread themselves out, and saw that to a man, they were all transfixed with the happenings within the City.

"I have been here before," Owen said, bringing her gaze back to him, "I can go on alone from here," he said sounding more confident than he felt.

"They have given me the charge of seeing you from our Realm," Aiya said sadly. "I also swore to protect your life with mine," she added.

"I know. About that, can I ask a favor?" Owen said awkwardly. Aiya smiled at him.

"You may," she said curious.

"I have to leave anyway, and I wasn't sure what you were planning to do now that everything was finished," Owen said, trying to find the right way of asking.

"I was planning on heading back to the Sidhe Nation for a time. Why?"

"I was just hoping, instead of you protecting me, you might consider going back to Quailan and watching over Orla for a little while?" Owen said meekly. How stupid of him to ask a renowned Sidhe Sword Maiden to go protect a young girl.

"It would do me no greater honor," Aiya said smiling. "I don't think our Princess would appreciate me as a body guard, however, so I will find another reason for my return to Quailan." Aiya looked at the boy before her. She had never met a more noble or selfless person in all her life, and to find it in a human after all the horrible things they had done to others and themselves.

"But about the City, I am to make sure you enter the Sacred Circle," Aiya added.

"I will. I'll go, I promise, I don't want to stay there," Owen said with a smile tipping his head towards the City. "You can trust me." Aiya nodded and stepped away from him and Boone for a moment, when she returned she brought with her the captain who looked pale and uneasy.

"The City is not in the state that I expected it to be," the Sidhe said to the captain. The soldier looked in the direction of the war torn city as they spoke.

"I can see that. My men are not thrilled about entering there just to have us all killed before we reach the circle," the small, dark Sylvan said. He removed his helmet and smoothed back his dark hair before placing it back upon his head.

"Owen has offered to go the rest of the way, alone," Aiya said watching the captain. The man's eyes widened a bit and looked at Owen, sizing him up, taking his measure.

"How are we to be sure he enters the City without an escort?" he asked.

"He has given me his word, and I require nothing further," Aiya said very firmly, inviting no argument. Making it very clear in her tone that if the captain required further proof of Owen, he and she would have a very serious disagreement.

The soldier nodded his approval. He looked back to Owen again with more of a saddened expression this time, as if he was sending the boy off to his doom.

"How do you plan on getting to the circle?" he asked Owen.

"With all the smoke and chaos, it should be simple enough to move quickly, directly to the circle. I remember the way from when I first came." Owen hoped he wouldn't happen upon any of the citizens of Cer'log de Mortem along his way. The captain nodded, but the expression did not leave his face, he did not expect Owen to make it to the circle.

The captain extended his hand to Owen, which he shook firmly. The Sylvan then turned and went back to his men. Owen looked at Aiya who was looking quite melancholy herself.

"I still don't feel right letting you go alone," she began.

He won't be alone, Boone interjected. The Sidhe smiled at the dog as Owen placed his hand upon the large animal's head.

"You're quite right, I apologize," she said with a smile. She had forgotten about the boy's *Duine Madra.* It did make her feel somewhat better about him leaving here at this juncture. And besides, the *Maou'r* had already made a request, which even though he didn't know it, she could not refuse. She would return to Quailan and act as Princess Orla's personal guard.

"It was an honor to meet you, Owen McInish, and more so to fight alongside you," she bowed gracefully in front of him, her long dark hair cascading down over her shoulders only to be thrown back again when she stood up.

"Me too," Owen said blushing slightly. He looked to Boone and then to the City.

"Well, no sense in prolonging this, eh?" he said to his giant dog.

He looked back to Aiya one last time and then headed off towards the City. They stayed to the forest edge for as long as they could, to where the forest approached the City at its closest point; that was where they then moved quickly across the barren ground. There was a short retaining wall along this portion of the City, which they were able to move quickly along until the came to the gate Owen and Orla had exited.

Owen and Boone moved quickly down the main street, sticking close to the buildings on the eastern most side of the roadway. The light was past noon, and was shining down from above the western side of the road. When they reached the end they could see the circle beyond. It was just the way Owen remembered it, surrounded by four flights of stairs, so no matter which way you approached it, there were stairs you could descend.

They had been able to move quickly through the City, the fires were spread out through the maze of streets, and only occasionally did they see any of the familiars flying through the air. The roads were, for the most part, empty.

"Let's go," Owen said. As he and Boone sprinted for the circle.

How does it work? the dog asked as they raced towards the ring.

"I don't know, I just assumed once we stepped into it, we would get sent back," Owen shouted over his shoulder to the dog. No one had given him anything, or told him to do anything in particular, so he just assumed all he needed to do was be in the circle.

"Hurry up, Boone!" Owen shouted as he reached the last stair. He bolted into the middle of the circle while Boone leapt from the last stair landing in the center next to his boy. Owen grabbed Boone by the scruff of his neck just as he felt a sudden uneasiness. He felt dizzy, as if the ground beneath him was moving. There was a shimmering light and then suddenly darkness.

112

And then there was light.

Owen almost fell, as if someone had been spinning him for pin the tail on the donkey, only faster and faster until the world around him was a blur, and suddenly stopped him in his place. He thought about vomiting, but was able to convince his stomach not to relinquish its hold on his lunch.

Looking down at his side, he was very pleased to find Boone looking how Owen felt. The dog's four legs were splayed apart in an attempt to keep himself upright and from falling over. The great dog, however, did raise his head to look at his master; in what Owen thought was an attempt at a smile. He felt the same way, he was very glad Boone had made the trip as well.

"Well, it's about time you got yourself here," a voice sounding like a bag of rocks said from behind Owen and Boone. Both turned, Owen instinctively reaching for his sword, Boone trying to regain his legs under him to be able to spring at any would be attackers. But what they saw when they turned was so unexpected neither of them knew what to do.

Sitting just outside the circle, at a small campfire, were Brule and Balor.

"C'mon now, don't just stand there, say something," Brule laughed. The great behemoth said slapping his knee. Balor punched him in his shoulder, an accomplishment for the much smaller man.

"HA! I told you! Look at their faces! Oh, if I could keep that look in my pocket forever!" the dwarf shouted.

"But how?" Owen finally managed, walking towards his two friends, exiting the circle, and now being unable to find his way back to it again.

"How?" he stammered again. Boone left the circle with him, cautiously sniffing his two old companions and comrades, not sure to believe their being there or not.

"HA! How indeed, well now, that's a story!" Balor said with a broad smile. He still lacked his beard, but a sandpaper shadow had grown across his face, especially just below his lip and over his chin.

"This big brute over here opened up another passageway when he brought the ceiling down between us. We fought our fair share of goblins mind you, they won't be forgetting our faces any time soon, but there were too many, even for the likes of us," Balor began. It was apparent to Owen and Boone that the stout man had been waiting some time to relate this story to them, or anyone else who would listen for that matter.

"So we took the passage, and it led us down deep under the mountain. The goblins pursued us. We stopped and fought them, chasing them back, time to time, but we pushed forward in hopes of reaching you again. But by the time we'd reached another passage heading out of the mountain some time had passed. As soon as we were out we made our way towards Narsus in hopes of meeting up with you there.

"Along the way, however, we ran into that Gray Pilgrim fellow, who told us you had already reached Narsus. He said that you would soon be heading south again towards Quailan, and then on to the City. How he knew all that is beyond me. I've never been one to quite understand those *Aingeal* folk. Queer they are, but anyways, he said we should head that way. He told us to make our way to the City and cross over into your Realm, and wait for you here," Balor said.

"Luckily," Brule interjected, "my horse met us shortly after that and we rode him all the way to the City."

"No *Fey* allowed with me?" Owen said with a slight smile.

Both the men smiled back at the boy.

"I'm no *Fey,* boy!" Balor said with mock indignation. "I'm a dwarf, there's a world of difference."

Brule chuckled as well, "And the *Fey* have pointed out my whole life that I'm a troll."

"HA!" Balor bellowed once more, "And did you see our handy work in the City?" he asked with a shrewd smile.

"All those fires and smoke?' Owen laughed.

"That was us!" the pair shouted in unison with uproarious laughter.

Owen and Boone joined their two friends for a late afternoon meal that they had already been preparing. During which Owen related their own adventures and the fall of Chamberlain and the Reunifiers. After they ate, Owen excused himself from his friends, and wandered down the hillside towards his home. He stopped at a large tree that blocked him from being seen from the road once he could see his small home. There was a stream of yellow police tape across the front door and along the driveway. The snow that had fallen had never been plowed, and there were no fresh tracks leading up the drive to the home. The building looked quite vacant.

That familiar pang in his chest and ache in his heart returned. He placed his hand on the tree he stood behind and leaned his head against it. The bark was peeling under his touch. He lifted his head and saw that it was an enormous yellow birch. One he had never noticed on this hillside before, which he had walked a thousand times if once. *Dad's favorite tree*, Owen smiled at the thought.

At that he heard a loud outburst from his friends back up the hillside. He wasn't alone.

Not alone, never alone, his parent's voices echoed through his mind.

Owen smiled, his parents were certainly gone, but he still had family with him. He wasn't alone; they all had made sure of that. Something bumped his hand and he looked down to see Boone staring up at him. He had nudged Owen's hand, placing it upon his head. Owen scratched the massive face in thanks.

He looked back at the yellow birch, and as he had seen Orla do many times, he said a quiet thank you. There were many things that had happened that would be hard to live with and be without, but there were still that many more to be thankful for, he could almost hear Orla's song bird voice telling him. He would never stop missing his mom and dad, but he did have a family who cared about him still. It would be hard living without them, but he would find a way, he had to, for them.

Printed in the United States
217363BV00002B/56/P